Praise for Katie Agnew

‘They don’t come much bigger or better than this … Throw plenty of scandal and sex into the mix too, and you’ve found the perfect beach fodder. Just don’t forget your SPF, because you won’t be shifting from that sunlounger all day. 5 *’ *Heat*

‘Escapism slathered with lashings of sultry glamour … Agnew’s pitch-perfect eye for detail will keep you captivated page after page’ *Sunday Herald*

‘Saucy, frothy, and entertaining, this tale of escapism, scandal and sex against the decadent backdrop of Monaco will keep you turning its pages’

Telegraph & Argus

‘Expect to see this tale of sex and scandal entertaining women on beaches and beside pools all summer long’

Daily Record

‘A grown-up novel that excites from the off: Agnew has a keen eye on the dark side of the high life as well as its shallowness, and her writing is as lively as her plotting’ *Metro*

‘You’ll be disappointed when this gritty, exciting and surprising novel ends – it’s unputdownable’ *Closer*

Katie Agnew was born in Edinburgh and spent her childhood in Scotland. She worked as a journalist for many years, writing for *Marie Claire*, *Cosmopolitan*, *Red* and the *Daily Mail* amongst other publications. Her novels *Wives v Girlfriends* and *Saints v Sinners* are also available from Orion. Katie now lives in Bath with her family.

By Katie Agnew

Drop Dead Gorgeous
Before We Were Thirty
Wives v Girlfriends
Saints v Sinners

Drop Dead Gorgeous

KATIE AGNEW

An Orion paperback

First published in Great Britain in 2003
by Corgi
This paperback edition published in 2012
by Orion Books Ltd,
Orion House, 5 Upper St Martin's Lane,
London WC2H 9EA

An Hachette UK company

A CIP catalogue record for this book
is available from the British Library.

Typeset by Deltatype Ltd, Birkenhead, Merseyside

Printed and bound in Great Britain by
Clays Ltd, St Ives plc

The Orion Publishing Group's policy is to use papers that
are natural, renewable and recyclable products and made
from wood grown in sustainable forests. The logging and
manufacturing processes are expected to conform to the
environmental regulations of the country of origin.

www.orionbooks.co.uk

For Mum

Prologue

There's an unfamiliar female voice talking to me on the phone. Her name is Rachel and she's asking difficult questions. She wants to hear stories I've long since banished to the darkest corners of my mind. Her voice is friendly, but she's taken a sledgehammer and smashed up my world. Why is she doing this to me? How did she get my number? Why now, when everything is perfect? Why now?

'Laura?' the voice is saying. 'Have you got time for a quick word?'

There are skeletons opening cupboard doors in every room of this big, old house and they're coming for me. I can hear their bones rattling in my brain, waking up sleeping memories with their heavy footsteps, headed my way. They're making my head spin. I feel dizzy. As if I'm going to drop the baby. I need to sit down.

The stone kitchen floor is hard and cold. I rest my head against the wall while the voice keeps talking. I want to throw down the phone, run into the garden and feel the freezing wind against my skin as it blows up from the beach. I could run straight into the frantic green waves and wash away the memories for ever. I need to be allowed to forget. That's why we came here. It was my only escape. But now they've tracked me down.

'So, can we talk?' she asks hopefully. 'Nothing too

personal. Just for a few minutes? Is that OK?'

'No,' I say. 'It's not OK. I don't want to ... it's not a good time.'

'When would be a good time?' she persists. 'Tomorrow?'

I know tomorrow won't be any better, or the next day, or the day after that. It'll never be the right time.

'It won't take long,' she continues. 'I promise. But my boss says I have to speak to you. She'll kill me if I don't. You know how it is. Please, Laura.'

The clock on the wall says ten past three. I stare at it and will it to wind back five minutes so I could go for that bloody walk I've been avoiding. The dog has been giving me those 'I want to go out' eyes for at least an hour and I've been determinedly ignoring the poor creature. Serves me right. If I'd done the right thing I'd have missed this stupid call.

I want her to go away and disappear back into her feng shui'ed office, but I know now that she's got my number she'll just keep ringing until she gets what she wants. I would have done the same in her shoes. And even if I put her off, someone else will get hold of me – eventually – and they probably won't sound as nice. She's young, I can tell, and her voice is kind. Should I let her talk?

'Why don't you want to speak to me?' she pleads. 'It's important.'

Maybe I should get this over and done with. It was bound to happen sometime soon. I've felt it coming: lying awake at night, like I used to in the old days, churning everything over in my head. When will it happen? Who will it be? How will I feel? Watching him dream beside me, his chest rising and falling in a deep, nightmare-free sleep. He has nothing to fear.

When we're awake, we're as close as it's possible for two

human beings to be. Blissfully happy. The perfect couple. At night, I cling to him so hard I hope I'll merge into his bones. But it's no use. After dark, we inhabit different worlds. He sleeps with a smile on his face, while I cry. Maybe tonight, when the worst has happened, we'll sleep together, our chests rising and falling, smiles on both our faces, lost in the same dream. If I don't talk now, will I ever get any peace?

'I don't know ...' I tell her. 'I'm not sure I'm ready.'

'It's been two years,' she reminds me gently. Has it really been that long? 'It might make you feel better, you know, to put the record straight. Especially now.'

There's something familiar about her voice. I can't quite put my finger on it, but I recognize her somehow. It takes a while to realize that it's me I'm hearing, or at least the me I used to be. My hand is gripping the receiver to my ear and I'm letting her words in.

'Go on, Laura. Tell me. Why did you give it all up?' she asks. 'Why did you just disappear? No one knew where you'd gone. Everyone was wondering. One of the tabloids even offered ten thousand pounds to anyone who knew where you were.'

'They did?' I say. 'That's ridiculous.'

My heart begins to beat more slowly and I think maybe I can handle this.

'So, why did you go? Did you have some sort of breakdown?' she perseveres.

'No,' I mumble, half to myself. 'Quite the opposite. I came to my senses.'

'Sorry? What do you mean?' she asks. 'What made you run away?'

And I know the answer to this one. That's easy.

'I wanted my life back, Rachel,' I say. 'I forgot who I was for a while there.'

The baby smiles up at me, sleepily. It's as if she's giving me her blessing. I make myself as comfortable as possible and then I tell Rachel the whole sordid tale.

PART ONE

Winter

I

'Stardom is making me depressed,' claims millionaire actress

The sex symbol looked at me with huge, watery blue eyes. She curled a golden lock (of hair extension) around her perfectly manicured finger and sighed deeply. As she did so, her pert (cosmetically enhanced) breasts rose gently out of their silk casing like a pair of golden globes before softly settling back into their bra. I stared at her pouty bottom lip as it quivered gently. She looked as if she was about to burst into tears. I was praying furiously that she wouldn't. I'd had celebrities laugh at me in interviews before, I'd spilt coffee over my favourite rock god and I'd even snogged the best-looking quarter of a boy band, but I'd never yet made one of the glitterati cry.

Lucy Lloyd – film icon, face of Chanel and object of many a grown man's sexual fantasy – had just confided in me (and hundreds of thousands of *Glitz* readers) that she was suffering from depression. She spoke in a strange mid-Atlantic drawl that fell somewhere between her luxury villa in Beverly Hills and the three-bedroomed semi in Stoke-on-Trent where she'd grown up. Like most celebrities, she was painfully thin – one of the dozens of Hollywood stars who were always being held up as terrible role models for teenage girls in the middle-brow, middle-England tabloids. 'ARE THESE WOMEN MAKING YOUR DAUGHTER ANOREXIC?' screamed one headline that week, alongside a photograph of Lucy looking willowy in a white, sequinned couture dress. Like all 'lollipop ladies', her head was too heavy for her scrawny neck to support, so it kind of flopped to one side and rested on her bony shoulder instead. The resulting look was strangely appealing, like one of those poor abandoned, malnourished puppies you see on *Pet Rescue*. The kind of look you know is unhealthy and yet secretly hanker for all the same.

I was trying hard to concentrate on what she was saying, but my eyes were inexplicably drawn to the girth of her bare thighs. They were minuscule, thinner than my forearms. We were sitting side by side on a cream leather sofa, in the most opulent suite of London's most exclusive hotel. With our knees almost touching, it was impossible not to draw comparisons. I looked from my denim sausage legs to her bronzed twiglets and back to my sausages.

How can she have so little flesh? I wondered. What sort of superhuman Pilates instructor knocks a grown woman into this sort of shape?

As I dragged my eyes away from her body I realized Lucy was still talking to me. Thank God I had my Dictaphone with me. It was great stuff.

'... You see, Laura,' said Lucy (nice touch, using my name, she must have been on a Positive Media Image course). 'When I was a teenager, I used to think, If I was beautiful I'd be happy; if I was rich I'd be happy; if I was famous I'd be happy; if I had a gorgeous boyfriend, *then* I'd be happy. Now I've got all that and I'm still miserable. I lie awake at night wondering, What the hell do I need? What *will* make me happy?'

A tear trickled down her suntanned cheek without smudging her mascara. If it was a performance, it was a bloody good one. In my experience, stars as big as Lucy Lloyd didn't usually conduct interviews without having a publicist or manager present, and I'd been pleasantly surprised by the lack of interfering busybodies when I'd arrived. A young PR girl from the film company had simply met me from the lift and ushered me into Lucy's room.

'Aren't you going to sit in on the interview?' I'd asked.

'No,' she'd replied. 'Lucy's an old hand at these things. We trust her.'

Lucy wasn't acting like an old hand, more like a frightened little amateur, and although I was delighted by this journalistic coup – 'Hollywood Star in misery shocker!' – I was also beginning to feel a bit uncomfortable about being alone in the presence of a broken-hearted celebrity. I passed her some toilet roll from my bag and tried to avoid eye contact – which wasn't too difficult with so many other interesting body parts to obsess over. What exactly are you supposed to say to a blubbering film star? I mean, it's hard to feel *too* sorry for a multi-millionairess who wears a size zero and has a bottom that defies gravity – especially one you've only known for half an hour. And yet, there was something so fragile about her, so broken, that I had to resist the urge to clutch her to my ample bosom and hug her until she felt better. I was utterly baffled by her unhappiness; the woman had *everything*, so why was she so miserable?

According to the red-top newspapers, the divine Ms Lloyd had been paid more than $20 million for her last movie. Back then, I earned just over a grand a month, and more than half of that went towards my rent. Her boyfriend, the actor Billy Joe Johnson, had just been voted the sexiest man in the world – for the third time running – while my other half, Pete, was once voted most likely to become a serial killer in the upper sixth and hadn't been awarded so much as a cycling proficiency badge since. She had the pad in LA, a massive work/living space in Shoreditch, a penthouse apartment in SoHo (New York, of course) and a whole entourage of yes people to pander to her every whim. I had an overpriced shoebox in Kentish Town, a fairly crap boyfriend and a flatmate who was allergic to cleaning products. But I had more than Lucy. Much, much more. At least I was happy with my life.

Professionally speaking, it was the best interview I ever did, the ultimate candid encounter – Lucy Lloyd uncovered, stripped to the bone, laid bare. The sound bites she'd given me were far superior to the half-truths, lies and clichés that most celebrities offered up as a poor excuse for an exclusive. I was used to conveyor-belt interviews, where every word uttered had been censored by the management and cleansed of emotion. This was something else entirely. What Lucy had said felt real. I knew I'd done well, but I also felt like a bit of a leech for sucking such juicy details out of her.

After the interview, Lucy kissed me on both cheeks – I remember it distinctly because her skin was slightly fuzzy like a peach – and then she promised to invite me to the VIP bit of her post-film premiere party the following week. I accepted gratefully. Celebrities often do this to journalists, but they never usually recognize you on the night, and you end up talking to some boring PR who wants you to write about sanitary products for her client. In fact, star-studded parties are never quite as flash as they appear to be when featured in *Hello!*. The free champagne lasts until 7.30, the big names arrive just before midnight and stay for five minutes, like Gucci-clad Cinderellas – Madonna never turns up at all – and all you're left with is a gaggle of B-listers powdering their noses in the ladies' room and several disappointed journalists standing around eating mini fish and chips. Still, I went to them all just in case.

I left Lucy, lost on the huge couch in her minimalist chic hotel room, and stepped back out into the drizzle of a November afternoon. Office girls in black trouser suits and mid-week shoppers were scurrying around Covent Garden, muttering under their breath about the tourists who had stopped in the middle of the pavement, crowded under umbrellas, poring over A–Zs. None of them knew how close they were to a real bona-fide, living, breathing icon. Nobody was aware that, for the last ninety minutes, I had been in the company of Lucy Lloyd. I wondered sometimes if I had a strange, enigmatic glow of importance when I left interviewees of this magnitude. A small childish voice always wanted to show off. I had an urge to tap a smart-looking City type on the shoulder and say, 'OK, so you've made five zillion pounds on the stock market this morning, but guess what *I've* been doing? I've just met Lucy Lloyd and she invited me to her party.'

It was at moments like these that I loved my job the most. The buzz of hanging out with somebody really important, the knowledge that I had some sort of secret 'in' with the in-crowd, would keep me smiling for days.

My iPhone rang.

'How was she?' demanded Pete.

Bear in mind that this was Pete who had absolutely no interest in my 'frivolous and superficial' job. Pete who thought I was a bit of an airhead because I enjoyed shopping. Pete who deliberately remained ignorant of popular culture in a vain attempt to appear intellectual. Pete who, despite all this, couldn't wait to find out what the world's most celebrated beauty was like.

'She was depressed,' I replied, happy to share my newly acquired wisdom on all things Lucy Lloyd. 'Really, really unhappy. I mean, I think it was genuine. She cried and everything.'

'Right, but was she beautiful?' he continued.

'Yes, gorgeous, but too skinny, like they all are,' I explained, stepping gingerly over a puddle. 'Look, Pete, it's pissing down and I've got suede boots on. I'll call you when I get back to the office, all right?'

'But do you think her tits are real?' he persevered. I could hear at least two male voices egging him on in the background, and I realized that the news desk of one of the most respected broadsheets in the country had come to a standstill while the staff fantasized about Lucy Lloyd's cleavage.

'Of course they're not,' I snapped, annoyed that he wasn't interested in any of the important stuff I'd discovered, like what she had to say, or how she felt, or what sort of human being she appeared to be. 'I'll see you later. Bye.'

I was desperately trying to hail a cab when my mobile rang again. Assuming it was Pete demanding greater anatomical knowledge of Lucy Lloyd, I said, rather rudely – well, it was raining and I was disillusioned by him ... again – 'What is it now?'

'Is that Laura?' asked an unfamiliar female voice.

'Yes.'

'It's Tina here, from Scorpion TV. We met last week.'

Oh – my – God. It's the TV girl, I realized, just as a free cab ignored my outstretched arm and covered me in muddy rainwater as it passed.

The week before I had been screen-tested for a hot new television show. This had been the most monumentally exciting event of my life so far. Better even than getting my first ever job on *Metro Miss* magazine. You see, I had always wanted to be someone. And not just anyone, you understand, preferably someone with fame, fortune, a clothing allowance and the ability to get a table at The Ivy. And then Scorpion TV called me out of the blue, saying they wanted someone 'young, witty and good-looking with a journalistic background' as their new presenter – I had apparently been suggested by someone.

I knew it wasn't that unusual for TV companies to approach journalists to audition as TV presenters. There are certain crossover areas between the two professions: we interview famous people, we have an unhealthy interest in popular culture, we crave seeing our names in print. For me, though, a move from occasionally having my face in *Glitz* to having it on terrestrial television was a quantum leap. Something I wanted so badly I ached for it. A chance to propel myself into another universe. In other words, an event so momentous that it couldn't possibly happen in the real world. Not to me, at least.

Being a journalist for a glossy magazine isn't exactly the worst way to make a living. In fact, it's pretty damn cool. You get free trips abroad, you get paid to meet famous people, you never pay to see your favourite bands perform, you get discounts in clothes shops and cabs on expenses. But you also live in the much less glamorous periphery of Celebland – the Media burbs, that is – and after a while you start to hanker for that gold-embossed invite to the VIP party. Scorpion TV had handed me the invitation, now all I had to do was get past the bouncers.

Being a confirmed insomniac, I hadn't slept at all the night before the screen test. I just lay there thinking about six-figure deals, diamond-encrusted Louboutin shoes and never having to get the tube again. Then I realized it was 2 a.m. and the panic set in. It was a familiar pattern.

Think, Shit, it's late. I'm only going to get five hours' sleep.

Decide that five hours is not enough to sustain me and that I will therefore totally fuck up tomorrow's screen test.

Run through countless nightmare scenarios of everything that could possibly go wrong.

Realize that the maximum amount of sleep I can now achieve is four hours.

Have a cigarette.

Know for a fact that I'll look dog rough the following day and that I won't be able to string a sentence together.

Spend two hours willing my brain to shut off. It won't.

At 5 a.m. the traffic on Kentish Town Road gets heavier, and I mean physically heavy: articulated lorries, mail vans, armoured tanks. The room shakes.

At 5.30 a.m. the first tube thunders past about five inches below my basement flat. My bedroom is at the epicentre of an earthquake reaching 6.9 on the Richter scale.

Fume silently for thirty minutes and then start to cry, thus making my already tired and puffy eyes red and piggy.

6.20 a.m., finally fall asleep.

7 a.m., alarm clock goes off, but I don't hear it due to deep, if belated, slumber.

9 a.m., flatmate, Becky, knocks on door and wonders if I shouldn't have left already.

9.10 a.m., try on outfit which I had deemed suitably gorgeous for interview. It looks crap.

9.20 a.m., trip out of the flat wearing trusty jeans dressed up with fuck-me shoes. Can't walk, but feel vaguely sexy – if thoroughly brain-dead.

Hail cab I can't afford.

I had arrived at Scorpion TV's studios two minutes late, wearing no make-up due to lack of time. This was not planned. The plan was to get up at seven after a restful eight hours' sleep, spend two hours choosing the sexiest, sassiest, most TV-friendly outfit in my wardrobe, before achieving a Cheryl Cole-style glow in the make-up department. Oh, and I was going to blow-dry my hair poker straight, like all those sleek Hollywood chicks I meet – quite an ambitious plan for a girl with corkscrew curls. I would then arrive at the studios exactly five minutes early – keen, but not too keen, with time to compose myself. Instead, the moment I arrived, Tina appeared and ushered me into a room the size of an aircraft hangar, full of cameras, wires and blokes doing odd things with microphones.

'It's great that you felt confident enough to do this without make-up,' she said. 'You'd be amazed at how much slap most girls wear for these things. And it's important we can see what you look like on camera, warts and all.'

A good-looking guy called Matt started helping me with my mike, which was fine by me. He clipped the sound box onto the waistband of my jeans and then threaded the tiny microphone up underneath my T-shirt, brushing my left breast on the way.

'Sorry, love,' he grinned.

Tina told Matt to stop flirting and asked me to sit on an upright stainless-steel stool plonked smack bang in the middle of the vast room, facing the largest and most intimidating camera. The crew obviously spent most of their waking hours in the studio. The assembled equipment required to make light-entertainment television had become as comfortable to them as my battered couch at home had to me. To the TV virgin, however, the soulless cavern of a room was filled with alien bits of metal, ankle-breaking wires and over-confident television types. I was absolutely petrified. No one explained what I was supposed to do, the procedure of live recording being second nature to them. I was already feeling a bit wobbly on the too-shiny stool when the lights were switched on and my warts-and-all complexion was illuminated by a million megawatt bulbs. For a nanosecond my head started to spin and I thought I was going to faint.

Tina's voice brought me back to earth. 'Just talk about yourself for five minutes to camera,' she said chirpily.

I felt like my mother must have felt when I gave her an iPhone for her birthday: excited, but totally baffled about what exactly I was supposed to do. Where do I talk? Who can hear me? Am I shouting? For the first time in my life I thought before I opened my mouth … and then I jumped off the cliff.

'Hi, I'm Laura McNaughton. I'm twenty-five and work as a feature writer for *Glitz* magazine …'

Sweating under the lights, with all sorts of wires stuffed down my jeans, I rambled on about my job, my flat, my boyfriend, my life, to a glass screen a couple of feet in front of me. It was all totally surreal and mildly uncomfortable. I desperately wanted to look at the human beings in the room, to tell my story to ears that might listen. But I'd been told to glue my eyes to the screen. The problem was, a machine gives you no feedback, no sympathetic looks, or reassuring sniggers when you say something witty. I tried the vulnerable Princess Di huge-eyed look, the sex kitten pout, newsreader deadpan and then the wacky, zany, 'I'm mad me' children's-presenter approach. But I was so self-conscious I probably just gurned. Can I blink? Am I talking too fast? Does the sweat on my top lip show?

I was unsure whether I'd been talking for five minutes, thirty seconds or three hours, but suddenly I just dried up. Finito. The end. The monologue over. 'Um …' I gazed over at the crew and smiled shyly. Had I just humiliated myself entirely? I'd been staring so unblinkingly at the camera that

I now had white lights flashing in front of my eyes and it took me a while to focus on Tina.

'Lovely, Laura!' she said, with what appeared to be genuine enthusiasm, and the crew gave me a clap. 'Now, this is Madeleine,' she continued.

A plump, middle-aged woman wearing a lime-green kaftan, too much make-up and a white turban-style hat appeared from nowhere and pulled up a stool beside mine. She hopped onto her perch rather gracefully for a large lady.

'Madeleine is a Madame in a dominatrix brothel,' announced Tina with a straight face. 'I'd like you to interview her for five minutes and find out as much as you can about her working life.'

Now I was on home ground. There was nothing *Glitz* magazine loved more than to feature salacious sex stories, and I'd spent many a Monday morning interviewing members of the sex industry and their clients. There was little I didn't know about stripping, whipping and dominating. I was, if you like, an old pro. Madeleine was putty in my hands and quickly confessed all: giving enemas to MPs, spanking media moguls while dressed as a schoolmistress and putting nappies onto business tycoons who were sick of being grown-up in the boardroom and craved the comfort of the cradle. Even Tina had to stifle a giggle, so I knew I'd done well. Five minutes passed in a flash.

In fact, I was feeling something approaching confidence until I slithered inelegantly off the stool and realized my bum had gone numb, which may well have been the reason I then tripped over a wire, went arse over tit and ended up flat on my face at Matt's feet. He made no attempt to conceal his hysteria while helping me up. He then whipped off the wires, revisiting my breasts on the way out, and gave me a filthy wink before Tina ushered me back out of the studio and the building.

'I'll give you a call in a couple of days, once the producer has seen your tape,' she had said while nodding at a six-foot-tall glamourpuss who was obviously being screen-tested next. One look at the competition and the little bit of hope clinging to the back of my throat dropped like a lead balloon to the pit of my stomach. I decided that the chances of hearing from Tina again were negligible, but at least I'd given them a laugh.

So, why was she calling me now? To break the bad news that I was never going to be a TV star?

'Darling, I just wanted to let you know that Jasmine, the producer, has seen your tape. She – loves – it,' enthused Tina in media speak, all staccato sentences and sugared hyperbole. 'Has to meet you. But I think it's safe to say, the – job – is – yours. If Jasmine likes you in the flesh, of course. When can you come in?'

I thought I was going to faint. This wasn't the sort of thing that happens to people like me. I mean, I was just a normal girl. My dad was a history teacher, not a movie mogul. I was brought up in the suburbs of Edinburgh, where life gets no more exciting than the arrival of a new alcopop. I went to a state school. I still hadn't come to terms with getting a feature-writing job on a glossy magazine, let alone this. Me on TV. How mad would that be? Somehow I managed to pull myself together enough to arrange an informal chat with the producer the following afternoon – nobody ever has an interview in the world of media. No, they're all so cool that they make life-altering decisions over drinks at Soho House.

With that I was left alone, standing in the gutter, soggy-haired in sodden boots and with a ridiculous grin on my face.

This is not the sort of news one should digest alone. I called Pete back. 'I've got a second interview for the TV job!' I screeched. 'The producer loves my tape.'

'That's nice.' He sounded distracted. 'I'd better go. Tokyo's just crashed.'

Right then, I made a mental note to find myself a new boyfriend as soon as I became famous. One who gave a shit.

Calling Mum was a much better plan. She'd be suitably excited. Hell, she never tired of showing her old ladies – she delivered meals on wheels – my byline in *Glitz*, even when the topic was 'How to give the perfect blow job' or 'Guaranteed orgasm for every reader'. Apparently I was already quite a celebrity at the local Miners' Club, which was now full of multi-orgasmic pensioners well-versed in the secrets of the prostate.

As predicted, Mum nearly crashed her car in disbelief. She was juggling her recently acquired iPhone on her lap with Bobby, the West Highland terrier, while driving at 15 m.p.h. on the dual carriageway. I was scared my news would cause a multi-vehicle pile-up on the Edinburgh bypass, but there was no sound of screeching brakes, so I assumed she'd managed to keep control.

Of course, I'd told Mum about my screen test, but she'd been even more dubious about my chances of actually ending up on the box than I'd been. Scottish Presbyterian pessimism kicked in, and after a half-hour chat with her, I'd convinced myself I'd be better suited to retraining as a nun than pursuing my media dreams. Even now, despite her evident pride at my success, in my moment of glory, she managed to put a dampener on the news.

'I mean, it's a wonderful opportunity, darling, but I watched a programme about Paula Yates last night, you know, Peaches and Pixie's mum,' she warned. 'I don't want you ending up like that. My advice would be to stay away from rock stars and drugs, dear, they're very bad for your health.'

'What about Dad?' I asked, hopefully. 'Will you tell him?'

'Um, no, dear. I don't think so. It's probably best to let things lie at the moment. I'm not sure he'd approve. You know what he's like. But he'll come round. One day ...'

Mum didn't sound convinced. Neither was I. Dad couldn't even bring himself to talk to me on the phone since I wrote what I thought was a rather hilarious account of my sex life in *Glitz* a couple of months earlier. He hadn't read it himself – he only ever read *The Scotsman*, *Scotland on Sunday* and the *Historic Review* – but unfortunately for me, most of his fifth-year pupils had devoured the article with relish. Poor Dad had endured weeks of jibes from a bunch of spotty sixteen-year-olds who now knew his daughter's oral-sex technique. I could see why he was upset, but I had tried to apologize. If only he wasn't so stubborn.

Next I called Fiona, my adorable, and adoring, little sister. Fiona and I were as close as two siblings could get without actually being Siamese twins. She was four years younger than me, but we looked almost identical, except that while my hair had dulled to mouse by the time I was twelve, hers had remained the same baby-blonde shade we'd been so proud of as little girls. Personality-wise, we often seemed to be negative images of each other. She was as quiet and thoughtful as I was exuberant and loud, as settled and careful with money as I was restless and irresponsible with cash. Fiona was a born carer who spent her working days making other people's children better as a paediatric nurse at Edinburgh's Royal Hospital for Sick Children, and her spare time looking after her friends and family. She was the good daughter and I was more of a handful.

Case in point: when Dad blew up the kitchen last summer while attempting to deep-fry haddock, Fiona was round there like a shot. She was the one who made the firemen cups of tea, cleaned up the mess, phoned the insurance company, found the petrified dog hiding under the next-door neighbour's car and mopped up Mum's tears. I was the one on the end of the phone finding the whole thing wildly amusing and being no help whatsoever. But at least I wasn't as useless as Dad. He just sat in the garden and sulked, apparently.

I always felt that Fiona was what I would have become had I made different decisions in life. Deep down, behind the public façades we had created for ourselves – as people do – we were very, very alike. We agreed instinctively on pretty much everything, from politics – free health and education for all – to animal welfare. There was a large part of me that craved her well-ordered life and her calm disposition. Likewise, my sister held up my life in London as some sort of fantasy existence. We were the ultimate mutual appreciation society.

'Oh, Laura,' she sighed when I told her about the TV audition. 'You are so clever.'

'Thanks, darling. But I don't think it's got much to do with intelligence,' I replied. 'Just luck, really. Anyway, I still might not get it.'

'Of course you will,' she insisted. 'I have a feeling. Oh dear, I think I'm going to blub ...'

Fiona has always had an abundance of feelings.

Back at the *Glitz* offices on the South Bank it was hard to contain my excitement, but I was determined to keep the news of my potential new job quiet until it was definite. The open-plan office was buzzing as usual. Three skinny adolescent models sat on the orange leather sofa in reception, clutching their books of photographs and waiting patiently to get the once-over from the fashion girls. Graham, the art editor, and Nat, my features editor, were bickering over the choice of Spotify playlist. The editor's PA, Cathy, was on the phone, lying to an unwelcome caller that the editor, Trudy, was in New York all week and wouldn't be available. Meanwhile, in the beauty department, the girls were squealing with delight over the arrival of a boxful of lipglosses in various shades of coral.

The *Glitz* offices had been redesigned at great expense to the company just before I'd started working there, with exposed brick walls, kidney-shaped desks, curvy orange chairs and state-of-the-art Macs. It would have been lovely if it wasn't such a bomb site, with piles of newspapers, magazines and empty coffee cups strewn everywhere. The only oasis of calm amidst the chaos was Trudy's minimal, white private office. The lack of clutter seemed to point out that the woman didn't actually do any work.

As always, Trudy summoned me into her office for a post-interview debriefing the minute she spotted me.

'Lau-rah!' she screeched, which was a cue for me to drop everything and run. She tried to carry it off as some sort of a professional meeting, when in reality it was a thinly veiled excuse for news, scandal and gossip from celeb world.

'So?' she asked, glaring at me from behind an enormous vase of rare black orchids. You'd be amazed at how much expectation can be loaded into two letters and a question mark.

I knew my part by heart. I had to tantalize Trudy with enough juicy morsels of celebrity scandal for her to believe I was a decent journalist, put whichever famous woman I had just interviewed down a tad in order to make Trudy feel better about the fact she was neither famous nor beautiful herself and share bitchy little observations that couldn't be printed for fear of pissing off Lucy Lloyd's influential management.

'Well, she's horribly skinny,' I confessed in conspiratorial mode. 'Definitely anorexic. She had that downy hair thing going on here.' I ran my hand along my jawline to show where I'd spotted the tell-tale peachy fuzz that indicates a body too thin to insulate itself without extra hair. In reality, the sight had upset me. Why would a woman with so much to offer the world want to take up so little space in it?

Trudy tut-tutted and looked smug. Which was rich coming from a woman who survived on a diet of nothing more calorific than multi-packs of Marlboro Lights and slimming pills. A star pupil of the A-woman-can-never-be-too-rich-or-too-thin school of philosophy, Trudy Wheeler gave a whole new meaning to being on a diet, and if it wasn't for her protruding nose, she really would have disappeared when she turned side on.

'And she's terribly depressed,' I continued, on a roll. 'She burst into tears and told me nothing makes her happy.'

I'd definitely earned Brownie points here. Trudy was positively glowing at the idea that Miss Hollywood Star could be half as dissatisfied with her lot as she was herself. Personally, I felt like a lowlife, bitching about Lucy, who had actually been pretty sweet to me, and added quietly, 'But she was really nice. Not too starry, just sad. Very, very sad.'

Trudy gave me a withering look and muttered, 'Stupid girl,' just loud enough for me to hear. She then informed me that she wanted the interview on her desk first thing tomorrow. It was 5.30 p.m. and I was supposed to finish work at six.

'What's wrong?' asked Natalie, my features editor, when I got back to my desk.

'The witch wants my copy tomorrow first thing,' I said, flopping into my chair. 'I'm supposed to be going out tonight.'

Natalie gave me a sympathetic look. The only thing that made working for Trudy palatable was the fact that the rest of the staff were not only lovely, but all in total agreement about how much of a bitch the boss was. Natalie reckoned Trudy was only horrible because she was jealous of all the pretty, young things working for her. A nice theory, but in my case, I knew Trudy found me uncouth.

'You can take the girl out of Scotland, but you can't take Scotland out of the girl!' she once proclaimed loudly at a *Glitz* party after one too many glasses of champagne.

OK, so I was having a drinking competition with Graham at the time, but, hey, a girl's allowed to have fun, isn't she?

Sometimes I tried to see myself through her eyes: big mouth, big boobs, big bum, big hair, and then, of course, there was the accent – it might have been toned down after four years of living in London – I knew my friends back home thought I talked 'posh' now – but I still rolled my Rs and dropped my Ts. God, she'd get a shock when she realized someone wanted to put me on the telly!

Trudy reminded me of a scabby old pigeon, all brown and withered, as if the life juice had been sucked out of her, with tiny birdlike eyes, a sharp, pointy nose and limp brown hair which looked, despite the best attempts of the Aveda Salon at Harvey Nic's, as if it might fall out if you gave it a good tug. No one seemed to know how old she was, but she'd been in the business for ever. Trudy hated children and animals, presumably because they're messy and leave dirty marks on calfskin sofas and Prada suits alike. She was a notorious bully who revelled in upsetting her employees. When off sick, staff were never genuinely ill in Trudy's opinion. However, Trudy herself suffered from such severe stress-induced migraines that she had to go home early at least twice a week. She was possibly the biggest egomaniac in London. Employees weren't allowed to interrupt her when she was speaking – such efforts would be met by an outstretched hand and a blunt, 'Shut up, I haven't finished speaking yet' – nor were they permitted to disagree or voice an opinion that differed from her own. For example, say Trudy held up a colour printout of next month's cover of *Glitz*, and asked the assembled staff members their opinion. If one of them thought that perhaps the cover star had been airbrushed a wee bit too much and now looked like an alien, well, it wouldn't be a good idea to point this out, because the point of the exercise was not to air one's views but to say how wonderful the cover was and to inflate Trudy's ego even further. Except I didn't quite grasp that at first and got into all sorts of trouble by being far too free with my genuine opinions rather than just saying what she wanted to hear. I soon learned.

The only thought that kept me sane when bearing the brunt of one of her rants was Graham's theory: he was always reminding me that Trudy's behaviour, like that of all bullies, stemmed from insecurity. He believed that Trudy – real name Gertrude – must have been terribly unpopular at school and that her entire career had been based on a need to prove herself cool to the trendy girls who gave her a hard time there. Indeed, Susie, Mary and Julie – or whatever their names were – would probably be working in M&S now, mothers, grandmothers even, and they must have been very impressed by their former schoolmate's success: 'Who'd have thought it. Gertrude Wheeler, the editor of a glossy magazine.'

I just wished they'd left her alone all those years ago. Then we might have had someone sane sitting behind the Conran-designed editor's desk rather than Bin Laden in a Prada skirt (beard and all).

Like Margaret Thatcher – Trudy's absolute all-time heroine. Enough said – our esteemed leader had a husband called Dennis. She treated him just like she treated us, but the poor man couldn't even escape to the pub at the end of the day, or keep his CV updated in the hope that a more desirable position would appear in the *MediaGuardian* on Monday. Dennis did something important in the City and earned even more money than Trudy, but she talked to him like a three-year-old who'd just wet his pants.

'Dennis, what the fuck are you still doing at work?' she was now screaming down the phone loud enough for the entire office to hear. 'We've got Vivienne and John Paul coming for supper. I need you to be home when the caterers arrive and I have a manicure after work ...'

Five minutes later she click-clicked out of the office in her heels towards the company car, which was waiting downstairs to take her to Knightsbridge.

'Oh right, so you've got to stay until you've written two thousand words and she's off to get her nails done. That's nice,' said Natalie, disappearing under her desk. 'Think we'd better open a bottle.'

Nat reappeared with a bottle of cheap Merlot. Working late was so much the norm that we had a secret booze stash to help us through the long, dark hours after six. We had a company tab round the corner at Oddbins, which we used rather too liberally for the accounts department's liking. Normally, I didn't mind working late. I knew it was a position for which a thousand girls would gratefully give their Manolo Blahniks. In a job market crowded with talented, keen, bright wannabe journalists, a writing job on a women's glossy was something to cherish. Even if it meant working until midnight, and even with Trudy as a boss. Tonight, Pete and his mates would be in the Oxo Tower without me, and I badly wanted to join them and celebrate my TV success by drinking my own body weight in Prosecco. But a girl's got to do what a girl's got to do, and I had an interview to write. And besides, I always enjoyed a drink with Nat.

'I'll stay and keep you company for a bit,' she said. 'Rob's at his mum's tonight, so no need to rush back.'

Nat was less enthusiastic about the whole magazine thing than me. She'd laugh when I got all excited about going to meet such-and-such a band, or so-and-so who was in that film last year – you remember, the one with the gorilla and the set that shook. She had an underlying cynicism I didn't understand. I liked Nat a great deal, but I suspected she'd begun to take the perks for granted. I thought she'd miss them when they were gone. You see, Nat had a plan to escape, which I found difficult to comprehend. All I wanted was to get deeper and deeper into the inner sanctum of the great media circus, while all she wanted was domesticity and normality. Madness!

She was the only person I knew in London who was under thirty and married. Hell, finding a boyfriend in that city was hard enough, let alone one who wanted to commit. Nat had single-handedly restored my faith in romance. She and the heartbreakingly cute Robbie had met a couple of years earlier, when he had represented her against a Dickensian landlord in the small claims court. Poor Nat had endured rats, a sewage leak and a near-death experience with a dodgy boiler while living in an East London hovel owned by a certain Mr Wright – and she had to pay £800 a month for the privilege. When she moved out, Mr Wright refused to repay the deposit, claiming Nat had left a stain on the carpet. Robbie was her knight in pinstriped cashmere, the lawyer who had won her several thousand pounds in compensation ... in return for her undying love. God, I loved that story. They'd been inseparable ever since. Nat's escape plan involved going home to bonk her Robbie stupid each night in the hope that he would impregnate her so that she could disappear into the sunset – pushing a very fashionable buggy, no doubt.

Nat was the only other 'common' girl in the office, and by that I mean she was one of the few who didn't have a double-barrelled name, and the only one, other than me, who hadn't been to Rodean, Benenden or Cheltenham Ladies' College. Nat was also the one who had employed me. Perhaps she wanted an ally. Physically, she was my opposite: tiny, neat and terribly chic, while I always looked like my clothes were too tight or needed a good iron. Natalie's nails were perpetually French manicured, mine were bitten and chipped, and she had an astounding array of crisp white shirts that never had unsightly stains down the front. Being five foot nothing, she lived in high heels and wouldn't be seen dead in Converse. I admired her attention to detail and always wondered how anybody could possibly look so squeaky clean when their mouth was so utterly filthy. Other than the obvious differences in appearance and outlook, we kind of understood each other without having to try. She was an Essex girl who didn't talk proper neither. But God, was she smart. All she had wanted as a kid was to prove that she wasn't a bimbo, which she had successfully done by becoming a features editor at the tender age of twenty-seven.

And now she had what she'd always wanted, she realized she didn't need it at all.

She showed me a property website she'd been perusing at leisure that afternoon, instead of getting on with forward planning the March issue, as Trudy had instructed.

'Look at this one!' she exclaimed, beaming at the photo of a three-bedroomed Victorian cottage in the north Essex countryside. 'We could sell our one-bedroom flat, in fucking Finsbury Park, and buy all this instead. It's got a water feature in the garden and everything.'

I smiled as enthusiastically as I could, despite my fear of all things rural. I had actually been known to come out in a cold sweat if I found myself more than a short tube ride from the nearest Whistles. Why on earth would an intelligent woman like Nat, with a fabulously glamorous job and a decent salary to boot – I once sneaked a look at her salary slip, so I knew this as fact – want to give it all up and move to the sticks?

'Why do you want to move to the sticks?' I found myself asking before my brain had time to connect to my mouth.

'Laura,' she said patiently. 'You like going to your nan's place, right?'

That was true: I did love going to Granny's house, which was a good 100 miles from the nearest Whistles, but only because I loved the old dear so much, and even then, two days at a time was quite sufficient.

'Yes, but not permanently,' I said. 'Won't you get bored? What will you do all day?'

Nat laughed so hard that she showered me in red wine – so that's where those unsightly stains came from. 'This career-woman stuff ain't all it's cracked up to be, believe me. I've done it longer than you have. And London, I hate the place. It's so smelly and everybody's bloody rude. I just want to move back to Essex, have babies, get a dog, go freelance and write decent stuff. No more of this fluffy sex and celebrity rubbish.'

I had no idea why she wanted to give up the day job, but had no doubt that she'd succeed in her plan. Pete often said she was the most talented writer he knew, which was rather insulting as I was a writer, too, and I was the one who gave him blow jobs and made him home-made chicken soup when he was ill! He said she'd get loads of work from the broadsheets, and he should know, he was the news editor on the best one. I worried that she'd miss the kudos of a swanky job in town, but she reckoned she was over that.

'You're mental if you think that's what makes you happy,' she said, sipping her wine daintily and grinning at me with a wicked glint in her eye. Nat loved to wind me up. Said it was easy. Rude not to, in fact.

She continued with gusto. 'Yeah, it's nice to show off at parties and tell everybody about your great job, and how you're the dog's bollocks and all that, but I couldn't give a flying fuck what anyone else thinks of me. All that really matters is being surrounded by people who love you. But then you wouldn't know much about that, would you? Your boyfriend's a shit – no offence, babes, but he is – your folks and your sister are hundreds of miles away and your old man isn't speaking to you anyway since you wrote that piece about your sex life.'

Nat was laughing and obviously didn't mean to be cruel, but the comments about Pete and Dad were a bit close to home and her sharp words hurt. I smiled and pretended to be thick-skinned, like I was supposed to be in my job.

'Oi! You commissioned me to do that,' I reminded her sternly, feigning anger.

'I know, I know and I'm sorry, but I told you to use a

pseudonym. It was you who wanted your real name on it. You know what Trudy says about you?' laughed Nat.

'No, what?' I asked.

'She says you're all ego, ambition and big tits,' Nat sprayed her wine over me again as she guffawed.

'Cow!' I screeched. 'I can't believe she said that about me.'

'Well, she did,' said Nat. 'Ego, ambition and big tits. Those were her exact words.'

'What, as opposed to ego, ambition and no tits?' I asked, sucking in my cheeks, flattening my breasts with my hands and furrowing my brow in my best Trudy impersonation.

Nat nearly fell off her swivel chair as we both cracked up.

'Anyway,' I continued. 'My tits aren't that big.'

I looked down at my cleavage, which was bursting out of a tight, V-necked sweater. Nat followed my gaze and raised one perfectly plucked eyebrow.

'I'm wearing a Wonderbra!' I insisted, but even I had to accept that perhaps Trudy had a point.

'Give me a drag of that fag,' gasped Nat, grabbing my Marlboro Light and inhaling deeply, having given up a few weeks earlier for the sake of her fertility.

She handed me back the cigarette and continued. 'I mean, seriously, darling, what are you going to do next? Become an editor like the wicked old witch? That doesn't look like much fun, does it?'

I realized this would be a good time to tell Nat my news. And anyway, it would be handy to have an ally in the office when I had to sneak out to meet Jasmine.

'Fucking hell,' shrieked Nat when I told her. 'That's unbelievable. Good for you, darling. I can just see you on telly. You'll be naked on the cover of *FHM*, like all those other TV dollies, before you know it. Don't think Pete would like it much, mind.'

I suggested Pete might be quite pleased for me, but Nat disagreed.

'He hates it when you're the centre of attention. He gets all bitter and then puts you down to make himself feel better. I've seen him do it at parties when some bloke's interested in what you're saying. Remember, when Shane from Boy Thing was chatting you up at that Brit Awards? Pete doesn't enjoy you being noticed. Honestly, love, I don't think he's going to like this.'

There was no point in defending Pete to Natalie. She'd never been a fan, and once her mind was made up about something there was no arguing with her. I was pretty sure that deep down he would be proud of what I'd achieved. OK, so he wasn't exactly the most demonstrative, touchy-feely type of boyfriend around, but he did love me – in his way. And he had his good points: he was handsome and intensely intelligent, he shared my love of football and good wine, he was well-travelled and well-hung. What more could a girl want? OK, so the odd compliment would have been nice, but hey, you can't have it all.

We polished off the wine and devised a cunning plan so that I could sneak out of the office the next day without making Trudy suspicious. Nat would tell her she'd sent me off to a very important film screening. That would buy me a good three hours. In return, I promised Nat all the exclusive interviews with me she wanted once I made it big. She'd be freelance by then, of course, so we'd offer the interview to anyone but Trudy.

By the time Nat left the office it was almost eight, I was half pissed, completely out of fags and still hadn't started my feature. In a last-ditch attempt to avoid doing any work, I called Pete to tell him I wouldn't be making it to the Oxo Tower. He didn't seem particularly bothered, nor did he have any interest in discussing my impending meeting with Jasmine.

'What should I wear?' I asked. A sensible enough question, I thought.

'Don't be ridiculous, Laura. It's not going to matter what you wear. They've got stylists to sort out that sort of thing. All this Jasmine will be looking at is your face, which was fine last time I saw it. I mean, it's obvious they're not looking for the Brain of Britain or they wouldn't have called you back in the first place, would they? Ha, ha, ha. It's probably your accent they like. Scottish birds present everything these days. Look, I've got to go. Ben needs a hand at the bar. I'll speak to you later. Bye.'

He hung up before I could say goodbye, and I realized with a pang that perhaps Nat knew my boyfriend better than I did.

There's nothing more depressing than being the only one left in an otherwise empty office with a pile of work to do, especially if you've just had a particularly difficult conversation with a boyfriend who isn't always as nice as you'd like him to be. I could see why Nat didn't approve of Pete. She and Robbie had such a romantic, tactile relationship. I would hear her on the phone to him at least half a dozen times a day, whispering 'I love you' and 'I miss you' and 'I can't wait to see you tonight', even though they'd eaten breakfast together before work that morning.

Nat often said that she thought I deserved someone more like Robbie and, to be honest, sometimes I wished Pete was more like Robbie, too. He treated her like a total princess, called her babe and sent roses to the office on Valentine's Day. Pete found that sort of thing terribly lowbrow. He said it was tacky. And he never called me babe, or darling, or love, or anything other than Laura. At school, my nickname was Naughty – what with my surname being McNaughton and kids being really imaginative – and I once told Pete this in the hope of encouraging a cutesy pet name – how sad is that? He just sneered. Maybe Nat was right. Perhaps my boyfriend was a bastard. Sometimes I felt sure I deserved more. But after two years together, I'd come to rely on him. And I loved him, despite everything.

I stared at my empty computer screen and willed the words to write themselves. They didn't. I opened another bottle of wine for inspiration and, after a hefty slug, decided to be kind to Lucy. She was depressed enough without me sticking the knife in.

2

Be careful what you wish for …

By the time I got back to the flat it was after midnight. The living-room lights were off, which was just as well because even the flicker of the television showed what a bomb site the place was. An empty pizza box, several cans of lager and the debris of a dope smoker were scattered around the purple-carpeted floor – we rented; it wasn't my choice of decor. The room smelled strongly of good Jamaican weed, and Becky was horizontal on the couch, joint in one hand, remote control in the other. Jerry Springer was talking to an obese redneck about the affair the guy was having with his stepdaughter.

'Been out?' Becky asked lazily, without getting up or taking her eyes off the TV.

'No, working. The witch made me stay late.'

I lifted Becky's legs up and dumped them on the floor, before falling onto the couch beside her. She held her arm out limply and said, 'You better have this spliff then, if it's been a long day.'

When I told Becky about my call from Scorpion TV she got as excited as it's possible for a very stoned person to be.

'That's pure brilliant, man,' she said in her Glaswegian drawl. 'Do you think you can give me a job when you're rich?'

'I haven't actually got the job yet, Becks,' I said.

'No, but if you do, you'll remember who your friends are, won't you?' she replied.

Becky and I moved to London together after being best mates at university. She was a bright girl with a law degree who had high hopes when she first came south. But she soon realized she had never wanted to be a lawyer, and a series of brain-numbing marketing jobs had rendered her practically unemployable. The girl had absolutely no work ethic and a serious problem with authority. She got sacked on average once every six months, and was currently working as a chef in a Thai restaurant in Islington, a job she had somehow managed to procure while partying in Koh Samui the August before. Actually, I knew how she got it: she slept with the owner's son.

'Hey, don't you celebrities have their own personal chefs?' she asked hopefully. 'I can only do pad thai and green curry, but you like those, don't you?'

Becky managed to drag herself to a standing position and into my bedroom in order to help me choose a suitable outfit to meet Jasmine. We decided on a pair of spray-on skinny jeans and a tight animal-print top. I tried them on with my red patent stilettos.

'You're a sex goddess, Laura,' announced Becky kindly. 'You were born to be famous.'

She was, of course, totally biased, but I appreciated the sentiment. We shared the last can of Stella and Becky rolled another joint for luck. She stared at me weirdly. 'God, you're so lucky. You get everything you want. I mean, I know you've worked hard and everything, but you've got this brilliant magazine job and now a shot at being a TV presenter. I really wish I was you sometimes. But I wouldn't want Pete,' she added, laughing.

'Oh, he's not that bad,' I said half-heartedly, but when Becky raised her pierced eyebrow I laughed with her. I gave my best mate a hug.

*

I was drunk, stoned and exhausted, but the minute I got into bed my sleepiness lifted as the familiar symptoms of insomnia kicked in and my mind started going over and over the events of the day. I thought about Nat and her dream of a simple life. I thought about Becky and her messed-up existence. And I thought about me and where my life was going.

Whenever I told anyone what I did for a living they were always deeply impressed. 'Oh my God, that's sooo interesting,' they'd coo. 'You must have met loads of famous people. Tell me all about it.'

And thus I'd spend many an evening in the pub recounting tales of P Diddy and Scarlett Johansson and how they're all so much smaller in the flesh. Once I'd told my best stories – I knew the ones that would impress off pat, and Lucy Lloyd bursting into tears had been added to the list immediately – the next question was always, 'And how did you get such a great job?'

With my eyes determinedly open and staring at the sagging damp area of the ceiling – when I eventually did get to sleep, I had nightmares about the building caving in on top of me – I thought about how I'd got here.

I have always loved magazines. I can remember being five years old and excitedly waiting in the car while Mum popped into the newsagent's to buy me *Twinkle*. By twelve I was reading *Just Seventeen*, at fourteen I'd progressed to *19*. A year later, my cousin, Catriona, two years older than me and infinitely more cool, showed me her copy of *Cosmopolitan*. That had sex in it, lots of sex, and sex was all anybody talked about at school, so obviously I had to start buying that, too, although I hid it under my mattress because Dad would have been mortified to discover I knew women could have orgasms – and multiple ones at that.

At about this stage, I began staring wistfully at the names on the mastheads of my favourite magazines – oh to be called Saffron, Tiffany or Saskia. It suddenly hit me that a few lucky ladies actually made a living from working on these hallowed publications. I figured that if I actually worked on a magazine, then my potential future life couldn't fail to be glamorous and glossy – the antithesis of my dull and uneventful teenage existence, which involved nothing more exciting than giving my friends make-overs and occasionally getting asked out by a boy from the year above. Unfortunately, we didn't go on proper dates to the cinema or bowling, like thcy did in the relationship features in my magazines. No, going out with someone meant that while me and my mates hung out on a park bench giggling and comparing eye-shadow, he would linger close by, smoking cigarettes and drinking cider with his mates. Then, about five minutes before I was supposed to be home, he would shyly approach and say, 'All right?' before manoeuvring me uncomfortably against a wrought-iron fence and snogging me, soggily, for half an hour. After a week or two I'd get horribly disillusioned with the relationship, which never progressed to the point of conversation and now involved him trying to get into my trainer bra at every opportunity. It was hardly a weekend in Paris. It seemed I wanted more from life than any sixteen-year-old boy in Edinburgh could offer.

And so, fresh copy of *Cosmo* in hand, I strutted on bad Nineties shoes – *Cosmopolitan*, May 1996, page 123 – to my school careers adviser's office and asked him about magazine journalism. School was a rundown comprehensive in the less salubrious suburbs of Edinburgh and the careers adviser was a world-weary middle-aged man called Mr Brown, who was up to his eyeballs in teenage dreams.

'Why do you all want to be racing drivers and actresses when this area is known for its coal mining?' he once asked my friend and budding actress, Vicky.

Mr Brown told me that periodical journalism is a competitive business, that there are very few jobs and that aiming for a position on the local paper might be more realistic. I looked at the grey-faced, brown-suited little man and thought, What the hell does he know? before rejoining my mates on the playing fields for a quick fag before double maths.

Reality didn't come into it. No, it was all about dreams. My dreams. And I was determined. Unlike most of my friends, whose parents and siblings had never even considered the idea of staying on at school or going into further education, I was the daughter of a teacher. It was expected that I'd do well. Law perhaps, or medicine. Journalism, OK, but only on a respected newspaper.

I worked hard at school, where doing well academically was considered deeply uncool by my peers. Luckily, my magazine obsession meant I was a slave to fashion if not style. All my pocket money was spent in Topshop and Miss Selfridge on cheap imitations of what the stars were wearing. Oh, to look like Uma Thurman in *Pulp Fiction*. I tried my best, but still had to do penance for being a swot, so I snogged as many popular, football-playing boys as is humanly possible, had many a fumble at the back of the school-hall disco with boys called Darren, Jason and Stu, and got a bit of a reputation. Better to be considered square but a bit of a slag than square and frigid. I played down my intelligence and the soupçon of good breeding a teacher's daughter can claim and tried to be one of the girls. There was an accent for home and another, more colloquial one, for school.

At Edinburgh University – Mum and Dad couldn't afford for me to go away to college, so I lived at home – I got a shock. Most people I met there had been to public school and suddenly I was considered common as muck, so I slept with as many well-bred, rugby-playing toffs as is humanly possible – Rupert, Julian and Tom, and that was just during Freshers' week – in the hope that some of their good breeding would literally rub off. I reverted to speaking like my new friends, and no one knew, unless they asked, that I hadn't attended St Margaret's School, like my new public schoolgirl chums. I never took my boyfriends home. My parents lived in a bungalow – oh, the shame of it.

I got an English MA; a first. And then moved to London at twenty-two, leaving behind a trail of concerned parents, a dumped boyfriend called Anthony, whose father owned half the fish and chip shops in Lothian, and a few ex-schoolfriends who had become neither racing drivers nor actresses – nor even coal miners, come to think of it, since the mines were closed by Thatcher in the Eighties.

'She's right up her own arse,' I heard one of my former classmates say to another the last time I drank at my local pub, The Hammer, before leaving for the bright lights of the big city. I spent half the night in the ladies', crying on Vicky's shoulder because nobody liked me any more. To be honest, other than my closest schoolfriend, Vicky – who was already pregnant by the time I left, having long since abandoned her dreams of becoming an actress – I was glad to see the back of them. I knew they were just jealous of the opportunities I'd had, but I hated being bitched about behind my back. I still wanted to be part of the in-crowd. But by now I knew there was a much bigger, brighter, more influential crowd elsewhere. And I was on my way to meet them.

After weeks of letter-writing and begging phone calls, I was accepted as a work-experience student – 'workie' for short; it's easier than learning names – making tea and screening phone calls for no money at all on a teen publication called *Metro Miss*. The features editor later told me that she thought I was bright, friendly and hopelessly impressed with the whole business. What's more, I was terribly keen to do all sorts of hideous chores that my wealthier, more sophisticated Home Counties predecessors had turned their pretty little noses up at. She allowed me to write a short film review and decided I had talent. After three months of slave labour, I got a permanent job as junior feature writer and the staff started to call me Laura.

And that's how I got my fabulous career. I worked at *Metro Miss* for eighteen months, interviewing a never-ending supply of manufactured boy bands. The pre-pubescent readers would develop enormous crushes for a month or two, the boy band would have two hit singles and then disappear into pop oblivion having already been replaced by another identikit group created by the same hit-making factory who'd bled the previous lot dry. I thought it was fabulous. After a year I was promoted to senior writer, and then a few months later I got a call from Natalie, asking me to come into *Glitz* for a chat about a writing job she had available. For the past couple of years I had happily spent about fifty hours a week writing about celebrities and real people – ordinary women who had extraordinary tales to tell for the real-life slot, or who just wanted a make-over from the fashion and beauty team.

For four years, I had lived in this strange bubble world, somewhere between reality and fantasy. I met all these famous people, but I didn't get to be their friend; I went to great parties, but I never got into the VIP area; I could walk into the fashion department and stroke a McQueen dress, but I could never afford to buy it and anyway, it would be a model size eight, so I wouldn't have been able to get it on. And now I had the chance to become a celebrity myself. I couldn't wait to hear how the news would go down in The Hammer. Luckily, I could still rely on Vicky to fill me in.

Eventually the fog of sleep began to cloud my mind, and as I drifted off there was just time for one last disturbing thought: if I was going to be a celebrity, I would no longer be a real person. And if I was no longer real, what on earth would I become?

3

Win a free designer wardrobe

I needn't have worried about meeting Jasmine Brown. When she ushered me into her office at the Scorpion TV studios in Soho, I warmed to her immediately.

'Call me Jazz,' she insisted. 'Everybody else does.'

Jazz had a massive frizz of curly Afro hair, a grin that was genuine, if verging on the cheesy, loads of freckles and large, kind brown eyes. We couldn't help bonding on the spot because she was wearing the same top as me.

'Hey, this girl's got fierce dress sense,' she said to Tina. 'I like her already.'

Jazz told me to sit down on one of the leather beanbags that were scattered around her office, while she and Tina flopped into theirs. I noticed that Jazz was barefoot. This television lark seemed terribly laid-back.

And so, lounging in a beanbag, latte in hand, I began to discover what my new life was all about. At no point did Jazz formally announce that I had the job; it was just kind of assumed. Up until now, Tina, who turned out to be the senior researcher, had told me very little about the programme. It had all been terribly cloak and dagger up to this stage, especially with me being a journalist – I mean, nobody trusts a hack, right? Jazz explained that my rushes (film clips) had been given the nod of approval from the suits upstairs and that she'd like me to be the female presenter for the pilot show. This would then be shown to various TV bods and small groups of target viewers, who would give it either the thumbs up or thumbs down. If they liked the show, but hated me, I'd be out and the show would go on without me. If they hated the show but liked me, Scorpion would keep me in mind for something else, but there were no guarantees. Jazz stressed that giving up a permanent job for this gig was a huge gamble and that I should think carefully before accepting.

I tried my best to look pensive for all of about thirty seconds before saying yes. The show itself had a working title of *The Weekend Starts Here*, and the plan was that it would go out every Friday night at 7.30 p.m.

'Everyone'll watch it while they get ready to go out on the razz,' said Jazz with infectious enthusiasm.

Its format was to be very much like that of a glossy magazine, hence their interest in journalists as presenters, and the target audience was eighteen- to twenty-four-year-olds of both sexes. Each show would be forty-five minutes long; there would be celebrity interviews, live music, fashion and beauty slots and a news bulletin that would focus on youth-friendly issues such as, um, sex and extreme sports. My co-presenter was to be a guy called Jack, who they'd poached from BBC Wales.

'He's far too sexy to be wearing a suit and reading the news in Cardiff,' laughed Jazz. 'You'll love him.'

We'd have ten days to do the pilot and then a fortnight's break while the market research was done. If it passed that stage, the pilot would be shown on prime-time television and audience viewing figures and reactions would be monitored.

'And if that goes well,' grinned Jazz, who obviously had no doubt that it would, 'we're sorted. Bingo! On air in January for a two-month run.'

The whole thing had been Jasmine's idea from start to

finish. She'd hand-picked her team, given up her other projects and dedicated herself entirely to *The Weekend Starts Here*. She talked about the programme with such gusto that I couldn't help being drawn in, and after half an hour I was almost hyperventilating with excitement about being part of the plan.

And it just kept getting better.

'Of course, you'll have a clothing allowance – about two grand a series, I think. And we'll have to do something about your hair,' enthused Jazz.

I fingered my curls fondly and asked, 'Do what to my hair?'

'Well, you'll have to go blonde,' stated Jazz matter-of-factly. 'You know? Girl on TV equals TV blonde. It's the law.'

'Oh,' I said.

'And we'll have to get your face out and about as much as we can. I'll wangle invites for all the best celeb bashes over the next few weeks. We'll get you out there, on the scene, wearing something short and tight, stand you next to one of the Saturdays and you're bound to get your picture in the tabloids, especially if I have a word in a few important ears. I've got mates in all the right places, you know. I can see the headlines now: WHO'S THAT GIRL?' said Jasmine, eyes misting over with the thought of all those column inches.

'I'm already invited to Lucy Lloyd's party next week,' I ventured.

'Fantastic!' said Jazz gleefully, clapping her hands together and grinning at Tina, who was nodding approvingly. 'That'll be the party of the year. That's next Wednesday, isn't it? Right, I'll leak your name to the press and make sure they know who you are when you arrive.'

I nodded and prayed silently that the megastar had been

true to her word and that the invitation would be waiting on my desk when I got back to the office. Please don't let me down, Lucy Lloyd, I thought.

'Well, we'll have to call in some clothes for that,' said Tina. 'Although you're not really a sample size, are you?'

I glared at the waif on the beanbag beside me and said proudly, 'No, I'm a healthy size twelve. And anyway, I don't mind wearing something from the high street. Karen Millen do some gorgeous dresses. I spotted a black, lacy—'

Jazz stopped me mid-sentence. 'Nonsense,' she scoffed. 'Your high-street days are over, girl. I've got good contacts at Harvey Nics. I'm sure they'll bike us over some dresses in your size. What d'you fancy? Gucci? Prada? Something by Stella McCartney?'

I nodded enthusiastically to all three, never having been able to afford anything more designer than a pair of J brand jeans before. Unless, of course, I counted the fake Louis Vuitton handbag Becky brought me back from Thailand.

'It's designer all the way from now on, Laura,' smiled Jazz.

'Thank you,' I said, wriggling with delight in my beanbag. 'Thank you so, so much.'

'No need to thank me, sweetheart,' she replied. 'It goes with the job. So that's decided. You can try it all on next Tuesday when you join us.'

'Um, how can I start next week? I've got to work a month's notice,' I interjected.

'Nah, we can get round that,' said Jasmine nonchalantly. 'Who's your editor? That Trudy Wheeler woman? I'll talk to her. What's her direct number?'

Jazz scribbled Trudy's number down on a newspaper, which she then tossed onto the floor, and went on to talk about which hairstyle and colour I should plump for. Before I left, she told me she'd give Trudy a ring sometime the next day and that I wasn't to mention any of this to anybody at work until she'd done so. I remembered my indiscretion in telling Nat about all this and hoped she hadn't blabbed. Jazz promised to call me on Friday to give me my official start date. Did I have any last questions before I went?

'Yes, who put my name forward?' I asked, intrigued.

Jazz smiled. 'Natalie Hill, your features editor. I know her quite well. Her husband's my lawyer.'

The little minx. And she did such a good job of acting all surprised when I told her. It wasn't until I was sitting in the Scorpion TV car, being chauffeured back to the office, that I realized I'd been so ridiculously over-excited I'd forgotten to ask about money. I called Fiona and we squealed together, 400 miles apart, until the car pulled up outside my office.

When I walked back into the office, Nat was sitting at her desk, grinning madly. She'd sent me an email which was waiting in my in-box.

'How did it go? Did you get it? Are you going to be the new Holly Willoughby? Or more Alexa Chung? Oh, and the witch wants to see you; she thinks you've been too nice about Lucy Lloyd. She wants more dirt. Not that you give a shit any more.'

I was about to email her back when Trudy shouted, 'Laurah!' and I had to run into her office.

'Your Lucy Lloyd piece was pretty poor. You were supposed to interview her, not give her a shoulder to cry on. I mean, the readers aren't exactly going to feel sorry for her, are they? The woman is obviously an ungrateful spoilt brat who doesn't know she's born. Make that apparent.'

I took a deep breath, controlled the urge to tell Trudy to stick her poxy job up her skinny backside, and said, 'But I thought we had to keep her management sweet.'

All the time, I was thinking, Please, please, please don't make me write anything cruel about her. Most celebrities claim to rise above criticism from the press, but I had a horrible feeling Lucy wouldn't be so resilient.

'We don't have to stay on her management's good side any more,' said the witch. 'Lloyd's their only A-list star. We've got her on the cover now and we won't need her again. Sounds like she's on her way out, and into the great celebrity loony bin, don't you think? She'll be in The Priory before we know it.'

Trudy laughed at her own hilarious observations and barked, 'Anyway, I want you to have another go at it and don't be so fucking wet this time. Now!'

I got as far as the door before she asked, 'How was the film screening?'

My mind went blank for a moment and I floundered, 'Um, the film screening. Oh yes, the film screening. It was fine. Very good. I'll tell you about it once I've rewritten Lucy Lloyd.'

Fuck, she'd sussed something was up. For all her dried-up old bagginess, Trudy always knew when she was being lied to. She gave me a stern look, as if to say, 'I know what you're up to, my girl.' Except, of course, she had absolutely no idea.

Trudy was in a particularly foul mood that day, even by her own high standards. Half an hour after she'd annihilated my Lucy Lloyd copy, I found her PA, Cathy, in the ladies', sobbing her heart out in the end cubicle.

'Cathy? Is that you?' I asked, peering under the door and recognizing her purple ballet pumps. 'You OK?'

I heard the door being unlocked from the inside and peered in tentatively. Cathy was sitting on the toilet with the seat down, head in hands, shoulders shaking.

'Is it Trudy?' I asked.

Cathy nodded and looked up at me. Her face was red from crying and her glasses were all steamed up.

'What's she done now?' I asked, kneeling down beside her and putting my hand on her knee.

'She, she, she ...' Cathy cried. 'She says she's going to fire me.'

'Why?'

'Because I forgot to collect her dry-cleaning.' Cathy sniffed. 'And now it's after five and the dry-cleaners will be shut and she needed her dove grey skirt for a function she's got on tonight. It's a really important meeting, and I'm the worst PA in the world, and what am I going to do, Laura? I need this job. I've got so many debts with my student loans and everything, and I really think she means it this time. Oh my God, how am I going to tell my mum I got fired.'

'Cathy, she won't fire you,' I said, giving her a cuddle. 'She'd never find another PA as good as you. You're the most over-qualified, under-valued assistant in town.'

Cathy had an MA in psychology from Oxford, which wasn't a necessary prerequisite for becoming an editor's personal assistant, but it did come in handy when dealing with Trudy's mood swings.

Cathy clung on to my shoulder, soaking my top with her tears. It broke my heart to see her so upset. She was the sweetest girl in the office – always eager to please, offering to fetch coffees, do photocopying and screen phone calls. She was also the most intelligent and the most badly paid. A walking testament to the fact that life sucks.

'Cathy, I promise she's just having one of her tantrums,' I said, stroking her shiny black bob. 'She doesn't mean it. Trudy would be lost without you. You run her life for her, and she knows that.'

'Do you think so?' asked Cathy, peering at me from over her steamed-up glasses.

'Cathy, I know so,' I insisted. 'We'd better straighten you up. We can't let her see you've been crying. Never let her know she's got to you, OK?'

Cathy nodded solemnly.

'Right, you stay here. I'll go and get your make-up bag and your hairbrush.'

I sneaked back into the office as quietly as possible and was just rummaging around in Cathy's bag when a gruff voice barked, 'What are you doing? Where's Cathy?'

It was Trudy. I mumbled something about Cathy needing a tampon and rushed back to the loos.

'She's looking for you,' I warned Cathy, who was still sitting on her toilet, comatose. 'Come on, babe. Let's sort you out.'

I stayed with Cathy while she splashed her face with cold water, put on some lippie and brushed her gorgeous hair.

'Beautiful,' I announced. 'Now, what did I tell you?'

'Don't let the bastard get me down,' said Cathy, smiling weakly.

'Just remember, Cath, she needs you more than you need her,' I said firmly. 'She'd never find anyone else to put up with her, and you could run the Bank of England single-handedly if you were given the chance. Christ, if you can handle Trudy Wheeler, you can probably sort out world peace while you're at it.'

'Thanks, Laura,' said Cathy, kissing me on the cheek. 'I don't know how I'd put up with this place if it wasn't for you.'

I felt a pang of guilt over my impending departure and wondered, briefly, whether Jasmine Brown might need a new PA. I made a mental note to ask her.

To my utter amazement, Pete called the minute I got back to my desk to ask if I wanted to go out for a meal at a new West Indian restaurant in Camden Town after work.

Perfect, I thought. I could tell him about my new job over a cosy meal for two. He would be so proud and we could celebrate together.

'Ooh, that'll be gorgeous,' I enthused.

'Yeah, well, something like that,' he replied, never one to be too romantic.

I rewrote my Lucy Lloyd copy as quickly as possible, mentioning her unnatural skinniness, the fake boobs and the hair extensions in as nice a way as possible, and ran out the door at five past six, before Trudy could grill me about the film I hadn't seen. Pete and I hardly ever did anything as a twosome, and I was determined to make the night special. We'd get pissed, discuss my fabulous new career, forget the arguments that had become the norm lately, go back to his place – because his pad in Maida Vale was far superior to my rabbit hole – and make mad passionate love into the wee small hours. That was the one thing we were good at doing together, after all.

We'd met in a pub during an England v Scotland football match. England won, I was pissed, upset by the score, and he happened to be the nearest Englishman, celebrating loudly, jumping up and down and treading on my toes. I ended up ranting at him about how downtrodden the Scots are and how England's full of evil bastards who have destroyed my brave nation of warriors. It was a strange experience. There I was, in the mood to despise everybody born south of Gretna Green, and yet I found myself inexplicably drawn to this guy in an England top. I had never encountered that base, animalistic urge to fuck a stranger before. I just knew we'd gel physically, and the feeling was obviously mutual.

We kept staring at each other hungrily, licking our lips in anticipation. He obviously found the whole thing a turn-on and ended up taking me back to his for some whisky to commiserate.

We had a brilliant night, and I woke up the next morning to find my clothes discarded in the living room. I had to count the used condoms to remember how many times we'd done it, and naked between crisp white sheets – clean linen is always a surprise bonus in a man's bedroom – Pete looked like a jolly good pull. Until, that is, we got dressed. Our social uniforms were immediate proof that we belonged to different cultural clans. My trilby, tapered trousers and All Saints T-shirt, showed membership of London's fashion-victim brigade. His mish-mash of traveller/City boy/dad's hand-me-downs displayed a flagrant disrespect for all things trendy. In short, we should have known immediately that we had absolutely nothing in common. It's the sort of thing I would normally have noticed at first sight, but he'd cunningly deceived me by wearing an England strip the night before, just like every other bloke in the pub. The football match was over, but we were still supporting opposing teams. A relationship can survive way past its sell-by date when lust and habit are involved – perhaps ours should have been a one-night stand.

Naked, Pete was an Adonis: six foot three, dark, lean, but muscular and tanned, even in February when the rest of us are blue. He had a solid, square jaw, strong unbroken nose and questioning green eyes. Fully-clothed, however, he was a disaster. To be honest, sometimes I was embarrassed to be seen with him in public. I kept him secret from my more fashionable friends for at least three months at the beginning of our relationship because I knew they'd be completely baffled by my sexual interest in a man who lives in a style wilderness. I mean, the man shopped once a decade for Christ's sake! I remember the first time I 'came out' with him. I was standing in some painfully cool Soho bar, surrounded by perfectly groomed magazine chicks, nervously downing a mojito, when he appeared at the saloon-bar door like some multicoloured Clint Eastwood: turquoise T-shirt, red jersey shorts and navy deck shoes without any socks. Even the normally kind-hearted Nat looked at me quizzically as Pete approached.

'He has the most enormous knob and he's brilliant in bed,' I explained swiftly.

Sexually, his technique was perfect. He knew just which buttons to press every time. Sex with Pete was gymnastic and orgasmic, like something out of a film. The only nagging doubt I had while shagging him the first time was that he must have pleasured a lot of women before me. And he had. While travelling extensively in his early twenties, Pete had made it his mission to get to know the local women – intimately. I knew this for a fact. I spent a very interesting afternoon, while Pete was playing football, reading his diaries from the period. All over Europe, Central America, the Middle East, you name it, Pete's leftovers could have held hands and created a ring of peace around the world. Making love to Pete would have been perfect if it weren't for the images of him frolicking with various exotic beauties that always gatecrashed my mind at the critical moment.

But it wasn't just the sex that attracted me to Pete. He was well-educated, intellectual and enjoyed a good debate – something I'd missed out on with previous boyfriends, who'd had no interest in politics, philosophy or literature. He introduced me to books I'd never read, taught me phrases in Spanish, Italian and Portuguese – mainly rude ones – and told me about countries, continents even, that

I'd never seen. Sometimes he let me do the teaching. He'd lie naked on his bed, smoking a joint and listening to me ramble on about Scottish history and folklore – occasionally, having a history teacher for a father can come in useful. I felt clever when I was with Pete. Interesting. Exotic even. He used to say I had a beautiful brain, that I was deeper than other girls he'd met. Although, come to think of it, he hadn't said anything like that lately. Or anything very nice at all, really. We'd obviously been through a rough patch, but tonight would be special – after tonight, everything would be all right again.

On the tube home from work I couldn't concentrate on reading the *Evening Standard*. I was too fidgety and impatient to get back to Becky to tell her about my new job. I jogged to the flat from the station and burst through the front door.

'Becks! Becks!' I shouted, running into the living room.

'Mmm hmm?' she said lazily from her habitual position, horizontal on the couch.

'I got the TV job. I got the fucking job!' I screeched.

Becky looked dazed for a moment as the news slowly seeped into her dope-addled brain. She sat up, appeared to be confused at finding herself vertical and then the penny dropped. She gazed at me open-mouthed.

'You are fucking joking, man,' she said, a look of sheer amazement on her face. 'You got it? You're going to be on telly?'

She jumped off the couch – and this really was a miracle – and threw herself into my arms.

'Laura, you are something else. I can't believe it!' she screamed. And then we jumped up and down on the purple swirly carpet, clinging to each other and screeching like banshees on acid. I hadn't even taken my coat off.

Becky popped out for a bottle of bubbly – Cava rather than champagne, due to our meagre finances – and we celebrated together in my bedroom while choosing an appropriately sexy outfit for my date with Pete.

'This is your lucky day,' said Becky, lying on my bed, swigging straight from the bottle, as I held up various outfits for her approval. 'Not only do you get picked to be a TV presenter, but Pete the Plonker actually takes you out somewhere nice.'

'Yeah, things are going to be good from now on,' I said, grinning. 'Everything's going right.'

I'd pulled the entire contents of my wardrobe onto the floor before we eventually decided on a backless black dress, worn with lacy tights and slut-red shoes.

'Gorgeous,' announced Becky as I did a twirl.

'What on earth are you wearing?' asked Pete, kissing me on the cheek, when I arrived twenty minutes late. 'You look like a hooker. Those tights!'

He was smiling, and obviously thought he was being very amusing, but it wasn't quite the beginning to the perfect evening I had planned.

I explained patiently that lace was deeply fashionable and pointed out that it was what all the best-dressed legs were wearing.

'And if all the best-dressed legs were jumping off cliffs, presumably you'd be doing that, too,' he sniffed.

'Yeah, probably, but only if *Vogue* said it was OK,' I answered with a sarcastic smile. God, he could be such a pompous twat sometimes. Served me right for going out with yet another jumped-up public schoolboy.

'Pete, I have to be trendy for my job,' I said patiently.

This was my standard excuse when he criticized my look,

which he did frequently. 'And who are you to comment? You dress more like your dad every day. Not that there's anything wrong with your dad, but he's sixty and you're thirty. I just wish you'd wear something younger occasionally. Why d'you want to be middle-aged before you are? God, you're so boring.'

'Yeah, right,' he said into a large glass of Chablis. 'You're totally rock'n'roll and I'm all pipe and slippers. I don't think so. I'm not boring, Laura; maybe I'm just a bit more mature than you.'

This was not going according to plan.

'Shall I come back in five?' asked the waiter tactfully.

'Yes!' we both snapped.

I took a deep breath and forced a smile. I would make tonight a success even if I had to choke on my good behaviour in the process.

'So, what do you think about my news?' I asked chirpily. 'Isn't it great? If the series gets commissioned, I should get paid pretty well, too, so maybe we could go somewhere exotic on holiday next year. You could take me to Argentina. It always sounds so wonderful when you talk about your time there.'

Pete was looking at me with a rather pained expression, as if he were watching a particularly untalented child sing in a school play.

'Look at you, all excited about some daft TV job,' he said. 'It's not exactly *Newsnight*, is it? Oh yeah, that Laura McNaughton, a nice bit of eye candy. That'll give you job satisfaction. When I met you, I loved the fact that you were more than just some bimbo. You were really feisty, you argued with me about politics and you knew your stuff. Now, here you are, with a first from university, but all you think about is what you're going to wear and which famous person you're going to meet next. I mean, it's embarrassing when we're out and you're telling everyone' – cue bad Scottish accent – '"Ooh yes, I interviewed so-and-so the other day. Let me tell you all about it ..." You sound like a total sycophant, Laura. No one's interested.'

'Why are you being so mean?' I asked, confused. 'I thought you'd be pleased for me.'

Pete snorted and said, 'Laura, quite frankly, it's embarrassing.'

I was shocked into silence. To be honest, Pete was often rude to me, but this took girlfriend abuse to a whole new level. I was blinking back tears when I should have been swinging from the chandeliers.

We ignored each other while ordering, and I tried not to stare too hard at the couple at the next table, who were snogging blissfully over their food – I noted that the girl's hair was dipping in and out of her soup as they kissed. I ordered a salad.

'Why are you having that?' asked Pete when my plate of leaves arrived. Which was a fair enough question seeing as I was usually a meat-and-two-veg kind of girl.

'Because if I'm going to be in the public eye I should probably watch my weight,' I explained patiently.

Pete spluttered through a mouthful of curried goat, 'See? That's exactly the sort of thing that winds me up. There's absolutely nothing wrong with your figure. You have a stunning body, it's perfect. It's your brain that needs work.'

I almost smiled. Pete thought my body was perfect. It was the nearest he'd come to giving me a compliment in a long time.

'Laura, please tell me you're not going to go on a diet and end up looking like those famine-victim girls in magazines.' Pete looked sad. Not just mildly pissed off, but gutted, like a little boy who'd lost all his Pokémon cards. He shook his head slowly and we continued to eat in silence.

It was one of those rare clear winter nights in London when you can actually see some stars, so after the meal – Pete insisted on paying which was totally out of character – we went for a walk along the canal. Pete had hardly said a word since the main course and I was beginning to worry that there was something seriously wrong. Generally, he loved putting me down; it was his idea of fun.

But Pete seemed different that night. Detached. I felt a sudden pang of something approaching fear as I wondered momentarily whether he might be questioning the validity of our fragile bond. I decided to placate him. I stepped closer to where he stood, leaning over the bridge, staring at the water below, and reached out to touch his arm.

'Pete, it's not going to change me, this TV thing. I'll still be me. It'll be great – for both of us.'

He turned round and stared at me intensely.

'Laura, you haven't been *you* for a long time. Not the you I like anyway. You spend your whole time talking about fashion and bands and watching crap TV. This new job, it's the final straw. It just shows me how caught up in all this media bullshit you've become. I don't want some bit of fluff for a girlfriend. You're a really good writer. Why don't you do something decent, like work for the *Guardian* or someone worthwhile?'

This hurt, especially as it echoed what my dad had said to me the last time we argued, before I disappointed him so deeply that he cut me off for good. But then, you'd expect that sort of reaction from a middle-aged schoolteacher who believed in modesty, a strong work ethic and jobs for life. It was not what I'd expected from my boyfriend. He should be proud, surely.

'Pete, I want to do this. It's my dream,' I explained slowly and deliberately, because I couldn't believe he didn't get it.

'Well, you're really showing your roots now, aren't you?' he sneered. 'Did all the other girls at your school want to be famous when they grew up, too? Did you all want to escape your working-class chains and make your mark on the world? How original.' It was said in an ironic, sing-song tone, and he was almost laughing, but as the street light caught the bright white of his teeth and eyes, casting a demonic glow over him, he looked totally evil.

I could feel a red-hot rage rushing to my head and I had to stop myself from pushing him into the rancid canal.

'How dare you be so patronizing,' I snapped. 'I'm not some two-dimensional cartoon character. It is possible to enjoy shopping and art at the same time. I can watch *EastEnders* and read James Joyce, you know. God, everything's got to be black and white with you, hasn't it? Laura likes clothes, so she must be thick; Laura downloads pop music, so she must have no soul. It doesn't work like that, Pete.'

I was shouting so loudly that he actually looked a bit scared, standing as close as he was to the edge of the bridge over Camden Lock. Tears were pouring down my face because when I looked at my boyfriend and the pained expression he was wearing, I knew what was coming. I just knew.

'Listen, Laura,' he said quietly now, trying to hug me.

I pushed him away saying, 'No, no, don't.'

We both knew where this was going.

'Laura, it's not working any more, for either of us.'

He'd said it now. The words were out there, floating around our heads, and I couldn't make them go away.

'No, no, you can't do this. Not today. This is supposed to be a perfect day,' I said, aware that I sounded desperate.

'Your perfect day, not mine. It's my idea of a nightmare. Listen, it's got to be over. It's making us both miserable because we want totally different things. You'll be fine. You'll get famous and run off with one of The Wanted.' Pete pretended to laugh, but actually he was crying, too.

'I don't want it to be over,' I whined, hating myself for being so pathetic.

We stood there on the bridge, staring at each other for what felt like hours. Suddenly all the doubts I'd had about Pete disappeared into the dark night, and all I could think about was the good stuff. For the first time, he seemed like the perfect man, and I couldn't bear to let him go.

'What about the sex. You'll miss the sex,' I said like some deranged madwoman.

'Yes, of course I'll miss the sex,' said Pete sadly. 'Look, I've got to go now. I need space. I have to get away from you. You're doing my head in.' And then, as an afterthought, 'This is best for both of us.'

Why do men always reach for clichés at moments like this?

'Pete, don't. Please don't,' I begged, the last dregs of self-respect having deserted me.

'No, I've got to do this. One of us has to.'

He stroked my cheek, but I jerked away as if he had a knife in his hand. Slowly, he started to back away.

'Look after yourself. I'll miss you, babe,' he said, before turning round and disappearing into the darkness. I lunged after him and reached my hand out to grab his coat, but Pete had gone.

And so I was left there on Camden Lock, sobbing for all the world to see, and all I could think was, He called me babe. He's just dumped me and for the first time ever he actually called me babe.

I stood there for a few minutes in a daze. I'd never been dumped before – well, not as a grown-up – and I didn't quite know what to do with myself. I couldn't believe Pete had finished with me. How could a day that started so brilliantly end up here? I started wandering home towards Kentish Town, slowly because of my shoes. There didn't seem much else to do.

An alcoholic tramp followed me up Kentish Town Road: 'Oi, love. You a whore?' he shouted. 'How much d'you charge? Fancy a shag?'

I started to run towards the flat, tripping and crying and muttering under my breath, 'I want to die. I want to die. I want to die.' I felt as though I was watching myself acting out the role of the heartbroken lover, and I hate to admit it, but there was a tiny part of me that was relieved to have a focus for all the disappointment the evening had brought. Cathartic, my English tutor would have said. Drama queen's probably more like it.

When I eventually got home, Becky was out, working the late shift at the restaurant. So I just lay on my bed, listening to a playlist of all my saddest songs. I wallowed gloriously in this oasis of misery amidst the desert of my otherwise charmed life.

I was languishing lavishly on my duvet, eyes smarting from salty tears, trying to absorb myself in the throes of heartache, but two niggly little voices in my head kept pestering me, trying to cheer me up. One was saying, quite loudly, 'Come on, Laura. You've just landed yourself a job on television. Don't be down. You're great.' The other one was just a faint whisper, 'Are you really devastated? Is it such a great tragedy that Pete's dumped you? Was he honestly the right man for you?' This second voice was bothering me. OK, I realized my love for Pete was totally conditional:

on what he was wearing, what he said, what music he was listening to, how drunk I was. And our music collection didn't cross over at any point – no record had ever been made that appealed to us both. It was true that he found my mates superficial, while I thought his friends spent most of their time up their own arses. But did that mean the relationship was doomed?

And so what if I made him cringe? When we went to dinner parties at the spacious and tastefully decorated homes of his stuck-up friends, I'd notice the look of horror on his face when he saw what I was planning to wear, but clothes aren't important in the grand scheme of things, are they?

It's true that I winced when they started discussing documentaries they'd seen on BBC2 about alcoholism in Scotland, or the plight of the working classes, or the state of comprehensive education. All right, so they didn't listen to what I had to say. They were far better – or more expensively – educated, and in their heads at least that made them better qualified to debate the chosen topic. The fact that I might have first-hand experience was irrelevant to them. They were much more content just knowing what they knew without confusing the issue with hard facts. Anyway, I had big boobs and a regional accent, therefore I obviously had no brain. They were the chattering classes, arrogance personified, and I hated them. But did that mean I should hate Pete?

When I got my job at *Glitz* and left the teen press for good, Pete's best female friend, Arabella, who had unruly unwashed hair and wore floaty, patterned things which I'd never seen in any shop, got very excited and asked cattily, 'Ooh, does that mean you're going to start dressing like a grown-up?' Pete laughed so hard I thought he was going to choke on his pak choi. Maybe I should hate Pete. 'Hate

Pete. Hate Pete. Hate Pete,' whispered the little voice.

Eventually, sanity began to seep back into my brain and the voices stopped. I breathed deeply and lit a cigarette, watching the smoke swirl up to the ceiling and disappear into the cracks. Then I did what I always did in emergencies: called Fiona.

'Laura, what's wrong?' she asked, when I sobbed hello. 'Tell me.'

I replied with a wobbly bottom lip, 'Pete's just dumped me. The bastard fucking dumped me.'

'Oh, sweetheart. It's all right. Everything will be all right.'

Fiona soothed, cooed and commiserated, while I howled down the phone.

'Laura,' she said gently after ten minutes of listening to me proclaiming it was the end of the world. 'Maybe, just maybe, Pete isn't the right man for you, you know? Maybe there's someone much better out there just waiting to find you.'

'Maybe,' I said, quietly. 'But why do I feel so awful, Fi?'

'Well, it's amazing how you can persuade yourself into loving someone – the wrong someone, I mean,' she replied. 'It's so much less scary to attach yourself to a bloke who makes you breakfast the morning after, than to trail alone through some depressing singles scene. I should know.'

Fiona had been single for two years and was now an expert on all things to do with flying solo, such as ready meals for one and celibacy.

'But I'm sure it's impossible to meet Mr Right in London,' I whined.

'It's not exactly easy up here, either.' Fiona laughed.

'Hmm. True,' I agreed, thinking about the fact that my gorgeous sister with the perfect bloke-friendly, easy-going personality hadn't had sex this decade.

'Christ, Fiona, if you can't find a boyfriend, there's no hope for the rest of us!' I concluded.

'Och, forget about men,' she said. 'They're so overrated as a topic of conversation. What about your new job. Let's talk about that instead. OK, so you're at a party with Colin Farrell, George Clooney and—'

'Fi, we're not to talk about men,' I interrupted.

Inevitably the conversation turned back to Pete. We chatted for an hour and Fiona said all the things I needed to hear, just like she always did.

'I suppose I've always known that it wasn't the real thing,' I admitted eventually. 'But it was enough for me, for now.'

'But you had your doubts, Laura,' said Fi. 'You were always phoning me up and complaining about him.'

'Of course I had doubts,' I said. 'It's the fact that he had doubts about me that really hurts.'

'And there's the rub,' said Fiona.

Half an hour later, after Fi had hung up, Becky came home. I told her my terrible news and she tried to be as understanding as possible, despite the fact that she'd hated Pete with a vengeance.

'Let's have a little joint. That'll make you feel better,' she suggested.

After a spliff and a hot, sweet tea I began to feel more human. Much less subtle than Fi, Becky had already pointed out that I didn't much like Pete anyway and that I was bound to bag myself a new boyfriend 'who doesn't dress like his dad and everything' very soon. She even managed to make me smile when she pointed out that I would quickly forget Pete, while he would have to watch me on telly every Friday night and face the fact that he'd recklessly dumped this fabulous famous woman.

We lay in my bed together into the night, watching mindless

American television and consuming twenty Marlboro Lights and a variety pack of crisps. It did hurt. Every now and then I'd remember what had just happened and begin to cry into a packet of cheese and onion, then Becky would remind me that I was going to be a TV presenter, the tears would stop and I would remember, on balance, that my life was pretty damn good.

4

Introducing Britain's most glamorous granny

When the alarm went off I had one of those weird moments when I couldn't remember exactly what had happened the day before. I remembered about the call from Tina first, and was just beginning to feel smug when the memory of being unceremoniously dumped by the canal seeped into my groggy brain. I slid back down under the duvet and let out a groan. Did I actually beg Pete not to finish with me? The videotape in my mind replayed the previous night's events. I did. How sad. I lay there, hiding from the world for half an hour, putting off the inevitable sympathetic responses I was bound to get when I told my friends and colleagues what had happened. I couldn't even redeem myself by telling everyone about my new job because it was all top secret. Shit, I got dumped. What does a girl wear to express the gravity of such a situation? Black? Well, at least it's very this season.

In the lift on the way to the fifteenth floor I practised an array of gloomy, poor-me faces in the mirror. They were all going to feel sorry for me anyway, so I might as well work it. I decided on the injured-toddler look, all big, sad eyes and pouty mouth. It worked a treat.

'Laura, what's wrong?' exclaimed Graham the minute I made my grand entrance. 'You look shattered!'

When I explained what had happened, he put his hands firmly on his slim hips and shook his head dramatically. He was wearing an original Seventies *Black Beauty* sweatshirt – without irony, which was strange as he was both black and beautiful – so it was hard not to crack a smile, but I reminded myself how humiliated I'd been and the frown returned easily.

'Poor, poor you,' he said with feeling, before announcing to the entire office, 'Listen, everyone, Laura's just been blown out by that idiot she was seeing, so everybody's got to be especially nice to her today.'

He turned back to me, put his hands on my shoulders and guided me towards my desk as if I were an invalid.

'I know everything there is to know about being dumped. Remember the state I was in last summer when that French croupier left me to work on a cruise ship? I was devastated. What was his name again?'

'Jean-Luc,' said Nat patiently.

'Oh yes.' A shadow crossed Graham's handsome face for a second as he recalled the nightmare of being rated second best to a P&O ferry, before turning back to the job in hand. 'What you need is a strong coffee, a chocolate croissant and a bit of Gloria Gaynor. Allow me.'

Graham flounced to the Bose sound system, thumbed through his extensive playlists – we had tried suggesting our own choice of music, but Graham was proud of his role as unofficial office DJ, and saw any outside contribution as a slight on his musical taste – and said '*Voilà!*' Then he jogged off to fetch me my breakfast.

'You all right?' asked Nat gently.

I nodded solemnly, and then we both started laughing, because it's hard to take anything seriously while listening to 'I Will Survive'.

When Graham returned he was accompanied by Trudy, who felt it was the editor's prerogative to arrive an hour after her staff. He had obviously filled her in on my personal tragedy, because I think she tried to smile sympathetically in my direction. It was hard to tell whether it was a smile or a grimace, unaccustomed as she was to any human kindness.

'And you be nice to Laura today,' said Graham sternly to the witch as she disappeared into her office.

'How on earth does he get away with talking to her like that?' asked Nat.

'Because he's the only bloke here,' I replied.

We often wondered if she realized he was gay. Although even Trudy must have picked up on the subtle clues like the two miniature poodle puppies he'd bought and christened George and Michael.

The one thing keeping my mind off Pete was knowing that Jazz was going to call Trudy today. Every time her phone rang and Cathy answered it, I asked, 'Who was that?' She was beginning to give me funny looks. By three, I was climbing the walls. Trudy wasn't acting any differently, except that she hadn't summoned me into her office at all; in fact she hadn't said a word to me all day. At five, she left the building in a cloud of Coco to go to an advertising meeting and announced that she wouldn't be back until tomorrow. What was going on?

On Friday morning, I was relieved to find a small silver card in my post, amongst the usual array of press releases and work-experience begging letters, announcing that Laura McNaughton (plus guest) had the honour of being invited to the post-premiere party for Lucy Lloyd's new film, *About a Girl* – the tale of a young woman so beautiful that she literally drives men insane – which would take place in a refurbished meat-packing factory in Smithfield the following Wednesday from eight till late. The dress code was 'glam'.

'You lucky bugger,' said Nat enviously when I waved it

at her across the desk. 'I've been through my post with a fine-tooth comb, but I haven't got one.'

'I thought you were over all those "media bollocks" parties,' I teased, referring to the conversation we'd had the night before last and wondering whether I should take her as my guest.

'I am,' she insisted. 'But it's Lucy Lloyd's party. That's different. I mean, *everyone* will be there – Posh, Becks, Brangelina, maybe even Prince Harry ... Ricky Jones.' She said the last name very slowly and deliberately and looked at me, wide-eyed. 'I wonder if he'll remember you?'

'God, I wish,' I said, developing butterflies just thinking about Sugar Reef's outrageously sexy lead singer, who I'd interviewed a few weeks earlier.

Graham was hovering by the sound system, pretending to be enthralled by the new Adele promo album, which had also arrived in my post. But it was pretty obvious he was eavesdropping.

'This Lucy Lloyd thing,' he ventured, tentatively, still staring at the CD cover, 'you wouldn't happen to have a "plus one" on the invite, would you?'

'Fuck off, Graham,' snapped Nat. 'If she has, I'm going. I'm her line manager.'

'Oh, well, if you're going to pull rank,' said Graham, spinning round to face Natalie, eyes flashing. 'I think you'll find that art director appears above features editor on the masthead of this magazine, and, therefore, I am the more senior member of staff and the one more entitled to represent the company at such events.'

Nat glared at Graham and Graham glared back.

'And I think you'll find that I'm the one whose name is on the invitation and I'll decide who comes with me,' I interjected. These two could get very competitive.

They both glared at me.

'So, you'll both have to be very, very nice to me until I've made my decision,' I added smugly.

Nat narrowed her eyes and stared at me, hissing, 'Excuse me, missy, but who gave you this job in the first place, with all its fucking perks?'

'Oh, just ignore her, Laura,' said Graham to me with a saccharine smile. 'She doesn't get out much these days. Would you like a skinny cappuccino? I'm paying.'

'I think you'll find Laura's a bit above bribery, you old queen,' snapped Nat. 'Anyway that ticket's worth more than a cup of frothy dishwater from the caff.' She turned to me with a toothy smile. 'Would you like to have lunch at Nobu today, babes? On expenses, natch. We'll call it a features meeting.'

This was getting tricky. Cathy was watching from her desk, giving me sympathetic glances every time Nat or Graham lashed out at each other. What was I to do? The answer was staring me in the face. Literally.

'Cath,' I called out. 'What are you doing next Wednesday?'

Cathy's mouth dropped open. 'Nothing.'

'D'you want to come to Lucy Lloyd's party with me, then?' I asked.

'That would be lovely, Laura,' she grinned.

Nat and Graham stared at me open-mouthed.

'What the fuck did you do that for?' snapped Graham. 'She's just the PA.' He spat out the letters 'P' and 'A' as if they spelt out 'dog shit on the sole of my shoe'.

'Yeah, and she's a lovely girl who works her arse off and never gets to go to anything glamorous,' I replied. 'If you two want tickets, sort them out yourself.'

Nat sent me to Coventry for all of about five minutes before conceding that it was really nice of me to ask Cathy.

Graham's fury lasted a good deal longer, and he avoided my desk for the rest of the day.

As the afternoon progressed I became increasingly twitchy about the fact that Jasmine Brown hadn't called Trudy. At least, not to my knowledge.

'Has she mentioned anything to you?' I asked Nat at 4 p.m. She shook her head, but there was a faint smirk on her lips.

At four thirty Pete called. He caught me off guard, and even though it had only been two days since I'd seen him, his deep, well-spoken voice started a tidal wave of nostalgia crashing through my brain, as if I'd just turned on the radio and caught a favourite song I hadn't heard in years. My stomach lurched.

'Just wanted to check you were OK,' he said in a much kinder tone than he'd ever used when we were together.

Knowing Pete, he wanted me to say, 'No, I'm miserable. Without you my life is a black abyss, filled only with longing for you, my liege.' Or something equally melodramatic. I was damned if I was going to give him the pleasure of knowing that he'd actually hurt me quite badly.

'I'm all right. Takes more than a broken heart to get me down,' I said as sunnily as I could manage, while stabbing my desk with a pair of scissors and imagining his chiselled face.

'Are you sure? Because we could meet up and talk about it this weekend if you'd like,' he continued.

It was tempting. God, was it tempting. There was nothing I'd rather do than curl up in his big strong arms and pretend everything was perfect. But there was a tiny sensible voice telling me not to. I knew that if we saw each other we'd end up in the inevitable place – bed – and then I'd have to go through all this again the next time he dumped me. Anyway, I still had my pride.

'No, honestly, Pete, I don't think we should see each other for a while. I will get over you, you know,' I said, although my voice must have betrayed me, cracking as it was, the words catching in my throat.

He sounded a bit disappointed that I didn't want to milk the whole splitting-up thing, but told me he still cared about me and that he hoped we could remain friends. I wasn't sure we'd ever been friends. When he hung up, I sat with the receiver in my hand for a while, staring at the phone. I could feel tears welling up again and I had to go to the toilets for a cry.

After reapplying my make-up and noting that there was only an hour of the working week to go – why hadn't Jazz called? – I wandered back to find the place empty. It took a few seconds to realize that the entire staff of *Glitz* had congregated in Trudy's office. Nat called me in to the sound of popping champagne corks.

'A toast. To Laura,' said Trudy, grinning. Grinning!

'And her wonderful new job.'

'To Laura!' shouted everyone, glasses raised. I was flabbergasted.

Trudy continued, 'Laura has been with us for nearly three years now, and she's always been a much-valued, hard-working member of the team' – news to me. 'We'll all, and myself in particular, be very sad to see her go, but she has, as they say, had an offer she can't refuse. Our Laura is going to be a television presenter. Isn't that exciting? I always knew you had a glittering future, my girl. Although perhaps not in magazines.'

She air-kissed me twice, somewhere in the region of my cheeks. This was the closest physical contact I'd ever had with Trudy, and it was incredibly awkward, but touching all the same. I could feel the waterworks being turned on again, but this time they were tears of joy. I couldn't believe they'd organized this for me. Nat handed me a glass of champagne and hugged me.

'Well done, sweetheart,' she said, handing me a perfectly pristine handkerchief.

Graham was on his mobile, telling some mate or other that his 'really close friend Laura is going to be on the telly and isn't that wonderful!' The fact that he wasn't actually speaking to me had obviously slipped his mind in the wake of my impending celebrity status. Trudy kept grinning at me broadly.

'Why is she being so nice to me?' I stage-whispered to Graham when he got off the phone.

'Because celebrities make her wet her knickers,' he explained eloquently.

'I know I was mean to you earlier,' he said bashfully, 'but you won't forget me when you're a somebody, will you?' he asked. 'I've always wanted to be someone famous's very best friend.'

'Graham,' I replied with certainty. 'I could never forget you. Even if I was kidnapped by Scientologists and brainwashed.'

Friday night and nowhere to go. I'd spoken to Jazz and I didn't have to go into the Scorpion offices until Tuesday lunchtime. I had no idea what she'd said to Trudy but I didn't have to work any notice and I was being paid until the end of the month. It was all so thoroughly perfect, the only hitch being that I had no one to celebrate my good fortune with. Becky had gone camping in Devon – in November! – with her crusty friends. She did invite me along, but I reminded her that I didn't do wellies and cagoules – or crusties come to think of it – even if I was suddenly single. Nat was going to her folks' place in Essex for the weekend. Graham was at a dog show in Derby with George, Michael and some guy called Jim, who was terribly important in canine dressage, and I was too ashamed to call any of my more peripheral friends, who I'd neglected dreadfully during my doomed relationship with Pete. And Pete? Well, there was no Pete now, was there? I made a mental note not to put dates before mates in future and settled down for a night – no, make that a weekend – in front of the telly with the half-hearted belief that it was all in the name of research for my new job.

I'm not very good at being on my own. Never have been. After half an hour I could feel a Bridget Jones moment coming on. Not a good look. There I was, chewing my nails and staring at the phone, hoping somebody – OK, Pete actually – would call and invite me out to some amazingly glamorous party or other – even if it involved his nauseating friends. I wondered if maybe I should take him up on his offer and meet him for a chat. After an hour, I found my hand inexplicably drawn to the telephone with my index finger hovering over the 1 button – speed dial; guess who was number 1? It stayed there suspended for a good two minutes while I had a serious word with myself and then I eventually dialled number 2.

'Hello.'

'It's me. Laura. What are you doing this weekend?'

'Oh, not much. Just pottering.'

'Can I come and stay?'

'Of course you can, sweetheart. You're always welcome.'

Forty-five minutes later I was on the overnight train to Aberdeen. Suddenly the idea of a weekend in the sticks seemed strangely appealing.

Everyone should have somebody they can turn to for unconditional love when they feel unhappy, unloved and unwanted. For me, it's always been Gran. When, aged six, I brought home a punishment exercise from school for talking during class; when on Christmas Day a couple of years later I had a tantrum while playing Monopoly and threw the board across the living-room floor; when Mum caught me smoking a cigarette out of the bathroom window; and even when I got alcohol poisoning at Dad's fiftieth birthday party and threw up on the headmaster's brogues – on all these occasions, while the rest of the family tut-tutted and told me I was a disgrace, she just laughed and said I had 'fire in my belly and a song in my soul'.

Maggie was never the archetypal grandmother. She didn't have long, silver hair tied back neatly in a bun, or glasses, or knitting needles or even a rocking chair. She always seemed younger – mentally at least – than my dad, with his pedantic need for order and obedience, and was as bemused as I was about her son's need to conform to some hypothetical, straight-laced idea of normality. She chain-smoked menthol cigarettes through an intricately engraved antique silver cigarette holder. As grandmothers went, she was pretty rock'n'roll.

She was on the platform waiting when I got off the train, wearing a scarlet mac and mock-croc stilettos, fag in hand despite the No Smoking sign above her head.

'You look well,' she said before kissing me on the cheek and branding me with a bright-red lipstick mark. As we all know, the word 'well' is a euphemism for 'chubby' when spoken by an elderly relative. I made a mental note not to eat any of her mouth-watering home-made scones over the weekend.

'So?' asked Gran as we clambered into her two-seater

Triumph Spitfire – as I said, she wasn't the archetypal grandmother – 'What's all this about? You haven't been to visit since May and here you are, arriving out of the blue.'

'Things are just a bit funny at the moment,' I said as we drove along Union Street. 'I wanted to see my granny.'

'You've torn your jeans,' said Gran, nodding at my knees.

'No, they're distressed, Granny. It's fashionable to have holes in your jeans,' I explained.

'How distressing,' said Gran.

I snuggled into my coat, shivering, before I noticed Gran's window was wide open.

'It's bloody freezing, Gran. Can you shut your window, please?'

'You've turned into a southern softy,' she said with a chuckle, winding up her window. 'Your mum told me about the television job. That's great news. So, what do you mean things have been funny? Funny ha ha, or funny peculiar?'

'Peculiar. Most peculiar,' I said, staring out at the view.

The north-east of Scotland is often sunny, a girl could freeze her tits off, it's that cold, but Aberdeen gets more hours of sunshine than most British cities. As we drove out of town, along the motorway that hugs the coast, there wasn't a cloud in the sky. Behind me, the sunshine glistened on the Granite City, making the entire place twinkle in the November frost. The steely-blue sea sparkled like a sapphire and white horses danced in haphazard rows as far as the eye could see. Gran was smiling as she drove along, comfortable in our silence, happy to have her granddaughter to herself on such a beautiful day. She was humming 'Scotland the Brave' while driving at 90 m.p.h. and smoking a cigarette. I felt a familiar, warm glow in my belly. With Gran, I always felt at home.

'Pete finished with me,' I announced after a while.

'Oh,' said Gran, raising a pencilled-in eyebrow. 'And how do you feel about that?'

She had a way of making me tell the truth, just by glancing at me with her imploring, pale blue eyes.

'Confused,' I replied. 'I mean, I know I wasn't going to marry him or anything. And I suppose, in a way, I didn't even like him that much. But then, I feel a bit ... oh, I don't know. I thought he loved me. I didn't think he'd finish with me. I feel as if ...'

Gran was smiling to herself. 'Your ego has been dented?'

'No,' I said. 'It's not that. Is it? Maybe it is.'

We looked at each other and laughed. Gran patted my knee.

'Laura,' she said. 'You're a bonny, clever, funny girl, but that doesn't mean you're perfect. Well, not for Pete, anyway. The only man you'll ever meet who thinks you're perfect will be the one you stay with for life. Your grandad thought the sun shone out of my ... well, you know what. It doesn't, of course. And most other men I've met have found me far too eccentric for their taste, but in Blair's eyes I could do no wrong. Of course, he annoyed the hell out of me sometimes. He wouldn't shave often enough and it used to scratch when he kissed me, and he was very uptight about swearing, like your dad. He used to go quiet on me every time I said bloody hell, which was quite often when I had three bairns in the house. And he pushed the boys a bit too hard, I think. Academically, you know. And your dad did the same with you. Like father, like son. Which is why wee Blair is the way he is, God love him. I just got a letter, you know, and a photo of him with his guru – what a fright. They're both wearing white robes. Oh, and Blair has this enormous beard. It really is ridiculous.'

We smiled at each other, knowingly, because Blair was

my favourite uncle – and if she was honest, Gran's favourite son.

We turned off the motorway into the pretty harbour town of Stonehaven, just south of Aberdeen, and then on along a twisting coast road until it appeared we would drive right into the sea. Gran turned sharp left down a tiny dirt track and there it was, Doric Cottage, huddled on the hillside, being battered by the wind, clinging to its cliff like a seagull in a storm.

Maggie McNaughton had been born in Doric Cottage and she grew up there, as wild as the wind that blew up the garden from the North Sea. Now, she was as much a part of the scenery as the gannets who lived in the rocks below. But it hadn't always been that way. A long time ago, Granny had had a twin brother called Neil. When they left school at fourteen, Maggie got a job gutting fish in the fish market while her brother went to sea as a fisherman. He drowned during a storm when he was just sixteen and his body was never found. After Neil had gone, Maggie wanted to escape the scene of the tragedy. At the time, she was engaged to be married to Willy Mackay, the boy next door, who was, according to Granny, 'a nice enough chap, with not much up top'. When Willy was sent off to fight the Germans, Granny took her chance. One morning, she packed a small case, hitched a lift into Aberdeen, caught the first train that arrived and finally found herself at Edinburgh's Waverley Station. Poor Willy was never any the wiser, dying as he did in Normandy two weeks later.

In the city, Gran spent her days hanging out with students from wealthy, professional families. Despite the fact that she'd left school at fourteen with no qualifications, she somehow managed to ingratiate herself with the in-crowd at the art college. She gatecrashed lectures, modelled nude for fine-art students and was the belle of every ball, where she drank, smoked and danced with handsome soldiers on leave from the Second World War. In the grainy black-and-white photographs that lived on top of her piano, she looked like a young Marilyn Monroe, all Cupid's-bow lips and outrageous curves. Even now, in her eighties, she refused to leave the house without matching high-heeled shoes and handbag, scarlet lipstick and a well-tailored coat, and still dyed her hair peroxide blonde, even though it had started thinning on the crown.

My grandparents had caused quite a scandal in their youth. Grandad, Blair McNaughton, was a second-year student at Edinburgh University when he met Maggie in Princes Street Gardens in the summer of 1948. He was revising for an exam in the sunshine and she was sunbathing in a bathing suit, which wasn't a common sight in those days, and certainly not in Edinburgh city centre. By the time they got married a year later, Granny was already six months pregnant with my father. Maggie's family were mortified and washed their hands of her, until the baby was born at least. Blair's parents – wealthy, God-fearing, Morningside folk – were so devastated by their son's poor match and immoral behaviour that they disowned him, his new wife and their unborn child for ever. Without his parents' help, Grandad was too poor to finish his degree and ended up down the mines like most of the men in Lothian. Two more sons were born and the family lived on top of each other in a one-bedroom tenement beside a brewery in Gorgie, until that was bulldozed and the McNaughton family was rehoused in one of the new high-rise council flats that had been built in the sprawling concrete wasteland of Wester Hailes – soon to become the heroin capital of Scotland, and therefore not exactly a des res.

Grandad died young like many coal miners – aged forty-four – of lung cancer, but he did live long enough to see my dad off to university. Apparently, his last wish was that my dad and his brothers, Michael and Blair Junior, would get good qualifications and live nice, clean middle-class lives. A wish my dad took a bit too literally in my opinion. As did Uncle Michael, who grew up to be a fat balding accountant. Uncle Blair, on the other hand, did too much acid in the Sixties, dropped out of polite Edinburgh society and was now living in an ashram in Goa, hence the beard and the guru.

After thirty years of exile in high-rise hell, Granny inherited her parents' idyllic cottage in Aberdeenshire. Perched on a cliff in the middle of nowhere, the whitewashed house had a magical garden that sloped right down to the beach, where angry waves crashed ashore and sleepy seals took forty winks. I loved that house more than anywhere else on the planet, and I loved Granny more than any other human being. Together, the house and the glamorous old lady were my little bit of heaven on earth – for forty-eight hours at a time.

'Welcome home,' said Gran.

As a child, I had christened the cottage The Tardis, because although it looked quite small from the outside, it was pretty massive inside. The rooms were vast, with old granite floors and immense open fireplaces. The windows were large and plentiful, with panoramic views over the North Sea. Most had deep window seats, made comfortable with pretty, handmade floral cushions, where a girl could sit and daydream for hours and maybe even spot a seal or two if she were lucky. The kitchen was the heart of the home, complete with Aga and well-worn oak table. My room was in the attic and ran the length of the house on the top floor.

It had exposed beams on the ceiling and two bay windows, with breathtaking views of the beach and the ocean beyond. It was four times the size of my room in Kentish Town.

When we arrived, I ran upstairs and dumped my bag, changed into comfy, warm clothes and scrubbed my face clean of make-up and London grime. When I got back downstairs, Granny had made a pot of tea and was busy spreading lashings of full-fat butter onto hot home-made scones. Bang went my resolution and my mouth watered on cue. We sat down opposite each other at the kitchen table and Gran poured the tea.

'Don't dwell on this Pete business,' she said, handing me a mug. 'It obviously wasn't meant to be. When you meet "the one", you'll know it's right. Look at your mum and dad; he knew she was the one the minute he clapped eyes on her. He went on and on about this amazing lassie he'd met; she was the most beautiful, intelligent, witty girl on the planet. He was smitten, talked about her non-stop for months before we even met her. She took a bit longer to come round, I think.'

'She did?' I asked, intrigued.

'Oh yes. There was someone else involved, you see. A singer.'

I was fascinated by this new insight into my parents' relationship.

'What singer? Someone she knew from the band?' I asked.

My mum had been a singer in a folk band once upon a time. I always found it hard to imagine that the plump, blow-dried, middle-aged lady I knew as my mother, was once the babe of the Edinburgh folk scene. But it was true. In the early Seventies she used to tour Scotland, performing in clubs and bars wearing kaftans and smelling of joss sticks. She even played the guitar. By the time I was old enough to have any memory of her, that part of my mother's past had been neatly folded away in a box in the attic, along with the kaftans. The guitar stayed in the cupboard under the stairs and came out at Christmas when Mum would wow us with her excellent rendition of 'Little Donkey'. Other than that, there was nothing left of the cool, hippie chick she had once been. Sometime during the early Eighties she morphed into a clone of every other suburban housewife I've ever met. Mum's idea of a big night is a glass of wine at the golf club, followed by a ready meal for two from Marks & Spencer, a G&T in front of the telly and then an early night with a trashy historical novel. She was quite the suburban teacher's wife. Fiona and I called her Hyacinth Bouquet. She cared terribly what the neighbours thought, all her clothes were navy and well-pressed, she owned two Barbour jackets – a smart one for public consumption and another for walking the dog – she was thrilled to bits when Dad invested in a timeshare on the Algarve – great golf, you see – and if Dad could have afforded a Range Rover, her life would have been complete. I could hardly imagine her with unruly hair, an afghan coat and twenty-inch flares.

I found both my parents rather frustrating. Deep down, I respected my dad and craved his approval, but the more I tried to impress him, the more I seemed to irritate him. It had always been that way. He was cold and distant, I was loud and in his face. Now, we didn't talk at all. Mum was easier to love on a day-to-day basis. She had always been there with cuddles and plasters and home-made chocolate cake. In fact, she was always just there, at home, the good little housewife. It was easy to take her love for granted because she gave it so freely. She never seemed to keep any for herself. Secretly I felt she'd sold out – her career, her independence and maybe even her true personality – for the sake of the man she loved, and I resented Dad for making her do it, but I resented Mum more for letting him. I made a pledge at a young age – ten years old, I think – that I wouldn't do what my mother had done. No man would stop me from fulfilling my ambitions. I would be strong, where she had been weak. From that point on, I guess I'd kept her at arm's length.

'What singer?' I asked again. 'I can't imagine Mum with anyone but Dad. Who'd have her?'

'You've got your mum all wrong, Laura,' said Gran. 'When it comes to your dad, she's always been the one in control. As I said, there was this singer.'

'Och, go on ...' I was intrigued.

'A laddie called Dylan James, who had a recording contract and everything.'

'No way,' I said, eyes popping out of my head.

'Oh yes,' said Gran, sucking on her cigarette. 'But then, your mother was an exquisite little creature. And she was wild – she smoked pot, she got blind drunk, she wore hot pants that barely covered her private parts. I didn't think your dad stood a chance. He was just some groupie who followed her around and bought her the odd pint of cider if he could get near enough. I mean, your mum was practically engaged to this Dylan chap, who, by the way, was absolutely the most handsome fellow I'd ever seen. Your dad's not a bad-looking man, but he was always a bit sensible. He was a bit of a square.'

'Still is,' I muttered under my breath.

Granny ignored me. 'Your Uncle Blair was after her as well,' continued Gran.

'No way,' I spluttered. A more unlikely pairing I could hardly imagine.

My gran nodded. 'And I was sure Blair was more her type, but he's a stubborn bugger, your dad.'

I nodded enthusiastically in agreement.

'No, Laura,' said Gran sternly. 'I mean stubborn in a good way. He never gives up. Sticks to his guns. And you should be grateful for that, because there wouldn't be any Laura McNaughton if he hadn't persevered with your mother, would there?'

'True,' I conceded. 'So how did he get his girl?'

'He happened to be at a gig one night when Dylan and your mum had a fight. Blair wasn't there, missed his chance, and it was your dad's shoulder that your mum cried on. He was the perfect gentleman and the rest, as they say, is history. She left the singer for your father, and eighteen months later they were married. It took Blair at least five years to give up trying to seduce your mother behind your dad's back.'

'That's mental.' I laughed. 'My mum the man magnet.'

'Oh she was,' insisted Gran, stubbing out her fag. 'Another scone?'

'Do you think Mum ever regrets giving up her career for Dad?' I asked through a mouthful of crumbs. 'She might have been the next Janis Joplin.'

'What? And end up dead of a drugs overdose!' Granny smiled. 'No, darling. She loves your father to bits.'

'But how can that be enough?' I asked, perplexed. 'She could have had a future, a career, maybe even fame and fortune.'

'Love's worth more than money,' said Gran.

'But she's a nobody, now,' I continued. 'She could have been somebody really important.'

Gran glanced up at me with a slight frown. 'She is

important, Laura. She's your mother and Fiona's mother and she's your father's wife.'

'Oh, I know,' I replied, suddenly feeling guilty about dismissing my own mother. 'She's lovely, but there's a whole other life she could have led ...'

Granny disappeared into the lounge and came back clutching an old photo album I'd never seen before.

'Here,' she said, opening the album and laying it in front of me. 'I found this in the loft last week. It's been up there since you were a baby, so you won't have seen any of these before. There are some photos there of your mum in her singing days.'

I pored over page after page of slightly faded colour photographs of my mum and dad as the people they used to be. It was them all right, but not as I knew them. I had never before seen evidence that they had ever been so young. All the framed photographs at home were of us all together as a family. But here was Mum, with waist-length golden hair, holding a guitar and gazing wistfully at the camera.

'You look just like her,' said Gran.

Dad was there, too, dark and handsome in a well-cut suit, staring adoringly at the beautiful girl at his side.

'They look so ...'

'Young?' asked Gran.

I nodded. 'And full of energy.'

Granny laughed. I carried on flicking. Mum in a smoky pub, surrounded by young men with sideburns, wearing brown cords and Aran sweaters. But she was ignoring the hangers-on and waving at the camera, presumably at my dad. Mum and Dad up a tree, both wearing outrageous flares. Mum in a minuscule miniskirt, perched on the bonnet of a red Mini. Mum and Dad's wedding day.

'Bad dress,' I said, pointing at the hideous Eighties

creation of billowing cream nylon, with a high neck and trumpet sleeves which Mum was sporting, proudly. Gran giggled and nodded.

Mum, heavily pregnant on the beach below the cottage. And then the final picture, Mum beaming in a hospital bed, clutching a tiny red-faced baby, and Dad, pleased as Punch, arm around his wife, gazing in awe at his newborn child.

'That's me,' I whispered. It was the first time I'd seen myself so young.

Gran nodded. 'Once you came along … well, they were in heaven.'

'Do you think Mum regrets any of it?' I wondered. 'I mean, she dumped a famous singer for Dad.'

'Don't be silly,' said Gran. 'She's a very contented lady, believe me. She just wishes you and your dad would make up whatever silly differences you have.'

'Hmph,' I said petulantly. 'That's up to him. All I did was write a feature about my sex life, for God's sake! I'm twenty-five, Mum was only twenty-one when he married her! Anyway, I was only doing my job.'

'I know, love,' said Gran. 'But your dad—'

'Is a square,' I interrupted.

'Yes, and he's also a very private man. And a teacher, who needs to command respect and authority. He was mortified that his pupils knew his daughter's favourite sexual position. They were taunting him, Laura. You can imagine what they were saying.'

'I know,' I said, giggling at the thought.

'Seriously, Laura,' Gran continued, 'you're as bad as he is. You're just like him, you know? You dig your heels in and refuse to budge, but one of you is going to have to make the first move or you'll end up with a full-scale feud on your hands. Your father adores you, Laura. And I know you love him to bits, too. This is just a silly wee argument that's been blown out of proportion.'

I sighed and looked again at the photograph of me as a brand-new baby. Dad did look chuffed to bits.

'OK, Gran. I promise I'll make more of an effort to patch things up,' I said.

'Good.' She smiled broadly. 'Now, let's put the telly on. We're missing *Strictly*.'

In bed that night I listened to the soothing sound of the waves and thought about my parents. I had never even asked them how they'd met. For the first time in months I drifted off into a deep sleep, images of my mum and dad when they were younger floating around my mind.

I spent Sunday morning walking on the beach in the blustery wind, collecting shells, wrapped in a parka, watching the seals as they bobbed in and out of view just offshore, and wondering what Nat would say if she could see me being such a good, clean-cut country girl. As I wandered back to the house, I spotted a van I didn't recognize in the drive; it said 'Knox & Sons, Master Builders' on the side. Through the kitchen window I could see Granny talking to a strange young man, and an attractive one at that. I smoothed down my wind-blown hair with my hand, licked my salty lips and opened the door.

'Well, London's a big place, Adam,' Gran was saying. 'Don't get your head turned.'

'Och, I won't,' the man replied. 'I'm going there to make something of myself. The last thing I'm going to do is start hanging out in trendy, overpriced bars or dating some silly London airhead ...'

I felt myself colour. Was I 'a silly London airhead'? Who the hell was this bloke and why did I feel so affronted?

'Laura, this is Adam,' said Granny, grinning broadly and blushing like a teenager who'd been caught snogging her boyfriend. 'He's my handyman.'

Adam was six foot two, with collar-length, black curly hair and bright blue eyes. He looked like a gypsy – all tanned, healthy and a bit dirty in his worn jeans and grubby white T-shirt. He was wearing the biggest boots I'd ever seen – big feet means a big ... – which were caked in muck. I couldn't help noticing, as he shook my hand, that his forearms were so muscular they were throbbing.

'Hi,' he said shyly, catching my eye for a split second, before staring at his grubby boots and muttering, 'I've just been emptying your granny's septic tank.'

I withdrew my hand quickly, wiped it on my jeans and said, 'That's nice.'

That's the problem with country boys, I thought. No class.

Granny winked at me as she took a tenner out of her purse and handed it to Adam.

'Och, put it away, Maggie,' said the handyman. 'I'm not taking your money.'

'You'll take some scones instead, Adam,' insisted Gran, handing him a Tupperware box. 'Your dad loves them.'

'Thanks, Maggie. I'd better get off, though. We're building some new halls of residence at the university,' said Adam. Then, turning to me, but avoiding eye contact, 'Nice to meet you, Laura. Might see you again sometime.'

I nodded and smiled through slightly gritted teeth. He picked up his tool bag and backed out of the door, tripping on the steps as he went and spilling spanners and screwdrivers all over the patio. His face turned a deep shade of beetroot.

What a prat, I thought.

'Adam's thinking of moving to London and setting up his own business,' said Gran proudly as we watched the van struggling up the dirt track to the road.

'He wouldn't last ten minutes in London. Country bumpkin like that.' I sniffed, knowingly.

'I wouldn't be too sure,' said Gran. 'The Knoxes are a fine family – they've always looked out for me, being so far away from you all – and Adam's a clever laddie.'

''Course he is, Gran,' I said, sarcastically. 'Builders are known for their superior intelligence.'

The old lady frowned at me and shook her head. 'You're not as smart as you think you are, Laura. But you'll learn. The hard way, like we all do.'

She busied herself with the dirty dishes, but I could sense, even though she'd turned away from me, that she was not amused. Her back looked angry. The soapsuds were flying out of the sink as she violently scrubbed a baking tray. Gran was fiercely loyal to her family and friends, and I should have known better than to criticize someone she respected. I hated being in Granny's bad books, so I took myself upstairs to lick my wounds. I sat on the window seat in my room, staring out to sea until the sky went black. Then I must have fallen asleep, there in the darkness, because the next thing I knew, Gran was calling from the bottom of the stairs.

'Laura! Supper's ready!'

All was forgiven. After a hearty plateful of home-made fish pie, we sat by the fire, stuffing our faces with more hot, buttered scones and discussing my new job.

'What do you think Dad will say?' I asked.

'He's not going to be overly enthusiastic,' said Gran with a sigh. 'He worries about you. To him you'll always be that cheeky little girl with bunches and plasters on her knees. He thinks the media's immoral. That it sucks people in, chews them up and then spits them out. He worries you'll get hurt. God knows what he'll say when he sees you on the box.'

'What do you think about me being on TV?' I asked, because I always looked for Granny's approval.

'I think it will be an adventure,' she said warmly. 'It might not be what you expect it to be, but life's for living and you're like me, you need to take chances or you get bored. You'll be OK. Whatever happens, it will happen for a reason, and you'll end up where you're supposed to be. You're strong, Laura. Stronger than you realize. You can weather any storm. Like me ...'

As Gran stared into the fire, a shadow crossed her face and her pale eyes watered.

'Are you OK?' I asked.

'Mmm,' she said absent-mindedly. 'I'm fine, dear.'

I wondered if she was thinking of Grandad, or maybe even her brother, Neil. It was stormy outside, and on nights like these she must have been reminded of him, still out there somewhere, under the waves. Dad once told me that the water in the North Sea is so cold that bodies don't decompose and float to the surface to be washed up on a nearby beach a few days later. They sink straight to the bottom and lie there for ever, never to see the light of day again. Perhaps that's why Granny moved back here, to be close to Neil in his watery grave.

On Monday, we bought fish and chips in Stonehaven and ate them on the pier, fighting off the world's largest seagulls by throwing them the odd chip. We drove up to the ruins of Dunnottar Castle – where they filmed *Hamlet* starring Mel Gibson, no less – and lay on the clifftop, upside down on our backs, getting dizzy from staring at the sky as it merged into the waves. Too late, we spotted an imposing grey cloud, the heavens opened and we got soaked as we ran back to the car. Gran drove me back to Aberdeen and put me on the four o'clock train to King's Cross for a seven-hour journey in wet jeans. Not something my mother would have done. 'You'll catch your death of cold,' she would have said.

'I'm glad you came, Laura,' said Granny as I cuddled her on the platform. 'I wanted to see you again before ...'

'Before what?' I asked.

'Oh nothing. Before you started your new job, that's all. Anyway, you take care and enjoy yourself. And don't worry about your dad. He'll come round – eventually.'

'That's what Mum says,' I replied.

'She's a wise woman.' Gran smiled. 'Now get on the train. It'll go without you.'

As the train pulled out of the station, I waved goodbye to my glamorous granny. It struck me suddenly, as she stood there alone on the platform, that she looked fragile and very old. I wiped the red lipstick from my cheek, sat back in my seat and got stuck into *Grazia*.

5

New job, new you

There were five envelopes waiting for me on the doorstep on Tuesday morning, and for once none of them were bills. There was a card from Vicky; it had congratulations emblazoned across the front, and inside it read, 'Dearest Naughty, you are a total star. I always knew it and now the rest of the world is about to find out. Loads of love. V. xxxxx. PS. In case you've forgotten, my telephone number is ...' There was another one from Mum, which she'd signed from Dad, too, but his signature was a blatant forgery. Fiona had handmade a good-luck card out of wallpaper and glitter glue, and Gran sent me a cryptic postcard of Dunnottar Castle. All she wrote on it was, 'Success has many fathers while failure is an orphan. All my love, Granny xxx'. And there was a hilarious card from work. Graham had superimposed my head onto Lucy Lloyd's pneumatic body, with the headline, NEXT YEAR'S SUPERSTAR! underneath. They'd all signed it, even Trudy. Becky had laid out a breakfast of fresh fruit salad and croissants, and left a coffee-stained scribble on last Friday's *Evening Standard*, which I think said, 'Knock 'em dead, babes!' but it was almost impossible to decipher. I sat there munching my fruit salad, fingering my cards and feeling all gooey inside because everyone had remembered what a big day it was for me.

I was forty-five minutes early for my first day at work at Scorpion TV, which wasn't particularly surprising since I'd been awake since 5 a.m. and wasn't due at the studios until 1 p.m. I sat in the window of a hip Soho café across the road and sipped a latte, while watching people come and go from the building. It appeared that nobody over thirty-five was allowed across the threshold – the blokes wore their jeans tight and their hair dishevelled, the women wore their jeans even tighter and their hair glossy. It was impossible to spot the lowly runners – glorified errand boys and girls, prepared to work for a pittance as a way in to television – from the presenters and producers, as everyone looked so damn cool. My coffee cup shook in my hand and the caffeine sat uncomfortably in my stomach. I was petrified.

There were still twenty minutes to go, but I couldn't wait any longer, so I crossed the road, took a deep breath and entered the building. The girl on reception was suitably glamorous in a Page Three kind of way. She was on the phone.

'Ooh, I know!' She sounded like Sybil from *Fawlty Towers*. 'I know! And his stitches haven't even been taken out yet. Dirty bugger.'

She eyed me lazily and continued her conversation. 'And the worst of it is, Denise, his wife doesn't even know about me. I mean, I ask you, what would you do in my shoes?'

I opened my mouth to talk to her, but she put up a well-manicured hand firmly and said, 'In a minute, I'm busy.'

'Sorry about that, Den,' she continued. 'Ooh, I know! That's the problem with older men, no stamina. But he's loaded ...'

I sighed impatiently.

'Listen, babes, hang on a minute,' she said to her friend, and then, in a loud whisper, 'I've got some ...' She looked me up and down again. 'Person here. She's probably just a courier. I'll get rid of her and call you back. Bye-ee.'

The receptionist put the phone down and said, 'Can I help you, madam?' with a false smile.

'I'm here to see Jasmine Brown,' I said without smiling. 'My name's Laura McNaughton and I start work here today. I'm the presenter on her new show.'

That was probably more information than she required, but I felt the need to let her know I wasn't 'just a courier'.

The girl's face turned puce and she stammered, 'Oh, oh, Laura. Yes, Laura, we were expecting you at one. You're early. I'm sorry. I was ... I was ... I was ...'

'Just talking to Denise,' I replied.

'Um, yeah. Sorry about that. I'll get Jasmine for you.'

She dialled a number and said, 'Jazz? I've got Laura here for you. She's early.'

The girl smiled at me shyly. 'I'm Julie,' she said. 'You'll probably be seeing a lot of me.'

'That'll be nice,' I said, although I wasn't sure I meant it.

At that moment, Jazz came bouncing round the corner, barefoot.

'Laura! You're early,' she exclaimed, kissing me. 'Have you met Julie?'

Julie and I nodded obediently.

'Right, come on then, Laura. There's someone I want you to meet,' said Jazz, taking me by the elbow.

As we got round the corner she whispered, 'Isn't Julie hilarious? She's completely inefficient but very entertaining. Our very own tart with a heart. She's having an affair with the MD, that's how she got the job, and she's sooo indiscreet. He's just had to have one of his testicles removed and she's told everybody. Now, whenever any of us have to go to his office for a bollocking, we know he's only got one bollock! God, she's priceless.'

I wasn't quite sure how to respond to this piece of inside information, so I just smiled blankly.

'Are you excited?' asked Jazz.

'God, yeah,' I replied with feeling. 'I can't believe this is happening to me.'

'Well, it is, Laura. Welcome to your new world. Come in.' She opened her office door and ushered me inside.

Tina was perched delicately on her beanbag, beaming, as we entered. Behind her was what looked like the third Mitchell brother from *EastEnders*, a short, thickset guy with a bald head and heavy brow, wearing cycling shorts, a Lycra vest and too many muscles. He was stretching his arms above his head for no apparent reason. Behind him was a television with an image of me frozen on it. The word 'Pause' flashed above my head.

'This is Trevor,' announced Jazz. 'He's your body doctor.'

'My what?' I asked, confused. Aren't all doctors body doctors?

Other than some first-day nerves, I felt perfectly well. Why did I need a doctor? Jasmine and Tina stared at me expectantly. Trevor carried on stretching. Was I being thick? Was I missing something here?

'Now, darling, don't get me wrong, you look fabulous and that's one of the reasons we've chosen you,' said Jazz. 'But this is TV, and you've got to be special. I'd have you just the way you are, but the suits upstairs have only agreed that you can be a presenter on the condition that you lose weight.'

Suddenly I realized what was happening. Trevor was here to help me shape up. They'd obviously been studying my rushes to evaluate my flab. Silly me. I thought I'd be taught about camera angles and autocues, but it appeared there were more pressing things for me to learn first, like how to get skinny – fast.

I felt like I'd been smacked in the stomach. OK, so I was no Kate Moss, but I was five foot nine and a size twelve. I'd never been called fat in my life. Curvy, maybe, womanly yes, but overweight? As if! I could feel my cheeks flushing and tears of anger and injustice stinging my eyes. It was one thing to compare my thighs unfavourably to those belonging to a world-famous sex symbol, but quite another to have a roomful of virtual strangers order me to go on a diet. Jazz and Tina looked at each other and bit their lips.

'Listen, Laura, I know it's not fair, but don't be offended. All those beautiful girls you see on telly every day have been told this at some point. You must know that, being a journalist.'

I did know that, but for some stupid reason I hadn't been expecting this. I should have seen it coming. I'd interviewed enough famous women to realize that the majority of them were a size eight or less, and that not all of them could be that slim without a hell of a lot of work. Suddenly, all the nerves that had been building up inside me all week, and all the doubts I'd had about not being good enough for the job surfaced, and I burst into tears. Trevor stopped stretching and left the room.

'I'm sorry,' I sobbed. 'This is really embarrassing. I'm not normally this sensitive, but it's been a weird week.'

I flopped onto the nearest beanbag and buried my head in my hands, mortified that I'd burst into tears at such an inappropriate time, and convinced I was about to get sacked after the shortest career in television history. Why was I being such a dork? It hit me suddenly that my period was due in two days' time. I was displaying all the symptoms of a mental, premenstrual female and, having always suffered terribly at the hands of Mother Nature, it was blatantly clear that I should never have left the flat that morning, let alone started a job in the precarious world of television. For three days of every month for the previous eleven years, I had become an emotionally fucked-up wreck. The only predictable behavioural trait during these dark days was overreaction to any given situation, whether it be with tears, fits of hysteria, anger or violence. Becky had actually banned me from going out in public during the three days leading up to my period after an incident which involved me breaking down in French Connection's flagship store on a busy Saturday afternoon because they didn't have a pair of trousers in my size. I'd had a full-on toddler tantrum, and the manager had had to ask me to leave the store.

Jasmine handed me a tissue and patted my shoulder.

'It must be very difficult to take all this in,' she said kindly.

'My boyfriend dumped me last week,' I said weakly, trying to excuse my childish reaction.

'I know, darling,' she said. 'Natalie told me. I'm sorry. I feel partly responsible. He wasn't very happy about all this, was he?'

I shook my head and blew my nose. 'It's not your fault.' I sniffed. 'He's a twat.'

She laughed gently and then took a deep breath. 'So, about this Trevor business. Are you OK with it?'

I nodded uncertainly and said lamely, 'I did order a salad the other night.'

Tina leaned towards me timidly, obviously frightened that I might smack her because she looked as if she wore a size four dress, and said, 'He's a kind of personal trainer cum nutritionalist cum psychologist. He'll help you work out, tell you what you can and can't eat and try things like hypnotism to sort out any problems you might have with overeating and lack of exercise.'

'It might be fun,' ventured Jazz. 'Think how many girls would kill to have their own personal trainer at their disposal?'

'Hmm,' I pondered. 'How much weight do they think I need to lose?'

'Not that much,' said Jazz. 'What are you? Nine and a half stone?'

'About that,' I nodded, thinking, and the rest.

'A stone, maybe,' she estimated. 'You need to be a sample size, really, like a model.'

'Why didn't you just get a model to present the programme, then?' I asked rather petulantly.

'Because I wanted somebody with a bit of spark. Someone who's not afraid to ask difficult questions. A woman with a brain and a bit of experience,' explained Jasmine. 'If it makes you feel better, Jack, your co-presenter, has a body doctor, too.'

'Does he need to lose weight as well?' I asked, hopefully.

'No, he's too skinny,' giggled Tina. 'He needs to build up a few muscles for the phwoar factor.'

My tears had dried up and I was able to laugh at the ridiculousness of the whole situation. I wondered if Jack and I would be dubbed the new Little and Large.

'This must all sound a bit rich coming from me.' Jazz looked herself up and down. She was even curvier than me, and a couple of inches shorter. 'But I'm not in front of the camera. I tried that. They made me lose weight, too, but my mum's Jamaican, and I couldn't resist her jerk chicken and deep-fried plantain. I decided it was easier being on the other side of the camera and eating like a pig.'

I forced a half-hearted smile.

There was a knock on the door and Trevor re-entered, smiling shyly. He looked like he'd overdosed on testosterone-laden steroids, so when he opened his mouth, I was expecting something gruff and manly to come out, but when he asked, 'Is everything all right?' it sounded as if he'd been breathing helium. It was the voice of Lisa Simpson trapped in the body of the Incredible Hulk. His voice was so squeaky and high-pitched that I had to stop myself from laughing out loud and asking, 'Are you taking the piss?'

'Everything's fine now, Trev,' said Jazz, seemingly oblivious to his comedy vocal cords.

'OK then, Laura. Come with me,' squeaked Trevor. I followed him like a dutiful puppy, out of Jasmine's office, along the corridor and into the lift, swallowing the giggle that was trying to escape. I'm not sure quite why I found it so hilarious. I can only assume it had something to do with nerves or raging PMT, or a dangerous combination of the two.

'Where are we going?' I asked, trying to make polite conversation.

It was a bad move.

'To the canteen,' he squeaked. 'To evaluate your eating habits.'

There were just the two of us in the lift. My giggle escaped, surprising both of us. It was louder than I thought it would be, and it seemed to go on for ever, reverberating off the walls of the lift as if it were the Royal Albert Hall.

'What are you laughing at?' he squealed like a piglet.

'I don't know. Must be stress,' I spluttered, before dissolving into a fit of hysteria, bent over double, there in the lift.

Trevor looked at me as if I was certifiable. I bit my cheeks, sucked in my breath and tried to contain my laughing fit, but my shoulders shook and I kept letting out involuntary sniggers in the process. I remembered that at school when this happened, which it did frequently when I was a teenager, I would make myself remember my treasured cat, Smoky, being run over by a motorbike. That would always stop the giggles. So, I forced myself to think about Pete and the heinous way he'd treated me. It worked to a degree. Slowly the laughter dissipated, and by the time we reached the sixth floor I'd managed to calm down a little, letting out just the occasional grunt. I felt terrible. I was sure Trevor hated me already, and he hadn't even seen my cellulite yet.

Trevor strode confidently into the canteen kitchen, nodding hello to the various men and women dressed in white, who were busy washing dishes or preparing jacket potatoes and chilli con carne. He opened a heavy door and entered the walk-in cold store. I followed him, shivering.

'Which are your favourite foods?' he demanded, waving his arms around, indicating the various yummy contents.

'Um, this,' I said, pointing to a jumbo-size box of cream cheese. 'And this.' Praline and cream ice-cream. 'These.' Frozen chips. 'Definitely this.' Mississippi mud pie. 'Oh, my favourite,' I enthused, clutching an oversized box of mini chicken Kievs. 'These.' Cans of full-fat coke. 'This.' Steak and ale pie. 'And these.' Meringues. 'And—'

'Thought so,' said Trevor. 'What about this?' He pointed to some lettuce.

'Nah.' I shook my head.

'These?' Brussels sprouts.

'No one likes those,' I insisted.

'Fish?' he asked, hopefully.

'I like fish and chips,' I confirmed.

Trevor frowned.

'You're going to have to completely relearn everything

you know about food,' he warned. 'How many sugars do you have in tea and coffee?'

'Three,' I replied.

'And how many cans of fizzy pop do you drink a day?'

'About four or five,' I ventured truthfully, perfectly aware it was the wrong answer.

'And how many litres of water?'

'Litres?' I scoffed. 'No litres. But I sometimes drink a pint of water before bed if I'm really, really drunk.'

'That's something else you'll have to cut right down on,' said Trevor, sternly. 'Alcohol.'

My face fell.

'You'll be drinking at least two litres of water every day from now on, and no more than eight units of alcohol a week.'

Oh joy! I thought.

We went back down to the ground floor and into Jazz's office.

'Don't mind me,' she said breezily from her ergonomically curved desk by the window.

Trevor presented me with a folder and various sheets of paper.

'This is what you are allowed to eat,' he said firmly, handing me a list of boring vegetables. 'We're avoiding a lot of carbs and cutting out fat almost totally.'

'Isn't that unhealthy?' I suggested.

'No, not in the short term. We'll reintroduce them in moderation once you've reached your target weight.'

For a man with a little girl's voice, he had a very authoritarian manner. I didn't dare argue.

'You'll also find diet sheets with recipe suggestions in your info pack and an exercise regime. Now, let's get you to the gym. Jasmine has some kit for you,' he said.

Jazz got up from her desk and produced a navy-blue T-shirt with Scorpion TV emblazoned across the front, a pair of cycling shorts and some rather funky Nike trainers.

To my amazement, Scorpion TV had their own private gym in the basement, which is where Trevor and I spent the rest of the afternoon. I'd become used to his high-pitched squeals and was in no mood for laughing any more. Especially when he ordered me to step on the scales. I took off my trainers to make me as light as possible. It was the first time I'd weighed myself in a year and I was absolutely terrified about what they would say.

'Ten stone four,' announced Trevor, typing the results into his state-of-the-art, hand-held electronic organizer. 'How tall are you?'

'Five nine,' I said, quietly.

'OK, then by my calculations' – he fiddled with his gizmo – 'you need to lose ... two stone four.'

'I haven't been eight stone since I was fifteen,' I said, flabbergasted. 'And anyway, according to those charts at the doctor's I should be at least nine and a half at my height.'

'Those charts are for the ordinary people,' sniffed Trevor. 'And you can't be ordinary if you want to look good on television. The camera adds several pounds, remember.'

Next, he did various tests on me to determine my fitness level. The most embarrassing one involved a set of pincers, which grabbed my flab and told Trevor my body's ratio of fat to lean muscle. Result? The flab was winning. Then he made me run on a treadmill, wired up to a machine, until I was gasping for breath, in order to figure out my cardiovascular strength. Result? I was heading for a premature coronary. After two hours in his company, Trevor had convinced me he had been sent from heaven to save my life.

After a lie-down in the shower – I literally couldn't stand

up – I staggered back to Jazz's office. She and Trevor smiled broadly at me.

'Well done, Laura,' announced my personal body fascist. 'You did really well. We'll have you in great shape in no time.'

'Excellent,' enthused Jazz, grinning. 'Let's go out for a celebratory drink.'

And so, red-faced from the afternoon's physical exertion, and still knowing zilch about television presenting, I ended my first day at Scorpion TV in Soho House with Jasmine, Tina and Trevor.

'What are you having?' he asked.

'Ooh, I could kill for a pint of lager,' I said, salivating.

'I don't think so,' he replied. 'You'll have a vodka and slimline tonic. And just the one!'

If this was what it took to get on the telly, I wasn't sure I wanted the job.

6

Exclusive! Behind the scenes at the party of the year

Getting to work the following day would have been physically impossible had Scorpion not sent a car to pick me up at 8.30 a.m. sharp. The mind was willing but the flesh was weak – and the muscles were throbbing like hell. When Trevor suggested a wake-up workout, I collapsed onto the nearest beanbag and groaned.

'The only thing that will loosen up those aching muscles is vigorous exercise,' he squeaked with demonic enthusiasm, offering me an outstretched hand.

And so I found myself on a treadmill – again – for what was to become my regular daily exercise regime. At an hour when most people are consuming their breakfast calorie quota, I was already burning mine off. And I'd only had a slice of melon.

For lunch, Jasmine took me to a swanky French restaurant where Jack was to join us for a 'getting to know each other' session. I sipped my fizzy mineral water nervously and watched the door for the arrival of my co-presenter. What if we hated each other? It was a bit like an arranged marriage. Jazz, as matchmaker, had decided we would work well together, but if we didn't, what then?

I spotted Jack the minute he walked in. He might as well have had 'TV Personality' emblazoned across his forehead. He was quite short for a bloke – small enough to fit inside the telly – but he exuded the kind of confidence that over-compensated for his lack of height. Something about his permatan and broad, gleaming smile shouted 'Famous!' even though nobody recognized him outside of Wales. Just watching him make an entrance made me feel like an amateur. Fellow diners sat up and looked, wondering, no doubt, where they'd seen him before.

'Jazz, darling!' he proclaimed loudly as he approached the table. 'You look even more yummy than usual.' There was no trace of a Welsh accent. He could have been from Putney.

Jack kissed Jasmine full on the mouth and then turned to me.

'And you must be Laura. Well, they said you were beautiful, but I wasn't expecting a goddess!' he exclaimed.

His cheesy grin was heading straight for my mouth, so I bobbed and weaved and managed to offer him a cheek instead. His lips were full, warm and wet. There was no denying that Jack was handsome in a textbook kind of way – small but perfectly formed. His cheekbones were high, his jaw square, his skin honeyed and his hair highlighted to perfection. He was groomed to within an inch of his life. Teenage girls would love him. My initial reaction? He made me want to retch.

'Waiter,' shouted Jack. 'Get rid of this for me.'

He threw his leather jacket on top of some poor Frenchman in a black waistcoat before sitting between myself and Jazz with a flourish of a napkin and a toss of his floppy blond hair. I smiled apologetically at the waiter in the hope he wouldn't spit in our food. Jack grabbed both our hands and smiled with twinkly green eyes.

'So this is the start of our adventure,' he said in conspiratorial tones, gazing from Jasmine to me and then back to Jasmine. 'How incredibly fucking exciting is this?'

I tried to throw a quizzical look in Jazz's direction, but she seemed lost in the Welshman's gaze. Was it only me, or was this guy a complete tosser? I had always prided myself on having highly tuned wank antennae, which could detect wankers, wankness and indeed all things wank at a hundred paces. These antennae had been vibrating violently since my co-presenter walked into the restaurant. But so far, only the waiter appeared to see what I could see. Jasmine, for one, was completely oblivious. I was already worried about the ratings. Would any sane person welcome this man into their living room?

Jack ordered steak to 'build up his bulk', as instructed by Trevor. Jazz plumped for chicken in a creamy, calorific sauce. I asked dejectedly for a seared-tuna salad. 'Without the dressing,' added Jasmine. Oh joy.

'So, did you manage to get me a ticket for tonight, gorgeous?' Jack was asking Jasmine.

'Would I let you down, handsome?' she flirted back.

'Oh, so are we all going to the Lucy Lloyd thing?' I asked.

'We certainly are,' smiled Jazz. 'And just wait until you see what I've got back in my office: a mound of designer dresses to die for. You can take your pick.'

'Well, at least I'll have a flat stomach,' I said through a mouthful of rocket.

'I'm sure you'll look absolutely divine,' drooled Jack as his hand rested on my thigh.

Oh great, I thought. I have to share a television screen with the lech from Llanelli.

After lunch, Trevor whisked Jack off to the gym and Jasmine and I were left alone in her office with thirty-four designer frocks for company. I was in my element. OK, so I was used to going to the changing rooms in Topshop with my arms laden with clothes, but this was something else.

These dresses were exquisite – every jewel was priceless, every pleat hand-stitched, every skirt length determined by a famous designer. I tried on a black, full-length column dress which had been hand-embroidered in Japan with turquoise birds and orange butterflies. It looked amazing on the hanger, but hideous on me. The dress hadn't been designed with curves in mind. I pulled a face of disgust.

'Hmm,' mused Jasmine. 'I think that one will have to wait until you've lost a few pounds.'

A sugar-pink, spaghetti-strapped, baby-doll number also caught my eye.

'This is cute,' I enthused.

'Try it on,' encouraged Jazz.

I stepped into the frothy little number, and it was looking good until I tried to squeeze my boobs in. Despite Jasmine's best efforts, the zip refused to do up.

'Never mind,' she said kindly. 'There are plenty more to try.'

I was standing admiring myself in the full-length mirror, wearing a white halter-neck silk top and matching wide-legged trousers, when Jazz asked, 'What do you think of Jack, then?' Her eyebrow was raised and her head cocked. I got the feeling she knew what I was thinking already.

'He's, um, very, er ...' I searched my vocabulary desperately for a positive adjective to describe Jack. 'Confident?' It was more of a question than a statement.

'You think he's an idiot,' said Jazz. 'Of course you do. Everybody thinks he's an egotistical halfwit when they first meet him, but, believe me, he grows on you. Wait and see. I'm not sure you're tanned enough to wear white, by the way.'

'Really?' I was disappointed. I thought the outfit looked great. 'Are you sure he'll grow on me?' I continued. 'He's so cheesy.'

'Babes,' she replied, throwing me another armful of dresses. 'Jack's a one-off. It's not an act, all that mwaw-mwaw stuff. He genuinely loves people. Never has a bad word to say about anyone. I mean, I know he can be a prat – that stuff with the waiter and everything – but he doesn't even realize he's doing it. It's just the way he is. And did you notice the size of the tip he left for the guy?'

I hadn't.

'Honestly, Laura,' Jazz continued. 'He's a born star. He's got some strange relationship with his mother. His dad left them, and she brought him up on her own as mummy's special soldier. The guy's been acting like royalty since birth. It all comes naturally to him. He believes his own hype, d'you know what I mean? And the camera loves him, so the viewers will, too. That's stunning by the way.' She nodded at the strapless scarlet dress I was clutching.

'It is, isn't it,' I agreed. 'But, Jazz, what if I don't like him?'

'You will, babes. Trust me. You will. Now try that one on. I think there are some Gina shoes here which will match perfectly.' Jasmine disappeared into a suitcase full of sandals, stilettos and boots before resurfacing with a pair of jewel-encrusted killer heels. '*Voilà!*'

The dress fitted perfectly in the way only very expensive clothes can. It hugged my curves tightly, skimmed my thighs in a satisfactorily slimming manner and stopped just at the knee. The shoes looked sensational, but were impossible to walk in, especially considering my aching calf muscles.

'Don't worry about being able to walk,' insisted Jasmine. 'You just have to stand there looking alluring. Which you do – very Jessica Rabbit.'

I stared at my reflection in disbelief. I'd never worn anything as beautiful before, and I could hardly breathe with excitement at the thought of walking into the party that evening dressed in this perfect red dress.

'Ooh, I can't wait for tonight,' I trilled, twirling around.

'You'll knock 'em dead,' said Jazz with a grin.

She glanced at her watch. 'Shit, it's three thirty. You've got a hair appointment in Mayfair in fifteen minutes.'

She picked up the phone. 'Julie, is Laura's car here yet? It is. Fantastic. She's just coming.'

'Right, here's the plan,' said Jazz, unzipping my dress. 'You go and have your hair done. It'll take about three hours for a full head of highlights and a trim, and then they need to blow-dry it straight. Daniel, the hairdresser, knows what to do, he's been fully briefed. A car will pick you up from Mayfair and bring you back here for sevenish. The make-up artist will be waiting. We'll have some bubbly while you get your face on, just to get us in the mood, and then we've hired a limo for you and Jack to arrive in. I've had a quiet word in a few ears – Fleet Street, Canary Wharf, you get my drift – so the press will know exactly who you are.'

'Oh my God.' I shivered with nerves and anticipation. 'I'll probably fall over or something stupid like that.'

'You'll be fine,' soothed Jazz.

'What about my friend, Cathy?' I asked, suddenly remembering my life outside Scorpion. 'She's coming as my guest.'

'Not a problem,' insisted Jazz, pushing me out the door. 'Give her a call, tell her to come here for seven thirty and she can jump in a cab with me. We'll be right behind you. Now go, Daniel doesn't like to be kept waiting. He had to cancel an It-girl to fit you in.'

In the car on the way to the hairdresser's I phoned Cathy. I was so busy enthusing about the red dress and the flash hair appointment that I almost forgot to tell her about the plans for the evening. She explained that Nat and Graham had managed to acquire tickets after all, and that she'd rather go with them than come to the television studios.

'It all sounds a bit flash for me,' she explained apologetically. 'But I'll see you in there around eight, yeah? And, Laura, thank you for inviting me. I can't wait. I've bought a new outfit and everything.'

Daniel Duchamps was born with a pair of silver scissors in his hands. At just twenty-seven, he already owned, and shared his made-up name with, the most exclusive hair salon in London – that season, at least. He had just been named Hairdresser of the Year and was responsible for the cut and colour of all the best-dressed heads in town. I was aware that a mere mortal would have to wait about four months for an appointment with this genius, and even then she'd have to fork out about £300 for the privilege. The fact that I was about to utter the words, 'I have an appointment with Daniel' was testament to the power of Jasmine Brown and Scorpion TV. I had a horrible feeling that the mousy-brown frizz I attempted to carry off as a hairstyle wouldn't be worthy of this man.

'Hi, you must be Laura,' lisped the super-slim manchild in black. 'I'm Daniel and I'm going to make you look like a superstar.'

While the surname was pure Rive Gauche, what emerged from Mr Duchamps' pouting mouth was more Merseyside.

I touched my hair self-consciously and mumbled, 'I'm sorry. It's a real mess. There's probably not much you can do.'

'Excuse me?' asked Daniel incredulously in his comedy accent. 'If I can handle' – he paused dramatically, comb in hand – 'actually I mustn't mention any names. Let's just say, if I can make a fat, balding singer/songwriter look attractive,

I think I can do something for you, Mademoiselle.'

Then he smiled broadly, to show me he wasn't offended. Not really.

'I'm going to turn you into a blonde bombshell,' he insisted. 'With a mane of shiny spun gold. Karen, fetch me the colour charts, please.'

A little elfin creature with a choppy peroxide crop scurried off and returned with a laminated card covered in loops of nylon hair in various shades of blonde, each with their own title, such as Titian Delight and Golden Glow.

'Looking at your colouring,' Daniel held back my hair and squinted at my face, 'I think we need to go for warmer tones. I'm going to use this honey shade here, with a bit of this gold, but mainly I'm going to use this.' Daniel pointed at the loop called Marilyn Monroe.

'But that's really, *really* blonde,' I said, alarmed.

'Let me explain something to you,' said Daniel patiently. 'On television, everything has to be brighter and bolder than in the real world and that includes hair colour. For most people I don't recommend going more than two shades darker or lighter than their natural hair colour, but for those clients who regularly appear on the screen – big or small, because I have many Hollywood stars on my books also, you understand – the colour has to be larger than life. If it washes your complexion out, who cares? That's what make-up artists are paid for. Forget the natural look, Laura. The whole thing is one big illusion. If you want to make it, you're going to have to fake it, girl.'

And with that, the Hairdresser of the Year clapped his hands and sent various little elves scurrying off to mix peroxide and fetch the foils, while the manicurist elf picked out an appropriate nail colour for my mani-pedi.

Three hours later, Daniel Duchamps was my new best

friend and I was no longer Laura McNaughton. I was someone else entirely. A young woman who holidayed on private yachts perhaps, and regularly ate lunch at Le Caprice before visiting the gym at the Harbour Club. I was high-maintenance woman. The owner of these golden locks couldn't possibly live in a north London hovel. No, she had to be Chelsea at least.

'Happy?' asked Daniel expectantly as I pranced and preened in the salon's hall of mirrors, admiring the back view, the front, the sides.

'Ecstatic,' I replied.

'So, I'll see you tonight, Cinderella. At the ball,' he said.

'You're going to Lucy Lloyd's party, too?' I asked.

'But, of course,' he replied. 'She's my most high-profile client. I'm going to her apartment to blow-dry her hair now.'

And so it was as a blonde in a £2,000 designer dress that I arrived at the party on the arm of a Welshman in a Prada suit. I had to admit that Jack looked magnificent, if a little short, next to me in my obscenely high-heeled shoes. Teetering up the steps towards the entrance, I thought I was going to hyperventilate with excitement. This was the moment I'd been waiting for all my life. Unfortunately, we made the mistake of arriving immediately behind Kylie Minogue, so I not only looked like a giantess, but the assembled paparazzi paid us absolutely no attention, despite Jasmine's tip-off. We must have looked the part, though, because the bouncers didn't even check our names on the guest list. They just ushered us into the throng of glamorous guests as if this were our natural habitat.

'God, this is amazing,' I whispered to Jack as we brushed past Kylie on our way to the free champagne.

'Be cool, Laura,' warned Jack sternly. 'Be cool.'

Cool, my arse, I thought as I spotted Nat, Graham and Cathy and gave them an unfashionably enthusiastic wave. I felt like Cinderella in my borrowed dress and newly golden hair. What if it all disappeared at midnight? What if the pilot was a flop? What if ...?

'I'm just going to introduce myself to that guy over there,' said Jack, interrupting my thoughts, sipping his champagne slowly and nodding in the direction of a group of important-looking middle-aged men. 'His name's Warren Clark and he's a shit-hot agent. Heard of him?'

I nodded. 'I've had to deal with him through work. I've interviewed some of his people,' I explained, emptying the first glass of bubbly down my throat.

'So, come over with me to say hello,' enthused Jack. 'We're both going to need a top-notch agent now. I've got a girl back in Cardiff, but she's just small-time; she'll have to go. I want the best, don't you?'

I hadn't even thought about getting an agent. Agents were for celebrities. We hadn't even made the pilot show yet.

'Coming?' asked Jack, eyeing Mr Clark keenly.

He was a huge, red-faced man with an air of self-importance, an enormous gut and a mean glint in his eye. Just watching him scared me. I shivered at the thought of trying to schmooze him. He might floor me with a glare, or belittle me with a cutting remark, or he might just sit on me. I shook my head.

'Nah, I think I'll just go over and say hello to my mates.' I grabbed a second glass of champers from a passing waitress. 'Cheers, Jack,' I said happily. 'To us!' I knocked back the second glass in one.

'Laura, we're here to network not enjoy ourselves,' warned Jack sternly. 'And don't get too pissed. It's very unprofessional to fall flat on your face at an A-list event and you're struggling to walk in those shoes as it is,' he added before disappearing into the crowd in the direction of Warren Clark.

'Fucking hell!' screeched Nat as I wobbled over to where my friends had set up camp at the bar. 'You look amazing.'

'Amazing,' repeated Cathy, open-mouthed.

'Baby, I could turn for you,' announced Graham, always the one to go too far. 'Who did your hair? It's fabulous.'

'Daniel Duchamps,' I said proudly.

'No! But I love that man,' said Graham, proving that he wasn't about to 'turn' for anybody. 'He's my dream boyfriend. I once pulled a sickie just because I knew he was going to be doing a make-over on morning television and I couldn't miss him for the world. He's French, isn't he? God, I love the French.'

I shook my head. 'Scouser. Definitely. He's about as French as The Beatles.'

'Really? God, I love Scousers,' said Graham wistfully.

'He's coming tonight. I'll introduce you,' I promised.

I leaned against the bar, third glass of champagne in hand, and gazed around the room. The stone floor, vast windows and double-height ceiling were all that remained of the meat-packing factory the place had once been. Red velvet chaises longues were dotted here and there, draped with the bodies of soap actors and teenage singing sensations. Smoke from a thousand cigarettes wafted up in spirals towards the glass domed roof high above. In the middle of the room a DJ was spinning the coolest tracks, his box surrounded by a gaggle of glamour models asking for personal requests. The whole building pulsed to the throbbing beat of garage, remixed to the sound of chattering voices and clinking champagne glasses. An England footballer in a tasteless striped suit was asking for a beer at the bar beside me. He turned towards me, took in the full effect of the tight red dress and winked approvingly.

'Looking good,' he said with a nod of his head.

He was obviously a wanker, and not even a particularly attractive wanker. But I grinned broadly nonetheless. I couldn't help myself. I had just been eyed up by my first celebrity. I bobbed to the music and lit a cigarette, following the smoke up, up, up. Above us, circling the entire building, I noticed a balcony. I could see the backs of two skinny girls walking towards a huge man standing in one corner. They stopped briefly beside him and then he pulled back a heavy curtain. The girls disappeared and the balcony was empty again, except for the sole bouncer.

'That's the VIP area,' I announced to my friends, pointing to the doorman on the balcony.

'But it's all VIP,' said Nat. It's wall-to-wall celebrities down here. Look, there's what's-his-name from *EastEnders*, and that guy there, he plays for Liverpool, doesn't he? Or Man United. Whatever. And she's from *X Factor*. And there's Kerry Katona ...'

'Kerry Katona,' I repeated. 'I rest my case. This is not the VIP area. So where are the *really* famous people? They're up there. I'm telling you. I swear I just saw Kate Moss disappear behind that curtain. And where's Kylie gone, eh?'

'Shall we investigate?' asked Graham, eyes glinting. 'Daniel Duchamps is probably up there with the proper celebrities. A guy like that isn't going to hang out down here with the plebs, is he? Come on, Nat. You're the queen of blagging. You can get us in.'

'Oh, I dunno,' pondered Nat. 'Let's get more pissed first. Dutch courage and all that.'

Graham was casing the joint maniacally. 'I see the

staircase,' he sing-songed gleefully. 'There. See?' In a darkened corner to our right was a tiny spiral staircase, completely cut off by the bulk of another burly bouncer.

'No,' said Cathy in a surprisingly authoritarian voice. 'We can't. We'll just humiliate ourselves. If Kerry can't get up there, how are we supposed to?'

'But—' Graham was just about to argue the point of our being cooler than Kerry when an audible ripple of excitement filled the party.

There was some sort of commotion in the direction of the door, and you could hear stage-whispered voices saying, 'It's her. It's Lucy Lloyd.'

'Shall we?' asked Nat, nodding towards the entrance. 'Might as well get a butcher's at what she's wearing, eh? Before she goes upstairs, too.'

We shoved our way as nonchalantly as possible towards the action and were just in time to see the glittering Lucy Lloyd and her boyfriend, the spectacular Billy Joe Johnson, float down the red carpet and into the party. She was a vision in Versace gold sequins, while he wore torn jeans, a white T-shirt, biker boots and at least three days' worth of stubble. Still, they made a magnificent-looking pair.

'Fuck me, she's thin,' said Nat as Lucy and her razor-sharp collarbone approached.

'Told you,' I replied in a whisper.

As Lucy and Billy got closer it became apparent that they were walking our way. Like the old hands we were, Nat, Graham and I turned our backs on the superstars and pretended to be engrossed in our own scintillating conversation. 'Celebrities? What celebrities? We see no celebrities!' screamed our body language. Poor Cathy, on the other hand, just stood there, gawping.

And then something amazing happened.

'Laura? It is Laura, isn't it? Billy, meet Laura.'

Lucy Lloyd had stopped right next to me, tapped me on the bare shoulder, kissed me on the cheek and was now introducing me to her boyfriend, the internationally renowned actor. The crowd looked on. I could just make out Jack, scraping his chiselled jaw off the floor, in the distance. Jazz had just arrived and was frantically giving me a thumbs-up sign. Meanwhile, Cathy had dropped her glass and showered Graham with champagne. Graham, in turn, was too shocked to notice that his crotch was now decidedly damp.

'I love your hair,' Lucy was saying. 'It suits you blonde.'

I closed my open mouth and tried to pull myself together. Lucy Lloyd was talking to me. It was too amazing. Too fantastic. Too weird.

'Thank you,' I managed to reply, touching my new hair self-consciously. The entire room watched us.

Lucy turned to Billy Joe and explained, 'Laura interviewed me for ...' She clicked her fingers three times and screwed up her tiny nose.

'Who was it again, darling?' she asked me. 'I've forgotten.'

'*Glitz*,' I reminded her gently.

'Oh, yes. That's right. They don't have it in LA,' she explained to Billy Joe. 'I was having a bit of a bad day when I met Laura. I cried. She was nice to me.'

'Cool,' said Billy Joe in a lazy Californian drawl. 'Most journalists are, like, total assholes. Hey, I need a drink.'

As if by magic three waiters appeared. They waited as Billy Joe downed five glasses of champagne and then belched.

'We should, like, vaporize,' he said.

'Pardon?' I asked, uncomprehendingly.

'Scram,' he explained. 'We've shown our faces, had our pictures taken, time to go.'

'Go? Already? But you only just got here. It's your party,' I said.

'We're not going home, silly,' giggled Lucy. She certainly seemed more cheerful tonight. 'We're going upstairs to my private party. Close friends only.'

She spoke the last three words very slowly and deliberately. I couldn't make out whether she was teasing me because I was a nobody or just making polite conversation. Either way, there was something deliciously flirtatious about her manner. Billy Joe had turned around and was heading for the stairs.

'Come on.' Lucy motioned for me to follow them.

I stood glued to the spot with shock. I could actually hear my heart beating in my mouth. I'm sure Lucy must have heard it, too.

'Come on,' she repeated a little impatiently, grabbing my hand.

'But I'm with my friends,' I blurted out automatically, amazed at my own loyalty. There was no way Nat or Graham would have been so charitable.

'Oh? Who?'

I pointed out Nat, Graham and Cathy. Lucy shrugged.

'They can come, too,' she said with a wave of her perfectly manicured hand, as if the whole thing was no big deal.

And so Nat, Graham, Cathy and I trailed along behind two of the most famous people in the world, walked straight past the first bouncer, up the spiral staircase, along the balcony, past the second bouncer and through the red curtain into a parallel universe where it was perfectly normal to walk smack bang into Russell Brand. Which is exactly what I did.

It was like visiting Madame Tussauds. In one corner the Beckhams were talking to Elton John. In another Lady Gaga was giggling with Katy Perry. Natalie Portman was deep in conversation with Cameron Diaz, while Brad Pitt nibbled the crudités. But best of all, facing me on a sofa, arm draped over the bony shoulder of a model I recognized from the cover of *Vogue*, was Ricky Jones. Ricky Jones, rock god. Ricky Jones, object of my sexual fantasies. Ricky Jones, the guy I spilled boiling coffee over in an interview a few weeks back. Nat had been teasing me about my crush ever since.

'So, what's with the new hair?' Lucy was asking.

'Oh, erm,' I dragged my eyes away from Ricky Jones, 'I've got a new job. Needed a new image. I mean it's nothing compared to what you do, but it's a TV-presenting thing and they wanted me to look a certain way, you know? But they think I'm too fat and they've put me on a diet and I have a personal trainer and, God, everything's changed since last week when I met you.' I was rambling. I had no idea how to converse with a megastar, but Lucy didn't seem to mind. She was probably used to being rambled at by nobodies.

'Yeah, they did that to me, too,' she said, 'in the beginning. Told me I needed to lose weight and all that. Dyed my hair. And I was only in a little lunchtime soap opera. Did you catch it?'

She must have known I'd seen the programme. She had played the part of a schoolgirl Lolita in the highest-rated daytime drama of all time. Lucy's character – or, more accurately, Lucy herself – had been such hot stuff that the tabloids could discuss nothing else. She was still a teenager, but she quickly became the nation's sweetheart, and within a year Hollywood had come calling.

'I remember,' I said. 'I used to watch it when I was a student. All the boys would congregate in the communal TV room at 1 p.m. sharp, just to catch a glimpse of you in your school uniform.'

'Oh, it was just a silly little TV thing,' she said, feigning embarrassment at having ever been so lowly. 'But everyone's got to start somewhere. Drink?'

Lucy handed me another glass of champagne.

'Take Ricky,' she continued.

I would have taken Ricky Jones gladly. He had a long, lean, feline beauty about him, as if he'd been carved by a classical Greek sculptor. He was a joy to behold: the lead singer of the most famous, and infamous, guitar band to come out of Britain since The Rolling Stones. Looking at Ricky, it was hard to believe he hadn't come out of his mother's womb a sex symbol.

'I remember seeing Sugar Reef at a festival about four years ago,' said Lucy, 'when they first started out. I was there with the Gallagher brothers and their crowd, I think. I can't quite remember. But I do remember thinking Sugar Reef were dreadful. They were booed off stage. I would never have imagined them being, like, super successful.'

'Is Ricky a good friend?' I asked, as if it were just a passing thought.

'He's the best,' smiled Lucy saucily. 'But he's a very bad boy. Gorgeous guy, terrible boyfriend material. Have you met him?'

I nodded. 'I interviewed him a couple of months ago. He wouldn't remember me, though.'

Lucy glanced at my cleavage, which was now trying desperately to escape from the obscenely expensive strapless dress I was wearing.

'Oh, he'll remember you, darling,' said Lucy. 'Ricky!' she shouted. 'Come here.'

Ricky obediently untangled himself from the endless limbs of the supermodel beside him, stood up, stretched like a cat who'd just woken up and casually pushed a slightly greasy lock of black hair out of his almond-shaped eyes. I felt my stomach lurch. He was just too damn sexy for words.

'You remember Laura, don't you? She's a journalist. She interviewed you.' Lucy slipped her arm around Ricky's slim waist. He was wearing a black shirt, untucked from his jeans. It was buttoned up the wrong way, as if he'd got dressed in a hurry, or in the dark. I noticed that the model's little black number was also suspiciously crumpled, and concluded that they'd probably had sex somewhere in the vicinity during the last half-hour. I was deeply envious.

'Ah, coffee girl,' drawled Ricky lazily. His voice was as confused as Lucy's in that it had no idea which side of the Atlantic it should fall – half Mockney, half LA. 'How could I forget the woman who left my testicles scarred for life?'

Lucy looked intrigued. 'Oh, yes?'

'I spilled my coffee in his lap,' I explained quickly, lest Lucy think I was some sort of madwoman.

'Lap?' said Ricky. 'Not lap. Scrotum. The least you could have done was kiss it better. Actually,' he continued, 'I thought about suing you for damages, but you were so pretty and you wrote such nice things about me.' He smiled, perhaps sarcastically. There was a hint of something slightly cruel about the glint in his devilishly dark eyes.

I cringed as I remembered the piece I'd written about Ricky. It had stated quite clearly that I loved him and wanted to bear his children. If he'd read the article, he'd know how much I fancied him. How embarrassing.

I couldn't help myself: 'Did you, um, read the piece?' I stared at my spangly shoes.

'Certainly did,' said Ricky. 'And very flattering it was, too. Pity you journalists make everything up. I'd be right in there if you meant every word you'd written about me, wouldn't I?'

I forced a laugh, but I could feel my face turning as scarlet as my dress.

'I just tell readers what they want to hear,' I muttered lamely.

'That's a shame,' said the rock god.

He was standing so close to me that I could smell him: an intoxicating mix of aftershave and sweat. He leaned forward, put his hand on my hip and kissed me briefly on the mouth with whisky breath. I thought my knees would buckle.

'It was lovely to meet you again,' he drawled, dropping his hand so it brushed against my bum. 'See you later. Maybe.'

The supermodel appeared at his side looking agitated. Ricky excused himself and turned to go.

'Your nipples are erect,' he whispered in my ear on the way past.

Perhaps I gazed too longingly at Ricky Jones's back, because Lucy repeated, 'He's a very, *very* bad boy.'

Before I could think of a fitting reply, I felt a hand stroke the back of my head. Ricky? I spun round to find Daniel Duchamps smiling warmly at me.

'What do you think, Lucy Loo? I did this. You like?' he asked, indicating my new hair.

'I love,' she enthused. 'She's two-thirds of the way there. Almost a TSB.'

The actress and her hairdresser laughed knowingly.

'TSB?' I was confused.

'Tall, skinny blonde,' chanted Daniel and Lucy in unison.

'The formula for success,' concluded Lucy knowingly.

From nowhere, Graham had appeared at my side, smiling expectantly in Daniel's direction.

'Daniel, this is Graham. He's a good friend of mine and a big fan of yours,' I said.

'Really?' Daniel gave Graham the once-over and appeared

to be satisfied. 'I do like to meet my fans. Would you care to join me for a drink, Graham?'

Graham nodded slowly, as if in a trance, and followed Daniel to the bar.

'I'd better mingle,' said Lucy suddenly.

I watched her wiggle gracefully across the room and into Billy Joe's arms. She kissed him on the lips, whispered something in his ear and then led him by the hand towards the toilets.

I stood alone in a roomful of stars, wondering how on earth I'd got there. Nat and Cathy joined me. I considered telling them about my brush with Ricky Jones, but something made me hold back. If I said it out loud, maybe it wouldn't be true. And anyway, he had sloped off into a dark corner with the supermodel again. Nobody would believe he was flirting with me when his date for the evening had appeared naked in last year's Pirelli calendar. And so we sipped champagne and drank in the atmosphere, soaking up every minute detail lest we forget anything when it came to telling the grandkids. On a sofa in the corner, Daniel Duchamps was nibbling Graham's ear. Lucy and Billy Joe emerged from the ladies' and joined Ricky and his supermodel in their corner. They were all so glamorous and beautiful and sparkling. Despite the dress and the new blonde hair, I suddenly felt painfully plain.

'Let's get absolutely wankered,' I suggested to Nat and Cathy, who had no objections to the suggestion.

An hour or so later the three of us had managed to acquire a sofa, a couple of lecherous film executives, a magnum of champagne and a tray of canapés, which we were guzzling in a drunken frenzy. My beautiful red dress was dappled with champagne and cream cheese and I had a sneaking suspicion that my professionally applied make-up was no longer where it ought to be. And as for the hair, it was just as well Daniel was too busy playing tonsil tennis with Graham to notice.

'Look,' I screeched. 'Graham's snogging Daniel Duchamps!'

'Good on him,' whooped Nat. 'Let's raise our glasses.'

We clinked champagne glasses clumsily and showered ourselves again.

'To our mate Graham, the star-fucker,' announced Nat.

'Star-fucker,' I shouted joyfully across the room.

'Laura, have you got a minute?'

I looked up through a drunken haze to see Lucy Lloyd swimming prettily before my eyes.

'Loothy,' I spluttered. 'Come and sit down. Have some nibbles.' I thrust some smoked-salmon terrine in her face.

'No, thanks,' she replied. 'Come with me. There's something I want to show you.'

I looked from Nat to Cathy. They both nodded enthusiastically. 'Go.'

'OK,' I giggled, shoving the salmon into my mouth. 'Somebody help me up.'

The fatter of the two film execs kindly gave my backside a shove.

'What are you going to show me?' I asked Lucy. 'Is it Ricky Jones with no clothes on?'

'No, we're just going to the loo,' said Lucy patiently, trying to guide me in my too-high heels. 'To freshen up.'

In the toilets, Lucy opened her Prada handbag and produced a hairbrush and make-up bag. She made me splash my face with cold water and then brushed my hair gently back into shape.

'Take a deep breath and straighten up a bit, Laura,' she said kindly as she reapplied my lipstick. 'If you want this TV job to work out, then you're going to have to learn the rules.'

'What rules?'

'Avoid the canapés for a start,' she answered. 'You've probably just consumed about 5,000 calories. What would your personal trainer say?'

'Oh, bugger him!' I replied.

'And make sure you look immaculate at all times, even when drunk,' she continued as if reciting the law of the land. 'Never leave home without these.'

She waved her hairbrush and make-up bag in my face.

'There are always people watching, waiting for you to make a mistake. And usually they have cameras with them,' she warned.

'Why are you being so nice to me?' I asked.

Lucy shrugged and said, 'You seem sweet.'

'Ahhh.' I tried to hug her, but she pushed me away gently.

'And finally,' she glanced round the room to check it was empty and then looked at me sternly, as if she was about to tell me a very big secret, 'if you want to really fit in, you'll need some of this.'

She opened her purse and produced a small rectangular wrap of paper.

'Drugs,' I said flatly. 'I don't do drugs. Well, not proper drugs. Just joints and only because my flatmate's a throwback from the Sixties.'

'Cocaine,' said Lucy patiently. 'Have you ever tried it?'

'No,' I said. 'I just like getting pissed. I don't want to get into all that heavy shit.'

'It's not heavy,' laughed Lucy, as if I was some naive little child. 'Everyone does it. Your mate does it. I saw him earlier with Daniel, asking Ricky if he had any spare. It doesn't *do* anything.'

'So what's the point if it does nothing?' I asked.

'It'll just wake you up, make you less drunk, stop you eating those nibbles, you'll see. Come on.'

Lucy led me into a cubicle and locked the door.

'Lucy, I dunno about this,' I said as she knelt down on the grubby, damp toilet floor in her full-length Versace gown. She put down the toilet seat as a shelf, opened the wrap, took a platinum credit card from her purse and expertly scraped a small amount of white powder from the paper. Then she cut the cocaine into two identical lines with the edge of the card before licking it clean.

'That's not very hygienic,' I warned.

Lucy ignored me as she rolled a £50 note into a tube.

'Now watch,' she instructed.

Lucy put the note to her right nostril, covered her left nostril, bent over the toilet seat and sniffed one of the lines of cocaine swiftly up her nose. She held her head back for a moment and sniffed again.

'Lovely,' she grinned as the powder ran down the back of her throat. 'Now you try.'

She offered me the rolled-up note. Suddenly I felt very, very sober, and I wasn't at all sure I wanted to do this. I'd managed to get through my teens without trying E; I'd watched university friends lose their minds on acid, but had never felt the urge to join them, and now here I was, aged twenty-five, in a toilet cubicle with one of the most famous film stars in the world being offered cocaine. This was how I'd started smoking: the cool girls offered me a fag and I didn't want to look like a square. It seemed I'd grown up very little in the last ten years. Lucy Lloyd looked at me expectantly.

'You'll like it,' she promised.

I took the note.

PART TWO

Spring

7

Who wants to be a millionaire?

It had been the first warm day of the year, or so Becky informed me when I eventually dragged my overindulged body out of bed at 6 p.m. The first weekend in April had produced the kind of sunny Sunday that wakes up an entire city full of depressed, winter-worn residents, persuades them to dress in pastels and relocates them from the centrally heated comfort of their living rooms to the bracing banks of the ponds on Hampstead Heath. By midday, my flatmate told me, the deli counter at Sainsbury's had sold out of pasta salad, while the Kentish Town Road had come to a virtual standstill as an entire army of ice-cream vans crawled out of hibernation, their shaky renditions of 'Greensleeves' reverberating all the way to North Finchley. At the men's pond, the beautiful bodies of a hundred gay men were on show for the first time that year. Some, Becky claimed with excitement, were wearing nothing but tiny Lycra swimming trunks and Hawaiian Tropic tanning oil. And I'd managed to sleep through the entire thing.

'We had a picnic on Parliament Hill,' she said as I switched on the kettle. 'There are some leftovers in the fridge if you're hungry.'

My concave stomach groaned at the thought of soggy egg-mayonnaise sandwiches.

'No, thanks.'

I made myself a coffee with shaky hands and glanced out

of the basement window to catch a glimpse of the sunshine. By peering up over the wall outside the kitchen window I could just about make out blue skies, but the daylight was too bright for my tired eyes. I winced and pulled down the blind.

'Got any fags, Becks?'

She threw me a cigarette and said bluntly, 'You look like total shit. What were you doing last night?'

'Oh, just the usual, you know,' I replied.

'No, I don't know.' She sounded touchy. 'You never invite me along.'

'Well, it's not really your scene.' That was lame, but I was in no state for an argument.

''Course not. Why would I enjoy meeting your new celebrity friends and hanging out at film premieres?' she replied sarcastically. 'I'm off to the pub. I'd invite you along, but it's not really your scene – we're meeting in a grotty beer garden in Holloway to catch the last rays of sun. Anyway, you're not dressed.'

The final statement was made with almost motherly disapproval. Only in this country could missing the first, and possibly only, day of spring be considered such a monumental crime. I'd even managed to offend the world's biggest dosser with my slovenly behaviour. But then, we weren't getting on too well any more, Becky and I. It was as if a door had slammed shut between us since I'd got my new job. For a start, we hardly ever saw each other. Since the full TV series had been commissioned, I was either busy leading my increasingly glamorous existence – filming, appearing on morning chat shows, doing photo shoots for TV listings magazines – or else I was out with my new best friend, Lucy Lloyd, international megastar, at some swanky bar opening or private members' club. Meanwhile, Becky had lost her job at the restaurant through lack of enthusiasm – she'd gone off having sex with the owner's son – and, other than helping her friend Ruth out with the second-hand clothes stall she ran in Camden Market, was unemployed, not to mention deeply in debt. I'd paid her rent for the past three months, because that's what friends do, but I hadn't pretended not to resent this act of charity. Indeed, had I not been rendered brain-dead from the previous night's recreational activities, I would probably have reminded Becky that she owed me over a grand and therefore couldn't afford to have picnics on the Heath or beers in the early evening sunshine.

The fact was, I was desperate to move out of our Kentish Town rabbit hutch and into something a little more fitting for an up-and-coming television personality. Since landing the TV gig I'd been gagging to buy my own place, but even with the money I'd got from Scorpion for the first series, I couldn't get my hands on enough of a deposit for a decent pad, my idea of a decent pad having changed dramatically since I'd first visited Lucy's luxury penthouse. I'd just made in three months what it usually took me two years to earn, but I had my new lifestyle to support. A girl can't wear Topshop for ever, you know. Paying Becky's rent every month wasn't exactly helping my financial situation, and neither, if I was honest with myself, were the regular Bond Street shopping trips with Lucy, or the nights out at Mayfair hotel bars – one bottle of champagne = £125. It wasn't much fun being skint when your new mates included actresses who commanded $25 million per movie. I was sick of being the one Lucy, Billy Joe and the rest of the gang took pity on. I felt like a charity case. Lucy had recently presented me with a real Louis Vuitton handbag because she was too embarrassed to be seen out and about with me and my fake one. This gesture, in turn, had upset Becky, who'd bought me the fake bag in the first place. She said she couldn't compete. I felt I couldn't win.

But all that was about to change. A few weeks earlier my agent, Warren Clark, had called explaining that the Superbra people, famous for their uplifting lingerie, wanted me, or more specifically my cleavage, to advertise their new Oomph range of bras and matching briefs. I'd spent a week shooting the TV ad campaign on a beach in Thailand and a couple of days back in London prancing around a studio in a 32DD and little else. Having just reached my target weight, I felt sleeker and sexier than ever before, and the test shots I'd been shown were brilliant – the wonders of computer retouching never ceasing to amaze me.

But the really, truly, unbelievable part was thc £1 million fee. I'll repeat that very slowly, just to make sure it sinks in. One – million – pounds. For a week's work! Can you imagine how it feels to be offered that amount of money? Lack of money had always been a problem for me. 'No you can't have a new pair of shoes,' Mum would say. 'We can't afford it.' While 'money doesn't grow on trees', was my dad's favourite line. Then came the student days of scouring second-hand shops for clothes I could customize, of having to live at home during the first year because we couldn't afford to rent a city-centre flat for me, of drinking in the student union because the warm beer was so bloody cheap. And all the time, dreaming and dreaming of the day I'd get out there and earn good money, live in a nice place and buy my own car. In London, nothing changed. In fact, I found myself worse off than ever before with the crippling rents of the capital and the student debts I had to pay off. For years, I'd been too scared to open bank statements. Instead, I'd just go to the cash machine, put my card in and pray it was feeling generous. For two weeks of every month it would inform me I had insufficient funds, even when I'd only asked for a tenner. I played the lottery religiously, just in case. If I could only win a million, then all my problems would be over. Life would be perfect.

When Warren told me how much I'd been offered for the campaign I fainted. Literally. Flat on my face on the shiny parquet floor of Wazza's office. It took two secretaries and a personal assistant to bring me round. I sat with my head between my knees, sipping a glass of water, but the room was spinning around me as I tried to grasp the idea of me as a millionaire.

'Why are they offering me so much money?' I asked Wazza in astonishment.

He shrugged his hefty shoulders nonchalantly and said, 'Well, I demanded twice what they offered initially, naturally, but a million is quite normal for an ad campaign of this profile. There will be billboards and television adverts. The entire nation will see you nearly naked – a girl has to be suitably compensated for that sort of exposure. And you're a great catch for them. You're a new face who has proved very popular with the public. An overnight sensation, I believe *The Sun* called you. Not to mention the fact that you have exactly the, ahem, assets they're looking for.'

Warren nodded at my cleavage in an embarrassed manner. His gaze lingered a little too long and I could see beads of sweat forming on his top lip. He was a rich, powerful man, many people were in awe of him, but he always reminded me of Benny Hill, so it was hard to take him too seriously. I crossed my arms firmly over my chest because he was old, fat and perpetually short of breath. He had a clammy unhealthiness about him that made me worry he'd have a heart attack at any moment. I didn't want my boobs to be the cause of his coronary, and nor did I want him leering.

For the past few weeks I'd enjoyed that delicious moment when you first wake up in the morning and remember that something really good has happened. I used to get it the morning after buying new shoes. Now I had the buzz of knowing that a cheque for £1 million – minus Wazza's 15 per cent commission – was about to be deposited in a high-interest bank account with my name on it. As soon as it arrived I was going to go house-hunting. Part of the deal I'd signed with Superbra stated that I was forbidden to disclose the amount I'd been paid for the job. So at first I'd told no one, not even my mum. In fact, especially not my mum – I had a surprise in store for her. I had, however, let it slip to Lucy last week. Cocaine loosens the tongue and mine had been particularly slack that night. She'd informed me enthusiastically that 'even in central London, you can still find a decent little des res for under a million', and promised to help me find the perfect palace for a TV princess. The only hitch was that I hadn't told Becky I was soon to be moving out, and I had a sneaking suspicion that she'd assume she could come with me. We'd lived together since our second year at university, and I knew she saw herself as part of my fixtures and fittings. But to me, Becky was now excess baggage I wasn't planning to pack.

'You've got to move on,' had been Lucy's advice. 'OK, so you'll have to leave some people from your past behind, but that's the price of success. Becky doesn't understand your world any more, so she can't be part of it.'

Fiona saw things rather differently. 'Laura, you can't just dump your oldest friends because you're famous and they're not,' she'd said in disbelief when I phoned her to discuss the Becky situation. 'She's always been there for you – remember when Pete dumped you. You've only known Lucy Lloyd for five minutes, but Becky's been your best mate for seven years. I'm not saying she has to move in with you when you buy your house, but you should at least tell her your plans. Don't just drop her because she doesn't have a private membership to Shoreditch House!'

Of course I knew Fi was right. And deep down I still loved Becky to bits, but as I watched her throw on a tatty old denim jacket and toss her dirty-blonde dreadlocks over her shoulder as she left to go to the pub, I couldn't imagine her ever fitting in with my shiny new life. Maybe if she smartened up her image a bit. She was a good-looking girl underneath the piercings and tie-dye, all she needed was a helping hand. I had suggested she have a make-over on my TV show's fashion and beauty slot but she'd declined the offer. In fact, she'd seemed rather offended by it. What more could I do?

'Oh, I almost forgot. Jack called this morning,' shouted Becky on her way out. 'You were supposed to meet him for a run at eleven. I gave you a shout but you were dead to the world. He didn't sound very happy. You should give him a ring. Apologize. Bye-ee.'

Who died and made Becky my moral adviser, I wondered as the door slammed shut. It was hardly surprising I hadn't been awake at eleven, having only got home at 8 a.m. I shuffled through to the living room, head pounding, mouth like a sumo wrestler's armpit, closed the curtains and collapsed onto the filthy sofa, spilling coffee and fag ash on the carpet as I did so. Bollocks. I'd completely forgotten about my arrangement with Jack. What was I thinking of, organizing a jog on a Sunday morning? I could just imagine the poor little thing, warming up in his pristine tracksuit and wrap-around shades, waiting patiently for me in Regent's Park. I'd arranged the fitness session on Friday night at the after-show party after ten glasses of champagne. I wondered how long he'd waited and how many autographs he'd had to sign while he did so. I found my real Louis Vuitton handbag on the living-room floor and rummaged around for my iPhone. There were five missed calls, four of them from Jack and one from Becks inviting me to join her on the Heath when I woke up. Oops. An increasingly familiar feeling of guilt washed over me as I dialled Jack's number and prepared to eat humble pie – only marginally more palatable than egg-mayonnaise sarnies after the night I'd just had.

To my relief it went straight to voicemail: 'Hi, Jack here. Sorry, I'm far too busy being an international man of mystery to take this call. Please leave a message and I'll get back to you as soon as I've finished making lurve to this babe. And if that's Laura, you can piss off. I hate you. Beep.'

I took a deep breath and grovelled, 'Jack, it's Laura. Listen, mate, I'm so sorry about this morning. I was out with Lucy last night and it turned into a big one. I didn't get to bed until, well, it had been light for a couple of hours, and I've only just woken up. I know that's no excuse and I should have gone to bed earlier, but you know how persuasive Lucy can be. Anyway, I am really, really, really sorry and I promise I'll make it up to you. Give me a call to let me know you still love me. Sorry again. Bye.'

Jazz had been right about Jack. He'd gradually won me over with his infectious enthusiasm and permanent smile. OK, so he was right up there with Bob Monkhouse in the cheese department, he lived for his work and had more blond ambition than Madonna, but deep down, beneath the sunbed tan and two layers of foundation, Jack was one of the good guys. Jack had covered for me and my lack of experience so many times in the early days of the show – like the time I couldn't for the life of me remember Ronan Keating's name as the Irish singer sat opposite – and although he rarely came along when I invited him out, preferring his beauty sleep to my nights of excess, the Welshman and I had become a real team over the past five months. And it had worked, *The Weekend Starts Here* was a rip-roaring success, watched by over three million viewers every Friday night. The last show of the first series had aired this weekend, and Jack Davies and Laura McNaughton were now officially household names, having appeared in *Hello!* and everything.

I found the work itself exciting. I loved interviewing people in front of the camera even more than I had for magazines. And any nerves had quickly disappeared as I'd realized people actually liked 'TV' me.

Fame had come relatively easily, but effortless glamour continued to evade me. I was still wearing an oversized Scorpion TV T-shirt and last night's make-up, having just managed to force down a slice of dry toast with my second mug of Nescafé, when the phone rang.

'Laura, it's Luce,' said Lucy Lloyd chirpily. 'Are you free tonight?'

'Lucy, what are you talking about? We only just finished having last night. I haven't even managed to get dressed yet. I was going to just veg in front of the telly.'

'Well, get dressed and get over to mine now,' she ordered. 'Or I'll have to come over and drag you out. Please don't make me do that. You know I'm allergic to that flat of yours; it stinks. And wear something spectacular.' I could hear the clinking of bottle against glass and was once again amazed at the girl's stamina.

'But—'

I was about to argue when Lucy announced, 'Ricky's back in town and we're meeting him at his hotel at nine. The band are having a party to celebrate getting home.'

I felt a sudden rush of adrenalin flush my cheeks.

'He says he can't wait to see you,' teased Lucy before hanging up.

It was the moment I had been waiting for. Ricky Jones had been recording Sugar Reef's third album in Jamaica for the past three months, and the closest I'd got to him since then had been reading the headlines about the band's debauchery in the Sunday tabloids. There had been pictures of him sunning himself on a beach with Miss Jamaica, and a story about him going out for dinner with the supermodel, not to mention the snaps the *News of the World* had managed to get of the entire band in a jacuzzi with a naked women's beach volleyball team. I'd been eaten up with jealousy every time another Ricky Jones exclusive hit the shelves. But now he was back and I was ready to make my move.

The tiredness lifted miraculously as I jumped in the shower – carefully keeping my hair out of the way because I'd had it straightened by Daniel the day before – shoe-horned myself into my new rock-chick jeans – size eight – a diamanté-encrusted backless top and a dangerously spiky pair of heels, did my face and called a cab. The butterflies in my stomach were dive-bombing with excitement. I couldn't wait to see Ricky again.

You see, we'd had a brief but intense affair just before he'd left. I'd gone home to Edinburgh for Christmas – my first break since filming the pilot for the show. Although Dad had barely nodded hello to me, it had been great to see Mum, Fiona and Gran, who was staying with my parents for the holidays again. They were all so excited about the television job, bombarding me with questions, and oohing and aahing over the new clothes the studio had bought me for the first series. The plan had been to stay up there for Hogmanay, but when Lucy called on Boxing Day and invited me to a New Year's Eve bash at a stately home in

Buckinghamshire, I couldn't exactly say no, could I? Fiona had understood, and didn't seem too upset that I wouldn't be going to the nurses' bash in Leith that she'd invited me to, Mum couldn't believe that she'd just answered the phone to an international superstar, and Dad disappeared to the golf club, muttering something about knowing where my loyalties lay on his way out. It wasn't until I was on a plane back to London the following day that it crossed my mind that Dad might have had a bit of a 'thing' about musicians, considering that Mum had her own rock god in her day.

On New Year's Eve, Lucy had picked me up from Amersham train station in her baby-blue Mercedes convertible. Even in real life, she always managed to look as if she was starring in one of her own movies. That day, she was a vision in a white fur coat, cream leather driving gloves and oversized black Chanel sunglasses. As I'd tripped out of the station, wearing a parka and beanie hat, bedraggled and creased, dragging my holdall behind me, I'd spotted Lucy immediately. It was the first time I'd seen her since the party the month before, although she'd insisted on calling me for girlie chats on a weekly basis since then. I was very confused by her interest in me, but way too flattered and excited to dare question why a woman like Lucy Lloyd would want to hang out with a nobody like me. I still had a niggling feeling that the whole thing was some sort of elaborate joke.

The temperature was hovering around the zero mark, and a thin layer of snow was trying its best not to melt on the pavement, but Lucy had the car hood down all the same, and her mane of golden hair extensions danced perfectly round her beautiful face in the icy wind. A group of teenage boys, wearing baggy jeans and clutching skateboards, hovered nervously a few feet away from the car, nudging each other and throwing furtive glances in Lucy's direction. 'You ask her,' 'No, you do it,' 'It's definitely her,' they whispered as I walked past. But they were too shy and too late. The minute I threw my bag onto the back seat and hopped in beside her, Lucy sped away, splattering her teenage fans with sleet as she went.

Lucy Lloyd was a better actress than she was a driver. We hurtled at breakneck speed along narrow country lanes, getting beeped at by Range Rovers and sensible family estate cars, and only just missing a herd of cattle who were innocently crossing the road to their cowshed, disgruntled farmer in tow. After a mercifully short journey, we turned onto a private tree-lined road and started towards a huge Gothic monstrosity of a stately home. The house had a grotesque cartoon-like quality about it, complete with snow-dusted gargoyles staring from the parapets. As we parked up on the circular driveway between a red Ferrari and a black Porsche, I half expected the folks from *Scooby-Doo* to run past, chasing a pesky ghost.

'Isn't it fantastic?' asked Lucy, breathlessly. 'So kitsch.'

'Who does it belong to?' I wondered out loud, suddenly realizing I had no idea whose party I was about to gatecrash.

'My good friends, the Right Honourable Lord and Lady Hurlingham-Jones,' said Lucy matter-of-factly.

I stared at her blankly. Lucy laughed.

'Ricky's mum and dad. They've gone to London; left this morning. They're attending a New Year's party at No. 10, no less. Master Richard Godfrey Hurlingham-Jones is throwing the annual bash at the family pile in their absence. It should certainly be a debauched affair.'

So, Ricky Jones was not only loaded but landed. It made sense. That Mockney accent fooled no one. I had always assumed that, like so many musicians, he was ashamed of his boring middle-class upbringing and liked to pretend to be a working-class geezer from the East End instead, as a way of gaining street cred. When I'd interviewed him for *Glitz*, I'd struggled to come up with much background info on him at all. I'd trawled through the newspaper cuttings for hours but only managed to discover that he was from Buckinghamshire, his dad was in the army and his mum was a housewife. This information fitted in with my Home Counties theory perfectly. What the papers failed to disclose was that his father actually *ran* the army, while his mother ran the stately home, as well as doing all sorts of charitable work, such as organizing balls at £500 per head to raise money for the poor and needy. During the interview itself, Ricky had cleverly deflected any questions about his childhood and schooldays, and I'd been far too awestruck by the man's beauty to probe. Now I knew the truth.

'Didn't you know Ricky was a toff?' asked Lucy with mock innocence, knowing full well I was shell-shocked. 'He went to Eton and everything. It's hilarious.'

An ancient manservant of at least seventy-five years old, wearing a pale grey uniform, had appeared from behind the immense front door and was trotting obediently down the snow-covered stone steps that led to the drive. I was terrified he'd slip and break a brittle bone or two. He arrived in one piece and opened Lucy's car door to let her out, nodding, 'Good afternoon, Miss Lloyd.'

'Ferguson, this is Miss Laura McNaughton,' Lucy introduced me. 'She's staying in the room next to mine in the West Wing.'

'Delighted to meet you, Miss McNaughton. I trust you will enjoy your stay at Hurlingham Manor,' said Ferguson as he walked round the car and opened my door.

'Thank you, Mr Ferguson. Please call me Laura,' I smiled, reaching for my tatty holdall.

'Let me get that for you, Miss Laura,' insisted the geriatric, struggling to lift my bulging bag.

I felt awful allowing this frail old man to carry my luggage, but Lucy was calling, 'Come on, Laura,' and frantically waving at me to follow her into the house.

The wood-panelled entrance hall was larger than my parents' bungalow and it smelled of polish and grandeur. A grandfather clock chimed half past three, and the eyes of dead creatures, who had presumably had the misfortune to be shot by some Hurlingham-Jones or other, stared down at me from where their heads were mounted on the wall. The ceilings were so high that when Lucy ran up the vast, sweeping spiral staircase in her high-heeled boots, her footsteps echoed on the shiny wooden steps like a percussion section in the Royal Albert Hall. I followed her to the first floor, past an enormous stained-glass window on the lofty landing, left along a mile-long corridor hung with portraits of Ricky's ancestors, right along another corridor, right again, left, left – there was no way I would remember my way back to the outside world – and eventually through a heavy oak door and into the most ridiculously opulent bedroom I'd ever seen, complete with mahogany four-poster bed and an enormous bay window offering views of the grounds.

'What do you think? Will it do?' Lucy threw herself onto the bed.

I knelt on the window seat and stared out at the snow-kissed manicured lawns and frozen ornamental pond. The view of the grounds was as eerily beautiful as the house was eerily grotesque.

'I've never been anywhere like this in my life,' I said in disbelief. 'I feel like I've walked into a Jane Austen novel.'

'Yup,' grinned Lucy. 'And we're going to have a ball.'

Five minutes later, Ferguson arrived, panting, with my bag.

'Master Richard wanted me to tell you that he has gone to see a man about a dog,' said Ferguson sheepishly. I got the feeling that the elderly butler found the young master somewhat distasteful. 'Mr Johnson has accompanied him. They aim to be back by six to dress for this evening. The other guests are due to arrive at seven thirty. Drinks will be served at eight.'

'Eight?' Lucy scoffed, glancing at her Rolex. 'Be a darling, Fergie, and fetch us a bottle of Lord Hurlingham-Jones's finest champagne. He did tell me to make myself at home before he left this morning.'

'Quite,' said Ferguson tartly. 'I shall bring it to you directly.' And with that the old man disappeared.

'Does Ricky know I'm here?' I asked Lucy.

'Of course,' she replied. 'It was his idea.'

As the afternoon went on, we consumed two bottles of champagne and raided Lucy's bedroom in an attempt to find something for me to wear to the party. She had briefly eyed the contents of my holdall with disdain, proclaiming even the new stuff to be 'bland'. By that time, with Trevor's help I'd already managed to lose two stone, and now fitted comfortably into a size ten, but most of Lucy's exquisite clothes were still way too small. Eventually we managed to pour my still-curvy body into a strappy, black, full-length number with real diamonds scattered across the breast and at the hem. It was outrageously tight, and I could hardly breathe once I had it on, but even I had to admit the result was pretty impressive.

'You can't wear a bra with that dress,' she informed me. 'And take your knickers off, you've got a VPL.'

I did as I was told.

Lucy fixed my hair up on top of my head, leaving a few blonde ringlets loose and falling into my eyes, which were now ringed with smoky eye make-up. She also lent me a diamond necklace from Tiffany, which I suspected was worth more than the Crown jewels. Even beside Lucy, who was wearing a white minidress that barely covered her bum cheeks, I felt like a babe.

'Does Ricky like me?' I asked Lucy shyly.

''Course he does,' she replied. 'You could have him like that.' She snapped her fingers. 'But I told you before, be careful. He'll sleep with you, but he's not going to be your boyfriend. He doesn't do the couple thing. In fact, I think threesomes are more his scene.'

But I was still hoping. Maybe with me it would be different. Perhaps I would be the one to tame the wild stallion. Since arriving at Hurlingham Manor my imagination had been working overtime, and I'd already planned the seating arrangements for the wedding reception in the great hall. As for the marquee, it would look divine beside the fairy-lit ornamental pond, with a string quartet playing on the jetty where the rowing boats were presently moored. My daydream was rudely interrupted by a knock on the door and in poured Ricky, Billy Joe and, to my horror, the supermodel.

'Girls!' shouted Ricky, a demonic glint in his eye. 'You look fucking gorgeous. Are you ready to party?'

Ricky had obviously already started his own private party and was off his face on something or other. Still, he looked as sexy as ever.

'Ricky's managed to acquire several ounces of Colombia's finest', said Billy Joe proudly, 'in deepest, darkest Buckinghamshire. That's like scoring in Salt Lake City,' he added to the supermodel, who was American and ignorant of British culture.

The supermodel appeared to be mute. As Billy Joe put his hands playfully up Lucy's minuscule dress and Ricky sat down at the nineteenth-century French dressing table to chop out five fat lines of cocaine, she stood in the doorway staring at me with a total lack of comprehension. Eventually, she opened her full, pouty mouth and whined, 'Ricky, what is the fat girl doing here?'

My cheeks burned with humiliation as I realized she was talking about me.

'What fat girl?' asked Ricky casually, still concentrating on the job in hand.

'That fat girl,' spat the supermodel, pointing at me.

'Oh, you mean Laura.' Ricky had looked up and was staring at me in the mirror, smiling with his eyes. 'Well, she's not exactly fat, is she, Venetia? Just because she has breasts and you don't, doesn't mean you have to get all bitter and twisted. Now come in and shut the door before Ferguson catches us. He'll tell my dad.'

Venetia refused to budge from the doorway.

'What is she doing here?' she repeated, staring straight at me, her voice dripping with venom.

I was beginning to wonder the same thing. I felt like a pawn in some elaborate game in which only the rich and famous know the rules.

'Sit down and chill out for fuck's sake,' said Ricky.

'I won't come in with her in the room. I don't like her.' Venetia's glare remained firmly on me.

I couldn't believe that an (almost) fully grown woman was acting like such a brat.

'What is your problem?' asked Lucy.

'Laura is Lucy's friend,' added Billy Joe indignantly to the stick insect.

This was getting interesting. Venetia had witnessed Ricky

flirting with me at Lucy's party and it had obviously upset her enough for her to feel threatened by me.

'She's here because Lucy wanted her to come,' Billy Joe was explaining. 'It has nothing to do with Ricky, so screw you, Venetia. You're a bitch, a total fucking bitch, and you've been annoying the hell out of me all day. Ricky, why don't you tell this ice queen to piss off?'

Ricky grinned but said nothing, enjoying the scene. I looked over at Lucy, who'd promised me it had been Ricky's idea I come here, but she was too busy drinking in the action to notice.

'He doesn't even like you,' continued Billy Joe, pointing at Venetia. 'He says that having sex with you is like fucking a teenage boy.'

Venetia frowned and managed to look almost unattractive.

'Ricky, are you going to let this ...' she glared at Billy Joe and spat, '... bastard talk to me like that?'

'If it pleases him,' said Ricky cheerfully.

'That's it, I'm going,' announced Venetia, stamping her foot like a three-year-old. 'I'm not going to stay here with you, you ...' her glare fell on me '... freaks!'

Venetia stood in the doorway for a moment or two, glaring at Ricky expectantly. Ricky ignored her, loudly snorting a line of coke instead. Then he did another one.

'I might as well have yours if you're leaving,' he said, shrugging at Venetia.

'Next?' He offered the rolled-up note around the room.

'You guys are really fucking screwed,' announced Venetia. The door slammed shut and she was gone.

Having accepted Ricky's offer of cocaine, Lucy had now collapsed onto the Persian carpet in a fit of hysteria and was rolling around, flashing a full Hollywood wax as she did so.

Her legs were so thin that she looked like a child. Billy Joe shook his head purposefully.

'Man, that is one crazy lady,' he said.

For a moment I wasn't certain whether he was talking about Lucy or Venetia, but then he added, 'I sure hope she really is gone, because I cannot spend one minute longer in her company.'

I realized he was talking about the supermodel.

Billy Joe took the note from Lucy's hand and did his line with practised ease.

'Laura?' he said, casually offering me the note.

This time I had no qualms about accepting. I'd been pleasantly surprised by the drug's effects at Lucy's party. At first I'd thought it wasn't doing anything, then I'd begun to taste its bitterness, crawling down the back of my throat. My tongue and lips had gone strangely numb and I'd felt a sudden rush of energy. Before I knew it I had sobered up and was talking to Lucy in an excited but coherent way. I couldn't wait to get back out to the party to socialize. I'd felt confident and attractive and on top of the world. Three hours and two lines later I was a convert. I hadn't felt out of it as I'd imagined I would, just pretty and witty and wild.

Venetia's outburst had left me shaken, but I was aware that I'd won some petty little battle in a war I'd stumbled into. With growing confidence, I took the note from Billy Joe. Ricky was still sitting on the stool in front of the dressing table, in charge of the drugs, the master of ceremonies. I tried desperately to remember the cocaine-snorting technique Lucy had taught me last time, as it would be very embarrassing to show myself up as the beginner I was in front of such an experienced crowd. I had to lean forward over Ricky's lap to reach the glass surface. I sniffed up the white line as hard as I could, but Ricky's portions were much more generous than Lucy's had been and I struggled to hoover up the entire lot.

'You've missed a bit,' said Ricky, his lips so close to my ear that I could feel his warm breath on my neck.

I looked up. His handsome face was only inches away from mine. He wiped his finger over the remaining cocaine and offered it to me. Perhaps it was the coke, or the supermodel's exit, but suddenly I decided I could handle him. I opened my mouth, took his finger deep inside and licked it clean of white powder. Ricky watched my lips with deep brown eyes that widened as I sucked a bit too hard and a bit too long. I slowly released his finger, reading the disappointment in his face as I did so, and stood up, licking my lips as if I'd just eaten something very tasty. I leaned closer to him. His face was now directly opposite, and almost touching my braless cleavage, so I waited there for a moment, allowing him to enjoy the view. He stared without embarrassment, and when I glanced down I could clearly see the bulge in his jeans. Ricky Jones was about to be mine.

Ricky and Billy Joe decided it would be appropriate to wear dinner jackets to celebrate the New Year. It was an incongruous look, seeing as they both had stubble and tattoos, but the stars of rock and film respectively made as handsome a pair as I'd ever seen when they walked into Hurlingham Manor's ballroom to greet the evening guests.

'You look very smart, Master Richard,' commented Ferguson with surprise. 'I don't believe I've seen you wearing a suit since your schooldays.'

Thanks to my new friend, Charlie, the night spun into a whirl of hedonism. I made confident small talk with actors and singers, cracked jokes with comedians and made an enormous champagne fountain with Lucy, which poured over the ballroom floor. Every half an hour or so, Lucy and

I would go up to her room and repowder our noses.

'What's the deal with Ricky and Venetia?' I asked Lucy as she racked up the coke.

'She's gone,' said Lucy. 'Her agency sent a car to pick her up and she went back to London.'

'No, I know that,' I said. 'But before today, what was the deal with them? Was she his girlfriend?'

'No, Laura, I've told you, Ricky doesn't do relationships. Venetia's just the girl he's been shagging for the past few weeks,' explained Lucy flatly. 'She's not even his type. She'd been after him for months and I think he just gave in at my party because she was so bloody persistent.'

'So, what is his type?' I persevered.

'Oh, you know, the usual,' said Lucy with a grin. 'Blonde, big tits, blue eyes. A bit like you actually!'

She looked at me and feigned surprise to find a blue-eyed, big-breasted blonde sitting next to her, and then she added, 'It's game on, Laura. I saw the two of you earlier. Just don't read too much into it, OK? I've spent too many nights mopping up the tears of Ricky's conquests. They're usually stupid cows like Venetia, but I like you, Laura, and I don't want to see you get hurt. If you can handle being one of Ricky's one-night stands, then go for it, but if you think you're going to get anything more than a few meaningless shags from him, you're wrong. Believe me.'

But by that stage there was no going back. Ricky and I had been giving each other loaded looks all evening, and ever since I'd noticed his erection earlier, I'd had a tingling sensation where my pants would have been had I been wearing any. Just the thought of having sex with Ricky Jones had kept me simmering on the brink of arousal for the past few hours. The foreplay had already begun.

It was a quarter to midnight when I finally saw him

heading purposefully my way through the crowds. He'd long since lost his dinner jacket and had undone his bow tie and the top button of his white shirt so a flash of tanned chest was on show, and he'd rolled up his sleeves to reveal a tattoo of a mermaid on his right forearm. Sugar Reef had just done an impromptu gig and he was hot from singing; I was hot from watching him sing. His dark hair clung in damp clumps to his forehead, which he wiped with the back of his hand.

'Phew, I'm burning up, man,' he said. 'I need a breather. Do you fancy joining me?'

It was a rhetorical question. He didn't wait for an answer, just expecting me to follow him, which, of course, I did. I followed him off the dance floor and out of the ballroom, down a corridor and through a door into a very large and ridiculously ornate bathroom, the walls of which were completely covered in Venetian mirrors.

'Lock the door,' he said, taking a wrap of coke out of his back pocket.

'The best surface in the house,' he announced proudly as he racked up a couple of fat ones on the polished marble counter.

Ricky went first and then, when I leaned over to do my line, he pressed himself against me and cupped my breasts in his hands. I felt the warmth of his penis as it grew between my bum cheeks and I had to catch my breath before sniffing up the line. I stood up and felt the drug buzz around my veins. In the mirror opposite I watched Ricky Jones kiss my bare neck and caress my breasts. They say that men are the voyeurs, but as I stood there being fondled by this amazingly sexy man I was definitely getting off on the view. It was like watching myself in my own private porn movie, except this was real.

'You are so fucking lovely,' he whispered. 'I've been wanting to do this ever since you interviewed me. I don't know what I said that day because all I could think about was touching you. I need to fuck you, Laura. I've been thinking about nothing else for weeks.'

There was something desperate and hungry about the way he was kissing the back of my neck, biting me almost, as he slid the straps of Lucy's dress off my shoulders. We looked at each other in the mirror. I was now naked to the waist and he was circling my nipples with his warm fingers.

'These are the most amazing tits I've ever seen,' he said, turning me towards him and kissing me lower, on the collarbone, then bare breast, taking one nipple in his mouth and then the other.

I thought my knees would buckle as I slid my hand up his shirt and touched the perfect skin of his smooth, hairless chest. Then I placed my hand on his swollen groin and massaged his dick through his straining trousers. He groaned. I undid the zip slowly and felt the tip of his bare penis poking out of his boxer shorts. It was already damp. I teased him briefly, touching him through his clothes, cupping his balls in my hand, and then I pushed his trousers and Calvins out of the way and released his throbbing dick. He lifted me up by the waist and sat me on the cold marble counter. My own groin was aching with anticipation. Spreading my legs and gripping his body with my thighs, I took his penis in my hand and started to rub it against myself through the flimsy fabric of Lucy's designer dress: faster, faster, faster.

'Oh my God, you are so horny,' he gasped as I rubbed him harder and harder against my clitoris.

I was writhing in ecstasy as I used Ricky Jones's penis as my very own vibrator. He placed his hands firmly under the dress and pushed it up to my waist.

'You're not wearing any knickers,' he groaned.

I placed his dick directly against my soaking wet pussy.

It only took a few seconds for me to come, hard and wet, against his bare penis, and then I thrust him deep inside me with my hands.

'I want it hard and fast,' I demanded in a voice that surprised even me. It must have come from the porn film I was starring in at that moment.

I watched the vision of our shagging bodies in the myriad of mirrors as I felt him in me as deep as I could take it. When I looked at Ricky's face I was amazed to catch him staring back at me, a look of tenderness in those huge brown eyes. My head was banging against the mirror behind me, but it didn't hurt. All I could feel was me and Ricky, Ricky in me.

'I'm going to come,' he announced suddenly, as men seem to do in these circumstances.

'So am I,' I shrieked, before experiencing my second crashing orgasm.

Ricky had a rather surprised look on his face as he came, as if the whole thing had been a bit of a revelation, and then I felt the heat of his orgasm as it filled me inside. His face was dripping with sweat and his damp shirt was clinging to his chest. We started laughing hysterically and then he dropped his head exhausted into my bare cleavage.

'This is my absolute favourite place in the whole world,' he announced from between my bosoms.

From somewhere very far away I could hear raised voices and clapping.

'Oh shit,' I said. 'I think we've just missed New Year.'

Back at the party, Ricky left my side and continued to socialize with his guests, but I didn't mind. I had a glow that no one could take away. Much, much later, we made love again between the silk sheets of a four-poster bed. It was the best start to any year I could possibly imagine, and when I eventually drifted off to sleep, it was with a rock god in my arms and a smile on my face.

I woke up confused to see Ricky, fully dressed and heading for the door.

'Where are you going?' I asked.

'Jamaica,' he replied. 'I'll call you when I get back.'

We both knew he didn't have my number. He closed the door quietly behind him and left me there, alone and naked in his stupid four-poster bed. Happy New Year.

8

There's no business like snow business

When I arrived at Lucy's opulent apartment building the doorman ushered me straight in. The lift carried me swiftly up fifteen floors and opened directly into the hall of the penthouse suite. I took off my sandals at the door and found Lucy sitting cross-legged on a floor cushion at the low cherry table in the centre of her enormous white, oriental-themed living space, wearing full make-up and a heavily embroidered Japanese robe. It struck me suddenly that I had never seen her without her make-up on, and nor had I ever witnessed anything more substantial than a rice cake pass her glossy lips. She looked tiny and doll-like in the huge room, a sad little Rapunzel, imprisoned in her ivory tower. In front of her on the table was an almost empty bottle of champagne and a mirror, covered in the paraphernalia of a cocaine user. She had obviously been sitting here alone, indulging in her drug of choice. I was pretty sure it wasn't healthy behaviour.

Sometimes I forgot how Lucy and I had met, because she'd opened up more to me as a journalist than she'd done since we'd become friends. Whenever I tactfully attempted to broach the subject of her depression or anorexia, she'd shrug it off by making a joke. The best opportunity to talk about her problems had come when my interview with her appeared in *Glitz*. I'd been terrified that our blossoming friendship would be over the minute she read the piece which, while still fairly sympathetic, had mentioned her unhealthy skinniness and the bursting into tears incident (thanks to Trudy's interference). Lucy had insisted on reading the magazine in the back of a limo on the way to Harvey Nics for a shoe-shopping excursion while I sat nervously beside her, studying her smooth forehead for signs of a frown. But she'd sat there expressionless, hiding behind her sunglasses, until she finished the feature. Then she'd gently closed the magazine and placed it on the seat between us.

'I like the cover photo,' she'd said.

'And the interview?' I'd asked tentatively. 'You don't think I was too harsh, do you? Because it really wasn't meant that way.'

'No, it's fine,' she'd said. 'I mean, everything you said is true.'

I'd opened my mouth to carry on, feeling brave enough to bring up the references I'd made to her eating disorder, but she'd known what was coming and jumped in.

'I'm thinking I might buy some of those Gucci knee-high boots with the wooden heels. Gisele was wearing a pair at that party I went to in LA and they look really good with bare legs and a tan. Then maybe we could have a glass of bubbly on the fifth floor.'

The moment was over.

In real life, Lucy Lloyd seemed to feel uncomfortable with emotions, which was ironic, really, because she was highly acclaimed for being an actress with a wide range of emotional capabilities. She'd played the part of a wretched homeless girl in her first film. It was a minor role, but at just eighteen she'd portrayed the broken girl's pain so astonishingly that film directors all over Hollywood began clamouring to have her in their next blockbuster movie. Her CV included roles as a heroin-addicted prostitute, a feisty single mother of an autistic child, a sexy Second World War spy and a dinosaur-hunting scientist. On screen, she could make you cry just by flashing her haunting blue eyes at the camera. She could have an audience in fits of giggles with a wink and make men fall in love with her with a coy smile. Off camera, she was a lot more guarded.

Sometimes I suspected that the reason she'd chosen me as a friend was because she'd accidentally exposed herself in that interview: she was worried I knew too much and felt safer having me close by, where she could keep an eye on me. And so we'd become party friends, forever dressing up and getting photographed together in all the best venues in town.

Lately she had begun to lean on me more, demanding my company and refusing to take no for an answer when I wanted a night off from partying. Billy Joe had gone back to LA to shoot a movie and Lucy was lost without him. I liked Billy Joe, he was a genuinely nice guy and was obviously smitten with Lucy. She seemed more grounded when he was around. While her boyfriend was filming a Western in the Hollywood Hills, Lucy was stuck over here until the summer, busy starring in a London-based costume drama in which she played a nineteenth-century prostitute.

Other than me, she didn't really have any female friends. She was universally loved by the guys, but women seemed uncomfortable in her presence. Of course there were the needy cling-ons – mainly lesser known actresses and ex-members of girl bands – who were continually popping up beside her at photo opportunities. But they were fair-weather friends, desperately clinging to her coat-tails in a vain attempt to sustain their own flagging careers. Worse were the professional piranhas. These people – her personal assistant, Karen; the film PRs, Martha and Charmaine; her agent, Sylvia Smith; the stylists; the personal trainers and even her psychiatrist – were all paid to look after her, but they weren't paid enough to like her. Whenever an unflattering story about Lucy appeared in the press, she knew perfectly well it had come from one of her staff. Lucy had made it her responsibility to take me under her wing as my own career took off. She always warned me, 'You can't trust anyone any more.'

As I bent down to kiss her fuzzy cheek, I could see that her mascara had run.

'Lucy, have you been crying?' I asked gently.

'Don't be silly,' she scoffed, flashing me her Oscar-winning smile – in fact, she'd won an Oscar for Best Actress only the month before. 'Here, have a glass of champagne and a line of charlie, and then I need you to help me decide what to wear before the Snowman arrives.'

Jim Snow, or the Snowman to his clients, was one of London's finest purveyors of top-quality cocaine. His clientele included pop stars, actors, minor royalty and a large section of the City's business community. Less important customers never met the great man himself, as he had several dozen employees to take care of their needs. Those at the bottom of the scrap heap – journalists, TV producers, bankers and the like – had to endure nerve-wracking exchanges in grimy Soho pubs and paid cash upfront. Lucy, on the other hand, dealt only with the Snowman, who gave her his five-star deals on wheels service, delivering to her door in his black BMW convertible, and allowing her to settle her bill on a monthly basis. They were an unlikely duo, but both had too much to lose to ever jeopardize their business arrangement. Confidentiality was all and they seemed to trust each other completely.

Folklore had it that the Snowman had murdered several

men during the course of his working life and that he was still embroiled in a bloody turf battle with a gang of particularly dangerous Yardies in west London. Jim Snow was in his forties, short, wiry, ginger-haired and pockmarked. His nose was flattened like a boxer's and a deep scar ran from the left corner of his mouth to his ear lobe. It made his smile seem both unnaturally wide and unbearably sinister. He scared the shit out of me, but Lucy had a deep respect for the man.

'I like him,' she insisted. 'He's a professional. Very good at his job.'

When the Snowman appeared silently at the living-room door, I jumped. He was wearing a full-length leather jacket and a wicked grin. His very presence seemed to sully Lucy's pristine apartment. Whenever I was in the same building as the man, the theme tune from *The Omen* started playing in my head.

'Awright, my lovelies?' He spoke out of the corner of his lopsided mouth in deep, gravelly Cockney tones.

'Jim,' smiled Lucy. 'How lovely to see you. Champagne?'

'I won't, thanks, darling,' he declined politely. 'I'm driving, and you know how I like to respect the law.'

He had a deep, throaty laugh. Jim made himself at home, sitting cross-legged between Lucy and me at the low table.

'This,' he said, 'is powerful stuff. Proper devil's dandruff.' He threw a clear plastic bag of white powder on the table. 'It's from a new source. Very, very pure, so be careful, my lovelies. Don't overdo it or you'll be up until next week. Only fifty quid a G. Would you like to try before you buy?'

'Ooh, yes, please.' Lucy's eyes were shining at the sight of so much cocaine. She was always worried about running out, so she'd started buying in bulk. But her stash wasn't lasting her any longer than before; she was just doing more – bigger lines, more frequently, starting earlier and earlier every day.

This stuff was potent. It nearly blew my head off when I snorted the line the Snowman offered me.

'Good shit, innit?' he grinned from Lucy to me.

'Fantastic,' enthused Lucy, her eyes widening. 'God, that's good. Phew!'

I always felt slightly uncomfortable with the fact that Jim never touched the stuff himself.

'Don't mix business with pleasure,' was his mantra.

'So, how many grams do you want?' he asked.

Lucy wrinkled her pretty little nose as she considered the question.

'Five, I think. You're not going away anywhere are you, Jim? I might need to see you later in the week.'

The Snowman shook his head to reassure her he would always be just a mobile phone call away and then turned to me.

'What about you, Laura? How much do you want?'

I'd never actually bought my own gear before. I just took what Lucy offered me. That way I didn't feel like a proper drug user. I told myself I wasn't like Lucy. I didn't rely on the stuff to get me through the day. But it would be nice to have my own stash. That way I could have a cheeky wee line whenever I wanted. It wasn't addiction, just convenience – that was my excuse.

'Um, I'll have a couple of wraps,' I said.

'Cool.' Jim produced some tiny electronic scales from an inside pocket of his leather coat and began dividing up the contents of the bag.

'I've just been over to see Ricky and the lads,' said Jim. 'He looks great; all brown and healthy. Don't know how he does it, mind. Sounds like he scored some heavy shit in

Jamaica. The guy should be dead by now with the amount of gear he does.'

'He's got the constitution of an ox,' said Lucy. 'It's those aristocratic genes. They're bred for excess, the upper classes. They don't need to be able to work, just drink and shag and party.'

'You're not wrong,' agreed Jim. 'You girls going over to see the boys tonight, then?'

We both nodded, in my case a little too enthusiastically.

Jim threw seven wraps of coke onto the table and stood up.

'I'll have to love you and leave you, girls. People to see, places to go, you know how it is. No rest for the wicked.'

He headed for the door.

'You can settle up at the end of the month. Laura, I'll set up an account for you, OK?'

And with that he'd gone and the apartment was clean again.

In true rock'n'roll style, Sugar Reef sent a chauffeur-driven limo to pick us up. I fidgeted nervously in the plush leather seat, not knowing whether it was the super-strong coke making me so jittery or the thought of seeing Ricky again. I asked Lucy five times whether I looked all right and she replied five times that I did. We were headed for the band's hotel, one of the grand old establishments on Hyde Park. It was a balmy evening and I could see through the window that girls were baring their legs for the first time that year, but I still felt cold and jumpy.

'You OK?' asked Lucy as we pulled up outside the foyer.

'Nervous,' I said as a portly porter in a ruby uniform opened the limo door.

She squeezed my hand reassuringly and smiled. 'It'll be OK.'

A handful of photographers were gathered behind a rope at the front door.

'Lucy! Laura! Give us a smile!' they shouted. 'Are you here to see the band?'

Lucy wiggled expertly past them, flashing her famous smile but saying nothing. I still felt like a ridiculous fraud under these circumstances – Lucy Lloyd's shadow – and kept my head down until we were safely through the revolving doors.

'We're here to meet Sugar Reef,' Lucy told the receptionist.

'Of course, Miss Lloyd. They're in the Windsor Suite. Fifth floor, turn left out of the elevator and you can't miss it. There's no one else on that floor.'

Ricky opened the door wearing nothing but a tan and a towel around his waist. His hair was wet and dishevelled and he looked even more dangerously handsome than I remembered.

'Baby, you're here!' He held out his arms and stepped towards us.

I assumed he was lunging towards his old friend Lucy, but he stepped right past her and gave me a bear hug before kissing me warmly on the lips.

'You look gorgeous.' He took a step back and eyed me up and down. 'You've shrunk.'

Lucy hit him playfully on the arm and they hugged.

'Good to see you, sweetheart,' he said. 'Pity Billy Boy's not around, eh?'

He grinned from me to Lucy and shook his head.

'It's so fucking great to be home. Come in, come in.'

Ricky ushered us into a testosterone-filled den of iniquity.

The four other band members – Lewis, Phil, Luke and Mal – were lounging on various chintz-covered couches, wearing denim, leather and black. The suite was dark and smoky and smelled of sweat and beer. The floor was littered with empty lager cans and the coffee table was strewn with white powder. Both Mal and Luke had their arms round pretty, giggly young girls. Lewis's girlfriend, Monica, a willowy Texan model with flame-red hair, whom I'd met and got on well with at Ricky's party, was pouring herself a G&T at the bar. Phil, the lead guitarist, was half-heartedly strumming on an acoustic guitar. They all looked kind of spaced out, but achingly cool, as if they were starring in the band's latest video. I happily entered their parallel universe.

'Do you guys want a drink?' asked Monica.

We accepted gratefully.

'Laura, I hear you got the Superbra gig,' continued the Texan, pouring generous amounts of gin into two glass tumblers. 'That's a great job. There are some models out there baying for your blood, they're so jealous.'

'Really?' I was flattered.

'Really.' Monica nodded her head firmly. 'And Venetia's one of them, so be careful. That girl has a major problem with you. Just make sure you're never stuck up a dark alley with her, OK?'

I laughed nervously, not quite sure whether Monica was joking or giving me a serious warning that I was in imminent danger from the six-foot-plus she-monster.

'She's not going to turn up tonight, is she, Ricky?' asked Lucy, reading my mind.

Ricky wore an angelic mask. 'Of course not,' he scoffed. 'I haven't seen Venetia in ages.'

'Ricky, we do read the papers,' said Lucy sternly. 'We saw you having dinner with her in Jamaica.'

'She was there doing a shoot for an ad agency. It was just a coincidence. I had dinner with her. Big deal. It was all perfectly innocent.'

'Yeah, sure,' said Monica, handing me the stiff drink I now urgently needed. 'And what about those naked girls in your tub, boys. Was that all perfectly innocent, too?'

'It had nothing to do with Lewis,' replied Phil a little too quickly.

Monica sat on her boyfriend's knee and stroked his beard in mock affection.

'Of course not. My Lewis would never have his head turned by another woman, would you, darling?'

Lewis smiled nervously at his girlfriend, and then she slowly poured her gin and tonic over his head.

The room went silent as we all wondered how to react. Lewis just sat there, dripping with gin, a look of startled amazement on his face. One of the groupies giggled quietly in the corner and Phil stopped playing his guitar. And then Monica threw back her head and laughed a long, throaty, sexy laugh. There was a group sigh of relief and we all joined in with the hilarity.

So that's how to handle a rock star, I thought in admiration.

Ricky was still wearing nothing more than a towel. He mumbled something about going to get dressed, took my hand and led me along a corridor to his bedroom.

'There really is nothing going on between me and Venetia,' he said gently as I closed the bedroom door behind us.

'None of my business if there is,' I replied chirpily. 'I mean, it's not as if I'm your girlfriend or anything.'

I was trying to laugh, to show him that I knew being his girlfriend was the most ridiculous idea in the world, when

Ricky pinned me against the door and stared into my eyes intensely.

'But you could be ...'

He kissed me hard on the mouth.

'... if you wanted to be.'

His hands crept up the back of my top.

'I'd like it if you were ...'

And he undid my bra with obvious expertise.

'... my girlfriend.'

He lifted my top over my head, then threw my bra across the room.

'You're just saying that to get me into bed,' I mumbled through his kisses, as he unfastened my jeans and peeled them down to my ankles.

'I don't think I have to say anything to get you into bed.' He slipped his hand into my knickers and I let out an involuntary groan of pleasure.

His towel had fallen to the floor and he stood totally naked in front of me. I could see the tan line where his shorts had been, which made him seem reassuringly boyish and less godlike. His willy was standing to attention, looking pale in comparison to his bronzed stomach. We tripped towards the bed, clinging to each other, but I fell over my jeans as I tried to step out of them in my high-heeled sandals. We collapsed giggling onto the carpet in a heap of limbs. I landed on top of him, and it seemed like the most natural thing in the world to just straddle him there and then. I was naked apart from my shoes. We both stopped laughing as I took him inside me and made love to him like I'd never made love to anyone before.

Afterwards, as we lay side by side on the carpet, sharing a cigarette, Ricky looked at me tenderly and said, 'Laura, I meant it when I said I wanted you to be my girlfriend.'

'Why?' I asked, intrigued. After all, according to Lucy, Ricky Jones didn't do relationships.

'Because I like you,' he said. 'You're different from the other girls I've had. You're just kind of easier to be with.'

Then he grinned his wicked grin. 'And you've got great tits.'

What Ricky didn't realize was that what made me different from the Venetias of this world was not my ample cleavage but my very ordinariness. If the man wanted a taste of something different, who was I to argue? I'd bagged myself a rock star boyfriend after all.

Waking up next to your idol is a funny old business. There are all the usual feelings of surprise, and even the faint dash of loneliness that comes from finding yourself naked beside an unfamiliar hunk of human flesh. His smell was alarmingly new, however intoxicating, and his skin felt alien, even though it was silky smooth. The early days of any relationship are filled with insecurity at the best of times. Will we have anything to say to each other in the brash light of day? Will he still fancy me now he's sober? Will he sneak out of bed and jump on the next plane to the Caribbean? That sort of thing. Wake up next to a household name and those anxieties are multiplied a thousand times. Last night he said he wanted to be my boyfriend; this morning would he even remember my name? The bedside clock said half past eleven. I watched Ricky sleep and waited.

An hour later he was still out for the count. As beautiful as he was, even I was bored of watching him by then, so I got out of bed as quietly as possible and found my way to the en-suite bathroom. I brushed my teeth with Ricky Jones's toothbrush and washed my face with his soap. In the mirror I could still see a flush of sex in my cheeks and when I looked down I noticed two huge carpet burns on my knees. I grinned at myself proudly – the cat who got the crème de la crème.

'Laura? You there?' Ricky called sleepily from the bedroom.

I wrapped a towel around me and walked back into the bedroom.

'Oh good. I thought you'd done a runner.'

Ricky did a long slow stretch and smiled at me with sleepy eyes.

'So, sexy lady. What do you want to do today?'

I opened the curtains a fraction. Yesterday's sunshine had obviously been a one-day wonder and rain now lashed the hotel window. Hyde Park looked bleak and uninviting.

'I don't know, it's pissing down,' I said.

'So get back into bed.' Ricky threw back the duvet and patted the warm space beside him. 'We'll order room service and hide out in here until it stops raining.'

I agreed. It seemed as good a plan as any.

The rain didn't stop for four days.

9

Property Special: Londoners forced to live in squalor as house prices go through the roof

Bad boy singer Ricky Jones of rock band Sugar Reef has a new girlfriend, we can reveal today. Jones, 27, spent the last *four days* holed up in bed with TV stunner Laura McNaughton, 25. Miss McNaughton, star of *The Weekend Starts Here*, arrived at the band's central London hotel on Sunday evening with her friend, Oscar-winning beauty Lucy Lloyd.

The band had checked into the hotel only hours earlier, having just returned to the UK from Jamaica, where they were recording their new album. While Miss Lloyd joined the rest of the band for a welcome-home party, Jones and Miss McNaughton disappeared into his bedroom, where the couple remained until yesterday morning!

A source close to Jones says, 'They obviously hit it off. From the noises coming from his bedroom, it was clear Ricky and Laura were doing more than playing tiddlywinks. Then, when they stayed in bed for four days, we decided they must be staging some sort of love-in, like John Lennon and Yoko Ono.'

Miss Lloyd was seen leaving the hotel during the early hours of Monday morning, but the love birds did not re-appear until just before midday yesterday. The couple refused to comment on their relationship when they were spotted getting into a limousine together outside the hotel.

Jones was his usual charming self, telling assembled members of the press to f**k off! Miss McNaughton, meanwhile, smiled broadly, looking every part the rock star's girlfriend in tight jeans, a leather jacket and designer sunglasses.

The news of Jones's new relationship has come as a shock to supermodel Venetia Tioni, who had been romantically linked to the singer for the past few months.

'I am disgusted by his behaviour and I don't know what he sees in that girl,' said Miss Tioni today, speaking from Milan. 'I thought I was his girlfriend and now I hear he's been sleeping with some cheap television presenter. It hurts, of course, but I'm not going to let this affect me. I've been called the world's most beautiful woman, Laura McNaughton is just a chubby little Scottish girl with no class.'

We can exclusively reveal that Miss McNaughton looks anything but 'chubby' in the latest Superbra campaign. Billboards featuring racy photographs of the tartan temptress are about to go up at a bus stop near you (*see pic, top right*). Industry insiders say that Miss Tioni had been favourite to star in the adverts until the obvious assets of newcomer Miss McNaughton caught the eye of advertising executives at the famous lingerie brand. 'Laura is blatantly better endowed for advertising bras than Venetia,' says a Superbra employee who could not be named. It appears that Jones agrees.

Of course, Jones is no stranger to woman trouble. Only last year he was cited in the divorce of Roy Wagstaff, head of Wag Records, Sugar Reef's record company at that time, when it emerged that the star had been sleeping with Wagstaff's wife, Jill. Sugar Reef have since terminated their contract with Wag Records and are now signed to American music giants P&G.

*

Nat was lying on my bed, cup of tea in hand, reading aloud from one of our nation's favourite tabloids. On the cover was a full-size photograph of me and Ricky outside the hotel with the strapline, 'Ricky and Laura spend four days in bed together – turn to pages 4 and 5 for the full story'.

'This is fucking hilarious,' she spluttered, spilling tea all over my duvet, but missing her pristine white shirt. 'I can't believe you're on the front cover. Mind you, at least you've got your clothes on in that one. This one, however.'

Nat held up pages four and five for me to see. There I was, taking up three-quarters of a page, wearing nothing but a push-up bra and a lacy black G-string.

I felt sick – half with excitement, half with fear. Part of me loved the fact that I was front-page news, that I was being held up as some sort of sex symbol and, most importantly, that the entire nation now knew I was Ricky Jones's girlfriend. But it scared me, too. As a journalist, I knew how the press could take control of a story and forget it was the story of someone's life – in this case, mine.

'Was there anyone hanging around outside?' I asked Nat, who'd arrived unannounced waving the offending newspaper excitedly five minutes earlier.

'Only that tramp in the wheelchair that's always there,' she replied. 'Why? Did you expect a crowd of paparazzi? 'Fraid not, darling. Not yet.'

Nat laughed again and reread Venetia's quotes.

'You've really got up that bitch's nose, haven't you, babes?'

'She's really scary,' I said. 'I think she wants a catfight.'

Nat smiled broadly and rubbed her growing belly subconsciously – she was four months pregnant and just beginning to show.

'So, is Ricky Jones as good in bed as legend would have us believe?' she asked.

'God, yeah,' I enthused. 'He's so fucking sexy.'

'Got a big ...?'

'Average, but he knows exactly what to do with it.'

'And you used condoms, right?'

'Um, no.' I knew this was the wrong answer.

'Laura, what the hell are you playing at having unprotected sex with that man? He's had more shags than you've had Marlboro Lights.' Nat looked deeply concerned.

'He swears he's had an Aids test recently,' I offered lamely.

'Well, you'd better pray he's telling the truth, babes, because that bloke is a world-renowned slut!'

We sat in silence for a moment, Nat munching a biscuit, me sucking on a cigarette and blowing the smoke out of the open window to avoid polluting my pregnant friend.

'So, how does it feel, now you've got what you wanted?' she asked eventually, breaking the silence.

'Fantastic,' I replied uncertainly. 'I think.'

Nat raised a neatly plucked eyebrow. 'You think?'

'Well, obviously it's amazing that I'm going out with Ricky, and the money for that ad campaign is a totally ridiculous amount, and d'you know what I really, really love?'

'What?'

'That Pete will have read this!'

Nat nodded enthusiastically. As a way of getting back at a tosser of an ex-boyfriend, shagging the country's most famous male sex symbol was indeed pretty impressive.

'But my dad will have seen this, too. Someone will have shown him; probably one of his delightful pupils. And he's already so pissed off with me. This is going to destroy him.'

Nat nodded again, less enthusiastically this time.

'But that was always going to happen,' she said gently. 'You can't have fame without the headlines. You know that, you're a journalist.'

'I know,' I said quietly, more to myself than to Nat.

Then a thought struck me. 'Nat, why are you not at work? It's Friday, isn't it? Trudy hasn't introduced a four-day week, has she?'

'As if,' laughed Nat. 'Nah, I was on my way to the office, saw this at the tube station' – she waved the paper at me – 'and decided to throw a sickie and come here instead. Best thing about being up the duff is that I've discovered a whole new range of medical excuses to use and no one ever doubts me. I've got really bad morning sickness today, as it happens.'

In fact, Nat looked a picture of good health; she was positively blooming as she tucked into her third chocolate digestive.

'Want one?' She offered me the packet of biscuits. I shook my head automatically.

'How silly of me?' scoffed Nat. 'You don't do food any more, do you? Anyway, why aren't *you* at work?'

'Because the next series doesn't start until the autumn,' I explained. 'I've got a few interviews to do next week to launch the Superbra thingy, but other than that I'm a free agent.'

'Nice work if you can get it, eh?'

We grinned at each other smugly. Nat had her baby and I had my fame. We'd both got exactly what we wanted.

Being front-page news made me very popular suddenly. The phone rang for the fifth time that morning. I'd already spoken to Jack, whose curiosity about Ricky forced him into forgiving me for standing him up the previous Sunday. Then Jasmine had called, desperate for all the details – I could hear Tina whispering questions in the background. Vicky had phoned from Edinburgh, gushing with excitement about my celebrity conquest. And Graham had been unable to resist an opportunity to compare notes now that we both had famous men in our lives – he and Daniel Duchamps had been joined at the slinky hips for months. This time it was Wazza, sounding even more breathless than usual because he'd just come out of a breakfast meeting to be shown my front-page splash and was practically wetting himself with excitement.

'Laura, this is fabulous,' he enthused. 'Do you know what this sort of publicity is worth? You are a clever, clever girl.'

He obviously thought that my relationship with Ricky had been born out of ambition, as part of some shrewd career plan.

'I've already had several requests for interviews from notable publications.' He was salivating at the thought of more column inches. 'We need to have a meeting a.s.a.p. Tomorrow morning. First thing. In the meantime, do anything to keep the rock star on side.' He laughed a dirty little laugh. 'And I mean *anything*.'

Warren had done his maths, and this was going to be a nice little earner for him. I knew the arithmetics of celebrity association as well as he did. It's a simple formula. I was, by definition, a mere C-list celebrity. And I was only registering on the scale at all because of my friendship with Lucy – A-list – Lloyd. British television presenters rarely manage to crawl out of the lower echelons of celebrity society, though, however important their friends are. Sex, on the other hand, sells. Ricky was a definite A-lister. He had the money, the looks, the ego, the sell-out stadium gigs and, most importantly, because British bands rarely break America, he had seven US number ones under his low-slung snakeskin belt. He was Mr Big. The fact that I was sharing body fluids with such a god immediately propelled me to at least B-list standing, and if the relationship lasted and we became a golden couple à la Posh and Becks, well, I would make the A-list in no time. This would make me a highly marketable commodity and Wazza an even richer, fatter old man.

I had long since realized that talent has absolutely nothing to do with fame. It's all about clever celebrity mergers – wearing the right dress to the right event, sleeping with the right sex symbol at the right time, signing the right deal with the right television company. It's as cold, calculated and cynical as that. But those rules didn't apply to Ricky and me – I just fancied the pants off the guy and he seemed to feel the same about me. We were young, healthy and full of raging hormones. I could have been a hairdresser and he could have been a mechanic, the same thing would have happened. Wouldn't it?

'Oh yes, I almost forgot,' continued Wazza. 'The money from Superbra is in your bank account. Enjoy. I'll see you at nine tomorrow.'

I skipped back into the bedroom and asked Nat if she fancied coming shopping with me.

'Why, what are you buying?'

'A new house,' I replied with glee.

'OK, so where do you want to live, ideally?'

We were sitting in Nat's car outside my flat, poring over a dog-eared A–Z.

'Well, it's got to be central and somewhere cool. Notting Hill's too much of a cliché,' I said. 'Everybody lives there, and I'm not really a west London girl, so I don't fancy Kensington or Chelsea, either – too posh. I'd love to be near the Heath, but Hampstead's a bit too grown-up, d'you know what I mean?'

Nat nodded.

'St John's Wood has never really appealed. It's not very happening, is it?'

'What about Camden?' asked Nat. 'You know it well, it's just down the road and you're a local at most of the pubs there.'

'Mmm,' I considered. 'Camden's OK, but it's a bit grubby and there are all those tourists at the market. I'm thinking somewhere near Camden but a bit more classy.'

'Primrose Hill!' Nat stabbed the A–Z with her finger. 'It's perfect. Walking distance to Camden, right on Regent's Park, loads of celebrity neighbours, classy, nice architecture, decent pubs. It's decided.'

And so it was.

My mobile started ringing. I glanced at the name of the caller and switched the off button with a pang of guilt.

'Who was that?' asked Nat.

'My mum,' I said.

'Why don't you want to speak to her?'

'Because she'll have seen the paper, and even if she isn't totally mortified by the public humiliation of it, my dad will be. I'll deal with the parents later; right now, I'm going to buy a house.'

'Whatever you say,' said Nat. 'But you're going to have to talk to them about all this sometime. Your family isn't just going to disappear.'

I stared straight ahead and thought about how much easier all this fame business would be if I had no baggage to carry with me. No Becky to fall out with, no mum to embarrass, no dad to disappoint. I was proud of what I'd done and pleased with where I'd got to, but they made me feel as though my pleasure was causing them pain. I felt a stab of isolation. Here I was, about to buy my first home but with no one likely to come and visit me there – except maybe Nat and Lucy (if she deemed it 'luxe' enough).

Staring in the window of the estate agent's on Gloucester Avenue, I realized how little £1 million was in terms of London property. I'd already decided to give £100,000 away to the deserving – Mum and Dad, Fiona, Gran and Becky. Call it guilt money if you will. Warren's fee was £150,000, and I had to keep back enough to live on until the next series of *The Weekend Starts Here*. I was left with about £700,000 to spend on a house.

'Wow, look at this one,' Nat was salivating at the sight of a Victorian, four-storey townhouse with conservatory and pond. 'It's only a couple of million ...'

'Bit out of my league, then,' I sighed.

'You could always get a mortgage,' suggested Nat.

'No, this is an investment. I just want to buy something outright. Cash,' I insisted, perusing the cards in the window.

'God, you're so flash. I'm going to enjoy helping you spend all this dosh,' said Nat, rubbing her hands together. 'What would Trudy say if she could see me here with you when I'm supposed to be having a meeting about a sex supplement in her office right now.'

She glanced at her watch and smiled happily at me. My face fell.

'You can't tell anybody about this.' I grabbed Nat's arm and looked her straight in the eye. 'Promise me. Especially not someone like Trudy. Not about how much money I've got, or where I'm looking to buy, or anything, OK?'

Nat was visibly hurt. 'As if I would. I'm your mate, for fuck's sake!' She pulled her arm out of my grasp and took a step back. 'Christ, you're getting paranoid, Laura. Too much coke, if you ask me.'

'Sorry,' I muttered. 'It's just that Lucy says I can't trust anyone any more. I just wanted to be sure.'

'What is it with you and Lucy Lloyd?' asked Nat, eyes flashing with anger. 'She treats you like her little project or something. The woman's a mess, Laura, but you think the sun shines out of her skinny little arse. She's trying to turn you into her clone. Do you really want to be a miserable, screwed-up, anorexic drug addict? Do you?'

She seemed genuinely upset and I was shocked by her outburst. What was she talking about? I was happier than ever. On top of the world. Perhaps it was her hormones – I'd heard that pregnant women could become irrational, but this was insane. I tried to calm her down.

'Nat, please, I like Lucy but I don't want to be her,' I insisted. 'I'm perfectly aware that she's got problems, but she knows what she's talking about when it comes to being famous. She just wants to help me, that's all.'

'Yeah, well just remember who your real mates are, all right?' Nat sighed deeply. 'I worry about you, that's all.'

'About me?' I was baffled. 'But my life is perfect.'

'Laura, nobody's life is perfect. It just appears that way until something goes wrong.' She gave me a hug but her eyes looked sad. 'Come on, let's go in and buy you your dream house.'

The subject was dropped.

I knew it was the one as soon as we pulled up outside. The house was at the end of a painfully smart row of three-storey, four-bedroomed terraces, a few streets back from Primrose Hill. It was tall, proud and imposing, and desperately in need of some TLC. All the others in the street were immaculately coated with fresh paint in white, blue or pink. Mine was the colour of dirty dishwater, but clinging to the tired façade was the biggest, most beautiful wisteria I'd ever seen.

'Oh, it's beautiful,' I sighed, as we walked up the steps towards the rotting front door.

Nat and the handsome young estate agent, whose name was Brian, exchanged puzzled glances.

'Well, it does have bags of potential,' agreed Brian. 'And it's an absolute snip at £750,000. You can't buy anything in Primrose Hill for that these days – not even a maisonette. The house two doors down went for over a million last month, but ...' He opened the front door with a creak and we entered a grubby unlit hall. 'You would need to employ a builder. It's not exactly habitable in its present state. But do have a look round, let your imagination run wild and see what you think.'

'It's not exactly *Elle Decoration*,' whispered Nat, as we stepped gingerly over broken floorboards into what had once been a beautiful living room. 'More *Steptoe and Son*.'

The house smelled musty and damp, there were random piles of newspaper lying around and a damp single mattress lay on the floor by the boarded-up fireplace. The nearest thing to a mod con was a camping stove in one corner. Paintwork and wallpaper had faded, peeled and merged into one vast, sludge-coloured horror.

'Yes, but it could be beautiful,' I enthused.

The living room opened into a dining room, which in turn opened, through broken patio doors, onto an overgrown jungle of a back garden, which would have been quite spacious had it not been for the bramble infestation. Downstairs was a basement, which Brian insisted had once been a large kitchen. All that remained as evidence of a sink were some dripping pipes sticking out of the wall. I could just about make out an old flagstone floor under the layers of grime, and there was a bricked-up door in one corner which would once have given access to the garden above by a wrought-iron spiral staircase.

'And this would have been the pantry.' Brian opened a door into a smaller room off the kitchen, a mouse ran out and Nat screamed.

'Oops, sorry about that,' said the blushing estate agent. 'Anyway, there's plenty of space to make this into a utility area, and here,' he opened another door, 'is a potential second loo.'

'It looks as if it's already been used as a toilet,' said Nat through pursed lips as she glanced into the filthy room and gagged. 'I think I'm going to be sick. I'm sure this isn't healthy for the baby.'

I was intrigued. 'Who lived here?' I asked.

'It belonged to a rather eccentric old lady,' explained Brian. 'She lived here for sixty-five years. Apparently the house was once a very smart property, but her parents both died when she was in her teens, so she just stayed here alone. When she ran out of money, she sold the furniture. By the time she died a few weeks ago, this was all that was left.'

'That is so sad,' I sighed.

'It gives me the creeps,' said Nat, shivering. 'Please don't tell me she died here, in the house.'

Brian shook his head. 'No, she had a fall and a neighbour spotted her through the window. They took her to the Royal Free Hospital. She died there.'

'Well, at least that's something,' said Nat.

'Mind you, I believe the parents passed away in the master bedroom. Consumption, or so the chap next door seems to think. That was a very long time ago, though. Nothing for you to worry about, Miss McNaughton.'

But the house's history didn't worry me. I found it all rather romantic.

Upstairs was an enormous master bedroom with a lovely bay window, which I was sure had a glorious view. Unfortunately, due to the lack of floorboards in the centre of the room, we couldn't actually get to the window to see. The bathroom boasted a freestanding Victorian cast-iron bath, which hadn't been cleaned for six decades. There was no shower and the sink had turned green where the tap had been dripping for sixty-five years. As for the toilet ... well, a description would be both unnecessary and distasteful. Bedrooms two and three were quite large but unreasonably squalid, while the fourth bedroom was little more than a cupboard. There was no central heating or running water, and although the electric lights worked in some rooms, Brian felt it might be wise to have the entire house rewired.

'I'll take it,' I said. 'But I'm paying cash, so I want a discount – £600,000, and you've got yourself a buyer today.'

'That sounds fair,' said Brian, who was visibly delighted to get the monstrosity off his hands. 'Let me just make a quick phone call.' He walked fifty yards down the street and made an animated mobile phone call. There was a lot of broad smiling and gesticulating of hands. Two minutes later he trotted back with a grin. 'You've got a deal,' he announced.

'This is a joke,' said Nat. 'You should see what half a million would buy you in Dagenham.'

Back at the estate agents, Brian faxed the deeds and various legal documents over to Warren's office for my lawyers to look over. After that, it was out of my hands. It would take a few days for the paperwork to be sorted out, but everyone agreed that, since the building was freehold, it was a done deal. I took Nat to a lovely little Greek restaurant for a celebratory lunch.

'I'm a homeowner,' I announced cheerfully, gulping a glass of champagne.

'You're a mad cow,' said Nat, sipping her orange juice. 'You should at least have the place surveyed.'

'Why?' I asked. 'It's quite obvious what a surveyor will say: the place is a shithole and it's falling down.'

'So why are you buying it?' Nat looked bewildered.

'Because I couldn't afford anything that was already nicely decorated. Well, nothing bigger than a two-bedroomed flat. This way, I've got a whole house and £100,000 left over to do it up exactly as I want it – new kitchen, bathroom, anything I fancy. In six months it'll be worth over a million but I'll only have spent £700,000 max. Do you know any good builders?'

Nat shook her head and replied through a mouthful of olives, 'My dad's best mate is a demolitions expert, though. Shall I give him a call?'

IO

How to make friends and influence people

My house was important to me because it was my future. OK, so right at that moment I was richer than I'd ever dreamed of being, but I also knew that fame was fickle, and that as much as I wanted it to last for ever, there might come a day when I'd be yesterday's news. The house was an insurance policy – something I could cash in if I ever found myself on the celebrity scrap heap. Ricky was as baffled as Nat by my purchase.

'Why do you need a house?' he asked me when I called to tell him my news.

'Because I need somewhere to live,' I explained patiently.

'You've got somewhere to live,' he replied, cool as you like.

'But, Ricky, it's a dive,' I said. 'You haven't even seen it. You wouldn't understand. It's smaller than your en-suite bathroom at Hurlingham Manor. And it smells.'

'So, why not just rent a bigger flat, one that's in good nick, with a cleaner and a porter and running water?' He was laughing at me.

'It might not have running water yet, but this place is going to be my dream home,' I insisted. 'Why not come and see it tonight?'

'There's a party on tonight,' he said flatly.

'Ricky, there's a party on every night. And anyway, you

can come and have a look at my place and then go to the party.'

'OK.' He didn't sound overly enthusiastic and I wondered momentarily whether he was bored of me already. Thankfully, he added, 'But then you'll come to the party with me, right.'

It wasn't a question. I'd learned quickly that Ricky didn't ask questions. He gave orders and I was happy to oblige. He said, 'Jump,' and I said, 'Hand me that pogo stick.'

Ricky was a natural-born nomad. Despite the obscene amount of money he must have had – and I never found out exactly what he was worth – he had no inclination to lay down roots. He took money for granted and was blissfully ignorant of the fear of having none. One day Hurlingham Manor would be his domain, but for now the man didn't own so much as a garage in which to keep his beloved Harley-Davidson. Theoretically, he could have afforded to buy a small nation, but he could always do that tomorrow, if tomorrow ever came. Because of this unique mindset, he was the perfect musician. The fact that he spent around 360 days of the year living in hotels and tour buses actually appealed to him. I gradually noticed he had very few possessions at all. He wore the same clothes day in, day out and carried everything of any personal value with him in a small battered leather suitcase.

I suppose that being born into a hugely wealthy family gave him a sense of freedom that few of us can ever truly enjoy. Ricky didn't hoard possessions as trophies of success like the rest of us do. There was no state-of-the-art TV, no villa in the sun, no rare pedigree dog or diamond stud in his ear. Instead, he wore his success in the hard set of his jaw and the steely black stare of his eyes. He had an unshakeable confidence – or arrogance, depending on your perspective

– which I have only ever witnessed in the incredibly rich. He never seemed scared of anything or anyone. He was the ultimate hedonist. The only thing he valued was having a good time. Nothing could touch him, not the police, not pain, not poverty. And it was all so bloody easy because he knew he was blessed. He had a special Ready Brek glow which nothing could penetrate. And so he would drive his motorbike at breakneck speed, without a crash helmet, after drinking a crateful of beer, and he would do more drugs, harder drugs, better drugs in his opinion, than anyone else was prepared to try. He also seemed incapable of feeling guilt, and I had a sneaking suspicion that there was a gaping hole where his conscience should have been. This made him dangerous. Very dangerous.

To become part of his world meant taking the same chances he did. It scared me shitless, but I desperately wanted to be let in. This fear was the most powerful aphrodisiac I'd ever known. Ricky Jones was more intoxicating than the cocaine I was becoming so fond of, or the headlines I was beginning to crave, or the beautiful new bones that had started to appear in my ever-shrinking body.

It was amazing how quickly and wholeheartedly a relatively good girl like me could slip from boring, middle-class normality into a heady underworld of excess. Except it didn't feel as if I was slipping, more as though I'd been caught up in some vast whirlwind that was spinning me round, making me dizzy, keeping my feet a hundred miles off the ground. And I was loving every adrenalin-charged moment.

I was happy – genuinely, sincerely, giddily delirious with the whole self-indulgent thing. I felt as if my life was building up to some huge, momentous, glittering event. I was being propelled towards an awesome bright light, and the excitement of the journey meant I could never quite catch my breath. The destination was unknown, but I was too caught up in it all to care. And the journey, oh that delicious, intoxicating journey. I was hooked. Anticipation became the one, dominant emotion. I was always looking forward to the next party, the next excuse to glam up to the nines, the next line of coke, the next click of a camera, the next time I could make love to Ricky …

I was wearing a Dolce & Gabbana bustier dress, hand embroidered with real precious stones, and sitting on the filthy hall steps of my lovely new house, waiting by candle-light. After what seemed like an eternity, I eventually heard the deep earth-trembling roar of Ricky's motorbike as it drew up outside.

'You alone?' I asked as his slim silhouette slid off the bike and swaggered up the path in the darkness. I looked down the street for paparazzi.

'Some photographers on mopeds tried to follow me from the hotel, but they were hardly going to keep up with this baby.'

He drew close and his face appeared out of the shadows. The fine, almost ethereal beauty of his features still made me catch my breath. And then he kissed me.

'So,' said Ricky, pulling away from my clutches. 'Let's see what you've been spending your hard-earned money on, eh.'

He strode into the hall, where the lights didn't work, and squinted in the candlelight.

'Mmm-hmm.' He wandered into the living room, the dining room, down the stairs to the basement, up the stairs to the bedroom with no floor, into the squalid bathroom and then down again and out into the garden before he passed judgement.

'I kind of like it,' he said, standing in the jungle, facing the house, head on one side. 'I don't know why, but it's got a cool vibe. Kinda freaky.'

I thought my chest would explode with pride. Ricky approved of my choice of house. He saw the potential only I could see. Perhaps he'd like to live in it with me.

'I gotta get the boys round here,' he continued enthusiastically. 'We're looking for a real creepy dive to shoot our new video in. This is perfect.'

That was somewhat insulting, but I forgave him because he was an artist, and artists see things differently from us mere mortals.

'It'll be really modern and comfortable when it's finished,' I said. 'And I've found a builder.'

'Mmm-hmm.' Ricky had wandered back into the house and was studiously examining every nook and cranny. He obviously wasn't listening to me, but I followed him and babbled on excitedly.

'A bloke called Adam. He's a friend of my granny's of all people. Well, his dad is, I think. Gran shouldn't really have friends under thirty at her age. Mind you, she's pretty funky, my gran. I phoned her earlier to tell her about this place and it turns out my timing's perfect. This Adam moved down here from Aberdeen in January and has set up his own business. Apparently all the guys he's employed are Scottish, too, so he's called his company the Tartan Army, which I think is quite funny really. He's got a tartan van and everything. He's meant to be very good. Been working for his dad in the building trade since he was a kid. I met him briefly the last time I was up in Scotland. He seemed like a nice enough bloke. And the best thing is, he can start on Monday.'

'What?' Ricky spun round and looked at me as if I was mad. I jumped.

'I said Adam, the builder, can start on Monday.'

'But what about our video?' Ricky looked confused. 'I just told you, this place is perfect for it. And we can't possibly get a video shoot organized by next week.'

'Ricky, I thought you were joking about the video. You can't expect me to put off having the work done on my home because Sugar Reef want to use it as a video location.'

By the look on his face I could tell that was exactly what Ricky expected me to do. Deep down, I knew he was being completely unreasonable, but I was desperate to please him, so I offered a compromise.

'OK, Ricky, why don't you decide which rooms you want to use and I'll make sure Adam's lot start work somewhere else, where they won't get in your way. OK?'

Ricky wore a pout a spoilt five-year-old girl would be proud of. 'Suppose so,' he said, moodily. 'But I'll definitely need the bathroom. And the kitchen. So they can't go anywhere near those places.'

'All right, all right!' Anything to put a smile back on that lovely face. 'So where's this party, then?'

And so it was decided. I was to have no sanitation and no cooking facilities until Sugar Reef had finished playing in my 'real creepy dive' of a house.

I soon learned that everything has a price and some things cost more than is stated on the tag. Pretty quickly, my house lost me a lot more than £600,000. Becky's bedroom door was open a fraction and I could make her out, or at least a creature I assumed to be Becky, sitting on the bed, curled up in a ball with her head shoved firmly between her knees and her fingers thrust deep into her dreadlocks. She was wearing purple pyjamas. There was a faint but distressing moan coming from somewhere deep under the hair and her shoulders shook gently. On the bed beside her was the letter I'd left in the kitchen the night before, explaining about the new house, and also the cheque I'd written her for £10,000. It was very, very early on a Monday morning and I hadn't expected to see her before I left to let Adam and his builders in. It was a cruel way to say goodbye, but I'd excused my cowardly behaviour by convincing myself that this was best for the both of us. We'd grown apart. End of story. If I just left quietly then there was no need for a scene. I'd packed my clothes, toiletries and make-up into two suitcases and booked a room in a small but exclusive hotel on Regent's Park. It was handy for the house and would be my home until the Primrose Hill pad was more habitable. I couldn't bear to live in the Kentish Town hole any longer.

Becky hadn't seen me and I knew I could just tiptoe past her bedroom and out of her life. I was tempted, but somewhere deep inside me was the old Laura whose heart broke at the sight of her best friend in such pain.

'Becks,' I said quietly, pushing open her bedroom door. 'Becks.'

She didn't look up, just mumbled, 'Piss off, Laura. Leave me alone.'

'Becks, I didn't mean to upset you.'

Becky lifted her head and glared at me with wild, tear-stained eyes.

'Upset me? You treat me like some fucking ...' She looked around wildly, trying to find the right word.

'Tramp! That's what I feel like, a tramp. If you throw some money at me then I'll just go away. Is that what you thought? Laura, I thought you were my best friend.'

The tears were pouring down her pretty face, taking last night's mascara with them.

'Why didn't you tell me you were moving out? I would

have understood. It's only natural you'd want to live somewhere better than this now you can afford it. Christ, I'm happy for you that you can. But why did you just want to sneak off without saying goodbye? I don't understand why we can't live different lives and still be friends. I could have found a new flatmate, we could have still seen each other. Couldn't we? But what I really don't get is this. Why did you leave me this?'

She waved the cheque at me.

'Are you trying to buy my silence? If I take this, do I just pretend I never knew you and keep schtum? This is your way of paying me off, isn't it?'

I could feel my own tears well up and my face burned with the shame of what I'd done.

'Becky, I'm sorry. I didn't mean it that way, I promise. I didn't tell you I was moving out because I thought you might just think you could come with me and live in my new house.' I was aware that I sounded like a prize twat, and a conceited one at that.

Becky snorted. 'Laura, I do live in the real world. Unlike some people.' She looked me up and down with disdain. 'I would never have expected to live in some designer show home with you. I mean, I know I owe you some rent, but I'm not a complete charity case. I do have some pride, and I can manage my life without your help.'

'I know, I just thought the money would help straighten you out a bit, financially. Get you back on your feet,' I said lamely. 'I can afford it.'

Becky lifted up the cheque and slowly ripped it, again and again and again, until it fell to the carpet like confetti.

'Now fuck off out of my flat,' she said. Her tears had dried up and she just looked angry now.

My tears were coming thick and fast as I begged, 'Becky,

please, I'm sorry. I fucked up, but I didn't mean to. I thought I was helping.'

I put my hand on her arm, but she threw it off as if I had leprosy.

'I hope you'll be very happy in your new home,' spat Becky. 'With your new friends and your new boyfriend and your lovely, new, shiny bright life. I hope you'll be so happy you choke on it.'

'Look, Becks, this is just a stupid misunderstanding. We can talk about it; sort it out.'

'No, Laura, I understand perfectly,' she said coldly. 'You don't want me in your life any more. I don't fit in. I don't look right. I'm not rich enough. It's been obvious since the minute you got that stupid TV job. You've just turned your back on everyone who isn't part of all that. Do you know how many times Fiona's called over the weekend?'

I shook my head sadly.

'Six times, Laura,' said Becky. 'Six times! She's your little sister for fuck's sake. I don't know what's happened to you. You were a really good person. You were the best mate I ever had.'

Her face crumpled and she started to cry again.

'Look, just go, Laura. Leave your new address so I can forward your mail and you can send someone over to pick up the rest of your stuff. I don't ever want to see you again.'

She pushed me out of her bedroom and shut the door in my face. I could hear her sobbing as I dragged my suitcases to the front door where a baffled Somalian cab driver was waiting to take my bags to his car. I cried all the way to Primrose Hill, but had the foresight to do so quietly behind large sunglasses, lest anyone should spot Laura McNaughton, TV personality, breaking her heart in the back of a clapped-out minicab.

For once I was grateful that the minicab driver spoke no English: I was hardly in the mood for a chat. And even when he went round the Camden one-way system three times looking for the way to Regent's Park, I couldn't have cared less. We stopped off at the hotel, where I checked in and dumped my suitcases. The room was large and opulent, with fine views of the park, but it still had that impersonal hotel feel, and I wondered what the hell I'd done, leaving the company of an old friend for the solitude of grandeur.

By the time we reached the Primrose Hill house I was forty minutes late. When I tried to pay the driver he shook his head and said, 'No, no. Your name, please,' and waved an unused receipt at me. For the price of a shaky autograph, I got my ride for free. It seemed grossly unfair, but the richer I got, the less I had to spend. Everything seemed to be free.

A large, ludicrously decorated transit van sat outside my house, and I guessed the Tartan Army had arrived. The door opened and something from a 1980s Athena poster got out. He was wearing torn stained jeans, gigantic brown leather boots and a slightly too tight white T-shirt. His boxer shorts poked out of a rip in his jeans, just below his right buttock. The words 'nice' and 'arse' sprang involuntarily into my head. I'd forgotten just how healthily handsome Adam Knox was. I'd become so accustomed to my new friends' fragile beauty – skinny, huge-eyed, cheekbones you could cut yourself on – that his robust, muscular physique shocked me. He was so big. Just the sort of chap to save a damsel in distress, or at least a TV star who'd just spent over half a million pounds on a ruin. Then I remembered the London airhead jibe and made a mental note not to be *too* nice to him.

'Hi, Laura.' He smiled broadly as he jumped out of his silly van, flashing perfectly straight white teeth.

I'd become a bit of a tooth expert lately, having recently

had veneers fitted to my own gnashers, plus a course of bleaching, naturally. Lucy, Billy Joe and Ricky had all had the same done years ago, and now we all had the identikit celebrity smiles that the rest of our ilk sported. But I noticed, with a stab of jealousy, that Adam's were the best I'd ever seen. And natural at that. I mean, they had to be. He was just a builder from Aberdeen, after all.

'Adam,' I said in the formal manner of employer to employee. 'Thank you so much for agreeing to do this at such short notice.'

'No worries,' he said cheerfully. 'You're a friend of the family, so you get priority.'

'Yes,' I said curtly. I was determined not to dwell on the family connection and to keep things as professional as possible. I'd heard how unreliable builders could be and I didn't want him thinking he could take the piss just because my granny baked scones for his dad.

'Anyway,' I continued. 'It's probably best if you come in and have a look round. As I said on the phone, the place is a real mess. It needs new floorboards and plumbing and heating and, well, it probably needs to be demolished and then you can start again.

I smiled half-heartedly at my lame joke.

'I'm sure it's not that bad,' he reassured me.

'I've got £200,000 to spend, including your wages. Will that be enough?' I'd persuaded the bank to lend me an extra £100,000, having seen how much work my house needed.

Adam shook with laughter. It started with a bouncing in his knees and then ricocheted up his body until he was practically having convulsions on my front door step. I noticed that a couple of clowns had clambered out of the van and were standing beside us, expectant looks on their faces, keen to be let in on the joke.

'She's got ... she's got two ... she's got two hundred grand,' spluttered Adam, 'and she's wondering if it'll be enough.'

The clowns collapsed into fits of hysteria. One was forty-ish, short, fat, balding and had a face the colour of beetroot; the other was also short, but skinny, blueish-white in pallor and red-haired. He looked about twelve. I stared, uncomprehendingly, from Adam to clown number one and clown number two.

'What?' I demanded. I wasn't in the mood for jokes.

'Laura, sorry,' said Adam, desperately trying to pull himself together. 'It's just we usually have a budget of about five grand in Aberdeen. I should think that £200,000 will probably be enough.'

'Good. Let's get started then.'

I ushered them all inside. It turned out that the fat clown was called Stevie and hailed from Livingstone, and the thin one was Goggsie and, to my horror, it turned out his parents lived in a bungalow two doors down from mine.

'I was at the same school as you,' he said warmly, as if this somehow made us kindred spirits. 'You were in the sixth form when I was in the first year. You were a prefect. You probably don't remember me, but me and my mates used to fancy you.'

'No, I don't remember,' I said, unnerved by the invasion of my totally unglamorous past into my glitzy present.

I was keen to let the subject drop, but Goggsie continued, oblivious. 'You had brown hair then and you had a bit more meat on you.'

'She had brown hair and a bit more meat on her a few months ago when I saw her at her gran's,' muttered Adam under his breath as he disappeared up the stairs.

Warren had arranged for his lawyers to prepare a legal document for Adam and his sidekicks to sign to safeguard my privacy and to ensure they kept their big gobs shut when they went for a few pints after work. They were forbidden to discuss our financial agreement, the location of the property or indeed anything they so much as saw, heard or smelled while working in my house with anybody.

'Not even my wife?' asked Stevie. 'She's really excited that I'm working for you.'

'Not even your wife,' I replied sternly as Wazza had instructed.

The sun was breaking through the clouds as I sat on the steps in my overgrown garden. I could feel the gentle heat of spring on my cheeks and it soothed my otherwise troubled mind. Adam and his lads were thinking about logistics, assessing the damage and deciding where to start work on the messed-up house. I was thinking about Becky, assessing the damage and deciding where to start work on my messed-up friendship. I phoned the flat: answer machine. I phoned her mobile: voicemail. I phoned the flat again and left a grovelling message. Then I phoned her mobile and left another grovelling message. I sent her a text message apologizing, phoned a florist and arranged for an obscenely large bunch of lilies to be delivered to her door with a card that just said sorry. Then I waited for her to call. She didn't.

I phoned Fiona instead, determined not to alienate all my nearest and dearest in one fell swoop.

'Laura? Laura who? I don't think I know any Lauras,' said my sister. Sarcasm wasn't usually her thing, so I knew she was pissed off.

'Sorry I haven't been in touch for a while. I've been manic,' I apologized.

'I know,' she replied. 'I've been reading all about it in the papers. You've had your hands too full of a virile young rock star to pick up a phone.'

Fiona explained that I'd also managed to upset Mum by not calling and that Dad had become mute since reading about my exploits.

'It's you he's annoyed with, but we're the ones who are suffering. I think you should come home and try to build some bridges,' she suggested. 'You could always bring Ricky.'

The idea of Ricky Jones sitting in the salmon-pink suburban sitting room of my parents' bungalow, surrounded by chintz and porcelain ornaments, seemed utterly ridiculous.

'I don't think that would be such a good idea,' I said with certainty.

'Well, you know best,' said Fiona. 'But you'd better do something soon or there won't be a home to come back to.'

'Maybe you could smooth the way for me. Have a word with Mum and Dad. Tell them that all that stuff in the news is just rubbish. They'll listen to you,' I suggested.

'Piss off,' said Fi, flatly. 'I do have my own life to get on with, you know. I don't have time to sort out your mess any more. God, sometimes it's as if you think I only exist for your convenience. You left, Laura; life moved on. I grew up. I'm not the pliable little kid I used to be. No more Mrs Nice Guy, OK?'

'All right, all right. I get your point.' I was shocked. 'I'm sorry.'

'Good,' said my not-so-little sister.

There was no emotion in her usually kind voice and I realized that she was very, very annoyed with me. I tried for the sympathy vote.

'Becky and I have fallen out completely,' I explained. 'She totally hates me.'

'Why? What did you do?'

I told Fiona about what had happened that morning and

waited for her soft words of comfort and wisdom. They were not forthcoming.

'You idiot,' she scoffed. 'I don't blame her. God, Laura, you'd better sort yourself out soon or you're not going to have any friends left.'

'But ...' This was not the Fiona I knew and loved. The one who thought the sun shone out of my increasingly bony arse. This was cold, hard, scary Fiona.

'But nothing. Imagine if it was the other way round. How would you feel? Think about it.'

'But ...' Had aliens abducted my sister and replaced her with a cold-hearted clone?

'Listen, I've got to go,' said the new Fiona. 'My shift starts in fifteen minutes.'

'Fi, don't be pissed off with me,' I whined.

I heard her sigh deeply. 'Laura, I love you, you know I do, I just don't think you're handling things very well at the moment. You seem so self-obsessed. Keep things in perspective and don't let all this go to your head.'

My little sister had grown up and now she was giving me lectures. I started to cry. Again.

'Remember,' continued the cloned Fiona, ignoring my sobs, 'you'll always just be Laura to us, so there's no use acting the diva. I really have to go now, I can't keep sick kids waiting, just because you're having a bad day. Think about what I said. You really should come home soon. Bye.'

I sat on the steps, watching a couple of baby starlings fight over a piece of bread and feeling sorry for myself. I wasn't trying to upset people, I was just getting on with my life. Why was everyone so angry with me? Eventually my thoughts were interrupted by Goggsie, whose muddy boots suddenly appeared on the step above me. He smiled shyly but wouldn't look me in the eye. I could tell he was intimidated by me and I felt mean for not being more friendly earlier. I smiled back as warmly as I could.

'Um, Laura. Can I call you Laura?' He blushed.

''Course you can.'

'We were just going to have a tea break and I wondered if you'd like a cup of tea from my flask, because I noticed you don't have a kettle yet.' He looked very earnest as he held up a Thermos and plastic cup.

It was only a simple gesture of kindness but it touched me.

'Thanks, Goggsie,' I said. 'That would be lovely.' And I meant it.

I followed Goggsie into the house and discovered the builders had already cleared out all the newspapers and swept the ground floor. Adam and Stevie were sitting on a clean dust sheet on the living-room floor, dunking KitKats into plastic cups of tea and poring over building-merchandise catalogues. They budged up to make room for me and Goggsie to join their powwow.

'What do you think of this one?' asked Adam, handing me a brochure for a very upmarket kitchen company. 'This is the best make: German, very functional, sleek lines, lots of stainless steel. It's expensive, but with your budget that shouldn't be a problem.'

'Gorgeous,' I enthused, drooling over the tastefully shot photographs of kitchens to die for.

'And with the bathroom – and this is just an idea – it might be nice to have that old bath restored rather than fit a new one. I mean, it's a mess at the moment, but genuine Victorian gear like that is pretty rare, and we could have it re-enamelled so it looks as good as new. You can get those cheap reproduction numbers, but they're nowhere near as classy. Obviously you'd need a new toilet and wash-hand basin, and you'll have to choose some tiles. Oh, and one of those huge chrome showers would look good, but the bath would make an interesting feature.'

'Lovely,' I agreed. I'd been thinking about getting an interior designer in to deal with the decor but Adam's taste seemed remarkably, well, tasteful.

'Where are you going to start?' I asked, eyeing a KitKat hungrily, but declining Stevie's offer when he tried to hand me one.

'The first thing to do is just clear out all this junk so we can see what we're doing. There's a skip being delivered this afternoon.' Adam paused to munch another biscuit.

'The floor upstairs needs to be fixed pretty urgently for safety reasons and it would be sensible to have the electrics, plumbing and heating done before we start any aesthetic work, but, basically, it's up to you which rooms you think you'll need done first. This room and the dining room don't need much doing to them structurally at all – the plaster's good and the original features are intact.' He pointed at the cornicing, ceiling rose and grand fireplace.

'And once these floorboards are stripped and polished they'll be very smart.' He gazed around the room, obviously relishing the thought of the transformation ahead.

'All in all, we should be finished by October.' Stevie and Goggsie nodded in agreement.

October! It was only the beginning of April. The enormity of the job hit me suddenly and I wondered whether I'd made a terrible mistake.

'When will I be able to move in?' I wondered, nervously, calculating my hotel bill and kicking myself again for the fallout with Becky.

'Depends what you're prepared to live with, hen,' said Stevie. 'Once you've got heating, lighting and water, then you can be comfortable enough, surely.'

'I'd wait for the kitchen, bathroom and one other room to be finished,' concluded Adam. 'We could make the bedroom a priority if you want us to.'

I nodded.

'If you choose your kitchen and bathroom today, we can get it ordered and it should arrive next week. Goggsie's a qualified sparky, so he's going to start on the electrics immediately, and me and Stevie are both Corgi registered.'

I looked at the men blankly.

'We can do your central heating, hen,' explained Stevie slowly, as if talking to a child.

'Then a mate of mine, Stu, who's a plumber, is going to deal with that side of things when we need him.' Adam devoured his fifth chocolate biscuit and my stomach rumbled.

'So?' I still didn't have an answer. 'When can I move in?'

'I'll aim to have the place reasonably habitable by June.' Adam swigged back the last of his tea and stood up. I gulped. The tea break was over.

'Have a look at these.' He threw me the pile of brochures. 'Pick a kitchen and a bathroom, but remember, we're keeping the old bath, and you'll need to decide on lighting and radiators, too. Just give us a shout if there's anything you don't understand.'

I nodded obediently. The man was indeed a masterful builder. His broad shoulders were just disappearing out of the room when he paused in the doorway and looked back at me with a mischievous twinkle in his bright blue eyes. 'I meant to tell you about a funny thing that happened.'

'Oh yes?' I was intrigued.

'Well, the first thing I saw this morning was you in your underwear,' he grinned. 'I opened my bedroom curtains and there you were, staring right at me from the billboard across the road, twelve feet tall and practically naked. I pointed it out to my girlfriend and told her I was starting work for you today, but I don't think she was too impressed. I reckon she thinks you must dress like that all the time and that you're going to seduce me or something.'

Adam chuckled to himself as if the thought of being seduced by me was totally ridiculous.

'Well, tell her she doesn't have to worry.' I could feel my cheeks burning with embarrassment. 'I'll make sure I'm fully clothed at all times.'

'That's a shame, hen,' laughed Stevie. 'Work might be more fun if we made this place a nudist colony.'

'Not for Laura, it wouldn't,' said Adam. 'You in your birthday suit? Now that would be a scary sight.'

'Aye, but our tool belts would cover our privates,' piped up Goggsie, warming to the idea.

'And believe me, my belt's fully loaded,' boasted Stevie, swinging his hammer.

'You'd have to be careful with your power tools, though,' I added. 'I was thinking of white for the walls and bloodstains would ruin the effect.'

I spent the day chain-smoking and lazily selecting items for my new house. It was the ultimate in retail therapy. I chose a white, high gloss kitchen with Corian work surfaces and polished limestone floor tiles. For the bathroom I decided on a simple white suite with white mosaic tiles on the floor and walls, the re-enamelled bath and a massive chrome power shower with a head the size of a dinner plate. Upstairs, I could hear Stevie and Goggsie singing along to their radio. They were surprisingly good, particularly at Elvis, so I clapped and whooped my approval. I felt comfortable in the builders' presence; they were so bloody familiar – their accents, humour and mannerisms – just like the boys I grew up with. It hit me that it had been a long time since I'd felt relaxed in the company of people just like me, and I realized with a pang of guilt that Becky would have loved them. I'd become drawn into Lucy's way of thinking: us and them. She was right, of course, there was a gulf the size of Glencoe between the haves and have-nots of this world, but given half a chance I was still one of them. As Trudy once said, 'You can take the girl out of Scotland ...'

I showed Adam my choices and he seemed to approve.

'That kitchen can be delivered by the end of the week,' he said. 'So if we get cracking down there ...'

'Ah.' I stopped him. 'Slight problem. My boyfriend's band want to shoot a video here and they need the kitchen to look' – I winced as I said it – 'like a real creepy dive.'

Adam stared at me in disbelief, as if I'd just suggested a dinner date with Osama Bin Laden, and then he shrugged. 'You're the boss.' But I could tell he thought I was a total airhead. So much for that professional demeanour I'd intended to cultivate with my employees.

'Hold off on the kitchen, lads,' he shouted to Goggsie and Stevie. 'Some rock stars need to shoot their video in there before we mortals can begin our work.'

As if by magic, the radio started to blast out 'Heaven Sent', Sugar Reef's latest No. 1 anthem. Stevie's portly frame suddenly appeared in the living room. He'd tied a rag round his forehead like a bandanna and was wiggling his hips, pouting his lips and holding an upside-down screwdriver as a microphone.

'My new girl is an expensive habit,
But when I see that body I've just gotta grab it,
And so all my money is spent,
I can't help it, she's heaven sent ...'

He sang along and danced in faux Ricky Jones style.

'Oi, that's my boyfriend you're taking the piss out of,' I shouted, not knowing whether to be amused or offended.

'I know,' laughed Stevie, gyrating across the floor. 'I've been practising this just for you.'

With that, the chubby little middle-aged builder fell to his knees and played air guitar to the instrumental.

'Ricky doesn't play guitar,' I scolded him. 'That's Lewis playing.'

Stevie ignored me and continued his guitar solo with his eyes closed.

'He really does love Sugar Reef,' said Goggsie, earnestly. 'He's not meaning to be rude.'

Adam scratched his head as he viewed the disturbing sight – Stevie's bare bum had escaped from his jeans entirely. There was nothing to do but laugh.

'Just don't do that when Ricky's here,' I warned as the song finished and Stevie got up, red-faced and puffing. 'He probably wouldn't find it very funny.'

The next day Lucy came round to view the premises.

I was in the garden, dreaming up designs, when Goggsie appeared at the patio doors, dancing from one foot to the other in a frenzy of excitement.

'Adam says to tell you that your friend Lucy Lloyd has just turned up outside in a white limousine,' he announced in obvious excitement.

His eyes were rolling around in their sockets and sweat was appearing on his forehead quicker than he could wipe it off with the back of his dirty hand.

'I really love Lucy Lloyd,' he gushed suddenly, as if unable to control himself. 'I've got posters of her on my wall in my digs and everything. She's a total honey.'

'She is,' I agreed. 'A total honey. Do you want to let her in? Tell her I'm through here.'

Goggsie ran back into the house without answering and reappeared a minute later with Lucy at his side. He was shaking as he looked at Lucy and pointed at me.

'Laura's there,' he said, stating the obvious, and then ran back into the house as fast as his skinny little legs would carry him. I could hear Adam's and Stevie's laughter reverberate through the empty house.

'Oh, bless,' said Lucy. 'I think he must be a fan. Any chance of a cuppa?'

Lucy was appalled when she realized I had no provisions in the house and found the thought of sharing a builder's flask unhygienic. Instead, she borrowed a pencil from a more-than-grateful-to-help Goggsie and wrote a list straight on the dining-room wall.

'Tea, coffee, milk, champagne, Marlboro Lights, what else are you short of?' She paused.

'Food?' suggested Adam from the corner, where he was doing something complicated with a tape measure.

Lucy wrinkled her nose and said, 'Nah, not hungry. You hungry, Laura?'

I shook my head, though my stomach rumbled in disagreement. Adam frowned and Lucy continued.

'One of those mini fridges to keep the bubbly cool, chairs to sit on, a kettle, whisky for Ricky – he's coming round later, isn't he? – and do you think this lot need some beers? Builders drink beer, right?' Lucy nodded her head towards Adam, as if he couldn't hear her.

'Adam, do you want some beers?' I asked.

'Not while we're working, thanks,' he replied. 'But a fresh cup of tea would be nice. I forgot my Thermos today and Goggsie's given all his provisions to you. Oh, and we all take sugar if that's allowed.' He flashed a cheeky grin at Lucy.

'Sugar? Do people still use that stuff?' she asked, horrified. 'It's terribly bad for you, you know.'

It crossed my mind that the white powder we preferred was a lot more harmful than sugar.

'I'll call Karen. She can sort all this out.' Lucy said 'PA' clearly into her voice-activated mobile phone.

'Karen, hi, it's me. I need some shopping done a.s.a.p. Write this down ...'

'It must be great, this celebrity lark.' Adam looked up. 'You don't even have to nip out to the corner shop for milk any more.'

He was smiling, but I was sure he thought Lucy's behaviour totally unnecessary.

'Well, Lucy's used to having things done for her,' I explained quickly. 'She can't really just walk the streets like a normal person. She'd get mobbed or cause a riot.'

'And what about you? Would you cause a riot if you popped to that newsagent's round the corner?' He was staring at me questioningly with intense blue eyes.

I shook my head in shame. 'Probably not.'

Adam's gaze shifted to Lucy, who was talking into her mobile impatiently. 'Make sure they're tasteful chairs, Karen. Try the Conran Shop. Leather would be good. If you call Ikea I'll sack you. And we need them today, OK?'

She turned towards me and gave me a 'you-just-can't-get-the-staff-these-days' look.

'So, that's something to drink, something to smoke and something to sit on,' she announced after hanging up. 'I've said white for the chairs because you can't go wrong with the clean, minimal look; they'll be my house-warming present to you. Now, Laura, give me the grand tour.'

The sun was shining, so Lucy was wearing white

everything – jeans, sandals, camisole and even shades. She stepped gingerly around the house and squealed every time a floorboard squeaked or a spider's web dangled in front of her face. In the bathroom she came face to builder's bum with Stevie, who was just in the middle of removing the old toilet.

'Awright, hen?' He grinned hello with a muck-smeared face.

'Hi,' said Lucy nervously, backtracking frantically onto the landing.

'So, what do you think?' I asked.

'It's, um, it's ...' I could tell Lucy was struggling to find the words. It was obvious she was horrified.

'It has potential,' she eventually announced uncertainly. 'I can see what Ricky meant about it being perfect for the video.'

'Shall we go and sit in the garden?' I suggested. 'I love it out there. I was just thinking of what I could do ... I mean, have done. I've been looking at some gardening magazines and I was thinking about railway sleepers for decking, and I'd really love a huge weeping willow tree and ...'

I realized that Lucy's eyes had glazed over. Gardening obviously wasn't her thing.

Half an hour later a delivery man arrived with the groceries we'd asked for, an hour after that a van arrived bearing the electrical items we'd ordered, and by early afternoon two beautiful white leather armchairs had arrived from the Conran Shop. Patience was not one of Lucy's virtues, but that wasn't a problem in her line of work. International megastars do tend to get exactly what they want, when they want it. And so Lucy and I lounged on the new chairs – I insisted on keeping them cellophane wrapped until the living room was decorated – with a chilled glass of champagne each while Goggsie made tea for the boys in the hole that was to become the kitchen.

'I approve of your choice of workmen,' said Lucy with a wicked grin.

'What? Goggsie?' I asked.

'No,' scoffed Lucy, 'the boss. The tall, dark, handsome one. He's absolutely toe-curlingly gorgeous.'

I looked over my shoulder and watched Adam working in the dining room behind me.

'Yeah, he's not bad, if you like that beefcake kind of thing,' I replied.

'I've always fancied a bit of rough,' continued Lucy, licking her collagen-injected lips. 'Might have a crack at him one day.'

I watched Lucy's face to see if she was pulling my leg, but she looked serious enough.

'What about Billy Joe?' I asked.

'What Billy Joe doesn't know ...' Lucy giggled. 'And anyway, he's away for months. Am I supposed to stay celibate for weeks on end?'

'Uh, yeah,' I nodded. 'If you love him. That's generally the way relationships work.'

Lucy looked at me and smiled patronizingly. 'Ah, you're young, but you'll learn.' She patted my head.

'I'm two years older than you,' I reminded her sternly.

'Yes, but you've only been in the fame game for five minutes,' she said. 'And we play by special rules.'

'What if he doesn't fancy you?' I teased, knowing that was a ridiculous suggestion. Everyone fancied Lucy Lloyd.

'I enjoy a challenge,' she said.

'He's got a girlfriend,' I added.

'Since when did girlfriends stop men from dropping their trousers?' asked Lucy.

Adam was a decent bloke and I was uncomfortable with the idea of Lucy treating him as some sort of project, but I never argued with Lucy. We were friends, but she was the boss. I could hear 'Heaven Sent' playing on the radio again.

'Come and see this, Luce,' I said, dragging her into the hall to watch Stevie's performance.

'That is just the funniest thing I've ever seen,' she giggled, spilling her champagne on the floor while she watched Stevie doing his Ricky impression with glee.

We were so engrossed in the comedy act that we didn't see Ricky's face appear at the bay window, which was a shame, really, because Adam, who did spot him, told me later that it was a picture.

'What the fuck is going on here?' Ricky asked angrily when I eventually spotted him and let him in.

Stevie stood glued to the floor, screwdriver in hand, rag around his head.

'Ricky, mate,' he said falteringly. 'I'm your number-one fan.'

'You're a fat, fucking arsehole,' spat Ricky as he shoved past Stevie. 'And you're certainly not my mate.'

He turned to me. 'What the hell are you playing at, letting them behave like that?' he asked in disbelief.

The party atmosphere was well and truly crushed.

'We were just having a laugh,' I said weakly.

'They're not paid to enjoy themselves.' He waved his hand in the direction of the builders.

I caught Adam's eye. He looked as if he had a nasty taste in his mouth.

'Get back to work,' ordered Ricky, 'or you're all fired.'

Out of the corner of my eye I spotted Stevie doing a little wiggle of his hips as he went up the stairs. I swallowed a snigger.

'Honestly, Laura, where did you find these cowboys?' Ricky tut-tutted as he helped himself to my champagne and wandered through to the living room. 'You really have to treat them like workmen; they won't respect you if you try to befriend them. These people only work well in an atmosphere of fear. I'll sort them out for you. Which one's the boss?'

'The good-looking one,' said Lucy, smiling sweetly, perfectly aware that such a comment would wind Ricky right up. 'He's called Adam.'

As far as Ricky was concerned he was the only good-looking man on the planet, and the idea of any sort of competition, albeit from a lowly builder, was too much for him to bear. He turned round and glared in the direction of the hall, where Adam was carrying a pile of floorboards with his top off, revealing a torso covered in rippling muscles.

'Behold, the good-looking one,' announced Lucy.

Ricky strode through to the hall and stood in front of Adam, preventing him from taking the floorboards upstairs. They were exactly the same height and brown eyes met blue. Adam stood firm, holding his load on his shoulder as they stared each other out like a couple of cowboys in a spaghetti western.

'This is like porn for girls,' whispered Lucy to me. 'They'll be wrestling naked on the floor any minute.'

'So you're in charge of that monkey, are you?' asked Ricky in a voice used to talking down to staff.

'I employ Stevie, if that's what you mean,' replied Adam without a trace of fear or respect.

'And are you going to let him get away with that sort of behaviour?' demanded Ricky.

'Sorry, mate,' said Adam. 'But I don't see that any of this is your business. We work for Laura, not you.'

Oh shit, I thought, don't drag me into it.

Both men turned and stared at me expectantly. The atmosphere was so charged with testosterone that I could practically smell the pheromones, and I had to say something quickly to diffuse the situation before a bare-fist boxing match occurred in my hallway – my money would have been on Adam, incidentally, seeing as he was a good few inches broader than Ricky and also armed with six solid timber floorboards as ammunition.

'Look, Ricky, I'll sort it out later. I'll have a word with Stevie and ask him not to do it again, OK? Just let Adam get on with his work and we'll go outside and have a drink.' I tugged on his sleeve, but he wouldn't budge.

'I'm not moving until I get an apology,' Ricky demanded.

I half expected him to add, 'Don't you know who I am?' but to his credit he managed to bite his tongue.

'Sorry, mate,' shouted Stevie from upstairs. He and Goggsie were obviously waiting on the landing, listening to every word.

'Happy?' asked Adam flatly.

'Delirious,' replied Ricky, sarcastically.

'Excuse me, but these are heavy and I need to get them upstairs.' Adam waited for Ricky to get out of his way, but Ricky stood firm.

'Ricky, stop being a prick and let the man past,' said Lucy suddenly, bored of the conflict.

She headed back towards the garden with a flick of her golden mane. After flashing Adam one last filthy look, Ricky trotted after her like an obedient puppy. It annoyed me that he always did as she said. Adam smiled at me sympathetically as he carried his load up the stairs. He didn't say a word; he didn't have to, I already felt about two inches tall.

In the garden, Lucy was showing Ricky a little contraption that the Snowman had given her, which neatly supplied a single line of cocaine without the need to faff about with credit cards and bank notes. They both took a hit and then handed it to me. I accepted, grateful for a chemical pick-me-up.

'Let's get out of here,' announced Ricky. 'There's a bit of a get-together going on at my hotel. There's a car waiting outside.'

To my horror, on the doorstep we found several members of the press.

'Laura, is this your new house?' asked a stupid young tabloid reporter.

'How much did you pay for it?' demanded a financial journalist.

'Are you keen on DIY?' asked the girl from an interiors magazine.

Lucy switched on her winning smile. Ricky growled, snarled and frowned as was expected. I stared at my feet and pretended they weren't there.

We pushed our way past and jumped into the waiting black Mercedes with tinted windows.

'How the fuck did they find you so quickly?' demanded Ricky as we threw ourselves into the back.

'I don't know,' I said, baffled. 'The builders have signed a secrecy clause, and other than them, only you and Lucy and Nat—'

'Nat?' Lucy interrupted. 'Would she tell them?'

'No way!' I was certain I could trust Natalie after the little chat we'd had on the day I bought the house.

'Who else, then?' asked Lucy.

It dawned on me slowly.

'Becky, maybe,' I said sadly. 'I left her the address so she could forward my mail.'

'And then you had a huge argument, didn't you?' Lucy nodded, knowingly.

'I think we've found the culprit,' said Ricky.

'I did warn you, Laura,' added Lucy. 'You can't trust anyone any more. Especially not old friends: they always sell you out in the end.'

I stared miserably out of the window. Would Becky really do that to me? Was she so keen to have revenge? But who else could it be? I could find no other explanation.

Back at Ricky's hotel a party was in full swing as usual. The boys from the band were pissed and high and acting like idiots, while their ever-changing gaggle of pubescent groupies looked on gratefully. I downed a couple of Bloody Marys, had some more coke and waited for the familiar buzz to lift my spirits. Ricky and Lewis were having an animated debate about who was the best guitar player ever, while Lucy and Monica were enthusiastically discussing the merits of Botox injections. I half-heartedly followed both conversations, but couldn't think of anything to add to either. Usually with cocaine I couldn't keep my mouth shut, but half an hour later I still felt flat.

'You're quiet tonight, babe,' said Ricky eventually. 'Everything OK?'

I explained that I was upset about falling out with Becky, that I was hurt she'd gone to the press, that my family were annoyed with me and that even my little sister was rapidly going off me.

'I think I want to go home,' I blurted out, 'to Edinburgh.'

'Cool,' shrugged Ricky. 'We'll go sometime. We can take the Harley.'

'Are you sure?' I was shocked that he'd want to come with me.

'No worries. A trip to Jockland. What harm can it do?' he shrugged.

PART THREE

Summer

11

Take the high road this summer

It was a long, hot, messy summer. By the end of July I'd visited places and met people beyond my wildest dreams. And yet my world had shrunk. Wherever I went – Cannes, LA, New York, even the VIP area at Glastonbury – I saw the same faces, heard the same conversations and enjoyed the same recreational activities as the week before in some other far-flung location. There was no routine to my life, as such, but there was an eerie Groundhog Day quality to my existence. Everything I did felt like something I'd done before. There were times when I didn't know what continent I was on, for God's sake, but every hotel suite looked the same. Days and nights blended seamlessly together, weekends and weekdays merged into one heady good time, and every morning the sun rose on another hot, sticky day. I rose with a stinking hangover and got up on a comedown.

My television career had taken off big time. Everybody kept telling me that I was good, really good. I was hugely flattered, but secretly I felt I was cheating them all. It didn't feel like hard work. So why was I being paid so much? And why did people keep telling me I was talented? My job didn't seem to require any particular skills. In June, Jazz announced that Scorpion TV were offering me my own show for the duration of the summer. It involved going to all the festivals to interview the bands, visiting Ibiza and Ayia Napa to chat to the DJs and flying off to LA and New York to catch up with the celebrity news on the other side of the Atlantic. I was delighted, of course.

It wasn't a regular nine-to-five job, that was for sure, and I never knew whether I was seeing the sunrise because I was still partying from the night before or because I had to be up at 5 a.m. to film an early morning appearance for my new series, which was simply called *Laura Live!* I have to admit that sometimes the party was too good to miss, so I'd go straight from night to morning without any sleep in between and face the nation on a drunken, drug-fuelled high. I found that strong coffee and a line or two of cocaine were enough to render me capable of facing a camera. No one appeared to find my behaviour unprofessional – as long as I was perky, smiling and perfectly groomed, Jasmine would be happy and gush, 'Fantastic, Laura,' at the end of every show. Despite zero sleep, the make-up artist simply painted out the bags from under my eyes and blended in enough bronzer to give me a pseudo-natural glow, and *voilà*, I was a natural-born beauty. The butterflies that had plagued my early TV appearances had long since fluttered off to bother some lesser star's stomach and I could easily flirt and giggle my way through an hour-long show. The camera didn't bother me a jot – for some reason I always looked more attractive on celluloid than in reality – even my addled brain could manage to read an autocue, and as the celebrities I interviewed were usually my friends, there was never any need to be nervous. Needless to say my guests included Lucy, Ricky and Billy Joe. Often we'd turn up at the studio together, interviewer and interviewee, in the same limo, fresh, or not so fresh, from the same party. Poor Jack, who went to bed early with a textbook about the workings of the media and drank nothing but five litres of mineral water a day, wasn't offered his own show. Instead, he had occasional slots on mine as a roving reporter covering the less glamorous events and less famous celebs. He must have hated me, but he never showed it. He was always there with a megawatt smile and no need for an autocue, having studiously memorized his lines.

When I reached the point where I needed sleep desperately but was too jittery and full of drugs to rest, the Snowman provided me with another magic formula. He just called them jellies. I think I might have been taking Temazepam, but I didn't care enough to ask. The pills worked, letting me snatch a few hours' sleep, just enough to recharge my batteries for the next party, and that's all that mattered to me.

Warren kept sending me cheques for silly amounts of money: my wages, fees from TV chat shows, newspaper interviews, voice-overs for breakfast-cereal ads, modelling jobs, special appearances, Superbra advertising campaigns, hell, I got paid for falling out of bed. Sometimes the crumpled cheques would languish at the bottom of a designer handbag for weeks before I'd find them again and hand them over to Cathy – I'd poached her from Trudy and made her my very own super-efficient PA. Cathy did her best to make sure every penny found its way into my heaving bank account eventually – she had to resort to rummaging around in pockets and bags, so Christ knows what else she found – but I'm sure the odd cheque for a thousand or two was lost along the way, probably discarded in a rolled-up state after being shoved up my nose. It didn't matter, I wasn't short of cash. Between them, Warren and Cathy were my surrogate parents. As I became increasingly irresponsible, they followed behind, clearing up the mess I left in my wake. I don't know which one did what, but the bills were always paid, my clothes were all dry-cleaned, the builders got their wages and I always had cash in my purse without ever visiting a bank. That meant I could concentrate on what I did best: having a good time.

I'd had no contact with my real parents since the story about the row with my dad had been splashed all over the tabloids and even my normally unshakeable gran was having trouble coming to terms with my behaviour. On the one occasion she'd managed to get through to me on the phone (I had a bad habit of ignoring the answer machine) she'd told me she was deeply disappointed.

'Laura,' she'd said. 'I've always stuck up for you in the past but you're so far off the rails now that I'm finding it increasingly difficult to come to your defence. I love you. You know that, but I don't think I like what you're becoming.'

They were harsh words from the woman I admired most and what she said hurt but I felt the criticism was unfair. Nothing that had happened was my fault, after all. I was the victim here. I was the one who'd been betrayed. It was amazing how twenty-four hours in May could change everything for ever.

I'd woken up early with a clear head and butterflies in my tummy. Having excused myself early from the party the night before, I'd managed to sleep well in Ricky's bed while the debauchery continued along the corridor. At some point, when it was already getting light, Ricky had come to bed and we'd made gentle, sleepy love, which now felt like a dream, then I'd floated easily back to sleep, happy because I knew I was going home.

I ordered strong coffee from room service, showered and dressed before shaking Ricky's sleeping body into life.

'What? What?' he moaned, trying to lift his head.

Ricky Jones looked almost unattractive. His cheek was criss-crossed with lines from the bedclothes, I noticed a small pool of dribble on the pillow where his mouth had been and his breath stank of stale booze. As the days and weeks passed, I was becoming less and less intimidated by Ricky and his rock-star status. I'd discovered that men are fairly straightforward creatures, full stop, however big their bank balance or their fan base.

'We're going to Edinburgh,' I said slowly, allowing time for the words to penetrate his befuddled head.

'Oh yeah.' Ricky sat up gingerly and winced at some unidentified pain.

'I've ordered some coffee,' I continued as I opened the curtains and let the bright spring sunshine flood in.

'Je-sus!' As the light filled the room, Ricky threw himself back under the bedclothes like the vampire he was. 'What are you on this morning? Perky pills?'

'No, I'm just excited about going home,' I explained.

After three black coffees and a long shower, Ricky was back to looking his glorious best. He rang reception and asked them to have his bike waiting for him downstairs. I felt like a proper rock chick as I pulled on Ricky's spare biker jacket.

'Ready?' I asked, chirpily, handing him his crash helmet.

'Almost,' he said, racking himself up a line of coke for the road.

I declined to join him. It was 9.30 a.m.

Ricky didn't usually rise until after midday, so we took the waiting paparazzi by surprise. They were too busy chatting amongst themselves and drinking Pret A Manger coffees to notice us appear through the revolving doors. A young valet had the bike's engine running and by the time the gentlemen of the press realized what was happening we'd left them choking on petrol fumes, dust and the pain of a missed photo opportunity. In my head, Ricky was Peter

Fonda in *Easy Rider*. He weaved expertly through the static London traffic at a terrifying pace and we hit the M1 flying. I thought I'd burst with the thrill of speeding at 110 m.p.h. on the roaring machine with my very own rock star between my thighs. We stopped briefly at a service station somewhere in the Midlands and giggled at a coachload of pensioners who were enjoying choc ices in the sunshine and nudging each other excitedly as they recognized the handsome young singer and his TV-presenter girlfriend. Ricky pointed out that you know you've arrived when the over sixties recognize you. I phoned home and was relieved when it was Mum who answered.

'Mum, it's me,' I said. 'I'm on my way home. I'm with Ricky. We'll be with you this afternoon.'

She was obviously thrown by the news, but her surprise quickly melted into delight.

'I can't wait to see you, darling,' she squealed. 'I'll make sure your dad and Fiona are here, too. How long are you staying?'

'We have to leave first thing tomorrow,' I explained. Sugar Reef's video shoot was beginning at my house the following afternoon.

And then we were back on the road. I held Ricky tight, leaned back and looked forward, watching the flat landscape of middle England give way to the bleak moors of the Pennines. When we passed a sign for Gretna Green, I knew I was almost home.

'God, it's beautiful,' I shouted as we took the coast road north and watched the North Sea become the Firth of Forth. Ricky couldn't hear me over the engine, but I wasn't really talking to him anyway. Across the water, Fife sparkled in the hazy May sunshine. And then, as we turned a corner on the top of a hill, Edinburgh, in all its glory, came into view.

I felt a rush of pride for its craggy geography and majestic architecture, as if I were somehow responsible for the surprising city-centre swell of Arthur's Seat or the breathtaking beauty of the castle, just by virtue of having been born there. I shouted, tapped and gesticulated directions to Ricky until we were deep in the bowels of the Southside suburbs, and eventually, after several wrong turns, we arrived in my parents' cul-de-sac of identical 1930s bungalows. Ricky took off his helmet and gazed around in astonishment.

'What?' I demanded. OK, so it wasn't Hurlingham Manor, but it wasn't exactly Hell's Kitchen either.

'It's so ...' he spotted the gnomes in Mrs Baxter's garden next door and chuckled, 'hideously suburban.'

I hit him on the arm. 'Oi, this is where I grew up, you snob. Not everyone has a stately home.'

'I know, I know.' He laughed. 'But I just can't imagine you coming from somewhere like this. And that's a compliment,' he added quickly, ducking to avoid my right hook.

I was grateful he'd never seen my Kentish Town flat. If he thought my mum and dad's neat little three-bedroomed bungalow was slumming it, what on earth would he have thought of that hovel?

'So, this whole estate is made up of identical houses, is it?' he asked.

'Yes, that's quite normal actually,' I replied patiently.

'And is it compulsory to drive a Ford Mondeo?' he persevered.

There were indeed three Mondeo saloons in a row in the neighbours' driveways.

'Actually, my dad's very proud of his Rover,' I said, pointing to the McNaughton homestead. 'That's us there.'

'Ah, I can see that your place is a cut above the rest.' He sniggered. 'You've got double glazing and everything.'

'Ricky,' I said as sternly as I could. 'Please behave politely. My mum's really house-proud, so don't take the piss or she'll get upset. And you know the situation with my dad. I want to make up with him, not give him more ammunition to disapprove.'

'I'll be on my best behaviour,' promised Ricky, but there was a glint in his eye that worried me.

Mum opened the door before we reached it and ran out to give me a hug.

'You're so thin, sweetheart.' She looked worried. 'You can't be eating enough.'

Fiona hovered at the door and kissed me. Her smooth skin felt good against my cheek.

'I'm so glad you came,' she said. 'Ooh, I've missed you.' We cuddled.

Dad was in the hall.

'Laura.' He nodded formally. There was no hug, no kiss.

Mum ushered us all into the sitting room and I introduced my family to Ricky. Mum was wearing her best M&S frock, Dad his smartest golf jumper, even the dog looked like he'd had a bath and Fiona, to my horror, was wearing much less than is appropriate when meeting one's big sister's boyfriend. The denim miniskirt and skimpy vest top – no bra! – she'd chosen weren't wasted on Ricky, whose gaze fell happily on the acres of twenty-one-year-old flesh on show. Dad, who was visibly uptight anyway, also noticed my boyfriend's approval and tensed up even further. Mum was oblivious to the tension in the room, or perhaps she was just experienced enough in the art of family diplomacy to pretend to be oblivious, and hurriedly set about organizing tea and sponge cake. Dad stood silently with his back to the window, swaying from his toes to his heels, arms held firmly behind his back; meanwhile, Fiona lolled with her naked legs swinging over the arm of her chair. Ricky and I sat upright on the oyster-coloured velour sofa and Mum blethered away nineteen to the dozen, trying to put everyone at ease.

'Did you have a nice drive up?' she asked, without waiting for an answer. 'It's a lovely motorbike you've got there. Did you see Richard's machine, Alastair?'

My dad nodded uninterestedly.

'So what do you do for a living, Mr McNaughton?' asked Ricky bravely.

'I'm a history teacher,' replied my dad curtly.

'Oh, an educated man. I'm impressed,' Ricky said.

'I believe you're a musician of some sort.' Dad knew perfectly well who Ricky was.

'Um, yes, I'm a singer in a band,' said Ricky.

'Your parents must be very proud,' replied my father.

'Actually, they'd rather I'd done something more academic,' explained Ricky, 'but I was always more interested in the arts.'

Dad raised a bushy eyebrow in amusement. 'The arts?' he asked incredulously. 'Is that what you call it?'

Oh bollocks, Dad had hit a nerve. I could see the colour rise up Ricky's face. If there was one thing the guy took seriously in life, it was his music.

'Yes, art,' he said curtly. 'Don't you believe that music can be art?'

'Certainly.' Dad was enjoying this. 'Bach, Wagner, Mozart, fine, Scottish fiddle music, perhaps, even some of the Beatles' early numbers, I'd accept them as art, but most modern rock or pop, or whatever you call it, is just noise pollution.'

'Actually, I'm regarded as one of the most gifted musicians of my generation,' Ricky boasted.

'By whom, exactly?' asked Dad.

'The *NME*,' explained Ricky, proudly.

My father looked at Ricky blankly and shook his head.

Fiona smirked, Mum busied herself cutting the cake and I flashed Dad a warning look.

'So, what do you do, Fiona?' Ricky turned his attention to a friendlier member of the family.

'I'm a paediatric nurse,' said Fi sweetly. 'I look after sick kids.'

'That's fantastic.' Ricky's eyes lit up, no doubt at the idea of my little sister in a nurse's uniform rather than with admiration for her worthy job.

'Yes, we're very proud of Fiona,' said Dad, meaning, We're rather ashamed of Laura.

'How's the new house?' Mum jumped in.

'A mess, but it'll be nice when it's finished,' I said. 'You'll have to come down and see it when it's done. We could go shopping in Harrods, see a West End show; it might be fun.'

'Oh, I'd like that, love,' said Mum.

'You too, Dad,' I added, hopefully.

Dad said, 'I don't think so, Laura. I'm not a fan of London. It's full of English people.'

He stared at Ricky and Ricky stared back. It was excruciating. Dad was acting like a thirteen-year-old – behaviour he'd no doubt learned from his pupils.

'Where are you from, Richard?' he demanded. 'I'm usually very good with accents, but yours is rather odd. You sound strangely American at times.'

'I'm from Buckinghamshire,' said Ricky. 'England. But I've travelled a lot. I spend a lot of time in the States because of my music. My art.'

'And were you privately educated?'

'Dad. What's that got to do with anything?' I couldn't believe how rude he was being.

'It's OK, Laura,' said Ricky. 'I don't mind. Um, yes, I went to boarding school, Mr McNaughton.'

This was Dad's pet subject. Being a proud member of the state-school system, he had a passionate aversion to anybody privately educated. I decided to get the worst of it out of the way.

'Ricky went to Eton,' I said.

A slow smile spread across my father's face. 'Oh really?' He smirked. 'How unfortunate for you. I can see now where you get your high opinions of yourself. You must have been told you were part of the elite so many times that you actually started to believe it. That's the trouble with public schools, they're too far removed from reality.'

'Cake?' Mum interjected, thrusting a strawberry-and-cream sponge in Ricky's face before he could reply and escalate the situation further.

We sat in silence, eating cake and drinking tea. It had been a long time since I'd eaten anything with such a high calorie content, but I knew Mum would give me a lecture on eating disorders if I said no to a slab of her cake. Its sickly sweetness stuck in my throat, as did the normally demure Fiona's behaviour. She appeared to be doing a special floor show just for Ricky, deliberately dropping a blob of cream on her bare thigh, scooping it up with her finger and licking it off seductively. She had a captive audience. I wasn't sure what had happened to her in the last few months, but she seemed to have suddenly discovered her sexuality. I made a mental note to kill her later. The gold carriage clock on the mantelpiece ticked loudly, but the hands moved very slowly indeed.

I'd just started to get over the cake nausea when Mum announced she had a meal ready. Ricky and I exchanged a look of horror at the thought of having to force down any more food, but there was no use protesting, as far as my mother was concerned guests were to be fed until they were incapable of doing anything other than languishing on the sofa for the duration of their stay – that way they couldn't escape. To say no to a three-course meal was to insult her hospitality and to refuse seconds was a slight on her culinary skills. Indigestion came with the territory.

Despite the fact that she'd only had a couple of hours' advance warning of our arrival, Mum had managed to make the meal an event – the kitchen table was laid with a red gingham cloth, the best cutlery and a vase of pink tulips. Mum's cheeks were flushed with the heat of the oven as she fussed around with bowls of home-made oxtail soup, plates piled high with roast chicken and all the trimmings and sticky toffee pudding and custard to finish. She chattered away self-consciously about the goings-on at the golf club, the babies my schoolfriends had had and which neighbour had painted their attic conversion which colour. It was blatantly obvious that, in her head at least, she was Ma Walton. Unfortunately, Dad was in no mood for playing Pa, and Ricky was never going to be John Boy.

'And how is Adam getting on in London?' asked Mum as she placed a second helping of pudding in front of Ricky.

'Yeah, fine,' I said, sneakily handing the dog a soggy handful of goo under the table. 'He's got a couple of blokes working for him and he seems to know what he's doing.'

'He's living in Shepherd's Bush, I hear,' she continued. 'With his girlfriend. She's a student – Italian. Very beautiful, according to Adam's mother. He met her when she was touring Scotland. It's a very romantic story actually: she was eating fish and chips at the harbour in Stonehaven with her friends when they got attacked by a giant seagull who was trying to eat their supper. They were screaming and dropping their chips everywhere when Adam came to the rescue, shooed the creature away and stole the Italian girl's heart. Have you met her yet?'

I could see Ricky smirking out of the corner of my eye.

'Mum, he's my builder,' I explained patiently. 'We don't exactly socialize in the same circles.'

Ricky snorted at the thought of getting friendly with a builder, especially that particular builder. Dad bristled.

'Adam Knox is a fine laddie,' he announced, after scraping clean his second bowl of pudding. 'Always used to look in on my mother every week without fail. She misses him dreadfully. You could do worse than get to know a young man like that. He might be a good influence on you, compared to these showbiz types you've been coming into contact with.'

He looked straight at Ricky.

'Alastair!' Mum was obviously appalled at her husband's behaviour.

'No, it's fine, Mrs McNaughton,' said Ricky calmly. 'I can see why a father might be nervous about my spending time with his daughter. I don't get a very good press, after all. But, sir, you really shouldn't believe everything you read in the tabloids.'

'I don't read the gutter press,' hissed Dad. 'And I have absolutely no idea what they say about you, nor do I care. All I know is that since Laura moved to London and got herself involved with rich young upstarts like you, she's become a spoilt, selfish, ungrateful, irresponsible floozy!'

I stared at my father in disbelief. His face was puce, and an angry vein pulsed in his forehead.

'Dad! You can't say that,' I spluttered.

'That's totally out of order,' Fiona backed me up.

'Apologize, Alastair. At once,' ordered my mother, who looked as if she might stab him in the eye with her dessert fork for ruining the glorious family atmosphere of her special meal.

'I will not,' he said petulantly. 'I meant every damn word of it and I've been meaning to say it for some time. Now, if you'll excuse me, I'd like to watch the evening news.'

He stood up and left the table, and the dog followed. Fiona shook her head slowly.

'He's lost it big time,' she said.

'Richard, I am so sorry.' Mum sniffled. 'I have no idea why my husband is behaving so badly.'

She turned to me and put her hand on my arm. 'Laura, he doesn't mean it, darling.'

'Of course he does,' I said, sadly. 'But it's got absolutely bugger all to do with Ricky, has it? I'm sorry, Ricky. Do you want to go?'

'No!' Mum shouted desperately, and then, 'No, please don't go,' in a smaller, choking voice. 'Why don't you give Vicky a call? I'm sure she'd love to see you. Get out of the house for a while and he, your father, will have calmed down by the time you get back.'

'Yeah,' added Fiona enthusiastically. 'We could go to The Hammer for a drink.'

I could see from Ricky's face that he loved the idea of going anywhere other than my parents' home. I wiped away a single angry tear with the paper napkin Mum had provided and went into the hall to call my oldest friend.

'Vicky. Guess who?' I said.

There was a screech on the other end of the line. 'Laura! Where are you?'

'I'm at my mum's. It's awful. My dad's being an arse and I need to escape. I thought we could meet at The Hammer. Fi's here, too, and my boyfriend, Ricky.'

'Ricky Jones?' asked Vicky in disbelief.

'The very fella.'

'God, I read about you and him in the paper, but I never thought I'd see the day when Ricky Jones was in The Hammer. I wouldn't miss that for anything. Shit, that means Kevin'll need to come, too. He'd kill me if he doesn't get to meet Ricky; he loves Sugar Reef. My mum's here, so I'll see if she can take the kids to hers for their tea.'

I could hear Vicky hollering to her mother, 'Mum, Mum, it's Laura. She's at home and she wants to go to the pub. Can you take the bairns? Please! She's got that sexy singer with her. You know, the one that was in the paper.'

I waited.

'No worries, that's sorted.' Vicky came back on the line. 'Right, give me an hour to clean myself up – I've got baby puke in my hair and I'm wearing Kev's trackie bottoms, so I'm not in a fit state to hang out with you glamorous people. We'll see you in there, yeah? God, I can't wait to see you, hen.'

'Me, too, Vick,' I said.

Back in the kitchen I told the others the plan and lit a much-needed cigarette.

'Oh, Laura,' said Mum in her most disappointed voice. 'You're not still smoking, are you? I really wish you'd stop. Open the back door so you don't stink the whole house out, will you? Tsk, tsk.'

I noticed that Fiona – a dedicated twenty-a-day girl – never lit up in front of the parents. It was beginning to dawn on me that my little sister wasn't quite the naive innocent I'd had her down as.

Ricky excused himself and asked where the toilet was. I knew perfectly well he was going to powder his nose, and who could blame him for turning to narcotics after an evening in the McNaughton household? Mum went to talk to my dad – or give him a bollocking – while Fiona and I washed up.

'God, Dad's such a prat sometimes.' She handed me a tea towel.

'Yeah, and he's not the only one,' I said. 'I'll wash up, you dry.'

I threw the tea towel back at her and elbowed my way in front of the sink.

'What d'you mean?' She pouted innocently.

'Well, what are you playing at, eh?' I said in a hissed whisper. 'Flirting with Ricky like that.'

Fi shrugged her bare shoulders. 'I've never met anyone famous before, that's all. I was only being friendly. And you want him to like me, don't you?'

'Oh, he *likes* you all right,' I replied. 'He can't help *liking* you. It's what he'd *like* to do to you that I'm worried about.'

'Sorry,' she said, giving me a look that suggested I'd gone completely bonkers, 'but I don't think you've got anything to worry about from me. For starters, I'm your sister, so I'm not likely to try and get off with your boyfriend, am I? Plus, you look absolutely amazing. Gorgeous. Fucking fantastic. He's not going to notice anybody else.'

Ricky reappeared.

'Everything OK?' he asked.

'Everything's just perfect,' I replied.

Mum came through from the living room looking tearful and told me to show Ricky, or Richard as she was insisting on calling him, to his room, which was in fact my old room and still decorated in teen-angst chic. I'd been relegated to the box room next door – it was separate bedrooms, of course. My room hadn't been decorated for a decade and there were posters of old bands everywhere, photographs of me and my friends in bad hair and old clothes, and even an old pair of trainers placed neatly at the foot of the bed, as if sixteen-year-old me was about to slip into them at any moment.

'Oh shit,' I groaned, mortified that Ricky should witness this.

He wandered around the bedroom, slowly picking up photographs and smirking at photos of me as a teenager.

'Cool,' he said. 'You look cute with all that hair. I would have had you down as more of a Take That girl, though.'

'As if!' I scoffed. 'I'll have you know I was one of the biggest indie kids in town. I was going to marry Kurt Cobain if he hadn't been tragically snatched from me.'

'So I see,' said Ricky, eyeing a childishly customized 'I love Kurt' poster on the wall. 'Just think, if he hadn't died, you might be with him now instead of me.'

'Oh, it's a certainty,' I teased. 'You're only my second choice rock god. I wouldn't have looked twice at you if he'd still been around.'

'Is that right?' Ricky kissed me full on the lips and we tumbled onto the single bed.

'Mmm-hmm,' I mumbled.

'So you don't really find me attractive at all?' he asked, perfectly aware that like 99 per cent of the female population I fancied the pants off him.

'Nope,' I lied. 'You don't really do it for me.'

Ricky tugged at my jeans and pushed up my T-shirt.

'Are you sure you're not just pulling my leg?' he continued, finding my left nipple and making me gasp. 'My third leg.' He took my hand and placed it on his cock. 'You see, I reckon you're gagging for it.'

He was right, of course.

'We can't do it here,' I protested weakly. 'This house is tiny. They'll hear.'

Ricky put his finger to my mouth and carried on undressing me. Once I was naked, he slipped his jeans down to his ankles and sat me firmly on his lap. I had to bite my lip not to groan as he slid inside me and I began to grind my hips against his body. The bed creaked slightly with every thrust and we laughed and shooshed each other as we kissed and fucked as silently as we could. Suddenly I was sixteen again and Ricky was the captain of the school football team. It was over in minutes, a quick teenage bonk. There had been no foreplay, but I felt naughty and excited and as scared of being caught as I would have been a decade earlier. It was delicious.

Afterwards, we dressed quickly and giggled like mischievous schoolchildren. Ricky got out his stash and chopped out some lines on the windowsill while I stood with my back guarding the door. First sex, then drugs, it was all so rock'n'roll. What would my dad have said had he known what was going on next door? Acting so abysmally in his house felt like perfect revenge.

'Are you two ready?' shouted Fiona from the hall.

'Just coming,' I called.

We stumbled out of the bungalow and became hysterical with relief as we breathed in the sweet smell of freedom.

'Well, that was a nice relaxing family gathering,' giggled Fiona.

'It went well,' joked Ricky. 'I think your dad likes me.'

'He'll be drawing up the wedding guest list as we speak,' I added, and then regretted it immediately, in case Ricky thought I wanted to marry him, which actually, right that second, I did, but I didn't want him to know that.

As we turned the corner onto the high street, The Hammer came into view. It wasn't the sort of drinking establishment Ricky was used to: there were no smart doormen dressed in black, no guest list, no rope to keep the riff-raff out, no neon signs announcing its name and definitely no limos parked outside, although there was a burnt-out Fiesta in the bus stop along the road, which had obviously been discarded by joyriders. In fact, The Hammer was an ugly, rundown suburban boozer that may have seen better days, but it was more likely, considering its location, that the place had always had a whiff of decrepitude about it. It hadn't been built to impress; it was a purely functional building, its sole purpose to serve cold beer and light relief to its downtrodden clientele.

'Fuck me,' said Ricky, as we approached. 'Are you sure it's safe?'

Thinking about it suddenly, and considering Ricky's reaction to Stevie, Goggsie and Adam, I realized he might have a point. The Hammer was going to be full of hard-working, hard-drinking hard men, just like it always was, and they wouldn't be impressed by Ricky's fame. Their girlfriends and wives, on the other hand, would be hugely impressed – decent talent of the male variety had always been pretty scarce in The Hammer – but that would just make the men bristle with resentment. If Ricky pulled the arrogant rock-star card there would definitely be trouble. I threw Fiona a concerned look.

'It'll be fine,' she said, but she looked worried too as we hovered on the pavement outside.

'I was joking.' Ricky laughed as he headed for the door with confidence. 'I do know how to act in the company of civilians.'

Fiona and I winced as Ricky strode towards the door.

Once again, my life became a scene from a bad western. Ricky flung the door open and entered with a flick of his hair, and Fiona and I followed five steps behind, hiding behind him as best we could. As the rock star made his entrance, fifty or so pairs of eyes looked up and the bar fell silent for what seemed like several minutes. I was glued to the spot. Then a slow murmuring began to filter through the room. It started with the table of teenage girls by the window, spread quickly to the older men propping up the bar and ended abruptly at the pool table, where the local nutters always held court. Then the bar was silent again. Nobody looked away. The Hammer was well lit and badly decorated, the jukebox played so quietly that it was hard to decipher the tune, and as my high heels click-clicked loudly towards the bar on the shiny, red vinyl tiles I felt my face burn with embarrassment.

'Laura,' said the barmaid without smiling.

'Hayley,' I said, grinning with relief on recognizing an old classmate behind the bar. She had thickened around the shoulders and waist, and had more wrinkles than was appropriate at twenty-five, but I knew her and that was something.

'How have you been?' I rambled. We'd never been friends as such, and I hadn't seen her in about seven years.

'Och, all right.' She shrugged uninterestedly. 'Just doing away, you know.'

'Yeah, me too,' I smiled.

A short girl at the bar next to me whispered something in her friend's ear and they both giggled wickedly. Fiona gave them one of her withering looks and they shut up. My little sister had been popular at school and still held a certain amount of respect among her peers.

'Drinks?' asked Hayley.

'A pint of lager, please, darling,' said Ricky, flicking his hair again and gazing round the room, staring out anybody who caught his eye. I suddenly realized how posh he sounded.

'Vodka and tonic,' I said quietly.

'And I'll have a bottle of Beck's,' said Fiona.

Hayley took a very long time to get three drinks together while I looked around tentatively to see whether Vicky and Kev had arrived. They hadn't, but I did recognize several faces from school. Everybody looked older than they should, and hardened somehow. I smiled my recognition at them all and they stared back unblinkingly, as if they'd never sat beside me in a maths class, let alone seen me on their television the week before, or semi-naked on the billboard at the bus stop as they'd walked to the pub that night.

'Six twenty-four,' said Hayley eventually, spilling the drinks as she plonked them on the laminated bar top.

'Six twenty-four – that's cheap,' announced Ricky loudly. 'You can't get a vodka martini for that in London.'

Hayley stared at him blankly. There was a mumbling of disapproval, and I'm sure I heard the word 'wanker' reverberate around the wood-chipped walls. I noticed that one particularly heavily tattooed pool player was holding his cue across his body like a weapon of mass destruction. I prayed that the shiny red floor would swallow me up.

'Let's get a table,' said Fiona, and I gratefully followed her to the darkest, most intimate corner, right beside the men's toilet, into which Ricky immediately ducked to powder his nose.

'Oh shit, not here,' I groaned to his disappearing back.

'Not here, what?' asked Fiona.

I had my back to the rest of the pub with my elbow resting on the wobbly wooden table and my forehead in my hand. I looked up at my little sister and whispered, 'Coke.'

Fiona looked blank and shrugged. 'Eh?'

'Charlie, laughing gear, nose candy ...' I continued quietly.

'Oh, *that* kind of coke,' said Fiona a little too loudly.

'Shh!' I scolded and looked round to make sure the middle-aged men at the next table hadn't heard.

'Has he got much?' she asked. 'I wouldn't mind trying some.'

'Fiona!' I was shocked. 'You're a nurse.'

'And that means what exactly?' She laughed at me. 'That I can't have a good time?'

'No, but not coke. You can't do coke. I won't let you.'

I knew I was being a hypocrite, but the idea of my lovely little sister adopting my seedy habits appalled me.

'Oh right, and I suppose you never partake yourself.' She raised a blonde eyebrow.

I shrugged. 'Now and again, maybe, but in London, in my crowd, everybody does it, so it's no big deal.'

'In London, in my crowd ...' she mimicked me. 'People do drugs here, too, you know. I just can't afford the expensive ones. But Ricky's quite rich enough to share his sweeties with me, isn't he? Speak of the devil ...'

Ricky sat down with a loud sniff and said, 'What?'

'Can I try some of your coke, please, Ricky?' asked Fiona, as sweetly as if she were a five-year-old asking for a wine gum.

I shook my head vigorously at Ricky.

Thankfully, just at that moment, Vicky and Kev arrived. I was shocked by the sight of the couple trotting towards me. Vicky had once been a gorgeous creature, with waist-length black hair, olive skin and startlingly exotic eyes the colour of Guinness. Her curvy little body had always filled her clothes just so, and all the boys loved her. Her body still filled her clothes, but the clothes were several sizes bigger these days. Her hair was shoulder-length and nondescript, hanging lifelessly around her face, which looked pale and puffy. She had dark rings under her eyes, though the eyes themselves were still unmistakably Vicky's. I composed my face into a warm grin and prayed that she hadn't noticed my look of horror. It had only been two years since I'd seen her, but she'd aged a lifetime. Her youngest son, Jamie, had leukaemia, and every heartbreaking, stressful, tear-jerking moment of his illness was etched on her face. Meanwhile, Kevin, who had been three years above us at school and quite the catch of the century, had gone completely grey and was thinning on top. Just looking at them made me want to cry.

'Laura, you look even better than you do on the telly,' screeched Vicky. 'How the fuck do you stay so thin? You bitch!'

She laughed and hugged me and kissed my newly straightened hair.

'It's so fucking good to see you, hen.' She kept looking at me and shaking her head as if I were a mirage. The pub looked on. 'What the fuck are you lot nebbing at? Nosey bastards,' she shouted to the audience. Fifty people simultaneously stared at their feet. Even the scary-looking bloke with the pool cue stopped glaring when she said to him, 'Jimmy, your flies are down and I can see your puny little cock.' Nobody messed with Vicky.

I introduced my friends to Ricky, and to their credit, they acted as if he was just some guy I'd dragged along. Fiona knew them both well already, little Jamie being a regular visitor to her hospital ward. I felt immediately at ease once Vicky and Kevin arrived, as if the fact that they were well-respected locals validated our presence, and I quickly found myself chatting away about the feud with my dad, my life in London and the ridiculously expensive house I'd just bought with no running water. Vicky, in turn, explained that they'd managed to buy an ex-council house on the estate behind the swimming pool.

'It's very up-and-coming,' she insisted, but I knew it wasn't.

She'd had to give up her job as a receptionist at the health centre because Jamie was so ill so much of the time, and now they managed on Kevin's wages alone. Kev worked as a steeplejack and was away a lot of the time. What they wanted more than anything was to go to Disneyland on holiday because that was Jamie's dream. Ricky could have done with an interpreter, but he managed to follow most of the conversation and when Vicky and Kev were at the bar he said, 'They're a really cool couple, but I can't believe how many problems they've got. It makes me feel guilty for being me.' I understood how he felt.

The vodka was flowing freely, or cheaply, and as the night wore on the atmosphere in the pub lifted along with my spirits. A hen party arrived on wobbly legs and they had no qualms about approaching Ricky and trying to snog him. For a man who'd been groped by some of the most famous women on earth, he looked absolutely terrified in the hands of Edinburgh's drunken wenches. I noticed a few cameras flashing, but assumed, at the time, that it was the bridesmaids keeping a record of the bride's last night of freedom.

At some point, much later, Ricky handed me a small envelope of charlie under the table and I sneaked off to the ladies' for a pick-me-up. Fiona followed and I was too drunk to resist her pleas. And so I demonstrated how to snort a line off a filthy toilet seat, just as Lucy had once shown me. She was far less nervous than I'd been.

At half past midnight, Hayley eventually managed to kick us all out and we staggered down the high street, arm in arm – me, Ricky, Fiona, Kev and Vicky – a most unlikely crew. Fiona hailed a cab to take her back to her nurses' digs in Leith.

'I miss you, Fi,' I sobbed drunkenly as we hugged on the pavement. 'Come and stay with me in London when you can.'

'Just try and stop me,' she replied. 'I want to go to all those glamorous parties and get off with famous blokes like you do.'

I pushed a cheque for £10,000 into the pocket of her miniskirt as she clambered inelegantly into the cab.

'That's for being the besht little sister ever,' I slurred.

Kev and Vicky walked with us to the corner of Mum and Dad's cul-de-sac.

'It was so good to see you again, Vick,' I said tearfully. 'I want you to have this, and I won't take no for an answer. Go to Disneyland with Kev and the kids, buy a new three-piece suite for the house, build a conservatory, make the neighbours jealous, I don't care what you do with it, just take it, please.'

Vicky looked at the cheque for £5,000 and protested, 'Laura, I can't. It's too much.'

Kevin and Ricky were singing a duet of Sugar Reef's old classic 'Notoriety' and were oblivious to the transaction taking place.

'Kev won't like it. He'll think it's charity. He's very proud,' insisted Vicky, trying to hand me back the cheque.

I was determined to give at least one of my friends some money after Becky's rejection.

'Vicky, it's not charity,' I said. 'I want you to have it. Please take it. For old times' sake.'

Vicky looked uncertainly in Kevin's direction.

'He'll understand,' I continued. 'You're my oldest friend and I really want to do this. Take it for Jamie's sake, if not your own.'

'OK, Laura.' She took the cheque gingerly, folded it

neatly in two and then slid it guiltily into her handbag. 'But I feel bad.'

'Don't,' I insisted. 'I bet the day comes when I need something from you.'

'What could you ever need from me?' Vicky smiled, but her black eyes were sad. 'You've got everything.'

We hugged goodbye and I made the usual empty promises to phone more often and keep in closer contact.

'We'll send you a postcard from Disneyland!' shouted Vicky as they disappeared into the darkness.

Ricky and I tried our best to let ourselves into the bungalow quietly, but keys and drunk people are always a bad combination, and we giggled and tripped and struggled to open the door until the dog started barking and Mum and Dad's bedroom light came on. Mum let us in, wearing a pink dressing gown and a thick layer of cold cream on her face.

'Shh,' she whispered. 'Your father's still asleep.'

With my mother watching there was no use resisting the separate-bed rule. I lay awake for hours, uncomfortable on the rickety old camp bed and haunted by the ghosts of home. I thought about Vicky and her poor sick child, about my dad and his anger and how he used to love me so much, and about Fiona and how she'd changed into a somebody much wilder since I'd moved away, no longer just a little girl under my control. I'd somehow thought that while I was in London, getting on with my life, everybody and everything I'd left behind would just stay where it was, waiting for me to come back and pick up where we'd left off. I was wrong: everything had changed.

Dad had already left for work by the time we got up, although why he had to get to school by seven thirty if it wasn't to avoid me, I don't know. Mum cooked us a full fry-up, which Ricky ate with gusto, while I resorted to feeding the dog under the table as usual.

'I could get used to this,' he said, digging in heartily as if food was the new, designer drug.

Mum cried inconsolably when it was time for us to leave.

'I worry about you,' she sobbed. 'There are a lot of bad people out there.'

'According to Dad, I'm one of them,' I said with a sigh.

'He didn't mean what he said yesterday,' Mum replied, but we both knew he did.

As we reached the corner of the cul-de-sac, I looked back, and saw her standing in the driveway alone with her tears. I hoped she'd be pleased with the cheque I'd left on the camp bed for £10,000.

'Can we just do something before we leave?' I asked Ricky as we turned into the high street. 'It won't take long.'

I directed Ricky to Arthur's Seat and instructed him to park up at Duddingston Loch.

'Where are we going?' he asked.

'Up there,' I said, pointing to the top of Arthur's Seat, the huge volcanic rock that sits in the middle of Holyrood Park, just behind Holyrood Palace and the Scottish Parliament.

It was a cold, clear, blustery day and the higher we climbed, the windier it became. Ricky managed to be every inch the rock star, even when hill climbing in a force-ten gale. The wind tousled his hair perfectly, as if he'd just walked out of Daniel's salon, his biker jacket blew open to reveal a tight black T-shirt over a lean, taut frame, and his shades remained stubbornly on. We passed a couple of Japanese tourists who nearly fell off the edge of the cliff they were perched on when they recognized Ricky – Arthur's Seat isn't known as a haunt of the internationally renowned, after all. After scribbling his name on each of the girls' backpacks in silver pen – they provided the stationery – his kissed them both on the cheek and left them giggling giddily, if not entirely safely, on their cliff top. It was possibly the strangest place he'd been asked for an autograph. We arrived at the top breathless and windswept, and sat huddled together on a rock, overlooking the city.

'It's beautiful,' said Ricky, staring out towards the castle. 'You must miss it.'

I drank in the view of my home town, gazed out over the Forth Bridge and tried to memorize that image of Edinburgh stretching out to the water, and of Fife sparkling in the sunshine beyond. I wanted to remember it all. I had a feeling I wouldn't be home for a while.

'I used to come here with my dad.' I tried to explain the special significance of the spot to Ricky. 'Just the two of us and the dog. We'd sit right here for hours on end and he'd tell me stories about Edinburgh's past. I loved it.'

'Cool,' said Ricky, but I could tell he wasn't listening. 'This would be a mental place to play a gig, don't you think?'

'Phenomenal,' I replied, half-heartedly. 'Come on, let's go. We've got five and a half hours to get back to London.'

I had one last lingering look at the Edinburgh skyline and then tripped back down the hill towards the Harley.

As we turned the corner into my street I realized that Sugar Reef's video shoot was not going to be a modest affair. In fact, my house and the surrounding area had been transformed into a Hollywood movie location in my absence. There was a lorry the size of a small office block parked immediately outside and two smaller trailers were double-parked next to it, completely blocking the road. Somebody had set up Portaloos in my front garden. The small group of paparazzi who'd been outside two days before had gone forth and multiplied into an army of microphone-wielding, camera-hogging TV reporters. Security personnel in black combat trousers stalked the area, holding back the press and whispering earnestly into their walkie-talkies.

'Well, I'm not going to be asked to join Neighbourhood Watch or the residents' association, am I?' I said to Ricky as we clambered off the bike and joined the throng.

Inside, my living room had been taken over by the band and their entourage, who were chain-smoking and happily dropping their butts on my soon-to-be-restored wooden floor. 'Yo!' they greeted Ricky with hand-slaps and high-fives. 'What's up?' It was as if they'd all been dragged up in Compton rather than privately educated in the Home Counties. I could feel my wank antennae begin to tingle and decided to make myself scarce.

I found the builders upstairs. Adam was busy laying floorboards in the bedroom and studiously ignoring the commotion, but Goggsie and Stevie were hanging over the banisters, straining to hear what the band were up to. I greeted them warmly, bummed a cigarette from Stevie and joined them at their perch, which had a perfect view of the front door and the comings and goings in the hall. I was as much of an outsider as they were. Just at that moment the front door was opened by a burly security guard and a tall, skinny woman in a white bathrobe was ushered in protectively. She slipped off the robe to reveal acres of tanned, bony flesh, covered only by a minuscule wisp of white gauze.

'Venetia.' I nearly fell down the stairs. 'What the fuck is she doing in my house?'

It wasn't really a question the builders could answer, but Stevie said, 'I don't know, hen. I've never understood the attraction myself. She looks like an alien to me.' Which was actually quite helpful under the circumstances.

Venetia looked up and caught me glaring.

'Laura, darling,' she cooed. 'What an interesting choice of property you have here.'

'So glad you approve,' I replied, flicking cigarette ash in the direction of her head.

'It's perfect for today's purposes, though,' she continued. 'When Ricky asked me to star in the video I couldn't exactly say no. He needed someone to play a beautiful, ethereal, waiflike ghost, and he just couldn't find anyone else who was up to the job.'

I made a mental note to chop Ricky's celebrity bollocks off later. Of all the models in the world, why did he have to go and book Venetia?

'I'm sorry to hear about you and your father,' called the stick insect from below.

'What do you mean?' I was confused. How could Venetia know about me and Dad falling out?

'Your family feud.' She smiled sweetly up at me. 'It's all over today's papers.'

My mouth went dry and my stomach crawled up to my throat. What was going on? I dropped my cigarette in sheer surprise and managed to burn a hole in Venetia's slip of fabric, which I quickly gathered was actually a unique designer creation and not a net curtain as I'd originally suspected.

'Adam's got the paper in there.' Goggsie nodded towards the bedroom. 'He said you'd be upset about it and told us not to make a fuss. We thought you'd have seen it by now.'

I stumbled on shaky legs to the bedroom. Adam looked up at me sympathetically from the floor, but I didn't want pity, I wanted to see the damage.

'Give me the paper, Adam,' I demanded.

He handed me the rolled-up tabloid, and as I spread it open on the bare floor I saw my face appear with Ricky, snogging in The Hammer. It had obviously been taken by one of the hen party the night before. And then I spotted a grainy photograph of my dad looking stern and school-teacherish. I recognized it from last year's school yearbook. The headline shouted 'LAURA AND HER DAD IN BITTER DISPUTE – TV PRESENTER'S FATHER HATES ROCK-STAR BOYFRIEND, RICKY'. It went on to detail, amongst other personal things, what my dad had said to me at the dinner table the night before. The story was on the front page. I felt the blood drain from my cheeks and the room swam.

'Adam, what's going on?' I pleaded. 'Why would someone do this to me?'

Adam shook his head sadly and scooped me up into his thick arms as my legs buckled. I stayed there, sobbing into his vast chest, despite the fact that he smelled of chemicals and his T-shirt was covered in sawdust.

'Shall I get Ricky?' asked Adam gently when my tears subsided.

'I don't know,' I said, confused. 'He's busy working and I probably shouldn't disturb him.'

'You don't think he might know something about this?' asked Adam, stroking my hair.

'Don't be ridiculous,' I snapped. 'What are you talking about? Why would Ricky want a story printed about me and my dad?'

Adam shrugged. 'Publicity?'

'No, he'd never do that to me.'

I pushed Adam away from me and wiped the sawdust from my wet cheeks. What did he know?

He reappeared a few minutes later with Ricky in tow.

'Well, it's obvious who's to blame,' said Ricky, shrugging. 'Your family wouldn't do this so ...'

I thought about it. The only people who knew about the fight were me, Mum, Dad, Fiona, Ricky and Vicky.

I remembered Lucy's words, 'You can't trust anyone any more.'

'It has to be Vicky,' Ricky continued. 'She needs the money, she's desperate and she's no longer a friend of yours.' Ricky gave me a half-hearted hug. 'It's no biggie,' he insisted. 'We all go through this when we hit the big time. Just call her and give her hell.'

I called her number from my mobile and when she answered I didn't let her speak.

'Vicky, you are a devious bitch and I hate you,' I shouted. 'How could you do that to me? I told you that stuff about my dad as a friend and you just went and sold it to the highest bidder. I thought you were better than that, but you're just cheap and nasty. I never want to see you again.'

I hung up, and when she tried to call back I switched my phone off. Adam, who'd witnessed my outburst, was pretending to be busy with his woodwork, but he kept throwing me concerned glances as I stood at the window and angrily smoked another cigarette.

'What?' I demanded eventually, sick of his puppy-dog eyes.

'Nothing.' He averted his gaze and concentrated on hammering a floorboard.

'You think I'm out of line, don't you?' I demanded, shouting to be heard over his banging.

Adam stopped hammering and shrugged. 'I think those were pretty harsh words to use on a friend when you've got no proof she was responsible, that's all.'

'No proof?' I spluttered. 'Who else could it have been? My mum? My sister? My boyfriend? And before you start, no it wasn't Ricky. You just want it to be Ricky because you're jealous of him.'

I could feel my cheeks burning with rage. Adam shrugged again.

'Whatever you think, Laura. You're upset, that's understandable, but I don't think you should go around throwing wild accusations until you know the truth.'

'You have absolutely no idea how difficult it is being me,' I shouted. 'How would you feel if your most personal details were splashed all over the tabloids? If your best mates betrayed you the minute some hack offered them a few quid? It's not easy, you know, being famous.'

It was my first diva-like temper tantrum. Adam looked at me with what can only be described as pity.

'Anyway, what does it matter what you think,' I continued. 'You're only the builder.'

'And that's all I've ever wanted to be,' he said flatly, picking up his hammer and getting on with his work.

'Good,' I said.

'Good,' he repeated.

Downstairs, it sounded as if the party was in full swing.

I noticed that Vicky never cashed the cheque I'd given her. I took that as an admission of guilt and added her name to Becky's on the list of those who'd betrayed me.

12

How to stay cool this summer

If my behaviour was weird, it was nothing compared to Lucy's. I was beginning to suspect she was seriously unhinged. It began at my birthday party in June. Warren and Cathy had organized a surprise bash at an exclusive private members' club in Holland Park. Ricky got me there on false pretences, promising a romantic meal for two at the restaurant downstairs. I'd thought it was an odd birthday treat, seeing as neither of us were particularly interested in good food, or food of any variety come to think of it. But when we arrived, the red carpet was out and the press were there with bells on, all shouting, 'Surprise! Happy birthday, Laura! Give us a smile!' I was a pro by then, confidently beaming and pouting for the cameras, just like Lucy.

Warren had invited everybody who was anybody on the celebrity circuit, which is how Venetia managed to sneak in, while Cathy had ensured that my real friends were there too. She had even invited the builders, bless her, because they'd been working so hard that they were ahead of schedule and below budget. Stevie and Goggsie were propping up the bar and taking full advantage of the free booze while ogling every passing celebrity babe. Adam had brought his girlfriend, Sophia, who was as dark, exotic and gorgeous as any of the famous women in the room, if a lot more curvaceous. Quite how Trudy managed to squeeze her skinny butt past the bouncers I'm still not sure, but there she was, brown-nosing for all she was worth. When I arrived, she'd cornered poor Jasmine, and was obviously trying to get herself a job. I was happier to spot Natalie bopping away on the dance floor with Rob. She looked resplendent in a tight red dress that showed off her growing bump magnificently. Graham and Daniel were cruising the joint, arm in arm, like an old married couple, telling anyone who would listen that they were expecting a new puppy now that George had sired a pedigree litter. They would call the pup Elton. Meanwhile, Jack was proudly showing off his new girlfriend, a Brazilian supermodel called Marina who I took an immediate shine to because she'd just knocked Venetia off the highest-paid stick-insect spot. They made an odd couple – she was half a foot taller than him – but he had a great view of her gravity-defying cleavage and they both seemed happy enough with this arrangement. The Snowman was there, too, of course, wearing a black suit and hair gel and sprinkling his magic powder over the guests.

The boys from Sugar Reef, who were perpetually horizontal when not on stage, had managed to secure prime positions, lounging sexily with long legs and long hair on the leather sofas that graced a raised platform in the centre of the room. That way they could be admired from all angles without having to circulate. Monica stood like a statue behind Lewis, drinking in the action and sipping a rum and coke. There was something regal about Monica; she always seemed to be detached from whatever pretentious antics were going on around her, as if she were somehow above all that, and I admired her for it. By contrast, the ever-shrinking Lucy fluttered maniacally around the boys from the band. She was wearing a skimpy wisp of a turquoise dress and a wild stare. She was so high her feet hardly seemed to touch the floor – Tinkerbell on amphetamines. When she spotted

Ricky and me, she threw herself at each of us in turn and kissed us both on the lips.

'Happy birthday, babes,' she gushed. 'I've got you the most amazing present, but it wouldn't fit in my bag. Has Ricky told you what you're getting from him yet?'

I shook my head, because the idea of getting a word in was preposterous.

'Haven't you told her yet, Ricky?'

Ricky shook his head. He never lost his patience with Lucy, however manic she got.

'Oh, can I tell her? Purlease,' she pleaded.

Ricky shrugged nonchalantly. 'If you like.'

'Well,' enthused Lucy. 'Tomorrow, you and Ricky are flying off to Cannes to spend a week on a luxury yacht that belongs to his friend Ahmed. Or to his father, at least. What does Ahmed's dad do again?' she asked but didn't wait for an answer. 'He owns a small Arab state or something. Anyway, they're loaded. Ricky and Ahmed were at Eton together, so they're toffs, but they're nice toffs.'

I smiled broadly at Ricky. 'That's so nice of you,' I said, bursting with love. 'It'll be great to spend some time together before you go off on tour, just the two of us.'

Sugar Reef's European tour started the following week, and apart from a brief catch-up at Glastonbury, where the band were headlining and I was filming a show, I wouldn't see him again until the end of July. The idea of a week on a private yacht, just me, Ricky and a bottle of suntan oil, was delicious.

'No, silly, not just you and Ricky.' Lucy giggled. 'We're all coming.'

The boys nodded at me from their sofas and Monica shrugged her elegant shoulders apologetically. My face fell.

'But I've got you something else as well,' Ricky interjected quickly.

He produced a small, exquisitely wrapped Cartier box from his leather jacket pocket. Inside was a solid diamond and platinum choker with a heart at the throat. It was breathtakingly beautiful and obviously cost a fortune, but I'd have swapped it in a moment for some time alone with my boyfriend. It wasn't until months later that I discovered the necklace had been painstakingly chosen for me by Monica.

'Now, where's that handsome workman of yours?' asked Lucy, staring wildly around the party.

'He's at the bar. With his girlfriend,' I replied. 'Leave Adam alone, Luce. He's terrified of you.'

Lucy hadn't given up her fixation on Adam and often popped round to the house after filming for a flirt. Adam, meanwhile, studiously deflected her innuendoes with monosyllabic replies and vibrant blushes. Goggsie and Stevie would look on in awe as their boss tried to ignore the advances of the world's greatest sex symbol. Lucy was not to be put off. No man had ever turned her down and she saw Adam's reluctance as some form of foreplay.

'Nope,' said Lucy. 'I'm not going to leave him alone. I haven't had sex in weeks and I feel horny as hell. I'm going to get myself a nice bit of rough tonight and he won't be able to say no.'

She lifted up her very short skirt and flashed a bare bum cheek. Ricky smacked it playfully and I winced.

'I'm not wearing any knickers!' she cried before running off in the direction of the bar.

'He's with his girlfriend,' I called after her, but she'd gone.

Ricky laughed satanically. He hated Adam, but obviously found the idea of Lucy toying with the poor bloke hilarious. I had come to like Adam. He worked hard and was always a calming presence around the house, even when the building was full of the sound of drilling and banging. I found Lucy's game really offensive: the powerful princess playing with the lowly builder. It wasn't as if she wanted a relationship with him – she was more than happy with the one she had with her internationally renowned actor boyfriend – Adam was just a nice little challenge to keep her occupied while Billy Joe was in America. I had a horrible feeling Adam would eventually give in and end up as Lucy Lloyd's road kill. Monica must have spotted the look of disgust on my face and squeezed my arm kindly, guiding me away from the boys so that we could have a private conversation.

'I've told Lucy, get a vibrator like everyone else,' she said drily. 'That's all she wants to use your builder for anyway, a sex aid.'

Monica handed me an unidentified cocktail from a passing waiter's tray.

'Lucy's spent too much time with those guys.' Monica waved her hand in the direction of Ricky, Lewis and the rest of the band. 'She sees how they treat women like sex slaves and she thinks that's how she's supposed to treat men.'

'And do they treat women like sex slaves? All of them?' I asked – paranoia about Ricky's sexual antics came with the girlfriend territory.

'Oh, don't be so naive, Laura,' Monica said with a frown. 'You don't honestly think those guys are faithful to us, do you?'

I shrugged. 'Maybe. Hopefully. Ricky says he is.'

'No, no, no.' She waved a long-nailed finger in front of my face. 'Laura, you have got to drop this little-girl thing you've got going on. Look at them.'

I watched Ricky and Lewis languish on their sofas. They were already surrounded by the giggling members of an all-new, all-singing, all-dancing girl band called the Pneumatic Puppies.

'Baby, those boys are megastars,' said Monica flatly. 'They have girls offering themselves on a plate, no questions asked, every night of the week. Young girls, beautiful girls, famous girls.'

Monica's green eyes narrowed as Lewis disappeared under the scantily dressed body of a teenage singing sensation. She continued with a sigh of resignation, 'And while we're here working our asses off in London, they're touring Japan or the States or Germany or wherever, it doesn't matter, there's nubile young flesh everywhere.'

'Bastards!' I spat. I tried to throw a hateful stare in Ricky's direction, but my glare was deflected by the pert bottom of girl band member number two.

'Oh, you gotta cut them some slack, honey,' Monica said sarcastically, turning her back on Lewis. 'They're only men, bless them, and they don't mean to shag around. It's not as if they go looking for it. They don't actually want to be unfaithful. Women just kinda fall over with their legs open right in front of them. What's a guy to do, huh?'

'But I can't be with Ricky if he's shagging around!' I announced defiantly. 'I'm going to have to finish with him.'

'Don't be silly.' Monica chuckled.

'Why do you stay with Lewis, then?' I demanded. Monica was such a strong woman, I couldn't understand why she'd put up with such blatant infidelity.

She sighed deeply and explained, 'I've been with Lewis for five years. I know he loves me. He thinks the sun shines out of my Yankee Doodle ass. Hell, we'll be together until we're old and grey. But it's his time to shine. As long as he comes back to me without VD and without getting some little tart pregnant, I'm not going to ask too many questions.

I can live with a bit of infidelity. Stars come with a sell-by date tattooed to their butts. In a couple of years, Sugar Reef will be has-beens, the groupies will have moved on to someone else and I can have my man back. And it's not as if I'm Snow White. I had flings with a couple of actors when Lewis and I were first together. Do you know, when we met, I was on the cover of *Vogue* and he was in some shitty little two-bit band with no record deal and no money? I thought I was doing him a favour. Now, he's the star and I'm past it. Funny old world, isn't it?'

Monica was the same age as me, which in modelling terms was practically geriatric. Having been spotted in a Texan shopping mall aged fourteen, she'd been on the celebrity circuit for well over a decade, so was well qualified to give lectures on superstar behaviour. Plus, she'd been with Sugar Reef from the start. She knew Ricky better than I ever would.

'I don't think I can live like that,' I said sadly.

'Your choice, honey,' said Monica. 'Just thought you should know what you've got yourself involved in.'

I felt sick. It was my birthday and here I was being told that my boyfriend was regularly at it with other women. I could feel my bottom lip begin to quiver and hot new tears were threatening to dislodge my sparkly eye make-up.

'Sweetheart, I'm sorry if I sound harsh,' said Monica gently. 'But if you wanna be with Ricky, you've got to face the truth and handle it, or you'll eat yourself up with wondering.'

I sniffed loudly and blinked hard, trying to stop the tears from advancing down my cheeks and ruining my flawless foundation.

'Just breathe, Laura. Take a deep breath. That's it. I'm not telling you anything you didn't already know, deep down,' Monica whispered in my ear.

I tried to compose myself.

'I see the stories in the papers,' I snivelled. 'I just kind of hoped they weren't true.'

'Listen, Ricky likes you a hell of a lot. I haven't seen him like this with any other girl, ever. Believe me, this is as serious as Ricky Jones gets, but none of those boys are keeping their knobs in their trousers. They think with their dicks, and no dick is going to say no to Lucy Lloyd if she's offering it to them on a plate.'

Monica's face fell as she realized she'd said too much.

The floor lurched beneath me as Monica's words bounced around my head. 'What do you mean about Lucy?' I asked desperately.

'Oh nothing.' Monica tried to brush off her last comment.

'No,' I demanded. 'You said that no man would say no to Lucy. What do you mean?'

'OK.' Monica sighed. 'So Ricky and Lucy used to sleep with each other. Big deal. It was never a boyfriend/girlfriend thing; it was just sex. As far as I know they don't do it any more. Why do you think she's chasing your builder? Ricky used to be her regular screw whenever Billy Joe was out of town. Then you came along, spoiled their little arrangement and now she's desperate.'

'She didn't tell me,' I said, feeling numb.

'She wouldn't. Lucy's not going to tell you anything that might jeopardize your friendship. It's not as if that little madam's got friends to throw away. Let's see. She's got you' – Monica pretended to be deep in thought – 'and you ... Oh, and then there's always you! You're the only pal she's got, for Christ's sake, Laura. She needs you more than she needs Ricky. Lucy can get sex anywhere, but she's not going to find another girlfriend who puts up with her madness the way you do.'

'I'm going to kill them both,' I muttered, downing my cocktail in preparation for the fight ahead.

Monica arched an elegant eyebrow. 'No, you're going to be cool,' she insisted. 'You're not going to say a word about this to either of them. Knowledge is power. Use it, girl.'

As I fought my way towards the ladies', everyone tried to grab a piece of me, to say hello to the birthday girl, but I just smiled as politely as I could and brushed past. I sat on the toilet for a long time thinking about what Monica had told me and wondering what to do next. Eventually, I realized she was right. There was nothing I could do, other than accept the situation and live with it, or get out. And I couldn't get out, it was too late for that: I was already in love with Ricky. I did a fat line of coke and composed myself to face my public. I was just reapplying my lipstick when the door burst open and Adam's girlfriend, Sophia, arrived in a whirl of tears and Italian swear words. Without asking, I knew exactly what was wrong.

'You OK?' I asked. Stupid question.

'The fucking bastard friend of yours,' she shouted angrily. 'That Lucy Lloyd woman; she try to seduce my Adam. She kiss him and she touch him here.'

Sophia pointed to her groin.

'She a little whore!'

Having just found out about Lucy and Ricky, privately I agreed. To Sophia I said, 'But Adam isn't interested in Lucy.'

'No?' Her eyes flashed wildly. 'Then why have they vanished? I can find them nowhere. One minute he's there, I turn to the bar for some drinks, I look back, he gone. She gone, too. I ask his stupid friends, "Where is Adam?" and they just laugh.'

'They're drunk,' I said. 'They don't know what they're doing.'

'Lucy Lloyd, she know exactly what she is doing,' shouted Sophia. 'And now she is doing it with my man! Well, she may have him. I am finish with that man. It's over.'

And with that, Sophia wiped away her tears, tossed her long black hair over her shoulders and flounced out of the ladies'. I followed her.

'Where's Adam?' I demanded of a very drunk Stevie.

He looked at me blankly with bleary eyes. 'Why's everyone looking for Big Ad? Sophia was asking about him, too. I dunno where he is. I'm not his keeper.'

I noticed that Venetia had managed to prise the little puppy off Ricky and had spread herself over him instead. She was whispering in his ear and he was laughing at whatever she was saying. Then he spotted me approaching, sat bolt upright and brushed her off.

'Babe!' He reached his arm around my waist.

'Where's Lucy?' I snapped.

He shrugged. 'No idea. Probably with that brainless builder. Have a drink.'

He tried to hand me a cocktail, but I shook my head and left him to Venetia's clutches.

I wandered round the club for what felt like hours, searching for Adam and Lucy, on a mission to split up whatever sordid little scene they were playing out, but they were nowhere to be found. Then Trudy cornered me.

'Laura, darling,' she exclaimed, air-kissing me twice. 'It's been so long. We do miss you at the office. Listen, my darling, I was wondering whether you'd do me an eensy-weensy, wincy little favour. I would absolutely love to have you on the cover of *Glitz* and I wondered if you'd have time to give us just a tiny bit of an interview. Nothing too taxing; I know you're a busy girl these days.'

I resisted the urge to tell her to fuck off and die.

'You'll have to speak to Cathy,' I replied with a false smile. 'She handles my diary and press requests. I trust her implicitly. She doesn't even bother me with the ones that she feels would be a waste of my time, so it's up to her whether or not I agree. She's such a good PA, isn't she? I'm so glad I hired her. Bye.'

I couldn't help smiling to myself as I left Trudy, open-mouthed in horror at the thought of having to grovel to her ex-PA. It was a priceless moment.

Eventually I spotted Nat's concerned face approaching me.

'Laura, come quick. It's Lucy and she's in a bad way,' she said, grabbing my hand and leading me towards a fire exit.

Outside, sitting in the gutter of the back alley behind the club, was Lucy Lloyd. I'd never seen her looking anything less than pristine before, but there she was, make-up smeared down her face, hair tangled in a bird's nest, dress covered in dust from the road and shoes who knows where. At first I thought she'd been attacked, but when she opened her mouth and sobbed, 'Laura, I've lost it. No one fancies me any more,' I realized she was just having a particularly violent fit of self-pity.

'I'll leave you to it,' said Nat. 'I've got to get home. My feet are killing me.'

'Thanks, Nat,' I said, kissing her cheek. 'I'll see you soon.'

She mouthed, 'She's fucking mental,' to me behind Lucy's back before waddling off in the direction of a black cab that was waiting at the end of the alley. I waved at Rob, who was watching from the taxi window.

Lucy stared up at me from behind huge mascara-smudged eyes.

'Adam said no,' she cried in disbelief. 'He says I'm not his type, that I don't do anything for him.'

I had to swallow a smile.

'It doesn't matter,' I said, sitting down beside her in the dirt, thankful I'd worn black. 'Every other man on the planet fancies you.'

Including my boyfriend, I thought.

'But, Laura, have you any idea how humiliating it is to be turned down by a builder?' she asked. 'I've had actors, singers, politicians ... and a stupid bloody workman says he doesn't find me attractive. Can you believe it?'

I shrugged. 'There's no accounting for taste.' I was half enjoying watching her suffer.

'Where is Adam now?' I asked, hoping that Sophia and he had worked things out.

Lucy shrugged. 'Dunno. He went after that girlfriend of his, but I don't think she believed him when he said nothing happened.

'Let's get you home,' I said, standing up and offering Lucy my hand.

She pouted. 'I don't wanna go home.'

'Remember what you told me about never letting anyone see you looking anything less than perfect?' I asked.

She nodded.

'Well, look.'

I handed her a small mirror from my bag.

'Oh shit,' said Lucy, staring at her reflection in disbelief, licking her finger and trying to rub off the wayward mascara.

'See what I mean? I'll get security to call you a cab. It can pick you up back here and the press won't see you.'

Lucy smiled weakly and took my hand.

'Thanks, Laura,' she said. 'You're my best friend, you know that?'

I pulled her to her shoeless feet. I knew what she'd done was disgraceful, but it was hard to be angry with her for long. She was a poor, pathetic, starved little creature, barefoot and friendless in a dingy London alleyway, and all she deserved was pity. When she threw her arms around me and cried like a baby, I stroked her tangled hair.

With Lucy safely sent off in a black cab I rejoined the party, but I wasn't in the mood to celebrate any more. Suddenly my life wasn't quite so shiny: my new boyfriend couldn't keep his dick in his jeans and my new best friend was a nymphomaniac who was almost certainly certifiable. What's more, the pair of them were not only screwy but quite possibly still screwing each other. When the club closed, the party moved on to the band's hotel. I followed out of habit rather than desire.

'You're quiet,' said Monica in the car on the way. 'Is it because of what I said earlier?'

We were alone in the limo. Ricky had gone on ahead with the rest of the band and their hangers-on.

'Not really,' I said. 'I just sometimes feel as if this whole world is a bit warped, you know?'

Monica sucked thoughtfully on a cigarette and nodded. 'None of it's real,' she said. 'And it won't last. It's just a temporary situation. Just enjoy the ride while you can.'

I didn't have a clue what she was talking about, but nodded anyway, in case she thought I was dumb.

Back at the Windsor Suite, the band were partying on. The girl band who'd been chatting up Lewis and Ricky earlier, were half undressed and dancing provocatively around the room.

'It's the first time these puppies have done drugs,' laughed Mal, looking on in glee.

'Their record company will be so pleased with you boys,' said Monica sarcastically, pushing an eighteen-year-old pop tart out of the way so that she could sit down.

'Where's Ricky?' I asked Lewis.

He pretended not to hear.

'Laura asked you where Ricky is, Lewis,' said Monica in her loud American drawl.

Lewis had apparently lost his hearing and was staring intently at his trainers.

'Is he with Venetia?' I asked, suddenly feeling bile rise to my mouth.

It was my birthday. Why was everything going wrong?

'He is with Venetia,' said Lewis eventually. 'But it's not what you think.'

Monica rolled her eyes heavenwards.

'It's the girl's birthday, for fuck's sake,' she shouted at Lewis, as if it were somehow his fault that Ricky had disappeared with the freak.

'Where are they?' I headed down the corridor towards Ricky's room, with Lewis following and Monica following Lewis.

'Don't go in, Laura. Leave it,' pleaded Lewis.

'Oh shut up, Lewis, you asshole,' spat Monica.

I threw open the door. Lewis was right, it wasn't what I'd expected. Ricky was slumped on the floor, head lolling against the wall, legs stretched out in front of him. His right shirtsleeve was pushed up and a piece of black rubber was tied tightly around his arm above the elbow. Ricky could see me – he was staring right at me – but there was no reaction at all. There wasn't even a flicker of life behind those black eyes. Beside him, Venetia was sitting barefoot on the carpet, a needle in her hand, injecting heroin between her toes. She sneered at me as she pushed the contents of the syringe into her bloodstream. I watched as her eyes rolled back and a big, sick smile appeared on her face.

'Holy shit,' said Monica.

'Whoops,' said Lewis.

'You fucking, stupid bastard,' I spat.

I could feel bile fill my mouth as I ran to the toilet. Monica followed me, and as I retched over the loo, she held back my hair. Afterwards, she sat beside me on the cold, shiny tiled floor.

'What is that all about?' I asked, still in shock.

She shook her head. 'I don't know. I've never seen Ricky do heroin before, or Venetia for that matter. I know some models are into smack – they inject it between their toes so the track marks don't show – but I didn't think it was Venetia's scene.'

Suddenly a terrifying thought hit me.

'Monica, I have unprotected sex with that guy and he's sharing needles with people!'

'Darling, he's sharing more than needles,' muttered Monica.

I shook my head slowly and said, 'Fuck, fuck, fuck, fuck…' over and over again.

'So, have an HIV test,' she said, lighting a cigarette and handing it to me. 'Chances are you'll be OK. But use condoms in future, for Christ's sake. I wouldn't let Lewis anywhere near me without a rubber on. And Jesus, I wouldn't touch Ricky's cock with Venetia!'

We sat in silence as I tried to get my head round the situation.

'I can't believe Ricky would inject heroin,' I said eventually. 'I mean coke, that I understand. It's a party drug. It's fun and it's harmless and it makes everyone have a good time but ...'

'Does it?' Monica looked at me with that raised eyebrow again.

'Well, yeah,' I continued. 'We all do it, right? So it can't be that bad.'

'I don't do cocaine,' said Monica.

'Don't you?' I was completely taken aback. All those times we'd all been together, sharing drugs, I'd never noticed her abstain. 'I just sort of assumed that you did.'

Monica shook her head. 'I can't stand drugs,' she said. 'I'll have a couple of drinks but other than that, count me out. That shit'll kill you in the end.'

I let her words penetrate my skull. She was the first person I'd come across in a long, long time who just said no.

'So what are you gonna do now?' she asked after a while.

'Go home,' I replied. 'Let his lordship sleep it off and see him in the morning. Aren't we all going to Cannes?'

Monica nodded as she stood up and smoothed down her dress.

'Well, I guess I'd better pack my bikinis and tomorrow I'll just get on with enjoying the ride,' I said.

'Good girl.' Monica held out her hands and pulled me to my feet.

When I climbed out of the taxi, I was surprised to see the Tartan Army van parked outside the house. Even Adam, with his Presbyterian work ethic, was hardly likely to be working at three thirty in the morning. There was a faint glow of light coming from the cracks around the doors. I banged loudly on the back of the van and shouted, 'Adam? You in there?'

The doors opened slowly with a creak and Adam's face

appeared. He looked most apologetic. I could see he'd been using a pile of black bin liners as a bed.

'Sorry, Laura,' he said. 'Sophia's kicked me out and I didn't know where else to go. I thought you'd be staying at Ricky's and wouldn't mind if I just dossed here in the van.'

He looked crumpled and uncomfortable, this huge great man shoved into the back of a small van, with all his worldly possessions in black plastic bags.

'Come inside, Adam,' I insisted. 'Let's have a cup of tea.'

We sat on diner-style stools at the stainless-steel breakfast bar of my state-of-the-art kitchen and drank huge mugs of steaming tea. Adam's night had been as eventful as mine. First Jasmine had offered him a job as resident handyman on her new DIY show. She had been quite insistent, apparently, and convinced that Adam's was the face of the future for Scorpion TV. Adam had politely declined.

'Why?' I asked, amazed that anyone would turn down a lucrative TV deal. It had been the making of me, after all.

'Because I don't think being famous looks like much fun,' he replied.

Just as he'd been getting over the shock of Jasmine's offer, Lucy had arrived with an even more ridiculous proposition. She had actually offered to pay him to become her resident gigolo while Billy Joe was out of the country. If any other man on the planet, other than the Pope, perhaps, had told me he'd turned down an offer of paid sex with Lucy Lloyd, I'd have thought he was lying, but Adam was so earnest and genuinely shaken by the experience that he was obviously telling the truth. Unfortunately, Sophia was not so trusting.

'She thought I'd gone off with Lucy,' said Adam in exasperation. 'I only went for a piss, and when I came back, she'd stormed off telling everybody who'd listen that I was sleeping with your nutter of a friend.

'Sorry,' I said.

'No, no, it's not your fault,' insisted Adam. 'You can't help it if your mate's a loony.'

The poor bloke had followed Sophia home only to find that she'd thrown all his worldly goods onto Shepherd's Bush roundabout.

'So I shoved the bags in the van and came here,' he shrugged. 'Didn't know what else to do.'

'She'll calm down,' I said. 'Talk to her tomorrow and sort it all out. You can stay here tonight. You'll have to sleep on the couch because I don't have a spare room, but that's your fault because you haven't built me one yet.'

'I'm not going back to Sophia,' said Adam thoughtfully. 'She's very possessive and jealous. I found all that passionate Italian stuff a turn-on at first but, to be honest, it's a pain in the neck. She wouldn't believe I wasn't sleeping with Lucy and she even thought I was sleeping with you when I first started working here.'

I looked up and caught Adam's piercing blue gaze. For a split second I wondered what it would be like to have sex with him. I looked away quickly, worried that he'd been able to read my mind.

'So, where are you going to live?' I asked.

'Oh, I'll just have a look in *Loot* tomorrow. Something will turn up. I only need a short let because I've decided to go home to Aberdeen once I've finished this place.'

'You have?' I was surprised. 'But I thought it was going well for you down here.'

'It is financially,' said Adam. 'But I'm not happy. I don't like London. The people are cold and unfriendly and it's too far from the sea. Anyway, I miss my mates.'

'Yeah, me too,' I said, thinking about Becky, who was a lot closer than Aberdeen.

'And I could do with having one of your granny's scones,' Adam grinned.

'Yuk.' I pulled a face. My mouth was numb with cocaine and dry from the champagne I'd drunk. I no longer craved sweet things. I had a constant empty feeling in my stomach, but I could never eat much. Food made me feel sick.

'You should eat more. You're too thin.' Adam blushed as he spoke and then apologized immediately. 'Sorry, that's none of my business.'

I was too tired to be offended.

'This is the shape I need to be to make it in television,' I explained. 'You need muscles for your job, I need to be thin for mine.'

'Fair enough, I suppose.' Adam picked up the empty mugs and rinsed them in the sink. He was very well trained.

'I guess I just like my women a bit more curvy,' he said, putting the mugs away in the correct cupboard.

I thought about Sophia's curves and felt a slight pang of something approaching nostalgia for the flesh I'd shed. Obviously, Adam didn't find me any more attractive than he found Lucy. He was one of those old-fashioned country boys who liked his women with meat on their bones and a flush of fresh air in their cheeks. We skinny London girls just didn't do it for him. With the air cleared of any sexual tension, I had an idea.

'Adam, why don't you move in here until the job's finished?' I suggested. 'It's just, well, I get a bit freaked out staying in the house on my own and Ricky's away on tour for most of the summer. I was convinced there was an armed robber in the garden the other night; turned out to be a reporter snooping around in my bins – lowlife scum! Anyway, what I'm trying to say is that I'd appreciate having a man about the place for security. I wouldn't charge you any rent and it would cut your commuting time by hours. What do you think?'

'I don't know.' Adam looked unsure. He was standing by the sink that he'd fitted, folding a tea towel neatly. Anyone would think he already lived there.

'I'd have to pay you rent,' he said thoughtfully.

'Rubbish,' I scoffed. 'How can I charge you for living in a house that you've built? Anyway, it's not as if I need the money.'

'That's not the point,' said Adam. 'Take a hundred pounds a week off my wages.'

'Fifty,' I compromised. He was a proud man.

'Deal,' agreed Adam.

We shook on it, even though his hands were covered in Fairy Liquid.

'So, you, better get one of those spare bedrooms finished quickly or you'll be on the couch for weeks,' I pointed out.

'Ricky won't like me staying here,' said Adam.

'Oh, who cares what he thinks?' I scoffed, picturing Ricky as I'd left him, smacked out on the bedroom floor. 'There are plenty of things Ricky Jones does that I don't like.'

And that was how the builder became my lodger. By the time I got back from Cannes, the second bedroom was finished and Adam had moved in.

13

The Incredible Shrinking Stars

'You're a disgrace!' Nat laughed, from behind her newspaper.

We were having a lazy Sunday afternoon, sheltering from the rain in my newly decorated front room. The hot weather had built up over the past few days into an airless inferno and London was suffocating. When the thunder woke me that morning and I heard the rain pounding the roof it was a blessed relief. Nat was lounging in my white leather armchair in my immaculate living room, perusing a pile of papers and magazines, her feet daintily sitting on a pink leather Moroccan pouf, while I painted her toenails scarlet. It was the end of July, she was almost eight months pregnant and her bump meant she could no longer reach her toes, so I'd been roped in as temporary pedicurist. I didn't mind, I hadn't seen her in weeks and it was good to catch up on news from the real world. Natalie and Rob had put in an offer on a seaside cottage on the Essex coast and were hoping to move in before the baby arrived. She had no plans to return to her job at *Glitz* after the baby was born. The thought of impending motherhood delighted her and she was more relaxed and happy than I'd ever seen her before.

'Why am I a disgrace?' I asked, concentrating on her little toe.

'Because you are one of the UK's Incredible Shrinking Stars!' she guffawed, turning the newspaper round for me to see.

There I was on Ahmed's yacht in Cannes, wearing white bikini bottoms and absolutely nothing else. I'd seen the photo a hundred times already in the past few weeks, and the sight of my naked breasts no longer upset me. This time, they'd placed it alongside one of the early promotional photos for Scorpion TV, taken the previous November when I was a hefty size twelve. The contrast was quite something and now, according to this particular paper, I was responsible – along with Lucy and a couple of supermodels – for giving the entire teenage population of Britain eating disorders.

'Cool,' I said. 'I hope my body doctor's seen that.'

'Cool?' Nat hit me over the head with the paper. 'It's not cool. You look emaciated.'

'No I don't,' I scoffed. 'You've just lost all perspective on what's normal because you're the size of a sumo wrestler.'

It was supposed to be a joke, but Nat frowned.

'I'm not the one who's lost perspective,' she warned me. 'And never, ever call a pregnant woman fat. She might sit on you.'

'Sorry,' I mumbled.

Nat went back to reading her paper in silence while I gave her toenails a second coat. She'd changed since she'd found out she was going to be a mum. There were no more wine binges, no shared Marlboro Lights, no late nights and she was even trying to stop swearing, scared that the little mite's first word might be an expletive if she carried on effing and blinding in her usual fashion. While I swanned off to parties and premieres, she spent her weekends in Bluewater shopping centre at Mothercare and Baby Gap. I felt as though I was losing her and it scared me rigid, because Natalie was the only real friend I had left from the days before the madness set in. With Nat, I didn't have to be Laura the TV Personality, I could just be myself.

'You didn't tell me much about Cannes,' she said eventually.

'Oh, it was fantastic,' I gushed. 'Like something out of an Eighties porn film. The yacht was absolutely fucking gigantic and totally OTT. Really tacky, actually. But so bad it was good, if you know what I mean. All money and no taste. Everything was gold-plated and embossed with the family coat of arms – Ahmed's dad has bought himself a title, Earl of Ealing or something or other. Anyway, I've never met anyone richer, and I'm friends with Lucy Lloyd! There were so many staff – Ahmed even hired topless models to carry solid gold trays of cocaine around. Can you believe it? They strutted around in G-strings and stilettos saying, "Excuse me, miss, would you care to indulge?" It was so cool.'

'Yeah, that's really cool, Laura,' said Nat sarcastically. 'You must be so proud.'

'Well, I enjoyed myself,' I said defensively. 'Apart from the press, of course. Christ, they wouldn't leave us alone.'

'Oh, I know,' mocked Natalie. 'Journalists, eh? Total scum.'

'I know, I know, you're a journalist, and I'm a journalist – well, used to be anyway – but it's different when you're on the other side, and I'm talking about the paparazzi anyway, not normal journalists. They followed us around in speedboats,' I explained. 'That's how they got that photo.' I nodded at the topless snap in the newspaper she was still holding.

'And you hated every minute of the attention, of course,' said Nat.

'Well, I suppose it's a wee bit flattering,' I giggled.

'Thought so.'

Nat tossed the tabloid onto the polished wooden floor and picked up a glossy Sunday supplement from one of the upmarket broadsheets.

'Time for something a little more highbrow,' she announced. 'Hopefully this won't be splattered with pictures of your tits.'

I blew on Natalie's toes to dry the nail varnish as she flicked, absent-mindedly, through the pages. Suddenly, she stopped and sat bolt upright, jerking her foot out of my hand and smudging her bright red nails.

'Well, fuck me,' she hissed, forgetting the no-swear rule. 'The little shit.'

'What?' Something in the way she was looking at me told me I wasn't going to like whatever it was she'd just found.

'You're not going to like this,' she warned me, holding the magazine to her chest.

'Is it Ricky?' I asked, my heart in my throat. Please don't let it be Ricky … again.

'No, not this time,' Nat took a deep sigh. 'It's that bastarding ex-boyfriend of yours. He's only gone and done a kiss-and-tell.'

'What? Pete?' I was flabbergasted. 'But he hates all that celebrity tittle-tattle.'

'Well, he has written it in a pretentious way, with a pseudo-psychological what-it's-like-when-your-ex-becomes-famous twist and it is in this pompous rag, but,' Natalie handed me the feature, 'it's still a kiss-and-tell.'

Pete had a photo byline. He was wearing glasses – although I'm sure they were for effect because there was nothing wrong with his eyesight the last time I'd seen him – and was staring out from the page with a grave frown of self-importance. LIFE WITHOUT LAURA was the headline, followed by a long-drawn-out first-person account of a relationship that bore very little resemblance to the one I'd had with Pete. He painted a picture of a super-ambitious but naive 'rough diamond' – me – who'd been plucked from the gutter by an intellectual and highly successful journalist – him. In true Professor Higgins style, Pete had polished and preened the little tramp into submission and created a highly marketable product. Then, when the TV offers arrived, the heartless little wretch had callously dumped the kindly professor – as if – and run off with a rascal of a rock star. Of course, the professor had had the last laugh, though, because the rock star turned out to be a womanizing heroin addict – how did Pete know that? – the fair lady developed an eating disorder – why did everyone think I was anorexic? – and they all lived miserably ever after. Except for the nice journalist/professor, who made pots of money from selling his story.

'Sue him,' said Nat. 'Not one bit of that story is true.'

'Do you know what?' I replied. 'I don't think I'll give him the satisfaction of reacting.'

I was getting used to reading about myself in the press. Sometimes it was hilarious, like the time some journalist supposedly traced my family tree and had me down as a direct descendant of Braveheart's, and sometimes it was flattering – I had been voted Britain's sexiest woman in one of the lad mags, beating Lucy and Venetia to the top spot. That moment of glory was only spoilt when I overheard Ricky and Lewis discussing the top ten. 'I've had eight of them,' boasted my boyfriend proudly. The press could even be completely harmless – I didn't mind at all when the papers picked up on the fact that Lucy Lloyd had bought me a baby-blue Mercedes convertible, identical to her own, for my birthday in June. It was when it got personal that it hurt. When friends were the ones behind the stories or when the hacks had been hounding my family. Poor Fiona was followed home to her nurses' digs in Leith by one journalist, who later wrote about the squalor she was living in while her big sister renovated a townhouse in a salubrious London location. I felt so guilty that I bought her a two-bedroom flat in a Georgian terrace in Edinburgh's New Town. And now here was Pete, the sad bastard, demanding his pound of flesh.

'But there's no way Ricky's going to let him get away with this stuff about heroin, is there?' asked Nat. 'That's got to be libellous. Shall I phone Rob? There's no point in being married to a solicitor if you can't get free legal advice when you need it.'

She reached for her mobile while I sat glued to the spot and said nothing.

'Laura?' Nat looked concerned. 'It's not true, is it?'

There was no way I could deny it so I said nothing.

'Laura, am I phoning Rob or is there something you want to tell me?'

Ricky had been rumbled.

'He dabbles. Sometimes,' I explained, in the words Ricky had used to excuse his behaviour to me. 'But it's nothing serious. He's definitely not an addict. He doesn't have an addictive personality, you see, so he doesn't need to worry about things like that ...'

'Laura, have you been visited by aliens and used in a scientific experiment that involved removing your brain?' Natalie looked incredulous.

'Not to my knowledge,' I conceded.

'So why are you spouting that shit at me?' she asked. 'I don't believe it, you don't believe it; and if Ricky Jones believes it, then he's even more brain-dead than your average smackhead. I presume, it was the Right Hon Richard who fed you that bullshit.'

I nodded, but at least I had the good grace to blush.

'Yeah, well, he's an adult,' I muttered. 'It's up to him what he does to abuse himself.'

'You haven't ... You wouldn't ...' Nat looked concerned.

'No!' I shrieked. 'Don't be ridiculous. I'd never touch heroin.'

'You used to say that about coke,' she said quietly, putting her shoes back on even though her nail varnish wasn't yet dry. 'I'd better get going.'

I didn't want her to go. I wanted to tell her about all the things that had been bothering me lately. Not just the heroin fiasco, but about Ricky's philandering and his weird relationship with Lucy and Venetia and God knows who else. Then there was Lucy herself. She was on the edge. The only reason she could still string a sentence together was because the Snowman kept her artificially afloat with enough uppers and downers to fuel a hot air balloon. She carried so many pills around in her handbag that it rattled; the only legal substance she took was the Prozac she'd been prescribed for her manic depression. I wanted to tell Nat about the HIV test I'd had and how scared I'd been waiting for the results – negative, thank God. About how difficult it was to contact Ricky when he was away on tour. His schedule was manic and he was hard to track down; he was never in the room he said he'd be in, or the right hotel, or city, or country even. But it seemed ridiculously petty to complain when I was sitting in this amazing house, with so much money in the bank and enough success to keep me in the headlines week after week. So I kept my mouth shut and saw her to the door.

'You're all right, aren't you, Laura?' she asked gently on the doorstep. 'I mean, you're happy, right?'

'Ecstatic.' I nodded, probably with a touch too much enthusiasm.

Natalie frowned and said, 'Hmm,' before waddling down the path, past the small group of press and my two resident stalkers, who were constantly camped outside the house. I watched her from the window as she met Adam at the gate, coming the other way. He grinned at her broadly and stooped down to kiss her on the cheek. I watched him put his hand gently on her bump, and although they were too far away for me to hear what was said, I could tell from the way he cocked his head to one side that he was asking questions about the baby. I realized that I hadn't even asked Nat how she was feeling. Adam was carrying an open bag of chips and I could see a can of lager shoved into his denim jacket pocket. He said his goodbyes to Natalie and then stopped to chat to the tabloid hacks on the way past, even offering them a chip. He'd been playing pool in a Camden Town boozer all afternoon with some Scottish mates, and from the silly smile on his face it was obvious he'd had a shandy or two.

'Hi, honey, I'm home,' he called in a bad American accent as he let himself in noisily.

'You're pissed,' I said accusingly.

'You're sober,' he replied, taking off his scruffy trainers obediently at the door. 'Makes a change. Quick, open a bottle of champers, dahling. You can't have the staff being more sozzled than you are.'

Actually, it was a relief to see Adam a bit worse for wear. I loved having him in the house because it made the place seem safe, but he could be a bit too much of a good boy for my liking sometimes. He was so clean-cut I felt kind of scuzzy in comparison. As far as I could see his only vices were the odd pint of lager and the very occasional roll-up, which he'd smoke slowly on the back step after he'd finished the day's work. Plus, he had a habit of asking me probing questions which I didn't want to answer.

'Nat's a nice girl,' he said, sitting cross-legged on the wooden floor with his chips laid out in front of him. He opened his can of lager without spilling any.

'She's lovely,' I agreed.

'Did you have lots of nice friends like her before?' he asked.

'Before what?' I knew exactly what he meant, but found the insinuation insulting.

'Before all this.' Adam swept his arm around the painfully stylish living room he'd created for me.

'I've still got lots of nice friends,' I said defensively.

'No you haven't,' said Adam with the honesty of a drunken man. 'They're horrible.'

'I like them,' I replied.

I stomped off to the kitchen to grab a bottle of champagne from the fridge as Adam had suggested. It was true that I didn't like to see my staff having a better time than I was. When I returned, Adam was still waxing lyrical about my choice of friends.

'What about Lucy?' he asked.

'What about her?'

'Do you like her. I mean, *really* like her?'

''Course I do.'

'It's just, I don't understand what there is to like.' Adam held up his bag of chips. 'Want one?'

I shook my head.

'I've got a theory,' announced Adam.

'Oh yes? The builder's going to try his hand at psychology, is he?'

'Yup,' said Adam. 'I don't think you do like Lucy. I think you just like the idea of Lucy liking you.'

'Don't be ridiculous, Adam,' I scoffed, reaching for my special box of goodies, which contained my drug stash.

'It's because you're normal,' he continued.

'Am I now?' I asked, racking myself up a line.

'You are. Still. A little bit anyway. And you think it's really cool to be liked by this big star. It's the same with Ricky.'

'Right.' I snorted a fat line loudly. Adam had seen me do it a thousand times and no longer seemed to notice.

'You think you're in love with him,' Adam carried on, 'but you just love the idea of being loved by him, which is a shame, because he doesn't love anyone but himself. Never will.'

'Adam, are you going to shut up now before I evict you?' I could feel the coke rush to my head and suddenly everything seemed a lot more amusing.

'You can't chuck me out,' said Adam. 'I haven't finished the downstairs toilet yet and anyway you need me as your live-in social secretary. Who else is going to field the endless phone messages that you never return. I spoke to your gran earlier, by the way. She'd really like it if you gave her a call. She misses you.'

'I'll do it tomorrow,' I promised but we both knew I was lying. The last thing I needed was another lecture.

As usual, I offered Adam a line of charlie. As usual, he politely declined.

'I don't understand that stuff either,' he said.

'It makes me more interesting,' I explained.

'No it doesn't,' said Adam, looking serious suddenly. 'You're a lot more interesting when you're being you.'

14

Screen legend collapses with exhaustion

Lucy was suffering from exhaustion – that was the official line, at least, when she was hurriedly checked into an exclusive rehab clinic in Surrey. I had arrived at her apartment as arranged. We were going to travel to Hampshire together to watch Sugar Reef headline at the last festival of the summer. I'd spent many hours and obscene amounts of cash getting ready for the big reunion with Ricky, and I was delighted with the slightly dishevelled, just-got-out-of-bed look I'd achieved with the help of Daniel's curling tongs and the chic assistants at Harvey Nics. In a vintage-looking tea dress and cowboy boots, I thought I looked suitably casual. It wasn't as if I was a festie virgin. Hell no. And I'd been in enough VIP areas to know that the celebrities who chose to wear high heels to such outdoor events just looked deeply uncool as they spilled warm beer on their overdone outfits and got their stilettos stuck in the grass. I'd gone to all the festivals the previous summer with Becky, so proud of the press passes I'd managed to blag for us from the organizers in exchange for a couple of pages of coverage in *Glitz*. Each time we slept in a tent, pissed in a Portaloo and went without washing all weekend. My rucksack never contained anything more glamorous than a hoodie, a cagoule and a pair of flip flops. There was no point in even trying to wear make-up – it would either be sweated or rained off – and hair had to be tied back at all times. I always arrived home looking like Stig of the Dump. It once took us seven hours to get the hire car out of the muddy field it was parked in and we didn't get back to London until Monday morning. I'd gone straight into the office wearing muddy jeans, wellies and a sweat-drenched T-shirt, and Trudy had given me a lecture on my scruffy appearance and explained that I should 'retain an aura of glamour at all times when representing the magazine'. I seem to remember I fell asleep in the fashion cupboard at lunchtime and didn't wake up until Graham found me at five to five. This time would be very different. We were being driven to Hampshire in Lucy's chauffeur-driven, air-conditioned limo and then helicoptered straight to the VIP area, where we'd be met by security guards and escorted to Sugar Reef's tour bus. Ricky and I had an hour or two to reacquaint ourselves with each other's bodies before the band were due on stage. The sun shone obediently for the occasion and the future was so bright I had to wear shades – Gucci ones. I couldn't wait to get going and hoped Lucy was ready.

When I got out of the lift I found Lucy's PA, Karen, lounging on the oriental cushions in the living room, tucking into a bottle of Bollinger, wearing her employer's best Chanel trouser suit and chattering happily into the telephone. Lucy was nowhere to be seen. Karen didn't notice me at first, so I stood eavesdropping in the doorway for a moment.

'Mum, you'll never guess what's happened now. She's in the nuthouse!' she was saying in the gleeful tones of somebody imparting top-notch gossip. 'The silly bitch has totally lost it this time. Her brain's frazzled by the charlie … Cocaine, mother, get with it … It's making her nose disintegrate, too … Yes, it was a bit frightening actually. When I turned up this morning she was still asleep and I couldn't wake her up. Honestly, I thought she was dead for a minute. I mean I could see she was still breathing, but there was this foam around her mouth and she looked kind of grey ... No, not so pretty any more. If her public could see her without her clothes and make-up they'd be shocked, I'm telling you. She looks like a prisoner of war. Anyway, I called her doctor in a panic ... Yeah, I know I should have phoned for an ambulance, but she'd got this real Rottweiler of an agent called Sylvia Smith, and I've been well briefed about what to do in an emergency. She'd have killed me if I'd got the authorities involved because it would be in all the papers tomorrow. So when the doctor arrived, he said she'd taken enough sleeping tablets to knock out an elephant. He had to give her an injection of something to get her to come round. Then, once she was conscious she started ranting and raving like a madwoman. She wasn't making any sense. Kept going on about her baby ... No, course she hasn't got any kids ... I suppose it is a bit of a shame, but she's brought it on herself, really. She's got everything, Mum, and she's just throwing it away. She's just so spoilt, with more money than sense. She spends more on drugs a week than she pays me a month ... Well, she's booked into rehab for two weeks and then she's got an appointment with a plastic surgeon on Harley Street to have a metal plate inserted in her nose to stop it collapsing ... It is sad, but at least I'll get a bit of a break for a while, with her locked away out of trouble ... Mmm, yeah, definitely time to look for a new job, Mum ... I know, you didn't bring me up to play skivvy to a jumped-up drug addict ...'

I could feel the colour drain from my face as I realized what had happened.

'Is she all right?' I demanded.

Karen jumped in surprise at the sound of my voice. She looked up at me, mouth open in horror.

'Mum, I'd better go,' she muttered quickly and hung up.

'Laura, I'm so sorry,' she began, looking sheepishly at the champagne glass in her hand and the designer clothes on her body, but I stopped her, holding my hand up firmly and narrowing my eyes in an attempt to look as disgusted as possible. The truth was, I couldn't really blame her for sharing the scandal. In her position, I'd have done exactly the same. Lucy couldn't really expect much loyalty from an employee she barely paid the minimum wage and referred to as 'that girl'. And it wasn't so long ago that I'd had a boss from hell myself.

'Is she all right?' I repeated.

'You won't tell Lucy about this, will you?' Karen's voice was shaky. 'It's just, I can't afford to be sacked if I don't have another job lined up, and I was only telling my mum. She won't say a word to anyone, I promise.'

'No, I won't tell her.' I shook my head and sat down beside her. 'I just want to know what's going on. Is anybody with her? Where's she been taken?'

Almost subconsciously I reached for the Bolly and took a hefty swig from the bottle. Karen looked at me as if I was as mad as Lucy.

Karen explained that Lucy had been taken to the Rainbow Clinic, which at £1,000 a night bore more resemblance to an exclusive health spa than a psychiatric hospital. There, she would be kept off the coke, forced into eating regular meals and be seen by psychiatrists, psychologists, physicians and beauty therapists.

I felt a pang of relief that Lucy was stepping off the crazy funfair ride for a while and wondered if I needed a break, too. But I quickly banished the idea – I was still in control, wasn't I? I thought about how scared Lucy must be feeling – but at least she was getting help. 'It'll do her good,' I thought out loud.

'I hope so,' said Karen. 'She's been a nightmare to work for these last few months.'

'You know, Lucy's not that bad,' I explained to her downtrodden PA as she put away the empty champagne bottle. 'Not deep down. She's just like a child, really, but all this mad stuff has happened to her and it's messed with her head.'

'Yeah, whatever,' said Karen. 'I'll just get out of this suit.'

With Lucy neatly dispatched to rehab, I was left with a rather serious problem: who would come with me to the music festival and how would we get there without Lucy's limo? It hit me again that I was becoming a bit short of friends, so in a fit of pity for the plight of the lowly PA I decided to invite Cathy. We could drive the Mercedes – it didn't get driven much because I was rarely sober enough to get behind the wheel – and meet up with the helicopter as planned. Cathy was the one who'd liaised with Ricky's PA to make the arrangements, so at least she'd know where to go. I was a bit surprised when Cathy said she couldn't make it because it was her boyfriend Gareth's birthday. I had to pull rank, have a mini temper tantrum *and* invite the boyfriend along too before she eventually agreed.

I'd never been in a helicopter before. Gareth seemed delighted by the change of plan for his birthday celebrations. I'd never met him before, but I wasn't surprised to discover that Cathy had chosen a complete gem for a boyfriend; she was a bright girl, after all. He was trendy and good-looking in a nerdy sort of way. The kind of bloke who wore black-rimmed media-whore glasses, collected old copies of *The Face* and knew everything there was to know about computer games and dance music. He sat up front with the pilot and drank in this new experience while Cathy and I sat behind, staring in awe out of the window at the Hampshire countryside.

'Well, you know what to get Gareth for Christmas,' I shouted to Cathy.

'Eh?' she mouthed back.

'Helicopter flying lessons,' I replied.

She nodded enthusiastically.

As the helicopter approached the festival site I began to make out fields dotted with makeshift campsites; hundreds of marquees housing dance tents, circus acts and bars; caravans selling hot pork sandwiches or housing cashpoints; and a playing field which had earlier hosted the celebrity football match Ricky had competed in. As we swooped lower, I could make out tiny little people thronging around the three stages. It was a blisteringly hot day, perfect festival conditions, and the crowds were out in force.

The helicopter landed in a field between Hospitality – for celebs, journalists, TV crews, industry insiders, sponsors and various VIPs – and the guest parking area. We waved our thanks to the pilot and jumped out of the machine. The blades caused a force-ten gale which we had to run through and I was glad I'd chosen the tousled look for my hair that day. We were collected by a security guard, who bustled us into a waiting Range Rover and sped us into guest parking, where we pulled up beside Sugar Reef's tour bus. Naturally, theirs was the biggest, boldest, brassiest, bestest bus in the place, a huge gold monstrosity of a vehicle with blacked-out windows. It had been imported from America and was approximately the size of an InterCity 125. I often wondered how it managed to actually move, let alone speed along the

UK's motorway network night after night. Apparently it could comfortably sleep twenty-five. Not that much sleep ever went on in the Sugar Reef tour bus. It had two bathrooms, a fully stocked bar, five separate sleeping compartments, a kitchen and an enormous lounge area with built-in bed settees and a cinema-sized flat-screen satellite TV. It played MTV twenty-four hours a day and the band always whooped with delight when they saw themselves appear on screen. As my dad says, 'Small things amuse small minds.'

The security guard knocked on the door while we waited in the Range Rover. He was greeted from the inner sanctum of the tour bus by another security guard. Both men looked around the car park commando-fashion before speaking into their handsets and nodding in our direction. It was safe to enter.

'Laura, I think we'll just head straight for the main stage,' said Cathy as we clambered out.

'Oh, don't you want to come in and meet the band, Gareth?' I was surprised.

Gareth smiled sweetly and said, 'No, you're all right. Cathy tells me you haven't seen Ricky for over a month. You need some time to yourselves.'

'Give me a ring on the mobile later if you want to hook up,' said Cathy. 'But we've got our passes and a tent in the rucksack, so don't feel obliged. We'll be fine. Anyway, we don't want to miss The Kills. They're on in half an hour. Bye.'

'Bye, then,' I said as they ran off excitedly in the direction of the gig.

I found Ricky sitting bare-chested and cross-legged on a sofa, head down, rolling a spliff on a copy of *GQ*. He wasn't wearing any shoes and his hair had grown so much that his long fringe now completely covered his face. I always forgot how sexy the man was whenever we were apart, so when he looked up and smiled lazily at me with those black eyes, my knees almost buckled.

'Princess,' he said in his slow drawl. 'You've arrived. Let the celebrations begin.'

He continued to roll his joint, but nodded for me to join him.

'Come here and give your old man a snog.'

I clambered beside him, held his beautiful head in my hands and kissed him so hard that he had to put down the magazine. I tried not to think about where those tasty, full lips had been over the last few weeks.

'So, where's little Lucy Loo?' he asked, peering behind me as if she might have been quietly waiting in the wings – Lucy. Quiet. As if!

'Rehab,' I explained. 'The Rainbow Clinic. She took too many jellies last night and Karen couldn't wake her this morning.'

'Heavy shit,' said Ricky, lighting his joint. 'Sounds nasty, man. D'you hear that, Lewis?'

For some bizarre reason known only to himself, Lewis was lying on his back on another sofa with a T-shirt covering his face, gently fondling his guitar. He removed the T-shirt and squinted over at us.

'Oh hi, Laura. Didn't hear you arrive. I was meditating, ready for the gig.' Lewis rubbed his eyes. 'What's happened to Lucc?'

'Rehab,' said Ricky. 'Again.'

'Heavy, man,' agreed Lewis before replacing the T-shirt and going back to his meditation.

'Has she been there before?' I asked.

'Sure has,' said Ricky. 'Couple of times. She hates it because she can't get her hands on any gear in there. Mind you, she's never actually OD'd before. Silly little thing. Does Billy Joe know?'

'Don't think so,' I said.

Ricky ordered one of his minions to get Billy Joe on the phone and spent the next half-hour talking transatlantically to his mate about Lucy while I watched MTV. I felt, somewhat uncharitably, angry that even safely tucked away in rehab she could still remain the centre of attention and get in the way of my long-awaited reunion with Ricky. By the time he got off the phone he had to start getting ready to go on stage.

This involved changing out of one pair of jeans and into another. All his jeans looked the same – well worn, Seventies-style, low slung, tight around the skinny hips and slightly flared. He pulled on a vintage Rolling Stones T-shirt and grinned at his reflection in the full-length mirror.

'My tribute to Mick,' he explained, proudly.

He finished off the look with his trusty old black leather biker boots and a slick of gel in his long hair. It had taken him less than five minutes to get ready, but he looked every inch the rock idol. Five security men were waiting at the door of the tour bus to escort the band to the main stage. They were already ten minutes late, but nobody seemed to be in any rush and the boys casually polished off a gram of charlie between them before strolling out, shades firmly in place, into the hazy late-evening sunshine.

The minute I stepped off the bus I heard it. 'Ri-cky, Ricky, Ri-cky!' It was muted at first, but as we got closer to the back of the stage it got louder and louder and louder, until I could feel the air vibrate with the fervent voices of 10,000 excited fans. I swear I could smell the anticipation in the air as I followed the band up the steps that led to the backstage area.

I grabbed hold of Ricky's hand and gushed, 'Wow! This must be more exciting than any drug.'

He had a wild glint in his eyes, like a tiger about to pounce on his prey. He kissed my forehead, not tenderly, but hard, like a head-butt, and said, 'This is the ultimate buzz. Better than drugs, better than sex, better than anything else in the whole fucking world.'

It was then that I realized I would never be Ricky Jones's number one. But it wasn't the other women I had to worry about, it was the music, and I could never compete with that.

'Ready, guys?' he shouted. The band nodded. 'Let's do it then!'

The other four ran on stage first to the manic screams of the crowd.

'Ri-cky, Ri-cky, Ri-cky!' The chanting reached a crescendo.

'Babes,' said Ricky to me as he wandered backwards towards his fans. 'I'll come off stage for a couple of minutes after "Notoriety". Have a couple of lines racked up for me, OK?'

And with that he swaggered arrogantly out onto his pedestal and scowled at the heaving ocean of adoring faces. Behind the crowd, the sun set perfectly over a field in Hampshire.

I stood in the wings and watched in awe as row upon row of blokes, long-haired Ricky wannabes each and every one, jumped up and down, mouthing his words back to him. Girls clambered onto their boyfriends' shoulders wearing Sugar Reef T-shirts and screaming, 'I love you, Ricky!' One pretty young thing with long, blonde pigtails, whipped off her T-shirt and jiggled braless to the music. Needless to say, the cameramen noticed and her naked torso was soon adorning the huge screen behind the band. Ricky noticed, too.

'That's it, girls. Get naked!' he shouted.

Five thousand Sugar Reef T-shirts were shed. Ten thousand naked breasts bounced for the band. Ricky grinned wickedly. He had the power. I was witnessing it first hand and now I understood what Monica had told me: there was no way this man could ever be faithful and it was something I was going to have to learn to live with. Ricky strutted around the stage, his skinny hips gyrating like a twenty-first-century Elvis, his full lips practically eating the microphone as his gravelly voice belted out hit after hit. No wonder the guy had elephantiasis of the ego. How could anyone receive this amount of adulation without beginning to believe he was actually a god? At that moment, I believed it myself.

15

Sisters are doing it for themselves

I rested my head on Ricky's bare stomach and gazed up at the blue, blue sky through the branches of the tree we lay beneath. Ricky was smoking a cigarette with one hand and twisting a lock of my hair absent-mindedly with the other while humming some nameless tune that would no doubt become an international hit once he'd thought up some lyrics to go with it. Through the cigarette smoke, I watched a bumblebee circle my head, then shooed it away gently when it looked as if it might land on my nose. We were lying on top of Primrose Hill in the late-afternoon sunshine, having polished off two boxes of strawberries and three bottles of champagne. Monica and Lewis dozed comfortably beside us on the cashmere blanket I'd provided. Their bodies fitted together like two spoons in a cutlery drawer, with his chest moulded to her back. Lewis's arm was casually slung around Monica's waist. They looked like a couple who'd been together for a very long time. It had been a glorious afternoon and my head swam with champagne and happiness.

'Lucy gets out tomorrow,' said Ricky, breaking the comfortable silence.

'She does,' I agreed.

'I think we should do something to celebrate,' he suggested.

'Such as?' I wondered.

'A party,' decided Ricky. 'A dirty, big, stonking night of hedonism. What do you think?'

Monica, who had appeared to be sleeping, said drily, 'That's a great idea, Ricky. Lucy's spent two weeks being detoxed and you want to pump her full of drugs and alcohol the minute she gets out. You're a real pal. You know I'm not Lucy's greatest fan, but even I don't want to fry what's left of her brain.'

'Hey, it's what Lucy would want,' Ricky protested.

'He's right,' murmured Lewis sleepily. 'She'll be dying to have some fun. A party's the least we can do for her.'

'If you say so,' said Monica. 'But if your little friend ends up back in rehab, you'll have no one to blame but yourselves.'

'Monica, sometimes I wonder what I'm doing with somebody so straight,' pondered Lewis.

'Yeah, you're like an old woman with all your worrying,' added Ricky.

'Jesus, if I don't worry about you guys, nobody will, and you'll all be dead by the time you're thirty.' Monica smiled but her eyes looked sad.

'Where will we have the party?' I asked, hoping nobody would suggest trashing my newly decorated dream home.

'At my place,' said Ricky.

'What place?' I asked. 'The hotel?'

'No,' he scoffed. 'Hurlingham Manor. The olds are in St Barts. We'll do it on Sunday. It always feels particularly decadent to have a party on a Sunday, don't you think?'

'Nice one,' said Lewis. 'An all-dayer?'

'It would be rude not to,' said Ricky. 'I'll let old Fergie know we're coming. Laura, I need to get my phone out of my pocket, can you move, please?'

I reluctantly sat up. The afternoon was over.

*

'You've got a visitor,' said Adam as Ricky, Lewis, Monica and I trooped into the house.

'Have I?' I wasn't expecting anyone.

'And she's a bit of a handful. She's in the bath.' Adam blushed.

My first thought was that it was Lucy, escaped from rehab and already throwing herself at Adam. It was hot outside and he wasn't wearing a shirt; she wouldn't be able to resist. I heard footsteps on the stairs and looked up, as did Ricky, Lewis and Monica. A long, shapely pair of bare legs descended the staircase, slowly revealing a short white towel and a waist-length mane of curly, blonde hair. It certainly wasn't Lucy, this body had curves.

'Fiona!' I shouted in surprise and delight. 'What are you doing here?'

Lewis and Ricky shared a certain look I'd seen before in the presence of nubile young beauty. Monica saw it too and rolled her eyes heavenwards.

'My little sister,' I explained to her apologetically. 'She's twenty-one.'

'So I see,' said Monica.

'I've come to stay for a week,' announced Fiona, pecking Ricky on the cheek as if he were some long-lost friend. He patted her bottom affectionately. 'Mum and Dad think I'm in Marbella. I'm banned from seeing you. You're a bad influence allegedly. The weather better be good or they'll wonder why I haven't got a tan.'

She hugged me so hard that her towel slipped, and when she disentangled her body from mine, a stray nipple was poking out for all to see.

'Oops,' she giggled. 'Can I wear something of yours, Laura? My clothes are so boring.'

'Fiona, you have no idea how brilliant it is to see you, but you should have called,' I said in a fluster. 'I might have been working, or away for a few days, or ...'

'In which case Adam would have looked after me, wouldn't you, Ad?' She smiled saucily at him, making him blush again.

'Just as well we're here then,' Ricky interjected, 'or you would have had a very boring time. You're not really going to see much of the high life hanging out with a builder, are you?'

'Oh, I dunno,' said Fiona. 'I've seen some interesting sights already.'

Adam muttered something about building a pergola in the garden and left – presumably to stop himself from bashing Ricky over the head with the spade he was carrying.

'Cute,' said Monica to his retreating backside. 'Nice ass.'

Fiona nodded in agreement as Ricky and Lewis seethed.

'So, what's happening tonight?' asked Fiona, bright eyes shining with anticipation.

'You're getting dressed,' I said, taking her by the shoulders and shoving her back up the stairs.

The others left, having arranged to meet us at a party in Chelsea later.

I found my little sister in my bedroom. To me, Fiona looked slim, so I was surprised to find she couldn't fit into any of my clothes.

'Size eight!' she said in disgust, throwing a pair of cropped red trousers onto the growing pile of designer clothes that covered my bed. 'Don't you ever eat?'

'Not if I can help it,' I replied.

'From a medical point of view that's not very clever. Got any tens?' she asked, stepping deeper into my walk-in wardrobe.

'Somewhere at the back is the stuff I was wearing in the spring. They should fit fine.'

I went for a shower and left my poor defenceless wardrobe in Fiona's hands. When I returned she was filling a little black strapless number obscenely well. She was more of a twelve than a ten, so her cleavage oozed over the top and her thighs strained the seams of the skirt, but somehow she got away with it.

'You look lovely,' I told her. 'A bit like a porn star, but lovely.'

Fiona stood, staring out of the bedroom window that looked over the back garden.

'What's so interesting out there?' I asked.

'Adam,' she replied. 'He's got his top off and I was just admiring his muscles. He really is a very fine specimen indeed. Don't you think?'

'Everybody fancies Adam,' I laughed. 'You, Lucy, Monica, Gran ...'

'You?' asked Fiona.

'Nah,' I scoffed. 'He's a bit too beefcake for me. Anyway, he's way too clean-cut. I prefer my men a bit dangerous.'

'That's one way of putting it,' said Fiona, without taking her eyes off the view. 'Ricky's definitely not safe, that's for sure.'

'What d'you mean? I thought you liked him.'

'I do. But he's not really the sort of bloke to settle down and live happily ever after.'

'Who says that's what I want?'

'That's what most people want, even super-successful career women like you. But not Ricky; he's not the settling-down type. I can tell.'

'So, do you think I'm stupid for seeing him?'

'No. I think it's a once-in-a-lifetime opportunity to shag

one of the sexiest men on the planet and I think you'd be mad not to.'

'Thank you. I think.'

'But don't get hurt, Laura. Please.'

'I won't. I'm just having a good time,' I promised, but I already knew that if Ricky ever left me I'd be devastated.

'Is Adam single?'

'Think so.'

'What do you mean "think so"? You live with the bloke. You must have noticed whether or not he's got a girlfriend.'

'He's never brought anyone back here, so I suppose he's unattached.'

'Good. Do you think I've got a chance?'

I looked at my little sister standing at the window, her body silhouetted by the sunlight and a soft halo of golden curls falling around her angelic face. I wondered if any man would be able to resist. I had a sneaking suspicion that my man wouldn't for a start.

'You could have him like that.' I clicked my fingers. 'I know he likes curves, so you're definitely his type, and he misses home, so the fact that you're Scottish is a bonus, but he can be quite shy sometimes, so take it easy. He can't stand flashy women – he's terrified of Lucy and he tells me I'm acting like a pretentious idiot all the time – so don't try to impress him. He's really boy next doorish, if you know what I mean.'

'The boy next door to us never looked like that,' scoffed Fiona, and we both laughed because poor Malcolm McAlistair at number six had never been much of a looker.

'D'you think he'll come out with us tonight?' asked Fiona.

'Who? Malcolm McAlistair?'

'Ha, ha. No. Adam.'

'You could ask him, but he's got a bit of a thing going on with Ricky, so I'm not sure he'll be too keen.'

'What do you mean, "a thing"?' asked Fiona.

'Basically, they hate each other,' I explained. 'They just rub each other up the wrong way.'

'He's probably just jealous.'

'Yeah, probably. I suppose a builder would feel a bit intimidated by a rock star.'

'No, silly.' Fi giggled. 'I meant that Ricky's probably jealous of Adam. He's so used to being the best-looking bloke in the room that he can't stand the competition.'

I was pleasantly surprised when Adam accepted Fiona's invitation to join us for the night. Flash model-agency parties on the King's Road were hardly his usual scene, so I was convinced the only reason he was tagging along was because he fancied Fi. I liked the idea of them getting it together and decided to do everything in my power to encourage the coupling. I quite fancied myself as a matchmaker. Adam was a lovely bloke and Fiona had been single for an obscene length of time. At the party, I manoeuvred them into a corner and tried to imprison them there by blocking their path to the bar and toilets. To my delight, they spent the entire evening giggling together over pints of lager while Ricky sneered, 'I don't know what she sees in him,' and Monica cooed, 'I'm jealous.' When Ricky, Lewis, Monica and I decided to go on to a private members' bar in Soho in the early hours, Fiona said she was knackered and wanted to go home to bed and Adam offered to take her.

'I think she's pulled,' smiled Monica as Fiona and Adam left together.

'Mission accomplished,' I agreed and we clinked cocktail glasses.

I got up at lunchtime and found Fiona pouring herself

a glass of fresh orange juice in the kitchen. She was wearing one of my bikinis and her skin shimmered with suntan oil. It was another scorching day and she'd obviously been sunbathing in the garden.

'So?' I demanded.

'What?' she asked.

'Did anything happen with Adam?'

She shook her head and sighed. 'No, he was the perfect gentleman. Paid for the cab, made me a cuppa and then went to bed. Alone.'

'Bummer. Never mind, you've got all week to work on him.'

'I know. He's out there now,' she said, nodding towards the garden. 'I thought this might work.' She indicated the itsy-bitsy bikini.

'Should do the trick,' I agreed.

I desperately wanted Adam to come with us to the party, but Ricky had made it clear, in no uncertain terms, that manual labourers were not welcome at Hurlingham Manor unless they were on the payroll.

'Listen, stay here for a minute,' I told Fiona. 'I'll just have a little word with Adam and see where you stand.'

'OK, but don't be too obvious, Laura.'

'Subtlety is my middle name,' I insisted. 'I interview people for a living, remember. Trust me, I'm a professional.'

Fi crossed her fingers as I took a glass of water out to Adam, who was laying railway sleepers for my decked area.

'Thanks, Laura,' he said as I handed him the glass.

'Why are you working at the weekend?' I asked.

He shrugged and wiped the sweat from his forehead with the back of his arm. 'I just want to get the job finished as quickly as possible.'

He emptied the pint glass in one go – glug, glug, glug.

'Can't wait to leave, eh?' I was slightly miffed at the insinuation.

'Well, time is money and all that,' he mumbled. 'You couldn't give me a hand quickly, could you?'

I wasn't exactly dressed for gardening. In fact, I was wearing a short white silk slip and nothing else.

'Um.' I scratched my head. 'OK. What do you want me to do? I don't think I could lift those sleepers.'

'No, no, no. Not that. I just want to get this magnolia planted and I need someone to hold it for me while I make sure it's central.'

I followed Adam carefully on tiptoe. I was barefoot.

'If you kneel down there,' he indicated a pile of dirt beside a large hole, 'I'll lift the magnolia into place and then if you could just hold it there while I have a look.'

I did as I was told.

'It's a beautiful tree,' I said through a mouthful of leaves.

'Yeah, it's a gorgeous plant, the magnolia,' Adam replied, squinting in the sunshine. 'Could you just rotate it to the left slightly. That's it. No, not that far. Back a bit. Yup, that's it. Perfect. Let's get her planted.'

Adam knelt down opposite me and took hold of the tree trunk.

'Come on then,' he said. 'Start filling the hole.'

'How?' I asked.

'With your hands, dizzy.' Adam smirked.

'What, with this dirt?' I asked.

'Yes, with the compost.' Adam laughed and the tree shook.

I did as I was told. It felt good to feel the sun on my back and the earth between my fingers.

'Come on, put a bit of welly into it,' encouraged Adam.

'Why am I doing all the hard work?' I gasped.

'Because it's your garden and it's my day off,' he teased.

My white nightie was filthy and the manicure I'd had the day before was completely ruined but I was having fun.

'Help me, Adam,' I pleaded. 'The tree won't move now, I've nearly filled the hole.'

Adam began shovelling the compost with his spade-like hands. Every now and then he'd spray me with earth and say, 'Oops.' By the time the tree was planted we looked like a couple of mud wrestlers. Adam and I lay side by side in the dirt and proudly surveyed our tree.

'We make a good team,' said Adam.

Suddenly I remembered about Fiona and the reason I had come into the garden in the first place.

'What do you think of my sister, then?' I enquired with the subtlety of a *Blind Date* contestant.

'She's a great kid,' he said, staring at the magnolia.

'Come on, she's hardly a kid,' I scoffed. 'Fiona's all woman.'

'Yeah. She looks like you did before you started doing your Posh Spice impersonation.' His eyes held mine for a moment. I could have sworn they flashed with anger, but I had no idea why.

Fiona tiptoed towards us in bare feet, trying to avoid stepping on stray nails.

'What are you two talking about?' she asked hopefully.

'Victoria Beckham,' said Adam before busying himself with his work.

'Oh,' said Fiona, looking disappointed.

'Sorry,' I mouthed.

'Why are you covered in mud, Laura?' asked Fiona.

'I've been planting a tree,' I said proudly.

*

Lucy looked amazing. When Fergie opened the door, she climbed gracefully out of her limo and onto the driveway of Hurlingham Manor. Her eyes shone like the midday sun, her skin glowed with good health and her smile was as bright as the twenty-four-carat diamonds she wore around her neck. It had only been two weeks since I'd seen her, but she'd obviously put on weight and the scrawny little bag of bones who'd been rushed off to the Rainbow Clinic now stood before us, resplendent in a fuchsia-pink organza dress. The transformation was mind-blowing, and I could fully understand why the clinic cost £1,000 per night if its results were this extraordinary. I wondered if I should talk to Warren about booking myself in.

'Gorgeous people,' announced Lucy to the twenty or so closest friends who had gathered to welcome her return. 'I missed you so much that I thought my heart would burst. I love you all to death.'

For some reason we gave her a round of applause.

'Let the celebrations begin!' she announced with a flourish of her arms and a megawatt grin.

So celebrate we did. Two dozen of London's brightest young things partied hard in the manicured grounds of Hurlingham Manor. Champagne and Pimm's flowed freely from the bottles and jugs that were offered by the waiters and waitresses who'd been hired at short notice by a rather stressed-out Ferguson. Beautiful, designer-clad bodies lolled about on red-and-white stripy deckchairs, rolling joints, snorting coke and petting heavily with fellow stars. There was a glorious air of decadence and glamour about the scene: teeth were bright white, skin was flawlessly tanned, sequins glimmered in the sunlight and everybody wore designer shades. Fiona held back at first. She stood awkwardly in my high-heeled shoes, nervously clutching a glass of champagne, almost hidden in the rhododendron bushes, painfully in awe of the celebrities surrounding her. I stayed with her for moral support until Lucy decided to take my sister under her experienced wing, introducing her to the assembled bunch of actors, singers, models and sports personalities. Gradually a smile spread across Fiona's face, and I watched with pride as she chatted easily to a BAFTA award-winning actress and flirted outrageously with a sexy Italian footballer. She could look after herself. It was time for me to relax and start enjoying myself. I looked around for the Snowman and found him doing some business with a Formula One racing driver.

Ricky and Lewis were sitting on the croquet lawn, nodding their long-haired heads, strumming their guitars and singing 'Sunny Afternoon' by the Kinks.

Monica and I whooped with delight and I thought I'd explode with the perfection of the moment.

Every now and then I'd catch a glimpse of Fiona being led by the arm from VIP to VIP by an exuberant Lucy. Luce did love to make projects of us ordinary girls. Fiona looked wide-eyed and oh so excited. I hoped she was on a natural high rather than one of Lucy's chemically induced ones, but knew that I couldn't say anything. Wasn't I the one who'd given her a line of coke in The Hammer that time? And how hypocritical would it be of me to stop her from indulging when I could feel the charlie pumping around my own veins? Still, I tried to keep an eye on her all the same.

'She'll be OK,' said Ricky, noticing my concern. 'Lucy'll look after her.'

'That's what I'm worried about,' I replied.

'How is Lucy?' wondered Monica. 'She hasn't overdone it, has she?'

Lewis laughed. 'Of course she's overdoing it. Do you think she's going to drink orange juice all day?'

Monica frowned. 'Listen, you guys, it's not a good idea for her to get totally off her face today. She's just gone through cold turkey. Her tolerance will have dropped.'

Ricky and Lewis guffawed and said, 'Old woman,' simultaneously. Monica shook her head and stared out into the sunset with a frown etched on her regal brow.

As it got dark, the grounds began to sparkle with a million fairy lights that were strung from the cedar trees in dancing rows. I shivered.

'Let's go inside,' said Ricky, pulling me up and leading me onto the grand verandah and into the house.

He took me to the library and locked the heavy oak door behind us. A real fire glowed in the hearth, even though it was the first weekend in August. We lay down on a bearskin rug in front of the flames and slowly undressed each other, languishing in the smooth beauty of skin on naked skin. As we made love, I watched Ricky's handsome face soften in the firelight, and I swear he gazed at me with such tenderness that, for a moment at least, I felt utterly adored.

'I love you, Ricky,' I whispered in the half-light.

'I know you do, babe,' he replied.

Afterwards, we wrapped ourselves in the bearskin and lay in front of the fire sharing a joint.

'My little Marianne,' said Ricky, kissing the top of my head.

'Pardon?'

'Marianne Faithfull,' he explained. 'I'm Mick, you're Marianne. Stately home, fur rug, you must know the story.'

'Oh yeah.' I remembered the infamous tale of the Rolling Stones' lead singer and his sex kitten girlfriend. Folklore had it that when the police raided the party, she was naked but for a fur rug. 'But didn't they get busted by the cops just about now?'

'So they did.' Ricky laughed.

It must have been late, although I still don't know exactly what time it happened. I'd been lying in Ricky's arms there in the library for some time, listening to him sing the new song he'd been working on. Slowly something seeped into my brain, a kind of consciousness that the world was carrying on outside the room and that it was somehow going horribly wrong.

'Did you hear something?' I asked Ricky, suddenly sitting up with a head spin.

'No.' He tried to pull me back down against his naked chest, but I was convinced I'd heard a strange noise.

I stood up and hurriedly threw on my clothes.

'Come on, Ricky, I definitely heard something. There. There it is again.'

'What?' He frowned. 'You're just being paranoid. You've probably had too much coke.'

I paused for a minute, wondering whether he was right, but then I heard it again, more clearly this time. It was very far away, but it was very definitely a scream. Ricky heard it too.

'OK, let's go and see what's going on.'

He pulled on his jeans, leaving his shirt and trainers on the library floor. We ran out of the house and back onto the verandah. The screams were getting louder and more persistent, and I felt the blood drain from my face as I recognized the voice.

'I'm sure that's Fiona,' I said with a shiver.

Ricky ran, incredibly fast for a shoeless man, towards the commotion. I followed on shaking legs, discarding my heels somewhere on the croquet lawn. The screams were coming from the direction of the boating pond. As we approached and our eyes became accustomed to the darkness we began to make out the figure of a girl on the jetty. She was soaking wet and her hands were thrust desperately into her waist-length blonde hair.

'Fiona!' I called to her. 'It's me. I'm coming. What on earth is wrong?'

When we reached her, Fiona stood pinned to the spot. She was still wearing my floaty summer dress, but it clung to her body like a sopping rag. Her face was alabaster in the moonlight, a look of stony horror etched on her features. She said nothing, but pointed a shaking finger in the direction of the pond. There, about ten metres from the jetty, floating daintily like a lily pad, was the body of a girl. She was face down, her golden hair billowing out around her head and the fuchsia-pink organza of her dress lapping gently around her still frame. It was Lucy.

'Oh my God,' I said, clasping my hand to my mouth. 'Oh my God. Oh my God.'

Ricky flung himself into the water and swam desperately to the body. Even drenched through Lucy didn't weigh much, and he scooped her up in his arms and swam back to the jetty as easily as if she were a favourite rag doll, accidentally dropped into the pond by a little girl. Fiona remained glued to the spot while I helped Ricky pull Lucy's lifeless body out onto the jetty. Her face was blue.

'Is she breathing?' I cried desperately.

'No, she fucking isn't,' he replied gravely, pinching her tiny nose and starting mouth-to-mouth.

'Fiona, call for an ambulance!' I shouted. She didn't move. 'Fiona, go and get help. Now!' Fiona remained frozen to the spot.

'I'll go,' I said to no one in particular and fled back in the direction of the house, where I'd left my mobile phone.

Hurlingham Manor was lit up like a fairground and I could make out the figures of party-goers enjoying themselves in its many rooms, all blissfully unaware of the tragedy unfolding outside.

When the paramedics arrived at the boating pond fifteen minutes later, Ricky was still desperately trying to revive Lucy. Fiona hadn't moved.

'I'll take over now, mate,' said one of the ambulance men gently to Ricky. He appeared not to hear.

'Ricky, the paramedics are here,' I said softly. 'Let them help her.'

He fell back, away from the body and yelled, 'Nooooooo!' We all knew she was beyond help.

Fiona was wrapped in foil and led zombie-like to an ambulance to be treated for shock. Ricky sat on the jetty with his head in his hands, wailing like a mortally wounded animal. I felt absolutely numb. The whole episode seemed so grotesquely unreal that I couldn't believe it had happened, even when I witnessed Lucy's body being stretchered off, covered by a green sheet.

By the time the police arrived, the Snowman had melted into thin air, but the rest of us were rounded up and kept in the ballroom under police guard. They searched our bodies and the premises and found enough illegal narcotics to keep a Colombian drug baron in business for a month. Fiona was questioned first as she was the only eyewitness to whatever had gone on.

Ricky stood apart from the group, alone at the window, gazing into nothing. I put my hand on his shoulder. It felt as hard and cold as a stone statue's. He turned around and looked, not at me but through me, with a haunted stare.

'She's gone,' he said, as if to himself. 'My little Lucy. She's gone.'

I watched as a light went out in his dark eyes. It was never switched back on again.

We were questioned one by one, charged with possession of whatever drug we'd been holding and then released until further notice. Only Monica was found to be clean. I was lucky, I had less than half a gram of coke wrapped up in my bra. The young policeman who questioned me explained that I would probably get away with a caution. The Buckinghamshire constabulary had a suspicious death on their hands, so criminal proceedings against the twenty-three assembled celebrities would have to wait. Fiona was taken to the nearest police station for further questioning. As I watched her being put solemnly into the back of a police car, I felt so guilty I wished I was the one who had died. The policewoman who drove me to the station to wait for my sister was kind enough, but I got the distinct impression that she thought we were silly spoilt brats who'd brought this tragedy on ourselves. She was right, of course.

Ricky refused to come with me.

'Don't you want to know what happened?' I asked.

He shook his head and snapped, 'I know what happened. She died.'

When I arrived at the police station, the clock on the wall of the waiting room told me it was 4 a.m. I sat on a bright-orange plastic chair, stared at a poster warning of the dangers of drug abuse and waited. I didn't let myself think about the fact that Lucy was actually dead. I couldn't, because somewhere, deep down, I knew that we were all culpable. Outside, the sun rose and a crowd of reporters, photographers and camera crews quickly assembled.

'We'll sneak you out the back door when they release

Fiona,' said the friendly middle-aged copper at the desk. 'You've had a bad enough experience without having to deal with that lot.'

'I'm used to them,' I said.

'I know,' he smiled kindly, 'but that sister of yours isn't, and she's pretty shaken up as it is.'

'I'd better organize a lift back to London.' I reached for my mobile.

'No need,' replied the policeman. 'Transport is already on its way. We had a phone call.'

I guessed that Warren had been rudely awakened from his sleep and forced into arranging our getaway. He would be furious. This wasn't exactly the kind of publicity he encouraged for his clients.

At half past six, Adam arrived. When I spotted his worried face approaching I got off my chair and threw myself at his broad chest. That's when the tears started.

'How did you know where we were?' I sobbed.

'I couldn't sleep, so I was watching TV. It was on the news,' he said.

Adam looked down at me. 'Laura, what the hell have you got yourself involved in?' he asked, not angrily, just concerned. 'And Fiona. Poor Fiona. How's she going to deal with this? They're talking about her on the news.'

'I don't know, Adam,' I said through my tears. 'I just don't know.'

Fiona was released without charge, guilty of nothing more than being impressed by Lucy Lloyd.

'Are you all right, Fi?' I asked when she was eventually brought to us by the kind policeman.

'What happened?' asked Adam gently, putting his arm around her shoulders.

Fiona looked shell-shocked.

'Lucy wanted to go for a midnight swim in the boating pond,' she said quietly. 'She thought it would be fun. I went with her because she asked me to. I don't know why. The water was freezing and it was really dark. I was scared and cold, so I got out, but Lucy didn't want to. She was laughing and swam into the middle of the pond. I couldn't see her; she swam too far away. And then everything just went quiet.'

Fiona shook in Adam's arm. I cried with grief for my dead friend and pity for my devastated sister.

'I waited for her,' continued Fi. 'I stood there for ages. I thought she'd come back. But then I saw something pink floating in the water. That's when I screamed.'

We drove back to London in Adam's van in almost total silence. Fiona sat shivering and staring blankly ahead at the road. I sobbed quietly beside her, unable to stop the tears now that they'd begun. Every now and then Adam shot us a sideways glance, his face full of concern. Back at the house, we had to fight our way through the hordes of press waiting outside.

'I want to go home,' said Fiona the minute we got inside. 'I don't want to be here any more.'

I knew how she felt. Neither did I.

'Fiona, I'm so sorry. You should never have been involved with any of that.' I clutched her cold body to me.

'It's not your fault,' she whispered.

We clung on to each other for dear life.

'Poor Lucy,' said Fiona into my ear.

'Poor Lucy,' I repeated as the reality of the situation began to sink in.

Needless to say, my parents were horrified at what Fiona had gone through in my debauched company. I could hear her sticking up for me when Mum phoned her on her mobile, but I guessed, correctly, that this time I'd gone too far and that there would be no more contact from my mother. Maybe even Gran would wash her hands of me this time. I arranged to pay for a chauffeur-driven car to take Fiona all the way back to Edinburgh – it was no time for public transport – and told her it would collect her at noon. Fiona sat on the couch beside Adam, who had his arm around her in a protective manner, and I wondered briefly whether something positive might come out of the tragic events of the past twenty-four hours. I decided to leave them to it and excused myself to phone Warren and Jasmine to discuss how we were going to deal with the negative publicity. One megastar was dead and twenty-three others had been charged with drug offences. It was the biggest scandal to hit the country since the Mick and Marianne bust.

Before she left, Fiona told me there would be no romance between herself and Adam.

'He's in love with someone else,' she explained. 'He just told me.'

I didn't pay much attention to what she was saying. I had other things on my mind.

Lucy Lloyd's funeral was a circus. She had already been dead for a fortnight. Her poor mother had to wait for the results of an autopsy and a coroner's inquest before the body was released for burial. When she'd drowned, Lucy had been five times over the drink-drive limit and had consumed, the pathologist estimated, between four and five grams of cocaine. If she hadn't drowned, she would probably have had a heart attack instead.

But Lucy would have approved of the event. Stoke-on-Trent had never seen such a glamorous gathering, as Hollywood's great and good flew in, each trying to outshine the others by wearing the most chic black outfit they could find. The church was full of Lucy's 'friends', including me, Monica, Lewis, Ricky, an inconsolable Billy Joe and even a smartly dressed Snowman, who had the courtesy to shed a tear – of guilt at providing her with her last fix or regret for losing his best customer, who knows. Outside, thousands of her fans lined the streets to pay their respects. An ocean of tears was cried.

Me. I couldn't take my eyes off Lucy's mum. She was such an ordinary-looking little woman. The kind of prematurely aged, forty-something lady you see in the supermarket every day. There was nothing about her that suggested she might have borne, and lost, such an astonishingly glamorous daughter, and after the service, nobody seemed to pay her any attention. There didn't appear to be a Mr Lloyd with her, just a little girl of about eight, who I guessed was Lucy's younger sister. I realized, far too late, that Lucy had never talked to me about her family and I'd never asked her.

Mrs Lloyd's face was crumpled with grief as she stood with the little girl in the graveyard after the ceremony. I approached tentatively.

'Mrs Lloyd?'

She looked at me with a glimmer of recognition.

'Laura,' she said warmly. 'It's so good to meet you at last. Lucy was so fond of you. She talked about you all the time. I think she found it difficult to know who to trust, but she said that you were a true friend.'

Guilt overwhelmed me. I wasn't a true friend. A true friend would have stopped a drug addict from pressing the self-destruct button; I just stood back and watched. But Mrs Lloyd didn't need to hear that.

'And you are Lucy's sister?' I asked the little girl.

She shook her head.

'No,' said Mrs Lloyd. 'This is Rosemary, Lucy's daughter.'

My jaw dropped.

'I ... I ... I didn't know ...' I stammered.

'Nobody did,' said Mrs Lloyd. 'Lucy had Rosie when she was fifteen. When Lucy got famous, we thought it was best if no one knew she was a teenage mum. But it doesn't really matter now, does it?'

I shook Mrs Lloyd's hand and offered my sincere condolences once more. As I wandered back towards Ricky and the others, the little girl with Lucy's eyes watched me leave.

It wasn't until after Lucy had gone that I realized how deeply Ricky had loved her. It's a cliché, I know, but when she died, part of him died with her. The good part. Ricky and I never made love again. We had sex, but there was no emotion and he always closed his eyes.

PART FOUR

Autumn

16

'Celebrity in public transport shocker'

It was a miserable wet Monday. Warren had called an emergency meeting with the Superbra people. The proprietors of the world's most famous sexy lingerie company were, and I quote, 'seriously considering dropping Laura McNaughton as the face of Superbra, due to excessive weight loss resulting in lack of adequate cleavage'. In other words, my once bouncing beauties had shrivelled into ickle-bitty titties and were no longer worthy of gracing the nation's advertising billboards. In another life, I would have been mortified by the news. Having been known as 'the girl with the nice tits' since puberty, I'd gradually started to identify myself that way. I could spot a gay man at a hundred paces because his eyes would land above the neckline of my top; all other men talked to my cleavage. It was a fact, or at least it used to be. Now I was a 32B, and a droopy one at that. I'd lost my crowning glories and I should have been devastated, but I was too busy mourning Lucy to worry about some missing bosoms.

Warren was convinced that my lack of flesh was only part of the problem with Superbra. After all, a talented graphic designer could do wonders with a Mac these days. No need for real curves when airbrushed ones would, and often did, do quite nicely. According to Wazza, this particular storm in a D cup had as much to do with PR as bras. Since Lucy's death and the surrounding scandal, my public profile had changed. I was no longer described as a 'TV darling', or 'cutie', now I was a 'troubled star', or 'bad girl', and one Sunday I was even described as drug addled, although Warren was in talks with our lawyers about that one. Right-of-centre newspapers and teen mags wouldn't touch me with a bargepole as I was far too dangerous, but picture editors at certain tabloids and weeklies paid highly for any snaps of me looking thin, drunk or in any way off my ever-decreasing tits. Witty young writers and sub-editors would then spend many an amusing hour thinking up bitchy captions to accompany the picture. Ironically, it was the really upmarket glossies and the edgy, too-cool-for-school monthlies who now considered me newsworthy. It was as if being outed as a 'troubled' 'bad girl' – à la Kate Moss, Lindsay Lohan et al. – made me somehow more glamorous – the kind of ideology that had got me into this mess in the first place.

So here I was, on a rainy Monday afternoon, summoned to Warren Clark's lair in deepest, darkest Covent Garden. Wazza's oversized frame was jammed behind his equally oversized desk. He looked decidedly cross and his face was even redder than usual.

'Laura,' he wheezed, sucking on a cigar. 'You look terrible.' This was rich coming from a man who looked like he'd just walked off an operating table in a cardiac unit, except that he was wearing a Savile Row suit rather than a green hospital gown, which was just as well considering the size of his lardy ass. Anyway, I digress. In short, the fat man was calling me ugly.

'Thanks,' I sulked, slumping into a chair to await my fate. The people from Superbra were due in fifteen minutes.

'You're clean now, right?' This wasn't a question, it was an instruction. In fact, Warren couldn't have cared less whether or not I was using drugs, he was merely informing me what the official line was for the meeting.

I nodded obediently, despite the fact that I'd just had a line of coke in the loo. Cocaine was no longer something I did at parties for a bit of a laugh; it wasn't even fun any more, just something I needed to get through the day. Cocaine was what I did when I got up in the morning, in between making a cup of coffee and lighting my first cigarette. There was certainly no way I could get through a meeting without a bit of snoz. I wiped my nose to ensure it was clear of white powdery residue and sniffed.

Warren examined me critically over the top of his wire-rimmed glasses. They were too small for his hippo head.

'Age is not on your side,' he stated.

'I'm twenty-six,' I reminded him, 'not sixty-six.'

He waved his hand impatiently to show that I was splitting hairs. 'That may be true, but television is an industry for the very young. Perma-youth, that's the word *du jour*. Actually, I was thinking about keeping you twenty-five for another year or so.'

This would have been funny if he'd been joking, but his humourless expression told me he was deadly serious. He continued, 'The only requirements in this industry are prettiness, perkiness and the mental capacity to read an autocue. There are countless girls out there who would quite happily kill you to take your job. What you need to remember, Laura, is that you're not *that* special, you're not *that* pretty and you're not *that* talented. If you look down you'll see a million nubile young blondes snapping at your stiletto heels.'

We both looked down at my feet. Warren seemed disappointed to find a pair of battered Converse trainers rather than a dainty pair of Manolo Blahniks.

'And you really must do something about your image,' he added in exasperation. 'You used to be so glamorous, Laura. Sort it out. I'm shocked that you would turn up for an important meeting looking like this.'

'Thanks, Warren,' I mumbled, shrinking further down into Adam's fleecy hooded sweatshirt which I'd recently adopted. It was chilly for October and I seemed to be feeling the cold quite acutely these days. 'You really know how to make a girl feel special. Oh, but of course, I'm not special, am I?'

'I'm telling you this for your own good,' he continued without sympathy. 'You've had a meteoric rise and I understand how difficult it can be to handle fame, but that's why you pay me: to advise you on how to deal with the complexities of stardom. And now I'm advising you that unless you pull your socks up, you'll be finished by Christmas. Only this morning I took on an eighteen-year-old – eighteen – who's on the shortlist for the new weather-girl job on *Wide Awake Britain*. She has a great future in front of her. So you see, Laura, you're not indispensable. Far from it.'

I drew my legs up onto the chair and hugged my bony shins, resting my chin on my knees. Warren continued to stare at me with a quizzical expression on his face. 'What's happened to your skin?' he demanded.

I put my hand up to my cheek. It felt like ice. I shrugged to show I didn't know what he meant.

'It's lost all its elasticity.' He leaned forward over his desk for a closer look. I could smell his halitosis. 'You've shrivelled up, woman!'

'No I haven't,' I argued. 'I'm just a bit rundown, that's all. I've got a cold.'

The truth was I had a perpetual cold. It was the charlie; it made my nose run and I had to sniff all the time. Wazza hadn't been a celebrity agent for twenty-five years without learning a thing or two about the signs of cocaine abuse. It went with the territory.

'You've always got a cold according to the make-up artist who rang Jasmine to complain about you last week,' he scoffed. 'She claims she had to use an entire bottle of make-up to cover up the red moustache under your nose and the black rings under your eyes.'

'Have you and Jasmine been discussing me?' I felt violated.

'Yes,' he retorted. 'And a bit too frequently for my liking. I do have other clients to worry about, you know.'

I stared out of the window and down onto the rain-soaked streets of Covent Garden below. I may have been crying, I don't know. I cried a lot in those days. Whatever the reason, Warren softened.

'Listen,' he said more gently. 'Why don't you go home. I'll handle the meeting with Superbra. I'll tell them you're ill or something. It's probably best they don't see you like this anyway.'

He was anxious to be rid of me. He walked round and put his hands on the back of my chair, ushering me up. 'Now, I've discussed it with Jasmine and we've decided to book you in for some treatments before the new series of *The Weekend Starts Here* begins – you've only got four weeks, remember.'

'Treatments?' I asked, bewildered. Was I about to be booked into the Rainbow Clinic?

'Beauty therapy,' he grinned, baring his too-big, too-white teeth. 'A bit of Botox for your forehead and a smidgen of collagen in those lips. It'll take years off you.'

'Oh, right.' I didn't have the energy to argue. It had all been arranged.

'You go home and catch up on that beauty sleep.' He shooed me off the chair.

'Shall I ask your PA to get me a car as usual?' I shuffled to the door.

Warren frowned. 'No, Laura. You can get a black cab outside like an ordinary human being. I can see I've pampered you too much for too long. I've spoilt you. What was I just telling you?'

'I'm not *that* special,' I chanted. Hell, I had no problem believing it.

'Good girl,' said my agent, dismissing me with a flick of his chubby, Rolexed wrist. 'Now run along before the Superbra folks see you looking so dreadful. We don't want them ripping up your contract on the spot. I'll call you later and let you know what's happening.'

I went to the loo again on the way out and then joined the hordes of ordinary people hailing cabs on Long Acre in the rain. Nobody looked at me twice because they were too busy huddling under umbrellas. I didn't have an umbrella, or a coat come to that. I was far too used to being chauffeured from door to door to think about anything that practical. The rain quickly drenched the fleecy top I was wearing, my jeans moulded their cold wetness to my thighs and my Converse squelched every time I stepped forward in a vain attempt to stop a passing cab.

'Season of mists and mellow fruitfulness', my arse, I thought as I sat dripping in the back of a taxi stuck in a traffic jam on Charing Cross Road. Everything looked grey and dank, as if London had lost its sparkle. It had lost September's sunshine to October's pouring rain; it had lost Lucy Lloyd to a watery grave; it had lost Ricky Jones to a stadium tour of the United States; it had lost Nat, Rob and new baby, Freddie, to an idyllic country cottage; and it had lost its place in my heart. The excitement I used to get from the sheer physical size of the city had been replaced by claustrophobia. The buildings seemed to rise up above me like gigantic bars in a concrete cage. The buzz I'd once felt from sharing airspace with ten million other people had gone too. Now I just felt like I couldn't breathe. I tried to slow my breathing down, but my heart was palpitating and I'd broken into a cold sweat. It was my first panic attack.

The taxi sat still behind a number 38 bus, which coughed fumes out of its exhaust into the damp London air. A bag lady limped past my window, dragging a bad leg behind her. She'd made herself shoes out of old carrier bags. Her face was expressionless and she looked about ninety, but I doubted if she was any older than my mum. I wondered what London had done to her. How did she get here? Limping up the Charing Cross Road on a rainy Monday afternoon in October with all her possessions in one Superdrug plastic bag. It crossed my mind that the money I'd shoved up my nose in the last few weeks might have been enough to save her. I was a horrid, wretched selfish cow and now I was suffering. I tried to slow down my heaving chest, but I just couldn't breathe. The windows of the cab began to steam up.

The taxi driver was watching me in the rear-view mirror. His look was one of simultaneous recognition and pity. I knew he was watching my discomfort and remembering those headlines: 'TROUBLED STAR'. 'BAD GIRL'. 'DRUG ADDLED'. To his credit, he said nothing, but I couldn't bear it any more; I had to get out.

'Just let me out here,' I shouted, with a voice that came from somewhere outside myself.

I stumbled out of the cab and thrust a £20 note in the driver's hand, even though the meter only said £8.20. I didn't wait for the change.

I think I heard the cabbie say, 'Are you all right, love?' but I didn't reply.

Huddled in a doorway, I lit a cigarette with shaking hands, hid from passers-by beneath Adam's hooded top and slowly waited as the panic subsided from my chest and my breathing gradually returned to normal. It was about then that I realized I was in serious danger of going completely bonkers, so I decided to do something as normal as possible. Could I make myself sane by doing something mundane? I caught the tube home.

The people in Leicester Square station must have recognized me as I refamiliarized myself with my Oyster card and made my way down the escalator towards the Northern Line's northbound platform, but this being London, everybody pretended to look right through me. Nobody said a word, and that suited me fine. The tube was quiet and I found a seat without difficulty, sitting opposite a stylish young couple in matching trench coats and loafers. Each had shiny cropped hair. The girl nudged the guy in the ribs as subtly as she could and they both glanced at me quickly and often from beneath their long fringes as we headed through Tottenham Court Road, Goodge Street and Warren Street. They got off at Mornington Crescent, and when the girl looked back at me through the closing doors I smiled. She smiled back. The tube trundled on towards Camden Town – my stop.

The rain had subsided into a dreary drizzle. Chalk Farm Road was awash with the debris from Camden Market which would have been teeming with students and tourists the day before. Soggy cardboard boxes floated in the gutter along with joint butts and discarded polystyrene boxes of half-eaten chow mein. I used to love Camden, with its weird hybrid population of pierced people, dope dealers, ageing bohemians, new media types and the overspill of young Blairite families from Islington. Now I saw it as dark, dirty and intimidating. Everybody I passed glared hungrily at me until I felt like a fish in a tank, waiting to be chosen for supper in a seafood restaurant. I scurried faster towards the footpath over the railway bridge which would take me to leafy Primrose Hill, staring at my sodden trainers as they half jogged along the pavement. Then I crashed right into Becky. Headfirst, literally. Smack, bang, wallop. We stood facing each other, dazed and confused, rubbing our foreheads where we'd bashed them together.

'Laura,' she said in surprise.

'Becky!' I cried, arms open, overwhelmed with relief at seeing that glorious, familiar face again. I'd long since got over her minor indiscretion. Hell, the press would have found out where I lived soon enough, whether she told them or not. I hugged her as she stood rigidly with her arms by her sides.

'You all right?' she asked guardedly.

I nodded enthusiastically. 'It's so good to see you, Becks. You look well.'

She did. She looked healthy and glowing and full of life. She'd had her dreadlocks cut off and her short blonde hair stood up in cute messy tufts around her pretty, round face.

'You look like shit.' She reiterated what Warren had said.

I shrugged, not knowing what to say. 'Do you ... do you want to do something?' I stumbled over the words. 'Get a coffee or ...'

Becky shook her head. 'No, I don't think so,' she said without smiling.

We stared at each other for a moment and then she said, 'Well, I'm off. I'll be seeing you.'

'Take my card,' I said in desperation, rummaging in my bag and fishing one out. 'Call me sometime.' I thrust it into her hand. 'I forgive you, you know.'

She gave me a withering look, turned and walked away.

'Becky,' I shouted after her.

She threw my screwed-up business card into the gutter with the cardboard boxes and half-eaten noodles. I watched her until she disappeared round the corner at Camden Lock and then slowly I made my way home.

I found Adam up the spiral staircase in the newly converted attic room with a broad grin on his face.

'Da-da!' he announced. 'Finished. What do you think?'

It was a lovely airy space, painted chalk-white with matching floorboards and two large dormer windows with sweeping views of the area. You could even see the giraffes in London Zoo if you leaned right out of the front-facing one. In the centre was an enormous white leather corner sofa, scattered with bright turquoise and fuchsia cushions. Adam had built chunky solid mahogany shelves into the eaves for my books and magazines. My brand-new state-of-the-art sound system was invisible behind an antique Tibetan console which Adam had sourced in Islington, and a huge plasma TV was fitted flush into the gable-end wall. Three large church candles lined the intricately carved Indonesian coffee table where a copy of *Vogue* had been casually tossed, just so. It was like something straight out of an interiors magazine.

'Your perfect chill-out room,' he said proudly. 'It's just what you wanted, right?'

'Adam, it's gorgeous. Really, really beautiful,' I said.

And I meant it. The room really was exquisite. But I hadn't expected him to finish it so quickly and I wasn't quite sure I was ready for him to leave just yet. It dawned on me that once Adam left, I would be alone in this sprawling house. Alone in this sprawling city. Lucy was gone, Ricky was touring, Nat was in the country, Becky was clearly not about to kiss and make up and now even my lodger was deserting me. I'd become used to having him around. I would miss him.

'So why do you look so miserable?' he asked, confused.

'Because this is the last room.' I sat down on the sofa with a sigh. 'And that means you're finished here.'

'Ah. Are you going to miss me?' Adam flopped down beside me in his dirty builder's clothes with a mischievous gleam in his blue, blue eyes. He was teasing me.

'Damn right, I am.' I leaned comfortably into his armpit, even though it smelled faintly of sweat. 'I've got used to having a flatmate.'

'Housemate,' he corrected me. 'And what a house, eh?'

'Yup. It's a stunning house, that's for sure,' I agreed. 'Thanks to you, my master builder.'

I kissed his cheek gratefully and he smiled sheepishly.

'I'll miss you, too, you know,' he said quietly.

'Thanks, Adam.' It felt good to know that somebody still liked me.

'We should celebrate,' I announced. 'I'll get a bottle of bubbly from downstairs.'

'I'd rather just have a lager,' called Adam as I started down the stairs.

'Some people have no class,' I shouted back. He did make me smile.

We toasted the house, me with my champagne flute of Veuve Clicquot, Adam with his can of Stella Artois. I'd put Sugar Reef's new album on my iPod to test the super-duper big-woofered speakers. Adam groaned.

'Must we?' he asked.

'Oi, that's the love of my life singing. Don't diss him.' I hit him over the head with one of the cushions.

'Don't you ever get bored of hearing his voice?'

'No,' I said, and then remembered that I hadn't actually heard his voice for three days, despite the messages I'd left for him at various hotels in the Midwest. 'Did he phone today? Were there any messages from him?'

Adam shook his head and looked away, suddenly very interested in the framed black-and-white photograph of Lucy and me that graced the back wall. He knew I'd be disappointed that Ricky hadn't returned my calls and didn't want to see the hurt look on my face.

'But Warren called to say everything was sorted, if that makes sense. And Monica phoned,' he offered by way of consolation. 'She wondered if you wanted to go to some party tonight in Fulham. Tom somebody-or-other is launching something-or-other. God, I'm sorry, I didn't really know what she was on about.'

I waved my hand nonchalantly to show it didn't matter.

'I don't really feel like going out tonight,' I explained.

Adam raised his eyebrows in surprise.

'What? Laura McNaughton in staying-in shocker?' he scoffed.

'Yeah. I want to enjoy my newly finished show home,' I smiled. 'And I also want to spend some time with my flat—I mean *house*mate, before he leaves the country.'

'Really?' asked Adam. He looked pleased.

'Really,' I insisted. 'Anyway, I didn't really enjoy myself this weekend. I think I might have overdosed on parties. It was as if all these really cool people were just wandering around, trying to find out where the action was, but there was no action because everybody was too busy trying to find it to actually have it. Do you know what I mean?'

'Sort of.' Adam looked confused. 'I think. Maybe. Actually, no. What do you mean?'

'I think it's because everyone is on coke. Nobody has a concentration span of more than five minutes. You'll be having a conversation with someone and really you're just talking over each other – blah, blah, blah, me, me, me – and you're both looking over each other's shoulder the whole time to make sure you're not missing out on something more exciting elsewhere in the room. It's all about talking to the right people, wearing the right clothes, being photographed at the right event. Plus, you have to go to the toilet all the time to stay high. It just gets a bit monotonous after a while, I suppose,' I explained.

Adam looked at me as if I was bonkers. 'So, where's the fun in that then?'

It was a good question. I shrugged. 'It's just what you do, isn't it?'

'It's not what I do,' said Adam. 'I go to the pub, meet a few mates, have a few beers, chat, catch up with what everybody's been up to, discuss the footie results, maybe have a game of pool, go to a gig ...'

'That's what I used to do,' I remembered, suddenly feeling a wave of nostalgia for the life I'd once had.

I reached for my box of drugs, but Adam's large hand darted out and caught hold of my wrist.

'Adam! What are you going?' I was shocked.

He let go. 'Sorry. I just wish you wouldn't for once. Just have one evening without it.'

'Piss off,' I snapped. 'Who the hell do you think you are? My dad?'

'No, I'm your friend ... I think.'

'Of course you're my friend, but that doesn't mean you can tell me what to do,' I retorted.

'I just think you're in a mess because of that stuff.' He hit the box angrily. I couldn't understand why he was getting so worked up about it. 'Look at yourself. You're a physical wreck. When I first saw you, I thought, Wow, what a lovely girl. I thought you were something special. But now you shove so much of that shit up your nose that you're like some spaced-out zombie most of the time. And your so-called mates and that tosser of a boyfriend of yours, they just encourage you. They suck you further and further into their disgusting little hole. You'll rot, Laura, if you don't get out of there. You'll end up like Lucy, and I can't bear to see that happen to you. I'm not going to sit back and let you die.'

My cheeks burned with rage. How dare Adam – the builder! – make such personal comments. It was all true, of course, but that just made it worse. When you know something is true, deep down, but are too scared to admit it even to yourself, the last thing you need is to hear it from a third party. It's as if once it's out there, spoken, it can never go away again. You can't bury it alive in the back of your mind because it'll just keep on rising up to haunt you. Damn Adam for saying it. Damn him.

'It's none of your fucking business,' I snapped, angrily racking myself up a hefty line of coke on the Indonesian table.

To my utter dismay, Adam took his hand and swept the line and the entire contents of the open wrap off the table and onto the floor.

'What the fuck are you doing?'

I scrambled onto the floor on my knees and desperately tried to pick up the white powder with my bare hands, but it was no use, the whole gram had just vanished into the seagrass matting.

'What have you done?' I wailed. 'I haven't got any more.'

'Good,' said Adam.

I rocked back and forth on the floor, hugging my knees to my chest and crying like a baby.

'Why did you do that, Adam? Why?'

Adam stood over me. His face had gone dark with some unreadable emotion.

'Because I care about you, you stupid woman,' he said, kneeling down beside me and holding my wet face in his huge hands. 'Why do you think I got the job finished so quickly? Why do I feel I have to go back to Scotland?'

'I don't know,' I wailed. 'You said you hated it here.'

'I only hate it because I can't stand watching you destroy yourself. I can't handle seeing you with that bastard Ricky Jones, I can't keep sleeping in the next room to you when all I really want to do is climb into bed with you and I can't tell you how I feel because you're this super-rich famous person and I'm just some builder. What is it that Ricky calls me? The hired help.'

'Adam, what are you talking about?'

'You just don't get it, do you, Laura?' He had a desperate look on his face.

'No.' I shook my head in his hands.

'I've fallen in love with you,' he said quietly, and then stood up and backed away from me.

The words penetrated my skull very, very slowly and then hit me with such a force that I almost toppled over. He loved me. The thought had never even crossed my mind. I'd had no idea he felt anything for me at all. We stared at each other for a long time. I knew I had to say something, but I didn't know what. The truth was, I didn't love him. I'd never thought of him in that way. He was the builder, who'd become a housemate, who'd become a friend. I liked him a lot, but I was in love with Ricky Jones.

'Don't worry,' he said quietly, his cheeks burning with

embarrassment. 'You don't need to say anything. I know you don't feel the same and that nothing's going to happen between us, but I just wanted you to know. It's been doing my head in for weeks. Months. Ever since I met you that time at your gran's. I only took on this job because I fancied you.'

I pressed the rewind button in my head, trying to recall the first time I met Adam at Doric Cottage almost a year ago. I remembered thinking he was good-looking but, even then, when I'd just split up with Pete, I hadn't thought of him as a potential love interest. My head had been full of my new TV job and my sights were set higher than some lowly builder. Strange, looking back, because in the last few months I'd begun to feel somewhat inferior to Adam, with his laid-back attitude and seemingly sorted life. After living with him for so long, I thought I knew him, and I was sure that, although he was fond of me in an 'ah, poor, fucked-up Laura' sort of way, I was pretty much the antithesis of everything he found attractive in a woman. How many times had he told me I was too thin? Too spoilt? Too big for my Prada boots?

'Look, I was going to hang around until the weekend to sort my stuff out, but I'll go tonight,' he mumbled, fumbling around with his empty lager can and his rolling tobacco. 'I'm sorry. I've just made a complete arse of myself. Here' – he took fifty quid out of his wallet and threw it on the carpet beside me – 'for the coke. That was none of my business and I had no right to throw it away.'

'Adam,' I said, struggling to my feet and trying to hand back the money. 'Stay. Please. We need to talk about this.'

'Why?' His blue eyes flashed. 'Are you going to tell me that secretly, deep down, you've been lusting after me, too?'

'No, but ...'

'But nothing.' He shook his head. 'Look, I'm a proud bloke and I've just made a twat of myself, so please, just let me go without a fuss, so I can keep a wee bit of dignity, OK?'

I nodded tearfully as Adam started to descend the spiral staircase. He stopped halfway down with his head in line with my ankles, looked back up at me one more time and added, 'I meant what I said about the drugs, though, and about Ricky Jones. They'll destroy you, Laura. I'm just pleased I won't be here to see it happen.'

My life was becoming too weird to handle. Certainly too weird to handle without the aid of narcotics. So as Adam noisily packed his belongings together in the bedroom below, I called the Snowman and invited him round. He said he'd be with me in an hour. I spent the next fifty-five minutes frantically pacing the floor of my chill-out room in a decidedly unchilled-out manner, biting my nails even though they were false – chewed plastic – yum – and staring wildly out of the window for signs of my drug supplier. Adam had messed with my head big time and I needed to get out of it a.s.a.p.

'Laura,' Adam called up eventually. 'I'm off. Thanks for everything – the work, the room and all that. Goggsie will be round tomorrow to fix that pipe in the downstairs toilet and then we're done. I'll sort my invoice out with Cathy. See you.'

He'd obviously been practising his exit speech while he packed and had plumped for the casual, professional, detached approach, which was ridiculous, really, considering the angst-ridden conversation we'd just had. I wasn't about to let him leave like that, so I ran down two flights of stairs to the hallway and grabbed his arm as he was about to shut the door. He wouldn't turn round so I could see his face and just muttered, 'Let me go, Laura,' trying to shake his arm free. Suddenly, faced with the fact that he was actually going for good, I desperately wanted him to stay. Not as a boyfriend, but as my one remaining friend.

'Please don't go,' I pleaded. 'Adam, turn round. Please.'

He stood there in the doorway with his back to me. Outside it was dark and wet and blowing a gale which swept into the hallway and chilled the house.

'I can't let you go,' I continued desperately. 'You're the only one I've got left. I don't want to be in this stupid big house on my own. Adam, please, I'm scared.'

Slowly, very, very slowly, he turned towards me. What I saw broke my heart. His face had literally crumpled. The huge, strong, cheerful man I knew had tears streaming down his cheeks and a look of such acute pain in his eyes that it hurt me to make eye contact. It was as if he was saying, 'Look what you've done to me, Laura.' I let go of his arm, feeling selfish, wretched and poisonous.

'I'm sorry, Adam,' I said weakly. 'I'm really, truly sorry. But I didn't ask you to fall in love with me.'

He just walked away. I stood at the door and listened to the Tartan Army van cough and splutter into life and then disappear noisily into the night. Eventually I closed the door, sat on the floor with my back against it and sobbed until the Snowman arrived with his little packages of chemical fun.

17

Hairdresser of the year marries gay lover

That Saturday Graham and Daniel got married in a lavish civil-partnership ceremony, conducted by a ridiculously camp 'vicar' – wearing a pink dog collar – on a boat as it meandered up the Thames. The grooms both wore white, Travoltaesque suits from the 'Staying Alive' era, with open-necked black shirts, enormous lapels and ridiculously tight trousers with a generous flare. George, Michael and Elton were bridesdogs or groomsmaids or something equally amusing. They'd been coiffed to white, fluffy perfection and each pooch sported a pink ruffled collar round its neck. I'd been looking forward to the event with the same kind of breathtaking anticipation that a six-year-old reserves for Christmas. Since Lucy's death, everything had been doom and gloom. If anyone needed a hefty dose of camp cheerfulness, it was me, and the occasion didn't disappoint.

'Laura,' screamed Nat from the starboard side. 'I haven't seen you for fucking ages. Oops, I'm a mum now, blooming ages. How are you, babes?'

'Oh, you know, so-so,' I smiled, giving her a hug. She was plumper than before the pregnancy, and her cuddle was warm, comfortable and mumsy.

She stood back and looked me up and down with a bemused expression.

'You look weird,' she exclaimed. 'What have you done to yourself? I think it's your mouth.'

I touched my newly pumped-up lips self-consciously.

'Collagen,' I explained sheepishly. 'Warren thought I was looking old.'

'And something else is different.' She squinted at my face. 'You look like a startled boiled egg.'

'I've had Botox, too.' I indicated my frozen forehead. 'No wrinkles, you see?'

'No facial expressions, you mean,' said Nat with mild disgust. 'It's not permanent, is it?'

I shook my head.

'Good,' said Nat with relief. 'Please don't do that again. You'll scare the baby and he's already freaked out.'

Freddie was screaming his little heart out and being comforted by Rob. The poor child had just been introduced to Trudy and had, understandably, found the experience a traumatic one.

'Shoosh, sweetie, shoosh,' Rob was whispering into his perfect little ear.

Nat walked over to her beautiful baby and started kissing his fevered forehead and stroking his shock of dark brown hair. Rob put his free arm around his wife's back and the three of them huddled for a moment in their impenetrable family unit. A lump formed in my throat. Partly out of joy for Nat, but also because I was suddenly aware of how horribly alone I was. Graham and Daniel snogged like teenagers in a corner, even Trudy was traipsing the terminally hen-pecked Dennis around from VIP to VIP while I hovered on the sidelines.

'Laura, come and meet Freddie,' called Nat. 'He's got something to ask you.'

'He wondered if you'd like to be his godmother,' said Rob rather formally.

'What? Me?' I couldn't believe they thought I was worthy.

'I'd absolutely love to,' I exclaimed. 'I'd be honoured.'

Nat and Rob grinned at each other proudly.

'But why me?' I asked. 'I'm the most irresponsible person you know.'

'Well, as long as he doesn't accept any medication from you, he should be OK,' teased Nat. 'Anyway, we thought the responsibility might do you good. Plus, you're the richest person we know, so you'll always give him fantastic presents. Now, hold your godson; he won't break.'

She handed me the tiny bundle. He was four weeks old and a minute, carbon copy of his mum. At first I was scared, frightened I'd hold him wrong or hurt him in some way, but gradually I relaxed and enjoyed the warmth of his tiny body against mine.

'You're gorgeous,' I cooed to him. And he was. 'My little godson.'

I kissed his teeny-weeny button nose and he stared at me with bewildered eyes. Nat and Rob smiled at each other rather smugly and I wondered if I'd ever be standing where they were. I couldn't imagine having anything so perfect in my life. Freddie was so fresh and clean and unspoiled – a perfect bundle of potential life – that he made me feel dirty. It was hard to believe that my mum had once held me the same way, kissed my tiny face and wondered what would become of me. She must have been so disappointed.

Later, over a dinner of prawn cocktail, gammon steaks with pineapple and sherry trifle – Seventies retro cuisine, apparently – I confided in Nat what had happened with Adam.

'Are you mad?' she asked me through a mouthful of gammon. 'Adam's lovely. Are you eating that by the way?'

I shook my head and she helped herself to my main course.

'Breastfeeding,' she explained. 'I'm starving all the time. You're a lucky bugger having Adam chasing after you.'

'Nat, I'm going out with Ricky Jones. I'm hardly going to get excited about having my builder lusting after me,' I said. 'I know Adam's good-looking but Ricky's an internationally renowned sex god!'

'An internationally renowned womanizing bastard, more like,' scoffed Nat. She'd had two glasses of champagne which had gone straight to her head – after nine months of abstinence her alcohol tolerance was at an all-time low. I remembered quickly how tactless Nat was when drunk. 'Babes, have you no self-respect left? You're a public laughing stock.'

'Natalie, I think that's a bit harsh.' I bristled, sick of everybody slagging off me and my boyfriend at every opportunity.

'Is it?' she asked wide-eyed. 'Did you see *Wide Awake Britain* yesterday morning?'

I shook my head. 'Of course I didn't. Only students and bored housewives with screaming brats watch that rubbish.'

'Too late, I realized that Nat, being on maternity leave, now fitted loosely into the latter category. 'Oops, sorry,' I conceded as she gave me a warning look.

'I'll let that go because motherhood has mellowed me,' she said, gulping down her third glass of champagne. 'I really shouldn't have any more of this. Freddie will get pissed on my breast milk, but it's just so lovely. Lovely, jubbly, bubbly.' She giggled.

'Nat, what were you saying about *Wide Awake Britain*?' I asked.

'Oh yeah. Well, they had a slot about infidelity – women who go back to cheating men time and time again, and they used you as an example. They asked, "What makes an attractive woman like Laura McNaughton stay with Ricky Jones when he's publicly unfaithful over and over again?" Laura, they had a psychologist analysing your relationship and then they had a phone-in on the subject with Sally from Solihull giving her opinion on your love life!'

I felt very, very small. 'And what did Sally from Solihull think?' I ventured.

'To cut a long story short, she thought you were a sad bastard and a poor excuse of a role model for liberated women. Although she didn't put it quite that eloquently.'

'I don't pretend to be a role model.'

'I know, but it comes with the territory, doesn't it? You wear a dress to a premiere and it appears in Topshop the following week because they know every teenage girl in the country will buy it. You have a bad-hair day and shove it back in a ponytail and beauty editors all over London start writing features on this season's must-have hairdo, as sported by Laura Mac. You go out with a philandering smackhead of a man and suddenly everyone wants one. I rest my case.' Nat hit the table with a baguette, which snapped in half and hit Graham's mother on the head at the next table. 'Oops.' Nat giggled.

I couldn't help smiling. Even when she was criticizing me, I loved being with Nat. However high I floated out into the ether of Celebland she always managed to catch hold of my shirt-tails and pull me right back down to the real world, usually just in time.

'God, I can't believe you didn't just shag Adam on the spot,' she continued with gusto. 'I would have.'

'Nat,' I squealed. 'You're a happily married mother of one.'

'Oh, I know, but I can dream.' She waved at Rob, who was on the other side of the boat, showing Freddie and his trendy baby jeans off to the girls from *Glitz*'s fashion department. 'You must fancy him, surely. Everyone fancies him.'

It was true. Nat, Lucy, Monica, Fiona, my gran, the list was endless. So, why not me? I conjured up a mental picture of Adam, stripped to the waist, muscles rippling, smooth, tanned flesh glistening with sweat and a naughty glint in those sparkling blue eyes.

'He is gorgeous,' I admitted. 'But I've just never thought of him in that way.'

'Because you're a snob,' announced Natalie.

'No, I'm not,' I argued. 'Anything but.'

Natalie put on her judge's hat again – it was obviously a role-play thing that she and Rob acted out in the privacy of their own home. 'Here is the evidence,' she announced. 'Your boyfriend is an aristocrat. Twice over, in fact.'

'What do you mean?'

'Well, he's a real, bona-fide, old-fashioned toff.'

'Yes.' I nodded. That was true.

'And he's rock royalty, too, which these days is way higher in the social pecking order.'

I looked at her with a bemused smirk.

'Who does our society worship?' she demanded.

I shrugged.

'Not God, not Charles and Camilla, but Posh and Becks.' Nat tried to rest her elbow on the table, but missed and nearly fell off her chair.

'Natalie, I do not worship Posh and Becks,' I told her as I helped her get upright again. 'I mean, I'm told they're very nice people, but they're not really my scene.'

'No, but you've happily thrown yourself onto the altar of stardom because you think it's the ultimate experience and, this is my point, the only reason you *think* you're in love with Ricky is because he's so famous. Conversely,' she stabbed the table with a fork, 'the only reason you're not in love with Adam is because he's way down in the pecking order. In fact, I don't think builders even register on your graph, do they?'

'I don't have a graph,' I explained, patiently.

'Now you do. Here ...'

Natalie made a graph on the table, using a knife and some sugar cubes.

'This is Ricky,' she explained, placing one cube right at the top, beside the point of the knife. 'And this is you' – she put me about an inch further down – 'a bit lower down because you're just a glorified TV presenter. And Adam is way, way, way down here.' She put his sugar cube right at the bottom of the handle.

'And where are you, Nat?'

'Well, I used to be about halfway up, but now I've fallen right off the table because I'm a stay-at-home mum and we don't count in society.'

'Right,' I said, shaking my head at her ridiculous theory.

'The thing is, it would take a brave woman in your position to consider having a relationship with someone like Adam. It would be like a Victorian lady having an affair with the stablehand. Very Lady Chatterley if you know what I mean?'

'No, because you're talking bollocks, Nat. You're pissed.'

'Drunk people talk the most sense,' she replied. 'Anyway, I haven't finished.'

'That's what I was worried about,' I said, feigning boredom. Actually, I was quite enjoying the old banter. It was the first time since Lucy's death that I'd felt a glimmer of happiness.

'Right,' continued Nat, fishing a pen out of my handbag. 'I'm going to write a list of attributes for both Adam and

Ricky. My theory is that if you were the old you, the not-famous Laura Mac, and Ricky Dicky wasn't a rock star, then you would pick Adam every time because he's fundamentally a more worthwhile human being. Let's go.' She picked up a paper napkin and wrote Ricky and Adam at the top. Then she scrubbed out Ricky and wrote Dick. I had a sneaking suspicion this was going to be a rather one-sided affair. 'We'll start with Dick,' she announced.

'Sexy,' I suggested.

Well, I suppose, if you like that scrawny, unwashed look,' said Nat.

'Millions of girls fancy Ricky,' I reminded her. 'They can't all be wrong.'

'OK, I'll let you have that one.' She reluctantly scrawled 'sexy' in his column.

'Talented,' I added, warming to the game.

'I accept the guy can hold a tune,' nodded Natalie. 'See? I'm not being biased.'

'Not much.' I laughed.

'Heroin addict,' she chanted with an innocent smile. 'Cheating, supermodel-shagging bastard.'

'Natalie,' I said, flashing her a warning look.

'Conceited.' She ignored me and carried on writing her list. 'Cruel, selfish, spoilt—'

'That's not fair,' I butted in. 'He's got good points.'

'So name them,' invited Nat.

'Um ...' I thought hard. Why did I love Ricky? 'Exciting! He's definitely exciting. Generous – he bought me this necklace. Caring ...'

'Who does he care for?' demanded Nat with a sneer. 'You? I don't think so.'

'He cared about Lucy,' I said quietly.

Nat didn't have the heart to argue and wrote 'caring' without another word.

'Now Adam,' she announced. 'He's sexy, too, so I'll put that down.'

'Good with his hands,' I added, meaning that he was a builder.

'I wouldn't know,' pondered Nat. 'I'd like to, though.'

'Down to earth,' I continued.

'Kind,' said Nat. 'Friendly, considerate, hard-working, good body ...'

'You always have to lower the tone,' I said. 'Tidy – he always cleans up after himself, and me. I'll have to get a cleaner now.'

'Honest,' added Nat. 'He admitted to you how he felt.'

'Proud,' I said thoughtfully, remembering how he hadn't wanted me to see the pain I'd caused him. 'Very proud.'

'Faithful,' continued Nat. 'He didn't get off with Lucy when he was with that Italian bird.'

'He definitely keeps it in his trousers, that's for sure,' I agreed. 'He even turned my sister down. Ah, but he did say he'd fancied me since we met, which means he was thinking about me when he was with his girlfriend.'

'That's different,' she argued.

'Why?'

'Because you're his "one"; he couldn't help it,' she replied wistfully.

'Natalie, you're being ridiculous, now. He just had a crush; he'll be over me in a couple of weeks.'

'Sure he will,' scoffed Nat, pouring her fourth glass of champagne and spilling it on the tablecloth.

'He will,' I insisted, trying to convince myself as much as her. I didn't want to feel responsible for Adam's unhappiness. I couldn't handle my own, let alone anyone else's.

'Whatever you say, babes.' She downed her drink and then neatly folded up the napkin she'd been writing on and put it in my handbag.

'I don't want to keep that,' I told her.

'Yes you do,' she insisted. 'Keep it for prosperity.'

'It's prosterity,' I corrected her. 'Or maybe it's posterity. What is that word?'

'Whatever.' She waved her hand drunkenly at me. 'Laura, I need some fresh air. Take me outside, please.'

When Natalie had finished throwing up over the side of the boat, we stood huddled together against the cold autumn night, leaning on the barrier and watching the twinkling lights of central London as we passed by slowly, Waterloo and the London Eye on one side, Westminster and Big Ben on the other.

'I don't think I like London any more,' I said quietly.

'It's got so many people, but it's got no soul,' agreed Nat wistfully.

'That was rather eloquent,' I complimented her, thinking how true her statement was.

'Gerry Rafferty,' she explained. '"Baker Street".'

I laughed until my stomach hurt, but then I remembered Lucy and felt guilty for being happy, for being alive.

'You must come to the cottage to stay for a few days,' said Nat. 'It's really lovely. It'll do you good to get out of this shithole of a city for a while. We're going to visit Rob's parents in Dublin next week. We'll be away for a fortnight, but after that, you'll come, yeah?'

I nodded. 'Filming starts again at the beginning of November,' I told her. 'But maybe I could squeeze in a visit the week before.'

'That sounds like a good plan,' said Nat. 'I worry about you. I wish I could see you more often.'

'Me, too,' I said.

She looked up at me with her big brown puppy-dog eyes and suddenly looked very serious. 'Promise me one thing, Laura.'

'What?'

'Promise me you'll come to me if you ever need help.'

I promised.

Rob appeared on the deck with a grizzly Freddie. 'He needs to be fed, love,' he told Nat.

'Oh dear, drunk in charge of a baby,' laughed Natalie. 'Time for me to shock the gay community by baring my breasts in public.'

Nat and Rob went to find a quiet spot amidst the madcap celebrations and I went to find the ladies' because I needed a fix.

When I got home I was struck by the emptiness of the house, just like I had been every day since Adam left. He'd gone on Monday and it was now Saturday. Usually when I got in from an evening out, he'd make me a cup of tea and sit me down in the kitchen for a chat. It didn't matter if it was 4 a.m., he was always there, smoking a roll-up on the back doorstep, waiting for me to return safely. He'd say, 'Oh, you're home then; I was just getting some air,' and pretend that it was a happy coincidence that he was still up, but I always knew he was waiting for me. I began to take it for granted that I'd never be alone in the middle of the night. I wondered if he'd been sitting there all those times I hadn't bothered coming home, the nights I'd partied right through until tomorrow and the times I'd stayed at Ricky's hotel. Was he on a step somewhere in Aberdeen thinking about me now? I wandered into the dark kitchen, but tonight there was no one waiting for me.

There were no messages from Ricky on the answer machine, just a sweet but rather odd one from my gran that said, 'Just wanted to tell you I love you. Take care, Laura.'

It was too late to phone her, but I made a mental note to speak to her in the morning. I hadn't been in touch for weeks. I tried Ricky's hotel in Chicago.

'Can I be put through to Mike Hunt's room, please?' I asked as politely as possible. Ricky always insisted on using schoolboy pseudonyms to check in to hotel rooms. It made asking for him highly embarrassing, which I guess was the plan.

'Whom should I say is calling?' asked the polite woman on the end of the line.

'It's his girlfriend,' I replied. And then added, 'Laura. It's Laura,' just in case the word girlfriend should cause any confusion.

'Hold the line, please,' said the woman.

I listened to 'Stairway to Heaven' for a couple of minutes while I was on hold and then the receptionist came back on the line and apologized. 'I'm sorry,' she said. 'But Mr Hunt can't be disturbed at present. Goodbye.'

I tried not to imagine what Ricky might be up to that would prevent him from getting to the phone and kidded myself that they were probably in the middle of some important band meeting. There didn't seem any point in having a cup of tea alone, so I popped a couple of the Snowman's sleeping pills and went to bed.

I was dreaming that the phone was ringing, and then the answer machine picked up the call and Dad was speaking to me. He sounded strange: sad, frightened and very far away. 'Laura,' he was saying. 'Are you there? I need to speak to you. It's urgent. Please pick up the phone.' It had to be a dream because Dad hadn't spoken to me since July, but it sounded so real. And then the fog of sleep slowly began to clear and I realized that his voice really was in the room. I grabbed for the phone beside my bed. The clock on the bedside table said 12.25 p.m.

'Dad. Dad, I'm here,' I said in a croaky voice. 'What's wrong?'

'It's your gran,' he said solemnly. 'She's dead. I thought I should be the one to tell you.'

My hand shot to my mouth and managed to let out a strangled, 'Noooo!' before I dissolved into tears.

He kept the call as short as possible. Gran had died in her sleep. Adam's dad had found her this morning when he'd popped round to mow her lawn. Gran's great big heart turned out to be a weak one. It had given so much that it didn't have the strength to beat any more. I thought mine would crumble into a million pieces it hurt so much to know she was gone. Dad told me the funeral would be held on Wednesday.

'She would want you to be there,' he said, implying that he wouldn't.

And then he was gone and I was left alone with a grief so enormous that I didn't know what to do with myself. How could Granny just die like that? I picked up the pink orchid from my bedroom table and threw it across the room. The pot smashed against the fitted wardrobes Adam had so meticulously made, chipping the wood and covering the floorboards with petals, earth and pieces of broken china.

18

Storms forecast for north-east of Scotland

When I phoned Ricky to ask him to come back for the funeral it was a test. I knew the band had a week's break after the Chicago gig before they played New York. The boys had planned a few days of partying in the Big Apple and I knew Ricky was looking forward to it, but I needed him to be with me. He had plenty of time to fly to the UK and back again before the first Madison Square Garden gig. So I asked him to make the sacrifice.

'Come on, babe,' he half laughed. 'You're not serious. I didn't even know the old dear.'

'Ricky, I'm deadly serious,' I replied earnestly. 'I've never asked anything of you before, but now I'm telling you that I need you to come with me. I can't face it on my own, and you know how things are with my family. Please, Ricky, I'm begging you.'

'It's just not possible, babe,' he said cheerfully. 'I've got stuff planned. I can't let everybody down now, can I?'

'But you'll let me down, right?' I asked tearfully.

'Laura, it's a hell of a favour you're asking. You can't expect me to drop everything and fly back just because your grandmother's died. Jesus, you're not my wife.' He was starting to sound mildly irritated. 'Anyway, you'll have your friend Adam to hold your hand, won't you?' He spat the word 'friend' out. 'He's from up there in the Outer Hebrides, too, isn't he?'

'Aberdeen,' I corrected him, amazed that such an expensive education could leave him so ignorant. 'It's the other side of the country and it's on the mainland.'

'Whatever,' he said dismissively.

'Adam and I have fallen out,' I told him.

'Oh yes?' Ricky sounded interested. 'Did he drop his hammer on your tootsies?'

'No,' I explained. 'It's a bit awkward really. He says he's in love with me.'

Ricky dissolved into fits of hysteria on the other end of the line. 'That is the funniest thing I've heard in ages,' he guffawed. 'What a total prick, man. Oi, Lewis,' he shouted into his hotel room. 'Listen to this, that builder of Laura's has only gone and declared undying love for her. I know, what an arsehole. That's hilarious, babe.'

'It was quite upsetting actually,' I scolded. 'He was really sad.'

'Well, what did he expect?' sneered Ricky. 'Did he honestly think you were going to dump me and get it on with him instead? Like, that's going to happen.'

'So, you're not going to come to the funeral with me?' I changed the subject back to the matter in hand. 'Even though I'm pleading with you.' I emphasized the word pleading with my girliest charm.

'Well, let me see.' Ricky was being sarcastic. 'A party in New York or a funeral in, where did you say?'

'Just outside Aberdeen.'

'No,' he said flatly. 'I'm not going to come. It'll be fine. Just have a wee dram for me and send the old lady off in style.'

'Oh, Ricky, please,' I persevered.

'Laura, don't turn into a whingeing cow. You know I can't stand clingy women and you don't want to annoy me, do you?'

'No,' I replied, beaten.

'Well then, shut up, OK?'

'OK.' I sniffed. 'I'm sorry.'

'That's better. Now I'm going to go and have some fun. Later, babe.'

The line went dead. I stared at the receiver in misery and disbelief. No tears came. I'd cried myself dry.

The small granite church was overflowing with smartly dressed, solemn-faced locals who had come to pay their last respects to Maggie McNaughton. I stood in the front pew for the service, beside Fiona, who held my hand tightly throughout. Gran wouldn't have wanted a scene, so we were both trying desperately to hold it together. Our shoulders shook gently as the minister spoke of her compassion, spirit and lust for life, and silent tears dripped from our noses onto the cold stone floor. Fiona had brought her new boyfriend – a tall, blond Australian doctor called Curtis – with her. Gran would have approved. Dad gave a reading with a grey face that had aged ten years in three days. He told the congregation that, even at his age, to lose a mother was to lose your childhood for ever, and Mum snivelled quietly into her hankie, heartbroken at the sight of her husband's pain.

Gran was buried beside her parents and grandparents in the family plot, which looked out over the angry North Sea and the body of her brother Neil. A headstone marked his passing, but he wasn't there. The graveyard was perched on top of a cliff on the windiest, bleakest spot on the coast. There were no trees, and the flowers left for the dead by the living had broken free of their containers and blew in manic, swirling dances around the graveyard. The minister's heavy black coat whipped around his body and his voice could hardly be heard above the sound of the wind and the crashing waves below. As I shivered by the graveside, I swear I could feel the breath of a hundred spirits on the back of my neck. I sobbed huge gulping sobs that the wind blew away. The coffin was lowered into the ground and with all my heart I wanted to throw myself on top of it, to stay with my granny for ever, but instead I threw in a single white lily – Gran's favourite flower. She'd had them in her wedding bouquet. Dad placed his hand very lightly and oh so briefly on the small of my back and gave me a flicker of a sad smile. Even in death, Gran was looking out for me, easing my way back into the family fold.

I couldn't bear to see the earth being shovelled over the coffin. It was just too final. Instead, I stared out over the ocean and watched the white horses ride to shore. I was miles away, remembering sunny days on the beach with Gran, when I slowly became aware of someone watching me. Adam stood on the other side of the grave, beside his parents. He looked magnificent in a black suit, with his black hair blowing in the wind. My heart lurched with an emotion I didn't recognize: loss, fondness, guilt? We held each other's gaze for a long time.

Back at Doric Cottage, Mum had put on a fine spread of sandwiches, sponge cake and scones – although they weren't nearly as good as Granny's. I found her in the kitchen, avoiding her grief by keeping herself busy making endless pots of tea. When I walked in, she put down the kettle, wiped her hands on her apron and held me tightly to her chest, as if I were four years old with a bleeding knee.

'Life's too short,' she whispered in my ear. And we both knew what she meant. I had never felt so happy, or so sad, before.

Later, Fiona and I escaped to the garden for a cigarette in the bushes, leaving Curtis to deal with Dad's third degree.

'He'll be fine,' said Fiona casually. 'He's a proper working-class lad done good. Dad'll love him. Where's Ricky?'

'New York.' I tried not to look disappointed.

'Oh well, probably for the best.' Fi shrugged. 'Dad's upset enough without being wound up by Ricky. Did you see Adam by the way?'

I nodded. Fiona knew nothing about what had happened between us and I intended to keep it that way. She might have a new boyfriend, but it was only a few weeks ago she'd been after Adam herself.

'Christ, he looks good in a suit,' she enthused. 'I almost fell into the grave with my tongue hanging out when I saw him.'

'Fiona, that's a bit disrespectful.' I frowned.

'Why?' She looked at me with wide-eyed innocence. 'Granny would have said the same thing if she'd been here.'

'True,' I conceded.

'In fact, if she could see this sorry lot' – Fi nodded towards the house full of grim-faced mourners – 'she'd tell them to lighten up.'

I smiled weakly at my little sister.

'I don't know what I'm going to do without her,' I sighed.

'Me neither,' agreed Fiona with a deep puff on her cigarette.

Back in the house I nervously approached my father.

'Dad?' I ventured bravely. 'I thought, what with everything that's happened, that maybe we could, you know, be friends.'

He looked old and broken, as if the fight had been knocked out of him.

'Laura,' he said softly, putting a hand on my shoulder. 'You are my daughter. I may not approve of the choices you make in life, but you will always be my daughter and I can't change that. I wouldn't, even if I could.'

'Thanks, Dad.' I smiled, but he held his finger up to stop me.

'The thing is,' he continued, 'I can't be around you when you're like this. When you're embroiled in this, this' – he searched for the word – 'sordid world. But if you ever decide to leave that behind and come home, then the door will always be open. I just want you to know that. It's your choice, Laura.'

He patted my shoulder weakly and walked off in the direction of Uncle Blair. It was progress, sort of.

I tried to find Adam. There was too much left unsaid and I felt the need to make amends. Besides, I missed him. I eyed the heaving living room, trying to find his head above the grey-haired throng.

'He's gone,' said a familiar voice behind me.

I jumped and spun round to face her.

'Fiona, how do you know who I'm looking for?' I asked.

'It's obvious,' she replied.

'But …'

'I saw how you two looked at each other earlier. I'm not daft, you know. Come on, spill the beans. What's going on?'

'Nothing's going on,' I lied.

'So why did he go home immediately after the funeral? And why are you so keen to find him now?' Not much got past Fiona.

'We had a slight disagreement,' I said.

'Mmm, and …?' Fi fixed me with the kind of stare you can't wriggle away from.

'OK, but this goes no further,' I warned her.

She took the news well, I thought. There wasn't a hint of jealousy.

'You should go for it,' she encouraged me. 'According to today's papers, Ricky's with Venetia again anyway.'

*

Gran had left me a heavy A4-sized manilla envelope, bound together with Sellotape. The day after the funeral, I took it down to the beach to open it. Inside were a set of keys and a letter. It was typically Gran. It read:

My dearest Laura,

I haven't left you any money. You have enough of the stuff already and it hasn't made you happy, so I've left it all to Fiona as I know the NHS doesn't pay very well. What you need, my girl, is somewhere to come home to, so here are the keys to Doric Cottage. It's all yours. The place isn't worth much money, but it comes full of love. Please keep it that way.
I love you. Be happy.

Gran xxx

PS. From what I've read in the papers, I don't think much of that Ricky Jones. Do yourself a favour and find yourself a decent man.

I looked back up at the cottage, clinging to its cliff. My life was in London. What on earth was I going to do with a house near Aberdeen?

19

Is this the end for Ricky and Laura?

When I missed the first period I put it down to the grief of Lucy's death. When I missed another I began to worry. I'd come off the pill months ago, convinced it was making me fat – fat chance – but I couldn't be pregnant, could I?

I'd insisted on using condoms since I'd found out about Ricky's dalliance with heroin and groupies. He'd complained, of course, arguing that sex wasn't the same when he wore a rubber, that the sensations were muted and his enjoyment impaired – the usual rubbish that certain men spout when faced with taking responsibility for contraception. But I'd been strong – at least until Lucy's death. Ricky had been depressed and about to go on tour in the States. The last time we had sex before he left for LA, I gave in and we used no protection. To be honest, I wanted to feel as close to him as was humanly possible, knowing that I wouldn't be able to touch him or feel him inside me again for weeks on end. All I wanted was to melt into his body and disappear. I no longer cared about taking risks. Life was short and cheap. Lucy had taught me that. And so had Ricky.

It was a week since the funeral. I was sitting on my loo, willing the pregnancy test in my hand not to reveal the second blue line that would confirm I was pregnant. It chose to ignore me: the second line appeared as clear as day. I did another test, just in case, but the same thing happened.

'Bollocks, bollocks, bollocks, bollocks.'

I threw the plastic test across the room. This wasn't what I had planned. OK, so the people from Superbra had given me six weeks to put on weight before the next shoot, but pregnancy was a bit of a drastic measure. My gut instinct was not so much that I didn't want a baby, more that I couldn't cope with one. Christ, I was having enough trouble looking after myself, without worrying about a little one. And then there was Ricky. He wasn't exactly the caring, sharing, homely type. What would he say?

I poured myself a deep bubble bath. In times of crisis, it was the perfect place to think. As I languished in the warm water I stroked my tummy and tried to find a hint of a bump. There was none, just the usual concave pit, but somewhere, deep inside me, was the beginning of a new life, and once that thought crept into my head I couldn't help but become attached to the fledgling embryo. Perhaps this was a sign, I reasoned, my wake-up call. I had lost too many people lately, through carelessness and death, but here was a new life. Maybe this tiny someone had been sent to save me. A baby would change everything; it would give me a reason to live again. I would love it unconditionally and it would love me right back. I even wondered, for a moment, if my gran could have had something to do with this new life.

Oh, it would be difficult. I knew that. But didn't teenage girls all over the country bring up babies all the time? According to the press they did. And if they could do it ...

I had money, lots of it. I could afford to give this child the very best start in life. It would be blessed, born into wealth and status, with a title and a stately home to inherit one day. The more I thought about it, the more the idea of impending motherhood appealed. Ricky would be shocked, of course, but he'd warm to the idea soon enough, just like I had. Funky young celebrities had kids all the time. It was practically de rigueur. Brad and Angelina, Posh and Becks. They all did it and survived. And maternity wear could look so stylish these days. Plus, it would bring me and Ricky together for ever. If I produced a mini Hurlingham-Jones, how could he fail to love me? Fatherhood would change him, I was sure of it. By the time the water turned too cold for comfort, I'd planned the wedding, the christening and the kid's twenty-first birthday party.

The first thing I did after dressing quickly was flush three grams of coke down the toilet. I prayed the drugs and booze I'd consumed in the last few weeks hadn't done any damage and promised myself I'd live cleanly from now on, for the sake of my baby. I made an emergency appointment with a top Harley Street gynaecologist for the following morning and booked a first-class ticket on a flight to New York, leaving from Heathrow in the afternoon, then I ordered a ham and mushroom pizza with extra cheese, garlic bread and a full-fat Coke for home delivery. If I was going to get fat, I might as well start at once. That night I slept without the aid of pills for the first time in a very long while, blissfully content to dream about the la-la land I'd created for myself, where babies solved problems and baddies turned into daddies overnight.

The perfectly polished air stewardess offered me champagne, but I asked for mineral water instead. The doctor had confirmed with an ultrasound scan that I was nine weeks pregnant, give or take a few days. I'd even seen my baby on screen: a tiny tadpole of a creature with a heart that was already beating. I couldn't concentrate on the film being shown on the personal TV that popped up out of the arm of my seat, all I could do was practise my speech for Ricky in my head. He didn't know I was coming; it was all to be one big surprise.

I noticed, as I strode through JFK airport, that Ricky's face was pouting from every newsstand on the cover of *Rolling Stone* magazine. He was naked from the waist up and wearing a crown on top of his long hair. 'RICHARD I OF ROCK' read the headline, and I remembered what Nat had said about Ricky being aristocracy twice over. If I had a son, he would be a prince, and a daughter would be daddy's little princess.

New York had never looked so inviting. The sun shone brightly on the yellow roofs of the waiting cabs. Fall had come later to the Big Apple than autumn had to the Big Smoke; it was positively toasty in comparison to Heathrow, and I shed my white sheepskin coat with glee. As the cabbie threw my leather Louis Vuitton holdall into the boot, I placed my Gucci shades firmly on my face and smiled. The cab headed for midtown Manhattan, slowly because of the midday traffic jams, while I wriggled impatiently in the back, ready to burst with anticipation. I had a feeling that this journey was the beginning of the rest of my life, and that whatever was about to happen would change my world for ever.

All the doormen at the hip Hudson Hotel looked like male models.

'Good evening, miss,' said the polite young man in the uniform with the chiselled jawline and floppy blond hair. 'May I take your bags?'

I followed him up an escalator into the perfectly polished lobby, with its clean wooden lines and impeccable staff. Sarah Jessica Parker was in the bar next door.

'May I help you, miss?' asked the breathtakingly beautiful girl behind the desk. I decided she must be a 'resting' actress.

'I'm here to see Ricky Jones,' I babbled. 'I'm his girlfriend. It's a surprise.'

'We don't have anyone of that name staying here,' said the girl sweetly.

'Oh yeah, sorry.' I blushed. 'He never books in under his real name. Um, which one is he using again?'

The girl looked at me blankly. She must have known perfectly well that Ricky was somewhere in the building, but she was way too professional to let on. After all, I could just have been some particularly expensively dressed groupie.

'They're always rude,' I explained. 'His pseudonyms, I mean. Give me a minute. It's coming to me. Um ... Crispy Cock. That's it, Mr Chris Peacock.'

How the receptionist managed to keep a straight face, I don't know.

'I'll just see if Mr Peacock is available,' she said with an award-winning smile. 'What name shall I give him?'

'Laura McNaughton,' I replied.

'Mr Peacock?' The receptionist had obviously got right through to Ricky. 'You have a visitor in reception. A Miss McNaughton.'

There was a pause. 'Yes. She's right here in the lobby, sir.'

Then another pause. 'Blonde, about five eight, very pretty ...'

The receptionist smiled at me shyly as she answered Ricky's questions.

'Yeah, sure. Here she is.'

She handed me the receiver. 'He wants to speak with you. I don't think he can believe you're actually here.'

'Laura?' Ricky's voice sounded thick with sleep, or maybe drugs.

'Hi, gorgeous,' I said chirpily. 'Surprise!'

'What are you doing here?' He didn't exactly sound over-awed with excitement, but I put it down to him having just woken up.

'I've got some news that I thought I'd tell you in person,' I explained. 'Shall I come up?'

'No.'. He sounded decidedly unenthusiastic. 'Gimme a few minutes. Just wait in the bar. Oh, and, Laura?'

'Uh-huh?'

'Order me a Bloody Mary.'

I thought it was strange that Ricky didn't just invite me up to his room but he'd sounded adamant I wait downstairs and I didn't want to begin this important reunion with an argument. So, I did as I was told ... and sat at a table with a view of the lifts so that I could watch for Ricky while I sipped my mineral water and fought off the urge to light a Marlboro Light. I tried not to stare too hard at SJP. Ten minutes passed, then twenty. I ordered another glass of water. Half an hour went by. I desperately needed to go to the loo, but I was too scared I'd miss Ricky if I moved from my seat. Forty-five minutes came and went. Still I waited. Almost exactly an hour after I had walked into the lobby, the lift opened and spewed out Ricky Jones, his hair still wet from the shower. He wandered casually towards me, stopping to air kiss a couple of immaculately groomed New York gals on the way.

'Hi.' I waved with a cheesy grin.

'Laura, this is a surprise.' Ricky seemed uptight.

He kissed me in the vague area of my lips while looking over my shoulder to check out who was in the bar.

'Your drink.' I passed him his Bloody Mary. 'But it might be a bit warm by now.'

'Cheers,' said Ricky with a forced grin. His eyes weren't smiling though; they were too busy darting nervously around the lobby.

'Are you looking for someone?' I asked.

'No.' He shook his head.

We sat there in silence for a minute or two. I watched Ricky closely, wondering when to start my speech about the baby, but I couldn't find the right words or the right moment. He seemed horribly distracted.

'So,' I said. It was something to say.

'So?' he repeated. 'What brings you here?'

'You do,' I replied.

Just then I spotted a tall skinny figure wiggling through the lobby in that weird, stamping, catwalk manner that only supermodels have.

'Is that Venetia?' I asked.

Ricky spun round as if someone had poked him up the bum with a hot toasting fork.

'No,' he said too quickly. 'Look, let's get out of here. I fancy some air.'

He downed his Bloody Mary, grabbed his leather jacket and put his shades on. He was the only man I knew who could wear his sunglasses indoors and still look cool. I followed him as he trotted down the escalator and out into the street. It had been Venetia, of course. I wasn't daft. But now I reckoned I had one over on the Stick Insect. I was going to be the mother of Ricky's children – beat that one, Freakoid.

'Where do you want to go?' asked Ricky, grabbing my arm and marching me down West 58th Street, away from the Hudson Hotel as quickly as possible.

'I don't know. You were the one who wanted some air,' I panted as I was dragged along behind him, narrowly missing a cab on 8th Avenue. 'It's a nice day. What about Central Park?'

'Cool,' said Ricky.

We turned left onto 7th Avenue and up towards the gates to the park. It was as beautiful a location as any to announce the arrival of Hurlingham-Jones Junior. Ricky gradually began to relax as he put a safe distance between me and Venetia.

'Ricky, can you hold my hand not my wrist?' I asked politely. 'You look as though you're abducting me and you don't want to get arrested for assault.'

We passed rollerbladers and dog-walkers, joggers and lovers, and then, deep in the bowels of Central Park, we plonked ourselves down on a bench.

'So?' asked Ricky again. We were back to where we'd been at the Hudson.

I took a deep breath and launched into my speech.

'Ricky, the thing is, and I don't want you to panic, but you see, I'm, I'm, I'm …'

'You're pregnant, aren't you?' he said, pretty casually considering the circumstances.

I breathed a huge sigh of relief. 'Yes, how did you know?'

'Well, you've never flown across the Atlantic to talk to me before. You usually just leave five hundred messages on my voicemail when you want to speak to me.'

'And you're OK about it?' I asked, bewildered at how easy it had been to break the news.

He shrugged. 'It's no big deal, is it?'

I was confused. 'Ricky, I'm pregnant. I'm going to have a baby. I'd say that was a pretty big deal, wouldn't you?'

'But you can get sorted out like that.' He clicked his fingers. 'My record company will pay for it. They always do.' Ricky lit a fag, leaned back on the bench and put his arm lazily around my shoulders. 'Don't stress, babe,' he said. 'It's a simple procedure, so I'm told.'

I shook his arm off my shoulders.

'I'm not going to have an abortion,' I said.

Ricky smirked. 'Oh yes you are. And don't give me any of that "it's my body" bullshit, either, because I've heard it all before. It's my sperm and I don't want it to be used to fertilize any eggs, thank you very much. I could sue, you know, for sperm theft.'

I gawped, open-mouthed, at him.

'You talk as if this is a common occurrence,' I said in disbelief.

'It is, babe,' he replied, cool as you like. 'You don't actually think you're the first to get "accidentally" pregnant by the Jonester, do you?'

I was flabbergasted at his callousness.

'Ricky, it *was* an accident,' I insisted. 'But I'm not getting rid of it.'

'Yes you are.' He drew deeply on his cigarette until his top lip puckered. 'Don't piss me off, Laura.'

Ricky narrowed his eyes. He looked so mean that a vague feeling of fear began to rise in my stomach.

'But I'm not just some one-night stand you can toss aside.' I stood up for myself. 'I'm your girlfriend.'

He shrugged in a non-committal way and said, 'Sort of.'

Anger rose like bile from my stomach and caught in my throat. I counted to ten and swallowed the fury, determined to keep things reasonable. Perhaps it was the shock talking; maybe I could talk him round.

'What are you going to do? Dump me because I'm pregnant? You're a twenty-seven-year-old man, not a scared schoolboy who doesn't know any better,' I argued. 'Think about it, Ricky. We're both adults, we have money, we're perfectly well qualified to be parents.'

Ricky threw back his head and laughed cruelly.

'You must be even more stupid than you look, darling. Do you really think that's going to happen?' he asked. 'You talk about it as if we've got a future together. Did you think I was going to get down on one knee and propose?'

He watched my reaction closely with a smirk on his face. I could see now that it was just a game to him, but this was my life and it was falling apart. I couldn't stop the tears any longer. My bottom lip had developed a life of its own, wobbling uncontrollably, the floodgates opened and huge gulping sobs escaped involuntarily from my mouth.

'I – I – I thought we were happy,' I stammered.

He looked at me blankly and said casually, 'We were. It's been fun, but I think it should end here before you get any more silly ideas into that pretty little head of yours. I thought you understood the rules, babe. I don't do commitment, I don't do monogamy and I certainly don't do the married-with-children thing. Not yet anyway.'

I took off my shades so I could wipe my eyes.

'Put your sunglasses back on,' ordered Ricky impatiently. 'You've got make-up all over your face and you look terrible. We might get spotted, and I don't want a scene.'

There was no one to see us except a red squirrel sitting on a tree opposite. I thought, rather irrationally under the circumstances, how nice it was to see a red one. You only get grey squirrels in London these days.

'So that's it. Over. Just like that?' I asked.

'God, you're quick, aren't you?' scoffed Ricky, throwing his cigarette butt onto the grass.

'Why are you being so mean to me?' I howled.

Ricky softened slightly and said, 'Look, it's a shame, I admit it. I've enjoyed your company, you're a nice girl, a good laugh, fantastic in bed, it has to be said, but we were never going to have a future. Even if I wasn't in a band and always away on tour, it could never happen. My future's been mapped out since birth and you're not the sort of bride my family have in mind for me. Christ, you're as wild as I am. You're totally off the rails. I'm a Hurlingham-Jones. If I ever get married it'll be to some sensible girl whose parents are friends of my parents. Do you get the picture? Someone who knows how to organize the staff, not some mental Scottish TV presenter.'

'And what about the baby?' I asked desperately. 'Our baby?'

'There isn't going to be a baby.' It sounded so final. There was no argument.

'You can't make me get rid of it,' I said stubbornly.

'Yes I can,' he said coldly. 'Because if you don't, I can make your life hell. Believe me, Laura, you don't want to go there.'

The mean glint in his eye made me shudder. I was scared of what would happen next. Ricky frog-marched me back to the hotel and up into his room. There were two empty glasses by the bed. One of them had a lipstick mark round the rim.

'Sit there,' he ordered, pushing me onto the unmade bed. 'I'm going to make a phone call and sort this mess out.'

'I won't have an abortion,' I sobbed.

Ricky ignored me and called his manager at the record company, taking the phone into the bathroom so I couldn't hear the conversation. I sat and waited for my fate to be arranged. Somewhere in my heavy heart I knew I didn't have the strength to fight this battle. I'd taken so many knocks in the past few weeks I felt punch drunk, weak; my head was spinning and my brain was numb.

Ricky came back into the room.

'It's all arranged,' he said. 'A cab will pick you up outside in five minutes and take you to Newark Airport. You're booked on an overnight flight back to London. Someone will be waiting for you at Gatwick and you'll be taken straight to a private clinic for the operation. It doesn't take long. You'll be home tomorrow afternoon.'

'And what about us?' I asked weakly. 'Will I see you again?'

'Hey, I'm sure we'll hook up at some party or other pretty soon,' he said light-heartedly. 'Maybe we'll even have a shag for old times' sake.'

He straddled me on the bed, held my wrists above my head and kissed me hard on the mouth. I struggled in his firm grasp, trying to turn my head away. He must have tasted the salt of my tears.

As I walked out through the lobby, I spotted Venetia sitting in the bar. She raised her champagne flute to me as I left.

20

Reality bites

I was broken. It was as if the part of my brain that dealt with emotions had been so overloaded with pain that it just shut down. I'd become a pawn in Ricky Jones's sick game and I didn't have the strength to break free. Instead, I surrendered totally and let myself be manoeuvred from position to position. When I stepped through the gate at Gatwick I spotted a man in a chauffeur's cap holding a sign with my name on it. A couple of photographers who did the airport shift took my picture, but I didn't respond. I walked like a zombie towards the driver, handed him my holdall and followed him to the black Mercedes outside. The rest is like a half-remembered nightmare, too painful to recall in detail. I don't remember the journey to London, or being bundled through a back door into the exclusive women's clinic that specialized in celebrity elective Caesareans with tummy tucks thrown in. Nor can I recollect being shown into a private room, handed a gown and told to lie on a trolley to be wheeled into theatre, but it must have happened. All I can remember clearly – very, very clearly – is seeing the anaesthetist coming towards me with a needle and suddenly waking up. I said, 'No,' in a clear, loud voice. 'No, I don't want to do this.' I know I said it. I'm sure. But the next thing I was aware of was waking up in a crisply made bed, in a pink room with white roses on the windowsill. My head was all fuzzy and there was a strange ache in my groin. I put my hand where the pain was and it came back covered in blood. The abortion had taken place despite my protestations. I had had a child stolen from my womb.

It was too much to take in and I must have shut down again. When I look back, I can vaguely see a female doctor in pale-blue overalls and glasses coming into the room to examine me. I know I told her that I'd been mutilated, that I'd changed my mind before the operation. She just said it was natural to feel confused after an anaesthetic. She told me I was fine and that I could go home, so I got dressed and waited for the driver to arrive and take me back to the car. When we got to the back door of the clinic, he covered my head with my sheepskin coat and guided me to the car, past the crowd of baying paparazzi outside. I could see the bright lights of camera flashes through my coat and feel the heat of their bodies closing in on me. Alien hands grabbed at me from all directions until the driver bundled me to safety. And then there was the cold leather of the car seats, hands banging against the blacked-out windows until the car rocked under their weight. I lay down on the back seat and stared into nowhere; I didn't even wonder how the press had known I was there. They must have followed us to Primrose Hill, because when we arrived at my house it was buzzing with journalists and photographers. I remember being bewildered and terrified as I tried to fight my way up the path towards my front door. I was shoved, poked and prodded, and they all shouted questions: 'Why have you had an abortion, Laura?' 'Was it Ricky's baby?' 'Does Ricky know?' My hands were shaking so much that I dropped my house keys on the doorstep and had to scramble to pick them up under the glare of the flashing lights. They made great pictures. There were tears streaming down my face and a look of complete terror in my eyes. I looked completely lost – lost in showbiz. It was a scary place to be.

When I got inside, I ran up the two flights of stairs to the attic room to hide from the world that had turned so nasty. I had to be as far away from the mayhem outside as possible. But as I curled up on the leather sofa I could still hear them knocking on the windows downstairs and shouting their questions through the letterbox. I didn't move for the longest time.

It got dark, and then it got light again. I could still hear them outside. My mobile was switched off but the landline kept ringing and ringing. Messages were left on the answer machine. Nat, Fiona and Mum all sounded beside themselves with concern. They phoned again and again. Was I all right? Was it true what they were saying in the papers? But I didn't know what they were saying. Warren wanted to know what the hell I was playing at. Did I have any idea how derogatory this publicity was? I didn't pick up the phone to any of them.

But I did begin to think. I was thinking how weird it was that the press had been waiting for me at the clinic when I'd come straight from New York. I'd told no one about the pregnancy, not even Nat; the only person who knew was Ricky. Ricky and the people from his record company.

Natalie called again. 'I know you're there, Laura. Pick up the phone. I don't know what's going on with you, but I do know you're in a mess. You promised you'd come to me if you were in trouble. Please, Laura,' she pleaded. There was a pause and then she said, 'OK, just turn on your TV. See what he's saying about you. Then call me, please.'

I reached for the remote and switched on the television. It was utterly surreal. A reporter with bouffant hair and a bad suit was standing outside my house. He was explaining that I hadn't been seen for twenty-four hours and wasn't available to comment on Ricky Jones's allegations against me. Then the picture flicked to New York, where Ricky stood outside his hotel, blinking back fake tears in the sunlight. He was surrounded by cameras. 'I don't know why she'd do this to me,' he was saying. 'I knew nothing about the pregnancy and was as surprised as anyone to hear that she'd aborted our baby behind my back. I need some private time to get my head around this, and I'd appreciate it if you'd let me have some space. I have no further comment. Thank you.' The picture flicked back to my doorstep. The cheesy reporter said, 'And that was Ricky Jones, speaking earlier from New York about the events that have taken place here in London. Obviously we haven't heard Laura McNaughton's side of the story, but Mr Jones is quite clearly a broken man. Now back to the studio ...'

As I switched off the television, something inside me switched back on. Suddenly it all made sense – the stories that were leaked, the private tit-bits which were whispered to the press, the personal photographs that miraculously appeared in the tabloids – it had been Ricky all along. It had to have been. He was the only common denominator. The only one who'd been there every time. But why would he want to destroy me? And then I remembered that I wasn't *that* special. In fact, it wasn't about me at all. Every time my name was mentioned in the press, Ricky's was there, too. Often he was portrayed as the hero – the man who stood by me when my family disowned me; the guy who helped me move into my new home; the poor, broken-hearted lover, whose unborn baby had been lost – and every time a story broke there was an album to sell, a tour to promote, a single to be released. I had been used until every last drop of life had been squeezed out of me. My shell sat huddled on the sofa, without the energy to move.

As the sun rose on the third day, I heard a key in the front door. I was terrified, convinced the press had somehow managed to break in. Heavy footsteps wandered around the house downstairs. I crawled into the corner of the room, under the eaves, curled up in a tight ball and hid my face in my hands. 'Please don't come and get me. Please don't find me,' I begged. Then the footsteps reached the first floor. Someone was calling my name, but I covered my ears and screamed until I couldn't hear a thing but my own high-pitched wail. When the hands reached out to touch me, I froze. I could feel strong fingers trying to prise my hands from my face and a voice shouting, 'Laura, Laura, Laura,' but I stayed in my ball, hidden from the world. It took the longest time for his voice to reach the part of my brain that recognized it was Adam.

'Adam, they stole my baby,' I said weakly.

Two days later, I woke up and found myself in bed at Doric Cottage. I recognized the local GP, Dr Robertson, as he stared down at me. I looked around the room, blinking in the sunlight, and found Fiona and Mum perched on the edge of the bed wearing worried frowns. Dad and Adam hovered in the background with furrowed brows and there were several bunches of fresh flowers dotted around the room.

'Hello,' I said.

They seemed delighted to have me back.

It turned out that I'd had some sort of mental and physical breakdown. I was suffering from 'exhaustion' in celebrity speak. Or, back in the real world, I'd collapsed from long-term drug abuse, malnutrition, a post-operative infection and acute stress. By the time Adam found me I had quite literally lost my marbles. He'd picked me up, all six and a half stone of me, carried me downstairs, out of the house, past the ladies and gentlemen of the press – who got some wonderful photographs – and placed me gently in the back of his tartan van, where I'd slept all the way to Scotland.

It took a few more days of rest, a hefty dose of antibiotics for the infection and bucketloads of Mum's home-made soup before I felt ready to get out of bed. After so long inside I craved fresh air, so I headed for the beach. I was sitting, staring out to sea, thinking about what I would do next, when Adam appeared and sat down beside me.

'It's good to see you up and about,' he said with a smile. 'What are you doing out here?'

'Just thinking.'

'About what?'

'About having to go back to London. About picking up the pieces. Above saving my job and reputation.'

'Is that what you want?' Adam picked up a handful of sand and then let it slip away through his fingers.

'No,' I said. 'I'd like to just stay here for ever and forget that any of that ever happened. But I can't, I've got to go back sometime.'

'Why?'

'Because I start filming the new series next week, because I've got to shoot a Superbra advert the week after that, because I own a house in London, because my friends are there ...' I trailed off as I remembered that I didn't really have any friends left. 'Just because.'

'You can do whatever you want to do,' reasoned Adam. 'If you don't want to go back to that life, just walk away. It's as simple as that.'

'But I worked really hard to get there. I can't just throw it all away.'

'Was it making you happy?' asked Adam.

'Did I *look* happy when you found me the other day?'

Adam shook his head. 'So leave it behind. Don't look back. You're not really living unless you keep moving forward.'

He stood up.

'Where are you going?' I asked.

'Home,' he said, wiping the sand from his bum. 'I was only hanging around to make sure you were OK.'

As I watched Adam walk away slowly along the shoreline, he seemed to take the sunshine with him and a cold shadow fell over me. The further he got from me, the lonelier I felt. Suddenly it became clear what I had to do. It was time to move forward. I ran along the sand as quickly as my wobbly legs would carry me.

'Adam,' I shouted. 'Adam, wait!'

He turned round and squinted into the sunset.

'Laura?'

'Kiss me,' I demanded breathlessly.

'What?' he asked confused.

'Kiss me,' I repeated with a laugh.

He stood there, frozen to the spot, looking baffled.

'OK, I'll kiss you then.'

I reached up on tiptoes and wrapped my arms around his neck, drawing his lovely, if confused, face towards mine. And then I kissed him. I kissed him with all the pent-up love that had been waiting for someone worthwhile, I kissed him with such hunger that I bruised my lips, and as I fell into the deep blue of his eyes I knew I'd found my home.

Jasmine was remarkably understanding about my decision to desert Scorpion TV at such short notice. It wasn't such a big deal, though, as Warren had once pointed out, the world was full of pretty little blonde things, dying to fill my high-heeled shoes, and she quickly found a new presenter for *The Weekend Starts Here*. Wazza himself was livid about losing his 15 per cent of the new Superbra deal, but wasn't he the one who said I wasn't *that* special? The house in Primrose Hill was sold to an eighteen-year-old weather girl for £1.2 million – enough to keep my bank manager smiling for life.

Cathy's last job as my PA was to pack up the huge collection of designer shoes, clothes and handbags that I'd collected over the year and send them up to Doric Cottage. They didn't fit me for long, but it didn't matter. There's no need for sequins and stilettos when you're eating fish and chips on the harbour wall of a Friday night. I kept some of them as a reminder of the person I used to be and I gave the rest away. Sometimes I'd go to the wardrobe and touch the beautiful fabrics, but before long I couldn't even remember the girl who'd worn them.

One evening, when the fish van beeped at the end of the drive, I realized I didn't have any cash for the haddock I needed for tea. I went to the wardrobe and looked in a Fendi handbag for a stray, rolled-up note from days gone by. At the bottom, I found a neatly folded-up napkin. When I took it out, I saw Nat's untidy handwriting scrawled all over it and I read what she'd written and smiled.

I spent much of the first six months at Doric Cottage in bed, sleeping off the mother of all hangovers. Adam would often come home after work and find me still in my pyjamas. He'd cook me something hot, fattening and delicious, run me a bath and put me back to bed. He was my saviour. Then, one morning in April, I woke up with a clear head and announced that I was bored of sleeping.

'Do something you love,' suggested Adam.

And so I enrolled as a mature student and did a course in

garden design, and then Adam and I set up a family business – he does the houses, I do the gardens. I spend most days up to my elbows in compost, and I've never been more content.

Comfortably back in the family fold I began to appreciate my parents for the wonderful people they were. It was as if, having almost lost them, I could now see how precious they were. I had a new respect for my mum and the choices she'd made to sacrifice her career for her family and I certainly understood why Dad had been so wary of the wild life I'd pursued with such a passion in London. But there were other bridges to build too and memories of the way I'd treated Becky and Vicky haunted me on a daily basis. It took me almost a year to pluck up the courage to contact Vick. We were in Edinburgh for the weekend, visiting Mum, Dad and Fiona, when Adam suggested I go round to Vicky's house. It took me three attempts to walk up the path to her front door. Adam had to physically push me there in the end.

'Ring the bell,' he demanded with such authority that I didn't dare chicken out.

Jamie answered the door with a gummy smile and shouted, 'Mummy, it's Auntie Laura!'

Vicky came to the door and stared at me with those huge, brown eyes of hers.

'Well, this is a turn-up for the books. What d'you want?' she barked.

'You know I once said that I might need your help?' I stammered awkwardly.

'Aye,' said Vick, eyeing me coldly.

'Well, I need the biggest favour ever. I need you to forgive me.'

She glared for a moment or two longer and then her face cracked into a grin and she laughed. 'Sorry, I can't keep a straight face. You look mortified. I'm no' that scary, am I? Come in, you idiot.'

Vicky always had a big heart and in no time we were gossiping over a cup of tea while Adam helped Jamie to build a hospital out of Lego. I knew I was lucky to have a friend who was so forgiving.

'Life's too short for petty arguments,' she explained, nodding in the direction of the son she'd so nearly lost.

Getting Becky back on side proved a little more difficult. I left forty-three messages on various answer machines and with friends and relatives in London and Glasgow before eventually receiving a postcard from New York. It read:

'Don't think I've forgiven you or anything. I'm still very, very cross. Just wanted to let you know that I'm living over here now with a Puerto Rican graffiti artist called Raoul and I'm working in a pan-Asian restaurant in the East Village. Anyway, guess who walked in today? Venetia! I spat in her bowl of seafood ramen for old times' sake. Hope you approve. Becky.'

There was no phone number or address, or any kisses after her name come to think of it, but it was a start. Three months later she called from Glasgow to say that she'd left Raoul and was now back home in Scotland. Her mum made her phone me because she was sick of passing on messages. Becky wondered if she could come up to stay because she wanted an apology straight from the horse's mouth and was looking forward to seeing me squirm.

'Jesus, you've put on weight,' was the first thing she said to me as she got off the train in Aberdeen.

It was a real table-turning moment. I'd come straight from work and was wearing wellies, muddy jeans and Adam's old holey jumper. Becky had returned from New York a new woman, perfectly groomed with a sexy, impish hairstyle, manicured nails and a wardrobe that the girls from *Sex and the City* would be proud of. She looked incredibly cool and very chic. But I wasn't jealous. It was about time Becky had her moment of one-upmanship. She made me kiss her pedicured feet – literally – there in the train station, which was pretty humiliating, but the least I could do under the circumstances.

'Repeat after me,' she demanded. 'I am a terrible mate and I will be eternally grateful if my ex-best friend Rebecca graciously agrees to forgive me for my heinous crimes against humanity.'

I did as I was told and repeated her mantra until we were both giggling stupidly on the platform and I couldn't spit the words out any more. Then we hugged and my laughter got caught in my throat as it turned into huge sobbing gulps.

'I'm so sorry, Becks,' I howled. 'I've been such a twat.'

'I know you have,' she said. 'But we're all right now.'

And we were. We were great. And we still are. Best friends for ever and ever.

Adam and I got married on a sunny July day with all our friends and family around us. Nat, Rob and Freddie travelled up from Essex; Graham and Daniel flew in from New York, where they've just opened a new salon; Becky drove over – she's now running a vegetarian sandwich shop in the west end of Glasgow; Jasmine couldn't make it to the ceremony, but she did give her indispensable PA, Cathy, time off to attend; Vicky, Kev and the kids were there, in high spirits because Jamie had just got the all-clear from the hospital; Jack sent a telegram from LA – he was trying to 'break' Hollywood, bless him – and even Monica and Lewis remembered, sending a video message from their beach house in Mexico – Lewis retired from showbiz after Sugar Reef broke up and is now the proud father of twins.

Dad said he had never been more proud in his life than the moment he walked me down the aisle. After the ceremony, Mum told me that marrying the man I loved was the most important thing I'd ever do. The bridesmaids looked stunning, despite the fact that Fiona had shortened her skirt by five inches and Becky's tattoo could quite clearly be seen in her backless dress. Adam bought me a golden retriever puppy as a wedding present. She was so blonde and beautiful that we had to call her Lucy. Needless to say, she's a bit of a handful and a real drama queen, but her heart's in the right place.

Three months ago, I gave birth to our baby, Maggie, and I thought my heart would explode with the sheer perfection of my life. Sometimes it feels as though the nightmare never happened at all, my mind has shut the painful memories out and when I look back at those dark days it's as if I watched them happen to somebody else, perhaps in a film. The only shadow that hangs over me is the fear of being found by the press. The one thing I've learned is who to trust, and I know that my real friends won't sell me out; they'd protect my privacy with their lives. But I always knew that one day the past would catch up with me. I could feel it breathing down my neck. I've been expecting this phone call for a long, long time.

Epilogue

I've been talking for hours, letting it all come flooding out, and now that I've purged myself I have to catch my breath. The receiver's shaking in my hand. There's a deafening silence on the line and I wonder if Rachel has long since hung up and gone back to her own life, bored of listening to mine. Eventually she speaks.

'Ricky's dead,' she says, so quietly I can barely take it in. 'That's why I needed to speak to you so urgently.'

'Dead?' My own voice rings in my ears before finally letting the meaning settle in my mind.

'Sometime last night,' says Rachel. 'It was too late by the time he was found this morning.'

'Dead,' I repeat, my head spinning. I don't know how to feel, don't know what to feel. I'm shocked, yes, but a part of me isn't surprised. This was always how it was going to end – sooner or later.

'Drugs?' I ask, although I know the answer already.

I let out tears I didn't know I still had for Ricky, as Rachel tells me what happened. Ricky Jones was found dead in his favourite London hotel, a needle by his side and vomit on his chin. The man who was adored by millions died alone.

'You know that Ricky apologized, don't you?' she says.

I don't, but for some reason I can't find the words to say so.

'Did you read the last interview he did?' she continues. 'It was in the papers last Sunday.'

I manage to retrieve my voice enough to whisper, 'No. No, I didn't see that. I don't really read the press any more.'

'Well,' she says with glee, 'I'll read it to you. OK, I'm quoting now ...'

As the words penetrate my skull my life flashes before my eyes. I see Lucy, so beautiful and frail. I see her in her coffin, tiny and perfect. I feel the baby that was ripped from my womb and, inexplicably, just for a moment, I ache for the man who nearly destroyed me. I grieve. My baby, Maggie, feels like a dead weight in my arms, even though she's only three months old. I'm still sitting on the cold kitchen floor. My legs feel numb.

The girl read on:

> 'Ricky Jones looks too old to be twenty-nine, too grey to be young. His reputation as the industry's biggest party animal is not in doubt, but his future must be. The man looks sick. Chiselled and handsome yes, but sick all the same. He admits his life has been in a downward spiral for months now. Rumours of heroin abuse abound in the inner sanctum of the rock world. When I ask him what his drug of choice is these days, he just shrugs and says, "Whatever."
>
> 'The death of his close friend, actress Lucy Lloyd, and the well-publicized split with TV presenter and überbabe Laura McNaughton can't have made life easy. "Oh, Laura," he says in a tired voice when I mention his ex-girlfriend's name. "Laura was something else. She was like a storm. She came from nowhere and turned everything upside down, changed everything, changed

me, and then she just disappeared again." I point out that she didn't exactly disappear; she left in a blaze of publicity after aborting Ricky's unborn child.

'Ricky Jones looks uncomfortable and stares at me with bloodshot eyes. "Listen, mate, I'm going to tell you something because it's been bugging me and I feel like a total shit for not saying this before. Laura didn't want that abortion. It was me. I made her do it. I wasn't ready. To be a dad, you know?" He smokes his umpteenth cigarette and stares out of the window over Hyde Park. "I mean, I tried to apologize, but by then she'd just vanished. Gone. I tried to find her but, I don't know, she obviously didn't want to be found. I've spoken to some of her old friends and they say she's doing all right, but she must hate me. God, she must hate me. The way she was written about in the press, like she was some total bitch, that wasn't fair. Laura was, is, a sweet girl. She's brave, you know. Different from the rest of the tarts out there. She's got more life in her little finger than most people have in their whole body. That's what freaked me out. She was too good for me and I couldn't handle it, so I screwed her. Totally fucking screwed her. I hope she's all right." Wherever Laura McNaughton is, I'm sure she's coping with the fallout better than Ricky Jones is.'

'Shall I go on?' asks Rachel.

'No, don't,' I say. 'That's all I need to know.'

Tears are streaming down my face as I gaze at my daughter sleeping sweetly in my arms. How bizarre the way things turn out. She could have been Ricky's baby; I might have been Ricky's wife. Would I be his widow now? Would he still be alive if we'd got back together? I'd known he was trying to find me. Nat told me, Jasmine told me, Jack told me. I didn't want to be found. I'd changed my phone number, my email address, my hair colour. I'd deleted my Facebook account, scrapped my website and turned my back on Twitter. Hell, I'd even changed my name.

I feel like my head's going to explode with the what-ifs swimming around there. It would have been so much easier to just put Ricky in that box labelled 'Evil' and leave him there to rot, but he redeemed himself before he died; he apologized publicly, something I thought was beyond him. Did he do it for himself? To purge some of the dirty shit he was carrying around inside? Or did he do it for me? Did he want me to read it? Maybe he needed to say sorry because he knew he was going to die? Whatever. It doesn't matter any more. A strange calm settles over me and I feel like the last ghost of those heady, horrid days has been exorcized. He wasn't bad, he wasn't good, he was just living in a very strange place where people do nasty things to survive. I make a new box in my head and label it 'Human'. Ricky can rest there in peace. With Lucy.

Maggie opens her blue eyes and stares at me quizzically. Perhaps she can sense her mother's discomfort because she begins to cry.

'I'll let you go now,' says Rachel. Her voice is gentle but she can't disguise the excited little wobble in it and I know she's desperate to get me off the phone so that she can share all the juicy morsels I've offered her. My life on her plate. 'I can hear that your baby needs you. Anyway, I think I've got everything I need.'

'Yes, me too,' I reply.

Rachel thanks me for my time and the phone goes dead. I imagine her back in her media bubble, scurrying into her editor's office on high heels, so keen to discuss my suffering, to pick over the sordid details, to wonder how and why. I know how she'll feel. She'll be so excited by her journalistic coup that she'll forget that there's a human being involved. I know because I've been there. I did an interview like that once. It was with an actress called Lucy Lloyd. I wonder where Rachel's life will lead and whether it will make her happy. I hope that what I've told her today will act as some sort of warning, but I know she'll learn the hard way. Like I did. I wonder if it will make her happy.

And me? I'll stay here in my world, where I can feel the flesh on my bones, my baby at my breast and the man I adore in my arms. I can wake up in the morning and taste the salt in the sea air. It makes my brown hair curl. I'll keep breathing, laughing, loving, living because I know who I am. I'm Laura – wife, mother, lover, daughter, gardener, friend. Just another ordinary woman, doing ordinary things in an ordinary world. But I'm alive. I'm real.